ATTACK OF THE UNHOLY

The bird—no, the *thing*—hovered some ten feet above the ground, its wings slowly beating; and its head, which was like a travesty of a dog's head but scaled and nacreous, turned with obscene deliberation to regard her. Its expression was contemptuous; a black tongue flickered and ropes of yellowish saliva hung from its jaws. Karuth clenched her teeth, struggling to remember the binding spell for higher elementals which, caught unawares as she was, had fled from her mind at the moment when she needed it. But, thank Yandros, memory clicked suddenly and her voice seared out.

"Creature of unhallowed dark, spawn of the Seven Hells, in the name of Yandros and in the name of Aeoris do I charge and abjure you—"

The monstrosity laughed. The sound was so like the giggle of a foolish girl that it threw Karuth utterly, and the power of the spell rising in her mind shattered, making her stagger back. As she tried to regather her wits, the creature laughed again—and suddenly there was the sound of booted feet scuffing on stone, and an outcry of new voices from the main doors. Karuth's head whipped round and she saw her brother Tirand's broad, stocky figure, flanked by four senior adepts, emerging on to the steps.

"What in blazes is going on?" Tirand's shout rang above those of the others. "Karuth—Handray—*what in the name of Aeoris is that th*

The Chaos Gate Trilogy
Book II

THE PRETENDER

Louise Cooper

BANTAM BOOKS

NEW YORK · TORONTO · LONDON · SYDNEY · AUCKLAND

THE PRETENDER

A Bantam Spectra Book / May 1991

ISBN 0-553-28977-2

Published simultaneously in the United States and Canada

THE PRETENDER

1

"Gentlemen, gentlemen!" Koord Alborn banged his pewter mug down on the bar with all his strength and shouted across the hubbub of talk and laughter that filled the smoky taproom. No one heeded him and he tried again, this time in the bellowing tones he used to drive out the last, reluctant stalwarts before shutting his doors for the night.

"Gentlemen!"

The noise abated, heads turned, and Koord, from his precarious position sitting atop the bar counter, thumped the mug again until at last he had the revelers' attention.

"Gentlemen! And ladies!" An expansive flourish; drops of ale flew across the room and someone swore good-naturedly. Koord grinned. He had reached the pleasant point between being drunk enough to lose his inhibitions and being sober enough to retain a modicum of control over his brain and tongue. "Good friends. Good friends all."

A woman in a startling green dress, her mouth painted scarlet and her dark hair spangled with a net of cheap sequins, made a rude noise, and there was more raucous laughter. As it subsided, Koord launched into his speech.

"Good friends all! As landlord of the Full Moons tavern and host of this night's happy gathering, it behoo . . .

1

it behoes . . . *behoves* me to propose a toast. A loyal toast, gentlemen and ladies, to she without who this occasion wouldn't have been!"

More laughter; a voice called out, "By the fourteen gods, Koord, you're on form tonight! Say it again, man, and we'll try to understand it this time!"

Koord waved his arms for silence. "She without who—" he repeated, then shook his head. "Ah, damn the lot of you; I'm being *serious!* A toast to our beloved High Margravine, for her birth-avi . . . anniversary two days from now!"

There was a roar of approval at this, and fifty voices rose to the roof, shouting the High Margravine's name in the traditional way. "Jianna! Jianna! Jianna!"

"Aeoris and Yandros watch over her!" someone added. A few maudlin murmurs echoed this, and the green-clad woman's feline gaze slid sideways to a man who sat close by in the ingle, on what for tonight's purposes had been dubbed the seat of honor.

"And maybe this year they'll send her the child she hasn't managed to get yet, eh? Or *someone* will, if they find half a chance!" She grinned lasciviously and jabbed an elbow against the man's shoulder. "How about you, Strann, eh? Eh?"

Lively and intelligent hazel eyes looked up at her from under the wide brim of a highly decorated hat, and the man's generous mouth widened into a grin. He got to his feet, smacking her firmly on the rump as he rose.

"You," he said, "are a shameless harlot. I don't know what I'm doing associating with you! Now, be a good girl and get me another drink before Koord starts on the next round of toasts."

She screeched with laughter, took his mug, and started

to shoulder her way through the press of people. Strann made to sit down again, but stopped as he realized that Koord had seen him and was shouting his name.

"Strann!" The landlord signaled imperiously to him. "Strann, stay on your feet and don't try to hide! Friends!" The mug crashed down again. "Friends all! There's another reason for our revels tonight, and that reason's been sitting there in the ingle eating my food and drinking my ale since the celeb . . . lebration began!"

"Shame on him!"

"Shame indeed!" Koord nodded vigorously. "Because we have in our midst the finest singer and storyteller in five provinces, returned to us after two years—"

"One and a half," Strann corrected him.

"Two, one and a half—what does it matter? Returned to Shu-Nhadek after a long absence! And tomorrow morning, he's to set sail—"

A chorus of groans and sounds of seasickness greeted this; Koord shouted the crude humor down.

"—set sail to Summer Isle, where the High Margrave himself, *in person,* has summoned him to sing his songs and tell his stories on our own High Margravine's special day! And so, and so in his honor, we're celebrating here tonight. And in rec . . . recognition of our generosity, I now call upon our good friend, our good friend Strann the Storymaker, to sing for his supper!"

The cheer that greeted this announcement was twice as loud as anything that had gone before. Pots and jugs trembled on their hooks, the old floorboards vibrated, and Strann, smiling, laughing, and shaking his head in mock self-deprecation, was manhandled across the taproom to the bar. This was a price he was always happy to pay, and

3

he made only a sham effort to resist as he was heaved up to sit on the counter beside Koord.

"Very well, then!" His voice rang out over the heads of the crowd. "What's it to be tonight?"

Requests were shouted, mostly songs known throughout all the provinces and perennially popular. Strann waited for long enough to get the measure of the crowd's mood, then held up his hands to still the babble and leaned over to where his most precious possession was stowed behind and under the counter, out of harm's way. Feet stamped approval as he took the long-necked, seven-stringed manzon from its case and settled it across his knee; he struck a chord, grimaced, and began to adjust the tuning while Koord proprietorially signaled for quiet.

The fourth string was out . . . ah, that was better. Now the sixth . . . just a fraction more . . . yes, that would do; tonight's audience wouldn't notice the occasional sour note. Flexing his hands, Strann fingered a swift series of notes—then froze as he realized suddenly what he was playing. A memory that he'd thought safely banished and forgotten slotted sharply into place in his mind, and he thought, *Oh, gods, not that. Not that, of all things.*

One and a half years ago, walking on the road out of Shu-Nhadek, Strann had made two promises to himself. Firstly he had vowed that he wouldn't return to this busy, prosperous province until enough time had passed to dull the aftertaste of his recent experiences. Secondly he had sworn that as long as he lived, he would never be fool enough to play the piece of music called "Silverhair, Goldeneyes" again without a very good reason.

Really, he'd overreacted to the whole affair. After all, nothing dire had befallen him as a result of what he'd done, and there was no logical reason why it should have.

But to Strann it seemed that logic hadn't had much of a hand in the matter; and what *had* occurred, though harmless enough on the surface, had been an experience he wasn't anxious to repeat.

He realized suddenly that a slow but steady stamping had started up all around the taproom. The celebrants were growing restive; his brain had been a hundred miles away and he was sitting on the bar like some slackmouthed harvest dumb-dolly. This wouldn't do. He had an audience to entertain, and the cloud lifted from his mind as he fingered another, less contentious melody to check the manzon's tuning and turned to face the room.

"Well, then." He took off his hat and dumped it on the counter beside him. "Let's see who's in good voice and who's too drunk to do anything but croak, eh?" He struck a loud major chord. " 'Good Luck to the Grape'—and I want to hear *everyone* joining in the chorus!"

Yells of approval set the jugs rattling anew. This was what they had waited for; they'd had good food and good drink, and now the real entertainment was to begin. Perhaps later, Strann thought a little wryly, they'd be tired enough for some more serious music, but until then who was he to deny them the simple, celebratory songs they loved? They'd been his bread and meat for more years than he had fingers to count, and whatever else he might be, he wasn't an ingrate. So, then:

A single chord whose complexity only a trained ear would have recognized and admired shimmered out over the taproom, and Strann grinned.

"Here's a health to us all luck at harvest time," he sang in his warm baritone.

The responding roar nearly lifted the tavern roof. *"And here's a good luck to the grape!"*

Stripped of her tawdry green dress, and with much of the paint wiped from her face, the dark-haired girl was far prettier than first appearances had suggested. Strann had suspected as much; he'd seen it in the glint of her eyes and the curve of her full mouth, and he hadn't been disappointed.

He watched her as she leaned out of the bed and reached for the ale jug, making two attempts to grab at the handle in the unsteady candlelight before she finally succeeded. She poured a full cup, drank deeply, said, "Ahhh! That's *good!*" and handed the cup to him.

Strann eyed her amusedly over the cup's rim. "What's good? The drink, or me?"

"Both." She rolled over onto her back and stared up at the ceiling. "I like you, Strann the Storymaker."

He ran his fingers lightly over her stomach. "And I like you. But d'you know something? You haven't yet told me your name."

She laughed throatily, covering his hand with her own. "You can call me Yya."

"Yya?" He suppressed an inebriate chuckle. "That isn't a name, it's a noise!"

"Yess." She rolled toward him. "It's the noise a woman makes when she's *pleased.*"

"I'd noticed. But what did your parents call you?"

"Something completely and utterly ghastly. But I'll make a bargain with you, my Storymaker: I'll tell you my real name if you tell me your clan."

She was touching him pleasurably, deliciously, and he couldn't stop himself from laughing. "No bargain, lady! I

6

reveal my clan name to no one. Not even beautiful creatures like you—and stop doing that; you won't persuade me!"

She did stop, and lay back again, her expression suddenly serious and curious. "Why won't you tell, Strann? Is it so important?"

"Probably not. But just as I don't parade the fact that I'm a Guild Master of the Musical Arts because the Guild wouldn't thank me for it I don't parade my clan name because my clan wouldn't thank me for it." He grinned. "It's called being the blot on the family escutcheon."

She laughed. "Well, then, that makes us two of a kind. Oh, and that reminds me: have you heard the news about your last little ladylove, here in Shu-Nhadek, Kiszi?"

A memory slipped into place of a pretty, pouting face surmounted by a cloud of golden hair—the wayward daughter of a minor aristocrat, with whom he'd had a brief but delightful dalliance on his last sojourn here. He'd almost forgotten Kiszi—and Yya's sly reminder brought a sudden stab of chagrin as he recalled the incident that had made the final breach between them. The last of the psychic experiences that had dogged his previous visit to this province. And by far the most unpleasant.

He followed Yya's gaze up to the ceiling, and abruptly his heart contracted. *Gods* . . . he'd known this was the same tavern in which he'd stayed the last time he was in Shu-Nhadek; he was, after all, a well-known and valued customer here, and it had seemed foolish to break an old habit because of one unpleasant incident. But this room . . . he recognized it now; recognized the pattern of smoke- and damp-stains on the ceiling boards, the lopsided window frame—damn it, even the lumps in the bed's mattress were familiar. This was the very same room in which *it*—whatever it was, and he still didn't pretend to know the answer to that question—had happened. The conjuring trick he'd tried to show Kiszi, spinning coins in the air with a sleight of hand that he couldn't quite make work. And then suddenly the coins had taken on a life of their own and had begun to spin and flicker in midair, and had formed a face. And words.

I am watching . . .

Yya said, "Strann? Where are you?"

The memory slid aside like a dream breaking, and Strann blinked owlishly in the candlelight. "What?"

She stared at him, surprised and a little indignant. "You haven't heard a word I've been saying!"

With an effort Strann dragged his mind back to join his more physical senses in the present moment. "I'm sorry."

If she sensed anything untoward, she ignored it. "I *said,*" she repeated, "that your little Kiszi is now betrothed to the second son of one of the wealthiest shipbuilders in Shu Province."

"Ah. Yes." He wasn't surprised; it was no more than he might have expected. Suddenly his eyes narrowed. "How do you know about me and Kiszi?"

"Oh, I miss little that happens around here. In fact," she nibbled at his long, ragged hair, "I'd a mind to win you for myself last time you were in Shu-Nhadek, but Kiszi was quicker." A broad, lascivious grin. "She knows of your return, and I hear that she's terrified you might stride up to her father's door and claim an old liaison with her." Yya giggled. "All I can say is, she must have a very high opinion of herself if she doesn't know better than that!"

"Mm?" Strann's mind had been wandering along unpleasant paths again; he pulled himself back. "What d'you mean, if she doesn't know better?"

"Ohh, Strann, Strann. *Everyone* knows about you. Love them dearly, promise them nothing, and be firm and true to your promise." She reared up and kissed his nose. "The wandering bard no girl has ever snared, nor probably ever will. I really think I could love you, if I was fool enough to let myself."

Strann smiled. "Love doesn't have to be a trap, Yya. Nor does it have to be forever." One hand traced gently across her jawline. "In your profession you must have learned that. How many men have fallen in love with you only to find they weren't the only light in your life?"

She acknowledged the point with a wry nod. "Enough. But I never promise them more than I'm prepared to give."

"Neither do I. Life's too short, isn't it? We travel through the span the gods grant us; aren't we wiser to take our pleasures wherever we can find them, provided we're not dishonest and we try our best to hurt no one?"

Yya considered this for a few moments, then hiccupped. "Oh, gods," she said good-humoredly. "So much for philosophy . . . but I think you're right, Storymaker. And for tonight at least you're *my* Storymaker, though I know you'll be gone from me in the morning and I probably won't set eyes on you again until the next time the High Margrave summons you to his table."

"I'd like to take you with me. You'd liven the Summer Isle court."

"I'm sure I would, and I thank you for the compliment because I suspect that you might just mean it. But for now, Strann, cess and damnation to High Margraves and all their fine feathers: tonight *I* have your full attention and no one else can take it away."

Her arms wound around his neck; in the dim candlelight her eyes were like elemental fires, alive with fond mischief. Ale and good company and the warm, lingering afterglow of a triumphant evening were fueling Strann's mind and body as Yya pressed close to him, her lips working expertly across his face, finally discovering his mouth. The candle guttered; he reached out with one hand and snuffed it, plunging the room into soft, comfortable darkness.

"Ah," he whispered, "Yya. Not a name. A noise. *Yya* . . . Pretty Yya . . ."

The quiet night closed in around them, and Strann's uneasy memories faded into the intimate concerns of deeper and more private pleasures.

Much later, when the first moon had set and the light of the second was no more than a filmy reflection on the drawn curtains, Strann lay wakeful. Beside him Yya was sound asleep, her breath ticking evenly in the quiet; but though he knew that he should follow her example, he couldn't persuade his body to obey his mind's desires. And he couldn't stop his mind from straying back to those few days in the spring of last year, and to the memories that tonight's celebration had brought streaming back into his thoughts.

It had been a bizarre time. In his years of traveling the world, telling his stories, singing his songs, Strann had grown accustomed to the bizarre, but this had paled other experiences into insignificance by comparison. Throughout his life he had never shown the smallest psychic talent, yet the events that had overtaken him on Summer Isle last year had hit at a core of occult instinct he hadn't known he possessed, and hit hard.

Now that the memories had been awakened once again, he couldn't push them back to some dark corner of his mind and forget them. Being honest, he had to admit that in unguarded moments they'd haunted both his dreams and his waking hours ever since his hasty departure from Shu Province. And one incident in particular had haunted him more than the rest. The High Margrave's wedding feast, to which he had been invited as a paid entertainer, and where through a chain of unlikely circumstances he had played what at the time had seemed a harmless duet with the High Initiate's sister, Karuth Piadar. That, he felt with a sure instinct, had been the launching point of the entire episode.

Strann had dreamed about Karuth on a number of occasions since that first and only meeting with her. Harmless dreams, nothing bawdy, which made a change from the usual run of his imagination's mill; but then, though Karuth was a fine musician and a handsome and intelligent woman, she was also neither beautiful nor available nor five or ten years younger than he was, and Strann had always cheerfully pursued women who fulfilled at least two of those three criteria. To judge her in such a way was nonsensical of course: Even he couldn't be so optimistic as to look on Karuth Piadar as a potential lover. But something else had swept the obvious considerations aside, dug deeper into his soul, and awakened a kind of fellow-feeling. And fellow-suspicion.

On that last night in Shu-Nhadek, Strann remembered, before his hasty departure in the wake of the last, intolerable psychic experience, he'd wondered whether Karuth was experiencing troubles similar to his own. Though she hadn't admitted it, he had a strong intuition that she, too, had been visited by the same apparition that had come to him after the wedding feast, the golden-eyed woman in the old-fashioned gown who had smiled so knowingly and stared so unnervingly into his eyes. To this day Strann didn't know whether it had been a dream or a vision—he wasn't even sure that he knew the difference—but it had terrified him. Nothing like it had ever happened to him before in his life, and the worst of it was, he believed he knew who his unearthly visitor had been. If he was right, then he had been the first man in nearly a hundred years to look on the face of the woman who had brought the gods of Chaos back to the world.

How many times since that night had he wished that he'd spoken out to Karuth instead of turning his back and trying to pretend that nothing untoward had taken place? Strann had always been chary of anything to do with occult matters; the gods and their affairs were, he felt, not a subject with which the layman should meddle if he had half a gravine of sense. But something had followed him back from Summer Isle, and that same something had haunted him for days afterward, culminating in the unnerving incident in this very room with the coins and the message they had conveyed. Only by leaving Shu-Nhadek altogether had he been able to shake it off. And—all right, call it intuition again, though he was becoming heartily sick of the word—he suspected that Karuth might have suffered experiences similar to his own.

Perhaps he should have written to her. His Guild training had given him a good grounding in scribe's skills, and he could have phrased a letter diplomatically and sent it to the Star Peninsula from a messenger-bird post in one of the larger towns. But every time the thought had occurred to him, he'd found one excuse or another to defer it. Now it was too late, for tomorrow morning—no, *this* morning, for it was long past midnight—he would put out from Shu-Nhadek to visit Summer Isle for a second time, and Karuth Piadar's views and experiences could be of no help to him.

What would he find waiting for him on Summer Isle? A celebration, yes; not as spectacular as the wedding of last year, but a grand occasion nonetheless. But what else? Was some residue of past events still lingering, waiting to haunt him again? Or was that old incident over and gone, and was he seeing ghosts where none existed?

A stirring beside him, and Yya's sleep-laden eyes opened, glinting in the darkness.

"Strann? What are you doing?"

He turned his head on the rough pillow and looked at her. "Just thinking."

"What about?"

A quick, faintly mischievous grin. "You of course. What else?"

"Liar." She yawned. "But seriously. What's the matter?"

Strann reached out and dabbed the tip of her nose with one finger. "Nothing's the matter, pretty one. I was simply engrossed in composing a sonnet in your honor."

She looked for sarcasm but didn't find it; his teasing was gentle. "Ohh . . ." she batted his hand away. "What sort of gullible empty-head do you take me for? Go to sleep, you ridiculous, lovable fool."

She'd broken his somber mood, and Strann was suddenly grateful to her in a way he couldn't have begun to explain. He laughed softly. "Is that an order, my lady?"

"It is. Go to *sleep. Now.*" She reached over to kiss him, then pulled him down farther under the blankets. "Sonnets, indeed . . ." Her voice was slurred with somnolence. "Good night, Storymaker."

Strann smiled fondly at her, though her eyes had closed again and she didn't see his expression. "Good night," he replied gently, and added, as a silent afterthought, *and thank you, Yya. Thank you for setting my feet back on the path of reason.*

2

Though he'd always been a good sailor, Strann firmly believed in the wisdom of not tempting Providence, and so an hour after dawn he was making his way toward Shu-Nhadek's harbor with two small offerings to cast on the sea in hope of securing a calm voyage. He was also nursing the grandfather of all headaches, but that was something he'd long been accustomed to, and the vile-tasting herbal draft he'd forced himself to drink before leaving the Full Moons would chase away the miasms soon enough.

There would be no ceremony to mark his departure. Those guests who hadn't managed to stagger to their homes after the night's revels were still snoring under Koord's roof, and even Yya had been dead to the world when he slipped out of bed and gathered his belongings together in the early light. It was a pleasant enough morning, fresh and bright after the squalls of the last two days, and the brisk westerly wind smelled bracingly of salt. A fair day to be putting out to sea, and by the time he arrived at the quayside where the cargo ship *Cloudfisher* waited for its quota of passengers, Strann's stomach and spirits felt considerably improved.

He made his offerings, throwing the two flower garlands on the tide's oily surface with due solemnity. One tribute to the gods of Chaos and one to the gods of Order;

it was prudent, he believed, to show no preferences. Some of the *Cloudfisher*'s crew watched him from the deck but made no comment, and at last, shouldering the bags containing his precious manzon and a few changes of clothes —Koord would take care of the rest of his possessions until he returned—Strann walked up the gently flexing gangplank.

In addition to the twenty or so passengers who had business on Summer Isle, *Cloudfisher* was carrying a fair tonnage of food and wine from Shu, Prospect, and Southern Chaun provinces to the High Margrave's court, and the smells of her cargo mingled headily in the cramped quarters below decks. Even though the herbal draft had settled his queasy stomach, Strann decided to find himself a place up by the forward rail where he could enjoy the fresher scents of the sea, and as the ship dipped out into the Bay of Illusions, seeming to curtsy an acknowledgment to her home harbor as she met the stronger currents, he settled down to enjoy the voyage. For some hours he sat comfortably propped against a pile of coiled ropes, alternately dozing and gazing at the steadily moving seascape ahead, until eventually he was awakened from a half-formed dream by a shadow falling across his face.

"Good day to you, Master Strann. How are you enjoying the voyage?"

Strann opened his eyes and squinted up at the silhouette that towered over him.

"Captain Fyne." He struggled into a more upright position and took off his hat in a courteous salute. "I'm enjoying the voyage greatly, and counting my luck in having a calm day for it."

Fyne Cais Haslo, *Cloudfisher*'s master, grunted agreement and hunkered down beside him. "We've been lucky, I'll say that. All the soothsayers predicted more rain."

"Which only goes to show that you shouldn't listen to soothsayers. I should know; I saw enough of their chicanery in my fairground days."

"I don't doubt it." Fyne smiled dryly. "Though that must be a good few years ago now, eh? From huckster to court favorite's a long road."

Strann wondered for a moment if there was a sour note lurking behind the captain's words, then saw the mischief in his eyes and relaxed as he realized what this was leading up to.

"True," he said, "but I don't forget my origins. And to save you the trouble of asking, yes, I'd be glad to help the ship's company pass the voyage with a song or two. I've a few new stories of events in Han and Wishet that may not have reached your ears yet."

Fyne reddened, but only briefly before his expression cleared and he laughed, a deep, chesty sound. "Well, you don't waste time tacking about. How did you know that I meant to approach you?"

"It's a hazard of my profession." Strann grinned. "When we landlubbers meet you seagoing men in a tavern, don't we invariably start talking to you about winds and tides and shiplore? Well, by the same rule, wherever I go, I'm asked to sing songs and pass on the latest gossip. And I'm always glad to oblige. Mind"—he looked about him—"I'll need to find a more sheltered place than this if I'm to play any music. Salt spray and my manzon don't make a happy combination."

Fyne nodded toward the stern. "There's plenty of space under the aft bulkheads, and they're well protected from whatever the sea throws at us."

"Well then, Captain, I'm at your disposal." Strann got to his feet. "How long, do you think, before we sight Summer Isle?"

"Oh . . . an hour, perhaps a little more if the wind teases us. Then probably the best part of another hour to reach harbor."

Two hours to harbor: say, then, an hour of entertainment. He could put on a fair enough performance in that time, Strann thought, and if he gave the crew good value, Fyne might see his way to refunding at least part of his passage fee at the end of the voyage. Even if he didn't—and it was unlikely, for Strann knew the captain to be a generous man—it would give him the opportunity to try out one or two of the new songs he'd prepared for the High Margravine's celebration.

He heaved his packs onto his shoulders and would have started along the deck, but suddenly a disembodied voice drifted down from above.

"Captain!" The lookout, high in the crow's nest at the top of the mainmast, was an indistinguishable black smudge against the brilliant sky, but his cry was clear enough. *"Storm!"*

Fyne's head jerked up. "What?"

"Storm ahead, sir!"

The captain said something that made even Strann raise his eyebrows, and swung around to scan the horizon. There was nothing to be seen but the calm ocean, the bright sun, a few placid and isolated white clouds.

Fyne raised his head again, and his voice bellowed up like a bull-roarer. "What are you raving about, you bloody idiot? There's no storm within a hundred miles of here!"

The lookout's voice floated back despairingly: "But sir"—

" 'Sir' be damned! Get down from your perch at the double, and don't—" And he stopped abruptly as a sudden gust of wind scudded across the deck, ruffling his hair and lifting the brim of Strann's hat.

Strann hastily clamped a hand to his hat to stop it from blowing away. The precaution was needless; the gust had vanished as swiftly and suddenly as it had sprung up. But Fyne's angry expression had changed to one of puzzlement.

"That gust came from the east." He spoke softly, glancing up to where the ratlines quivered as the lookout began his agile descent. "Odd . . ."

Strann frowned. "Pardon my ignorance, but why 'odd'?"

"What?" Fyne looked at him in some surprise, as though he'd momentarily forgotten his existence. Then abruptly his eyes focused. "Why? Because it was in direct opposition to the prevailing wind, and that's not natural."

"It was just one gust," Strann said, hoping he sounded more nonchalant than he felt and surreptitiously touching the iron band on a nearby belaying pin for luck. "Probably means nothing."

Fyne grunted noncommittally. "Maybe. Nonetheless—"

This time the sudden cold slap came from the south, and it snatched Strann's hat off his head before he could react. He opened his mouth to shout an indignant protest, but the wind whipped his voice away too, and he and Fyne both staggered under its onslaught. They heard a yell from the frightened lookout, still suspended in the rigging; *Cloudfisher* heeled sharply, and the sails roared as the squall filled them and beat them against the masts. For a few seconds there was nothing but shouting, buffeting confusion—and then, just as before, the wind vanished in the space of a moment.

"Gods . . ." Strann's ears rang in the sudden quiet; he found himself clinging to the rail as though it were a long-lost lover, and slowly slackened his grip. "What in the name of the seven hells was *that*?"

Fyne didn't answer, and Strann walked unsteadily along the deck to retrieve his hat, which lay forlornly some twenty paces away. As he returned, the lookout, who by a combination of instinct and grim determination had managed to keep his hold on the ratlines, came scrambling and slithering down to the deck, jumping the last ten feet. His face was the color of bilge water.

"Captain, I—"

"All right, all right." Fyne silenced him with a sharp gesture; this wasn't the time for superfluous words. "What did you see out there?"

"L—lightning, sir." The sailor's teeth were chattering, and he had difficulty forcing the words out. "Dead ahead. Southeasterly."

A sensation like a kitten's claws at the base of his spine made Strann's flesh shrink abruptly as memories stirred and mingled with an unpleasant sense of premonition. Fyne, unaware of his disquiet, glared at the lookout. *"Lightning?* In a clear sky?"

"It's what I saw, sir. It couldn't have been anything else." A pause. "But . . ."

"But *what*? Spit it out, for the gods' sakes!"

The sailor met his furious stare unhappily. "It was *red* lightning, sir. Crimson, like blood." He shivered. "And not a cloud anywhere. I've never seen anything like it before!"

Oh gods, Strann thought. *But I have . . .*

Fyne swore softly. "Unnatural squalls, unnatural lightning—if I'm not drunk or deluded, then there's something uncanny afoot." He swung about, staring hard at the sea as though challenging the elements to play some new trick, but nothing happened. Fyne paused for a moment, considering his next move, then abruptly turned back to face the lookout.

"Right. I want every man at his station and the ship made ready for storm conditions." His voice was suddenly crisp and decisive as his mind moved on to familiar territory. "Send the first mate to me here—but don't do anything that might disquiet our passengers without my order. This may be a false alarm, and there's no point in creating needless worry."

The sailor saluted and sprinted away along the deck. When he was out of earshot, Strann said dryly, "I fear, Captain Fyne, that one of your passengers is already very disquieted indeed."

Fyne looked at him and was surprised by what he saw. Strann's face was sickly pale under its tan, and beads of sweat were banded across his forehead despite the wind's briskness. His studied nonchalance was slipping, and the effort he made to sound and seem lighthearted failed badly. Unaware of the underlying cause of his agitation, Fyne grinned sympathetically.

"Don't worry, Strann. The gods have never yet sent us a storm that *Cloudfisher* couldn't ride out, so you've little to fear apart from maybe a dose of seasickness." He hesitated. "All the same, I'd go below if I were you, and take your gear with you. At least that way you'll keep dry, and your talents might help to take the other passengers' minds off their predicament if we do get a rough blow."

Strann was tempted to say that the other passengers

could rot or riot for all the difference it would make to him in his present state, but held the words back. He was beginning to feel sick with the peculiar and unmistakable queasiness of apprehension; his legs were growing less willing to support him with every moment, and he was suffering the first sensations of vertigo: all a warning that if he didn't get a grip on himself quickly, he was in danger of losing control and panicking.

Red lightning, out of a clear sky . . . An ugly, involuntary sound bubbled at the back of his throat, and Fyne said, "What?"

"Nn." Strann shook his head, dismissing the captain's query with a hasty gesture. "Nothing; nothing. I'll . . . ah . . . take your advice, I think."

Fyne peered at him uncertainly. "You're sure you're all right? You're as white as a dead fish."

Strann wanted to be truthful and say, *No, I'm not all right, there's something very unpleasant in the wind, and because I'm a craven coward, I am at this moment terrified half out of my mind.* But he wouldn't say it, firstly because he didn't want to make a fool of himself in Fyne's eyes and secondly because he didn't want to give the embryonic panic any fuel on which to feed by admitting the truth aloud.

"I'm fine, Fyne." He tried to grin at the unintended joke, but failed, and started to move along the deck, resisting an urge to grip the rail to steady himself. "I'll just go below, and—*oh, Yandros!*"

The appalled yell startled Fyne, and for a moment he didn't see it; he knew only that Strann was staring out to sea and that his eyes were bulging in their sockets, his mouth working, gasping like a newly landed fish. Then, belatedly understanding, the captain looked toward the horizon.

The cloud was purplish black, the color of a fearsome bruise. It towered into the otherwise empty sky, and it was boiling into the shape of a vast anvil, the flattened, tapering head rising two miles or more above the sea. And it was moving—no, Fyne thought; this wasn't possible, it wasn't *possible!* No cloud could move at such a speed: Seconds ago there had been nothing on the horizon, and now the entire southeasterly sky was filling with darkness as the monstrous thunderhead rolled toward them. This was no natural storm—it was something from a hell beyond imagining!

Suddenly the suffocating quiet was ripped apart by a stentorian voice from the ship's bows. *"Storm ahead! Storm ahead!"* To Strann it was like a physical blow, breaking the hypnosis that gripped him. He reeled back from the rail with a cry of horror and despair and cannoned into Fyne as the Captain started toward the source of the shout.

"Get below!" Fyne took Strann by the shoulders, spun him violently around, and shoved him in the direction of the companion steps. "Don't stand there gibbering, you fool—*get below!*"

Intelligence snapped back into Strann's eyes, and with it a renewal of his fear. He didn't speak—he couldn't, words were beyond him—but lurched away, hampered by his packs, staggering along the deck. He vanished through the hatch with a stumbling clatter, and Fyne swung around to face the approaching horror again. Now he could see what the lookout had seen: the lightning, the flickering, crimson tongues spitting like demonic fire in the heart of the darkness. Minutes—minutes, no more—

and it would be on them. And for the first time in his life Fyne knew what true terror was.

His hand went to his belt and he snatched from it a short brass horn. In all his days of seafaring he'd never used it, for the signal it sounded was a warning of the direst emergency and danger, and until now Fyne had been a lucky man. Now, though, his luck, and the luck of his ship, had run out.

He put the horn to his lips and blew. As the sharp, clear, and urgent note rang out, bringing the crew racing to their stations, the first bawl of thunder rolled across the sea to swamp *Cloudfisher* in a deafening wall of sound.

Even from the vantage point of this highest of all the palace towers, the horror unfolding in the Bay of Illusions was far beyond the scope of human vision. But the eyes that gazed down from the tower and across the well-tended acres of grounds to the distant harbor and the sea were not entirely human, and the mind behind the lovely face in its frame of jet-black hair was capable of reaching beyond ordinary dimensions to see and hear things that no ordinary mortal senses could discern.

She hadn't moved for upward of half an hour. She had an uncanny ability to remain so still for so long that any observer could easily have taken her for a bizarrely lifelike statue, and only the slow, controlled rhythm of her breathing betrayed her and intruded on the silence.

Outside, the heavy overcast was almost complete, and sunlight broke through only in a narrow, brazen scar to the south. In the tower room's deeper shadows, away from the window, a second figure sat hunched and watching the woman with an unwavering gaze. He was naked, and his red hair gleamed like embers in the semidarkness, hanging in ropes about his stunted and distorted frame. One hand rested on a nearby table; now and then the taloned fingers moved idly over the polished surface as though caressing it. He waited; and at last there was a long, gentle expulsion of breath, the woman's shoulders relaxed, and she turned to face him.

"We will have guests before too long, Father," she said. "I must make myself ready to receive them." A smile parted her lips, voluptuous but feral. "Our very first visitors from the mainland."

The red-haired demon returned a smile that more than matched hers. "Go then, child. And make sure they see you at your most magnificent."

"Oh, I will." She glanced back toward the window. The sliver of sunlight had vanished, swallowed by cloud, but at a gesture from her hand another light began to creep in from the world outside. It was dull, copper-colored, and as it grew stronger, it began to fluctuate like the pulse of a slow and massive heart. The woman smiled again, and when she turned back to face her father, the light flung her figure into silhouette and throbbed behind her like an ominous aura.

"What shall you do with them?" the demon asked softly.

"I haven't yet decided. But I'll find a use for them. One way or another, I'll find a use." Silk rustled as she began to move across the room, then by the table she paused and looked down at a small, ornate casket that rested on the surface. It was a deliberate mockery of another and far older box, which she'd never seen but which all the history tracts described in detail, and it amused her

25

to think of the use to which this virtual twin was now being put. Her fingers hovered near the catch; the demon looked obliquely up at her, and she held his gaze for a moment, then withdrew her hand.

"No," she said. "I don't need to see it again. I know it's there: that's enough." She looked into a small, oval mirror that hung on the wall behind the demon and pushed her hair back from her face, turning her head to study her reflection from a variety of angles. Then she threw a last glance over her shoulder.

"Watch the audience room in the scrying glass, Father. I plan to entertain our guests in ways that I suspect you'll find quite amusing."

The demon listened to the sound of her light footsteps skimming away down the tower stairs. For a few moments after they had faded, there was silence, then a thin, silver-tongued bell sang somewhere below, and he heard his daughter's voice calling sharply for her servants. He smiled once more, indulgently and yet with faint cynicism, and ran his hand fondly, possessively over the lid of the casket before rising and moving toward the window, from where, unseen, he could observe the outside world and await the guests' arrival.

The hoarsely shouted words *"Land ho!"* were, Strann thought, the sweetest he had ever heard in his eventful life, and more precious to him than the truest promises of love or money or acclaim. With a great creaking of damaged timbers and groaning of torn canvas, *Cloudfisher* lurched through the choppy water, and the grimly determined chants of the rowers at their benches below decks vied

with the noises of the elements as what was left of the sails
bellied to the sudden thrust of a strong following wind.

Strann picked himself up from the floor of the big
communal cabin, trying to ignore the stinks of sweat and
vomit that were threatening to make his stomach rebel
afresh. He'd long ago lost his breakfast, not from seasickness but through blind and shaming fear; and even when
the danger and the horror were over, it had been a long
time before he could force his muscles to move. He didn't
know how long the storm had lasted or even how bad it
had been. Throughout its duration—minutes? hours?
days?—he had been in the grip of a terror that had reduced him to a piece of physical and mental flotsam
curled among his hapless fellow passengers on the cabin
floor with his eyes tight shut and his fingers jammed into
his ears. Only when he had forced himself to believe that
the scream of the gale and the crack and thunder of the
lightning bolts had finally ceased had he regained any self-
control, and even now his grip on himself was precarious.
He didn't want to think about the storm. He didn't want
to think about what the *Cloudfisher*'s crew, battling in the
midst of black mayhem to save their ship and passengers,
might have seen and faced up on deck, and he certainly
didn't want to think about his own cowardice. All he
wanted was to feel solid ground beneath his feet, dry land
where he could crawl away and nurse himself back to
something like sanity. And—if his stomach would only
tolerate it—a very, very large quantity of liquor to send
him into blissful and dreamless sleep.

He realized, as he found his feet and began to move
slowly toward the companion steps, that he was alone in
the cabin. He must have been the last to recover his wits,
and the knowledge made him feel ashamed of his weak-

ness in giving way to the terror and the panic. Damn it, he was a Master of the Musical Arts, a true bard and not some posturing amateur! He of all people should have been ready to distract his companions and soothe their fears, but instead he'd shivered like a rat in a trap and proved himself worse than useless. He was disgusted with himself—the more so as terror receded and his confidence started to crawl back—and for a moment he saw in his mind's eye the face of his old master at the Guild Academy of Musicians; the same man who had subsequently, and successfully, pressed for his removal from the Guild's roll of honor for disreputable behavior. The old vulture would have liked to see him now, Strann thought. He would have nodded his head sagely and smiled the smile of triumphant vindication. At this moment Strann couldn't in all conscience have argued with him.

He reached the steps and started to climb unsteadily toward the deck. Daylight was slanting down from above, cold air laden with the tang of salt slapped against his face, and he paused to take several deep and grateful breaths before completing the climb. As his head emerged through the hatch and he instinctively looked up, he had a sharp shock, for where the sails should have towered in their full glory, only a few tattered remnants clung to the masts and struggled to hold and take advantage of the wind. Beyond them the sky was washed to a clean and hard blue: all traces of the storm had vanished, but it had taken its toll on the ship. The top third of the mainmast itself had snapped off, leaving a jagged spear pointing toward the sky, and broken spars and torn rigging were tangled like monstrous seaweed in the sails' remains. *Cloudfisher* was listing sharply to port; and over the noises of sea and wind, shouts, running feet, and, from somewhere below, a rhythmic thumping as men frantically worked the bilge pumps, the voice of the first mate roared orders and encouragement in equal measure.

Strann shook his head in an effort to clear his mazed mind, then looked about for Fyne Cais Haslo. At last he saw the captain in the forecastle, surrounded by a knot of anxious-looking passengers. Fyne was holding a spyglass to one eye, and Strann hauled himself out of the hatch and made his way along the wet and slippery deck to join the group. As he reached them, Fyne lowered the spyglass, saw him, and nodded brief acknowledgment. His expression was tense and uncertain.

Strann swallowed back the sickness that the lurching of the ship had brought welling up again. "Is something wrong?"

"No. No, I don't think so." But Fyne's eyes belied his words. A painfully thin woman beside him suddenly reached out and clutched at his arm.

"We're going to sink, aren't we?" Her voice was shrill, on the edge of hysteria. "The ship's holed! We're going to be drowned!"

"Madam, I tell you again, the ship is *not* holed." Fyne turned wearily toward her trying to prise her fingers from his sleeve. "She's battered and bruised, but she's still perfectly seaworthy—I assure you, you're in no danger!"

For the first time Strann saw clearly just how exhausted the captain was, and it shamed him afresh. It was almost impossible to imagine the sheer skill and seamanship that Fyne and his crew must have displayed in bringing the ship through the storm: he and the other passengers owed these men their lives, and that was a sobering realization. Yet he had a disquieting feeling that all was not entirely well. Not the ship herself: Strann had no reason to doubt Fyne's assurances to the frightened woman that *Cloudfisher* was in no danger of sinking. But something else. Something else . . .

He said, "We're in sight of land?"

"Yes." Fyne couldn't quite suppress the small frown that appeared on his face. "Summer Isle's in sight. We should put in to harbor within half an hour." The frown deepened. "That in itself's a miracle from the gods. I'd thought we'd been blown miles off course by that—that *thing.*" He shuddered.

Strann couldn't help it; his curiosity was stronger than his prudence, and goaded by the uneasy instinct. "That . . . *is* Summer Isle ahead?" he ventured.

Fyne shot him a filthy look. "Of course it's Summer Isle. What do you take me for?"

"No, no; forgive me, I didn't mean to imply any slight. But you seem a little . . ." Strann paused, then reasoned that he'd already cast tact overboard and caution might as well follow. "You don't look entirely happy at the prospect of making landfall."

Fyne turned fully to face him. *"Happy?"* he repeated incredulously. "After what my crew and my ship have been through, you don't think I'm *happy* to see land ahead of me? Aeoris's eyes, man, you must be either jesting or mad!"

Several of the other passengers laughed at this, releasing nervous tension, and even the thin woman managed to smile. But as Fyne made his excuses and left the forecastle, Strann stared thoughtfully after him, then on impulse followed him down the steps and along the deck toward *Cloudfisher*'s stern.

"Captain Fyne."

Fyne stopped and turned around. They were out of

30

earshot of the other passengers now, and Strann looked the other man directly in the eye. Gently, he said, "I don't believe you."

Fyne stared back, and for a moment Strann thought he might have overstepped the bounds. But then with an abrupt gesture the Captain held out his spyglass.

"Summer Isle lies thirty degrees off our starboard bow," he said brusquely. "Take a look through this, and tell me what you see."

Strann took the glass and put it to his eye. At first he could see nothing but the blurred images of the torn sails; then Fyne guided his arm until the glass was focusing on the sea. A coastline slid into view—Strann was impressed by the glass's power, for the image was clear and sharp— and then he saw the familiar curve of harbor walls, like two arms reaching out to embrace the ocean.

"I see Summer Isle harbor," he said.

"Yes. And what else?"

Strann was nonplussed. "What else should I look for?"

A pause. Then Fyne said, "Try looking for ships."

Realization dawned. Slowly Strann lowered the glass, and his hazel eyes narrowed as he turned to stare at the Captain.

"The harbor's empty."

"Precisely."

"But—"

"But with guests coming from all over the provinces for the High Margravine's celebrations, there should be vessels of every size, shape, and color you can think of at anchor in that harbor today." Fyne took the glass from him; Strann released it as though all the strength had suddenly gone from his fingers. "Why, Strann? You're the storyteller: What manner of story is this?"

"I . . ." Strann's voice caught; he tried again. "I don't know."

"Neither do I. But there's something peculiar afoot, and now that the passengers can't hear me, I'm prepared to admit that I don't like the look of it." Suddenly he scowled. "I don't want anyone starting an alarm, do you understand? If you say one word to anyone—"

"No," Strann assured him hastily. "You have my promise. And I apologize"—he nodded back toward the forecastle—"for speaking out of turn." He paused. "Though I don't know how much difference my silence or yours will make. They'll see the truth for themselves soon enough."

"Maybe so. But by then we'll be dropping anchor and there'll be no question of turning back. The men are exhausted, and I won't sanction a return voyage to Shu-Nhadek in our present state. I intend to put in to harbor and I don't want any arguments about it. Whatever's waiting for us can't pose a greater risk than trying to get this ship back to the mainland without repairs."

Strann nodded. "I understand. And, self-preserving coward that I am, I agree that it's the only sensible course."

"Sensible?" Fyne eyed him sharply. " 'Sane' would be a better word with the damage we've suffered; and that's something else that I don't want you babbling to all and sundry."

"Depend on it."

The captain continued to look at him for a few seconds more, as though trying to decide whether or not Strann could be trusted to keep silent. Then, abruptly, he nodded.

"Well, then. There's work to be done, and I'm not about to leave it all to my subordinates. We'll reach harbor in about half an hour, as I said: then we'll see what's what."

He strode away, leaving Strann alone and distinctly unhappy.

Despite Fyne's hopes, the realization that something was amiss on Summer Isle couldn't be avoided as *Cloudfisher* approached harbor. A chance word from a thoughtless crewman, sharp eyes and sharp minds among the passengers, and the heightened state of tension that already existed on board all played their part, and as the ship yawed toward the twin arms of the harbor wall, her bows were crowded with people staring anxiously shoreward. Strann was among them, though he wasn't overanxious to shoulder his way through to the rail for a better view. And when the murmuring began, and rapidly swelled into cries first of chagrin and then of alarm, he felt the sinking crawl of horror in the pit of his stomach.

"What in the gods' names—?"

"I've never seen anything like—"

"What is it?"

"Aeoris! Look there—look!"

"There! There's more of them!"

"They're all— "

"Back now, ladies and gentlemen." Fyne strode into the midst of the crowd. "Stand back now, please." His voice was steady, but his eyes gave away the feelings and the fear that he wouldn't allow himself to show. Three crewmen followed behind him, gently but firmly shepherding people away from the rail, and slowly the press began to clear. Fyne flashed a quick look at one of the sailors and spoke quietly.

"Take them below, and persuade them to stay there in their own best interests."

"Sir." The passengers began to move away, and for the first time Strann had a clear view of the scene beyond *Cloudfisher*'s bows.

The harbor wasn't entirely empty. A solitary ship was moored to the main pier, rocking gently on the water's surface. The vessel—of a design like nothing else Strann had ever seen—was entirely black from stem to stern: black hull, black masts, black sails hanging unnaturally still like crows' wings at rest. Her prow bore no figurehead and she boasted no name. She looked utterly deserted.

And then Strann saw that, contrary to first impressions, there were people on the quayside. Or at least men. With the momentary appalling clarity that shock brought to his senses, he realized that there must have been a hundred or more of them, some in sailors' or stevedores' or harbor officials' garb, others in the distinctive uniform of the High Margrave's personal guard. A hundred or more, littering the docks and the harbor front beyond in a bloody carnage of broken, twisted corpses, and without a single survivor to be glimpsed among them.

3

<hr>

The first mate had pushed a sword into Strann's unwilling hand and told him to stop arguing and hold on to it. Strann didn't want to hold on to it; he had no skill with weapons and had never before handled anything more lethal than a short-bladed knife, and he didn't want the responsibility of this heavy and cumbersome blade. But Fyne Cais Haslo's order was unequivocal: Every able-bodied man or woman for whom there was a weapon to spare must be armed, and there could be no exceptions. Fyne, hard-eyed and under icy self-control, had addressed the assembled company and announced that, as he was unwilling to risk putting the storm-damaged *Cloudfisher* to sea again, they must steel themselves to the horrors of what they had found here, and take immediate action to discover what had happened and assess the danger to themselves. The crew and passengers would therefore split into two parties, one to stay with and guard the ship, the other to strike out for the High Margrave's palace.

Strann was very reluctant to be included in the exploratory party, but his pride, and the knowledge that any protest would achieve nothing, deterred him from saying so. There was, though, one brief skirmish with the mate over the question of what was to become of his manzon. The mate argued that the bulky pack would hamper

Strann and thereby slow the whole party's progress, but this was one issue on which Strann wasn't prepared to back down. The manzon went wherever he went, he stated flatly, and that was an end to it. Eventually his stubbornness prevailed, and as he slung the extra burden on his back, he tried to cheer himself with the thought that at least he would get away from the grisly scene on the harbor front and from the stench of decaying human flesh. Fyne and one of the passengers, a physician from Prospect, had risked their stomachs to examine some of the dead men, and the physician had concluded that they must have been slaughtered at least a full day before *Cloudfisher*'s arrival. His use of the word *slaughtered* was no exaggeration: the victims of this carnage had died horribly, their bodies torn and mutilated by wounds of a kind that the physician declared he'd never seen in twenty years of medical practice. No, he couldn't say what had made those wounds. But he'd stake his reputation that they were not inflicted by any normal blades.

That knowledge did nothing to aid Strann's faltering confidence as the shore party set out on the road, with Fyne himself at their head. The High Margrave's court lay some two miles inland, sheltered from the prevailing sea winds by a chain of low hills. They wouldn't have their first sight of the palace until they were less than half a mile from its gates, and Strann suspected that his companions were preoccupied by the same speculation that plagued him. What would they find at the palace? What would be waiting for them in the lee of those hills?

They strode along in grim silence. Everyone had noticed but no one was willing to be first to voice the fact that as far as the eye could see there wasn't a soul in sight. A few deer grazed in the distance and the occasional sea gull sailed overhead, but there was no sign of any human life. Strann, striving to hold on to the sweat-slicked hilt of his borrowed sword, flicked his gaze nervously this way and that and tried to ignore the tension that twisted his gut as his fertile imagination ran riot. First his premonitions in Shu-Nhadek, then the unnatural storm, now this. Gods, what were he and his companions walking into? They should turn back. Never mind the damage to *Cloudfisher*; they should leave this island, get away—

"Captain!" The sudden shout made him jump with fright, and he dropped his sword. As he bent to retrieve it, he heard Fyne swear softly, other voices joining in, and when he straightened and looked up, Strann saw what had captured his companions' attention.

They were climbing the gentle hill that hid the Summer Isle palace from view and were perhaps thirty yards from the crest. Above the crest a light had appeared. Not sunlight, for even without the heavy cloud cover the sun would by now have moved far around toward the west. Besides, the sun didn't pulse with an eerie rainbow of dark colors, amber and green and crimson and indigo . . .

One of the sailors glanced at Fyne for permission, then, hefting a cutlass in one hand and a heavy stave in the other, hastened on ahead of the party. He reached the crest, hesitated a bare moment, then turned and beckoned agitatedly. "Sir, up here! Quickly!"

Fyne broke into a run, the others—Strann lagging a little—behind him. They reached the crest, and the entire party fell silent, stunned and staring.

The High Margrave's palace lay before them, surrounded by the huge, verdant swathe of its gardens and grounds. The outer walls of the gracious old building were faced with quartz, and the quartz's countless facets were flickering under a hellish glow, so that the entire palace seemed to throb like a vast heart. The source of the light hung unsupported in the air above the tallest tower. Pulsing its beams out from a dark core in implacable rhythm, swelling and fading, swelling and fading, was a monstrous seven-rayed star—the emblem of Chaos.

Someone in the middle of the group moaned softly. Two or three others fell to their knees, making the splay-fingered sign of reverence to the gods, and Captain Fyne began to swear, very quietly but very, very intensely. Strann's eyes met those of the sailor who'd been the first to see the grim phenomenon. The man had seemed paralyzed, but abruptly the contact with another human gaze broke the spell that held him. His jaw worked spastically for a few seconds, then cohesion returned.

"It's *their* work." He started to shake with reaction; light from the pulsing star reflected coldly on the quivering cutlass blade in his hand. "All this . . . and the slaughter at the harbor . . . it's *Chaos*! Sweet Aeoris, what are we going to do, what are we—"

"Be quiet!" Fyne had recovered his wits, and his words cut sharply across the crewman's hysteria, jerking him back from the brink of panic. The Captain turned to face the company, his figure grotesquely haloed by the dark glow, and held out his hands, palms downward in a pacifying gesture.

"Please—all of you!" The rising tide of mutterings and exclamations began to ebb; after a few moments there was silence. The star continued to pulse ominously. Fyne swallowed.

"The emblem of Chaos hangs over the palace. It's an awesome sight, but it does *not* threaten us. Do you understand me? We're all true servants of the fourteen gods—

why should we fear Yandros's own sign?" His gaze flicked swiftly from one face to another to another; he was, Strann knew, aware that his authority hung by a thread, and was equally aware of the urgent need to maintain control of the party.

"It would seem," Fyne continued, "that the palace is under Chaos's protection and we can therefore consider it a safe haven. I assure you, there is *no* danger to us here." He flashed a scathing look at the frightened seaman, who didn't have the courage to meet his stare. "We have nothing to fear from the forces of Chaos, and I'd remind you all that those we left behind to guard the ship are depending on us to bring back help. We must go directly to the palace without any further delay."

It was like watching a flock of beasts following the herder's lead. Heads nodded, uncertainty coalesced into thankful accord; even the frightened sailor hunched his shoulders and capitulated Relieved, Fyne turned, ready to lead the group away down the hill.

And, sharply and without any premeditation, Strann said, "No."

Fyne stopped and looked back. "What?"

"I said no." A chilly and unpleasant sensation crawled over Strann's skin as he looked into Fyne's eyes and realized that he was about to be challenged to justify himself. He couldn't. He had no logical arguments to put forward, no evidence to present, simply an ugly and implacable presentiment of danger.

"I'm not going to the palace," he said, and his voice was shaking despite his efforts to keep it on an even keel. "And if you've a gravine of sense, Fyne, you'll stop anyone else from going. Turn back. For the gods' sakes, turn *back.*"

"Don't be a fool, Strann." Fyne was clearly irritated, but his anger was tempered by something he saw lurking in Strann's eyes and he spoke more moderately than he might otherwise have done. "That's Chaos's own sign hanging over the palace—we're far safer here than at the harbor!"

"We're not. And if that star has anything to do with the gods of Chaos, then I'm the long-lost son of the Margrave of Prospect."

Fyne's temper began to quicken at what seemed to him a piece of frivolity. "Don't be ridiculous, man! You don't know what you're talking about, and you're verging on blasphemy!"

"I don't think I am," Strann said flatly. The chill feeling had suddenly grown far worse. "I don't know why I feel as I do; I just know it's the truth. I'm scared, Fyne. I'm scared to the deepest pits of my soul. I believe we should get away from here, before something happens to stop us."

One or two others began to murmur something akin to agreement, and Fyne realized that if he didn't act quickly, the party's prevailing mood would swing dangerously toward panic again.

"Nothing's going to happen!" he snapped furiously. "Damn it, man, what are you made of—flesh and blood, or piss and wind? You may not have the spine to face the gods' own symbol but, by Yandros and Aeoris, you're the only one who hasn't! Do as you please—sit here and weave daisy chains, if that's all you're fit for—but the rest of us are—"

He was interrupted by a harsh scream from someone at the edge of the group, and at the same moment a sailor bellowed, "Sir! Sir, *the palace!*"

Strann heard their noise rolling across the sward from the direction of the palace gates before he saw them, and his stomach contracted so violently that he thought he might be sick. Then he did see them, and shock and fear fused into sheer, stark terror.

They were neither hounds nor giant cats but some unholy miscarriage between the two, and four times the size of any dog ever whelped. Their bodies were seamless black, their eyes scarlet, their tongues silver, and as they streamed out from the palace gates, their hideous baying sounded like the war horns of the Seven Hells. Strann's stunned mind, working on some reflexive level beyond his control, counted twenty of them . . . fifty . . . a hundred. Then a new sound tore through the throbbing air, an insane, ululating, howling chorus, and a horde of riders on pitch-black horses erupted through the gates on the heels of the houndcats, and the whole monstrous pack came thundering over the turf toward the paralyzed and horrified watchers.

Fyne whipped his cutlass from its scabbard, and his voice roared above the mad din of the oncoming attackers. *"To me! To me! Close in, quickly—form a line of defense!"*

Strann realized what the captain was trying to do, and every instinct he possessed rebelled violently. "No!" he bawled with all his strength. "Fyne, don't be a fool; we can't stand against this! Run—*run for your lives and souls!"*

He swung about, ready to flee whether or not anyone else chose to follow him, then yelled in terror as a huge, dark shape seemed to explode out of the ground in front of him. An appalling image of something that looked like a skinned but living horse, ridden by a human shape with a black and featureless body, smashed into his brain, and then the thing was screaming and rearing above him, and Strann was screaming, too, twisting about and running like a scalded animal, anywhere, he didn't know where and it didn't matter, anywhere that would get him *away* from it—

Other yells mingled with his, and suddenly Fyne's embryonic phalanx collapsed into chaos as people scattered, shouting, in all directions. Strann slewed to a halt as he saw what was happening, saw the earth opening and the other huge, dark shapes rising in a sweeping, curving line around them, cutting off their retreat. The houndcats' baying dinned in his ears, the shrieks of the grisly horses and their unhuman masters battered against his skull, and through the mayhem he heard Fyne's desperate rallying cry, *"To me! To me!"* like the howling of a lost soul. Then the black tide was on them, and Strann found himself fighting for his life with the wild desperation of the unskilled, the unfamiliar sword seeming to take on a life of its own, dragging him helplessly with it as, off-balance, he lurched this way and that. He didn't want to kill, he wanted only to survive, to fend off the snapping teeth and flying hooves and shimmering black blades that hacked down like lethal rain into the melee. Ducking, weaving, dodging—he couldn't fight, he didn't know *how* to fight, not like this—he sprawled at last into a clear space, and though the hiatus was brief, it enabled him to see the terrible truth that his embattled companions hadn't yet comprehended.

A burly sailor, his cutlass a blur as he frantically defended himself against five snarling, slavering monsters, cannoned backward into Strann, almost knocking him off his feet. Strann grabbed the man's arm as the houndcats fell back a pace, and yelled in his ear.

"You can't kill them with a blade! Gods help us, don't you see? *They're not flesh and blood!*"

Shock registered on the man's bloodied face; seeing their advantage, the houndcats closed in again. The sailor howled in defiance, the cutlass swung in a savage arc—and passed through the bodies of the two leading beasts without the least effect. The screaming sailor went down under an onslaught of claws and fangs and Strann, moaning aloud in horror, stumbled back from the carnage. He had to warn the others! They didn't know, they hadn't realized—these monstrosities were phantoms, creations of black sorcery! They could kill, they could tear, they could rend, they could rip; but they themselves were impervious to weapons and therefore impossible to defeat.

"Fyne!" He couldn't see the Captain, but he bellowed his name despairingly. *"Fyne, where are you? There's no hope—flee! Flee if you can!"*

But even if any of his friends could have heeded the warning, understanding had come too late. They were dying, falling one by one as though scythed, and the grass underfoot was turning red and slick with their blood. Strann, still twisting and turning, still, incredibly, alive, lost all control at last and cried out his fear and his loathing and his sense of sheer, bitter injustice, cursing demons and sorcerers and gods alike, pleading for help, pleading for sanity as he flung himself to the ground, hands clasped over his head in a last, futile effort to protect himself from this madness.

Then suddenly, shockingly, the battlefield was silent.

Strann lay still. He didn't know whether he was alive or dead and he dared not move to find out. The silence was awesome and there was something unnatural about it. He couldn't claim to know much about such things, but he felt instinctively that in the aftermath of such carnage there should be noise: men shouting, feet stamping, the moans of the wounded. But there was nothing. *Was* he dead, and was this some limbo between dying and whatever afterlife the gods had decreed for him?

Very cautiously he tried to move. His limbs responded, but he immediately felt dampness spreading across his stomach and thighs. He froze, convinced for a moment that he was bleeding, then realized that it wasn't blood but something far less heroic. Strann felt his cheeks flaming with shame. He was alive after all, and the only stigma he had to show for his ordeal was a disgraceful lapse of self-control. Disgusted with himself, he began to move again—and stopped still for a second time as he heard a footfall in the grass beside him.

Something reached down, and hard fingers took a grip on his coat, hauling him to his knees. Blinking, Strann looked up at a black silhouette, manlike in shape but devoid of any feature. It didn't speak—he wasn't sure that it was capable of speaking—but pointed with its free hand to where three men stood huddled some way off under the guard of several of the hideous horsemen.

Strann began to shiver uncontrollably. Ignoring the reaction, his captor lifted him to his feet and propelled him at a staggering half-run toward the others. He felt the manzon bumping on his back, but the borrowed sword was long gone, and even the scabbard had fallen from his belt. They neared the dismal little group, and Strann saw that it consisted of two of *Cloudfisher*'s crewmen—he didn't know their names—and Fyne Cais Haslo himself. Fyne had been wounded; there was an ugly gash down one side of his face, and with his left hand he clutched his

44

broken right arm hard against his side. But he was alive. At least he was alive.

Strann whispered, "Fyne . . . who else . . . ?" He couldn't finish.

The Captain stared back bleakly. "No one else." His face was stiff with drying blood and his mouth formed the words with difficulty. "Just the four of us. The others are all dead."

Strann looked away. Shock was setting in now and beginning to numb him, but the stark tally still struck home hard. He wanted to say more to Fyne, though the gods alone knew what could be said that was worth anything under such circumstances, but before he could speak again, their captors gestured toward the palace gates. Between the legs of the grisly horses the houndcats slavered and leered, their silver tongues licking the air as though tasting man-scent, and Fyne let his shoulders slump, accepting the inevitable. His eyes were dull with defeat, Strann saw. Knowing Fyne, he surmised that the Captain had hoped to die quickly and with some dignity, but he made no protest as the black horsemen pushed them forward and the monstrous animals chuckled and chivvied at their heels.

As they were hustled away, Strann forced himself not to look back at the battlefield where the rest of the black houndcats were now feeding rapaciously but to turn his face to the palace before him and pray silently to whatever powers might be listening to grant him a chance, just a chance, to survive this nightmare and emerge on the far side with his soul and his sanity intact.

The palace had changed. Strann couldn't claim intimate knowledge of it, for he'd only visited the Summer Isle court once before, and that briefly. But he remembered the atmosphere of the place, the sense of security and tradition that soaked through every stone and imparted its own blend of comfort and awe into the mind of natives and newcomers alike. Now that atmosphere had vanished utterly and something else had taken its place. Something equally strong and secure, but redolent of a darker and more malevolent force, not secular as the High Margrave's rule had been but shot through with veins of supernatural power. The palace, he thought, stank of evil.

They were marched along corridors that Strann dimly remembered and arrived finally before a set of ornate double doors at the palace's heart. The party halted, and Strann's memory, unbidden, conjured images of the great audience hall that he knew lay beyond, filled with music and light and all the brilliant splendor of the High Margrave's wedding celebrations, where he had danced with the High Initiate's sister after their triumphant duet.

When they had played that damned piece from the Equilibrium *epic, and this whole hideous chain of events had begun . . .*

One of their guards raised an unhuman fist and struck the doors. A metallic boom set Strann's teeth clenching, and as it echoed away through the palace, the doors began to grate open. Vivid light spilled through the widening gap, and blinking in its glare, Strann had an astonishing impression of a great and colorful gathering filling the hall, a celebratory crowd like the wedding guests of last year. Then three things hit his churning mind at the same time. There was a desperate edge to the gaiety of the people thronging the hall. He could see them more clearly

46

now, see the smiles and hear the laughter that only barely
masked the terror in their eyes. Threading through them
like a cancer were black and faceless shapes, not human
but kin to the horrors that had come shrieking from the
palace to slaughter Fyne's party. Guardians, sentries,
watchers; whatever term the tongue devised, their function was the same: to control.

At the far end of the great hall, on an immense and
alien throne raised above the heads of the crowd, a solitary figure sat in the High Margrave's traditional place of
authority. Strann looked at her and knew that she was the
loveliest and most physically perfect woman he had ever
imagined. He watched as she leaned forward with lithe
and easy grace, watched her hair falling like a black cat-
aract around her, took in her porcelain complexion and
the sapphire brilliance of her eyes. She smiled, holding out
a hand in a mockery of felicitous greeting. And Strann
knew that, until this moment, he had not understood the
true meaning of evil.

Ygorla rose. Immediately the hall fell utterly silent,
and she turned slightly to one side and snapped her fingers. A figure—a silhouette, no more—stepped from behind the throne, and at first Strann thought that the staff it
held in its hands was crowned with a standard, perhaps
this woman's personal emblem. Then from somewhere in
the middle of the throng came an agonized cry. It was
quickly stifled, but not before Strann had traced its source,
and his eyes widened as he saw the blond woman at the
front of the crowd, held there by two faceless guards who
had pinned her arms tightly against her sides. Jianna, the
High Margravine herself—but she was barely recogniz-
able, for the beauty Strann remembered had been wiped
out and in its place was a dead-white mask of a face,

cheeks grimed and streaked with tears, lips bitten and blis-
tered, eyes red and hollow from weeping. She was staring
at the standard-bearer with the blank, desperate near-
madness of disbelief; Strann quickly followed the direction
of her gaze, and his gorge rose with a violent jolt as he
saw, crowning the pole in the black creature's hands, the
severed and grotesquely smiling head of the High Margrave, Blis Hanmen Alacar.

Ygorla moved to the front of the dais and stood looking down at the four captives with sweet pity. Then she
smiled.

"Welcome," she said. "I am Ygorla—your new High
Margravine, and your Empress!"

4

There was a short exhalation of breath, then a dull thud as
one of Strann's companions dropped to the floor in a dead
faint. The other sailor hadn't seen the horror; he was
hunched over, clutching at his rib cage and trying to stem
the gentle but implacable flow of blood from a wound just
above his stomach. Fyne, though, stared at the black-
haired woman without flinching. His face was quite expressionless; Strann didn't know him well enough to know
what that portended, and besides, he felt too numb to pay
Fyne more than the barest heed. He had managed not to
vomit simply because his stomach was already empty, but
he felt nauseous and giddy, and the scene before him
seemed to swim through a dreamlike fog. He wanted to
wake up. He would have given anything at this moment—
all his talent, his singing voice, even the use of his hands—
to wake up and find that this was nothing more than a
nightmare.

He sensed that the black-haired woman was staring
down at them. He didn't raise his head; he didn't want to
look her in the eye. Then she spoke again.

"Well, this is a poor showing." Her voice was as lovely
as her face, but underlying its sweetness Strann heard an
acid note that implied an appalling threat. "Four travelers
come to pay homage to their new ruler, but it seems they

have nothing to say for themselves. No compliments to pay me, no pretty words to praise me, not one single plaudit. I am disappointed." She paused. No one made a sound. The heels of her shoes clicked on the dais's quartz floor as she moved slowly back toward the throne.

"Perhaps our new friends are so overwhelmed that they find themselves at a loss for words? That would be understandable, would it not?" She looked around her at the silent throng, and her eyes flashed venomously. *"Would it not?"*

This time they answered her, and Strann's gut curdled at the sibilant *yes, Majesty*s and *indeed so, madam*s that rustled from the throats of her terrified courtiers. It occurred to him that these people, among whom he recognized a good number of Blis Hanmen Alacar's personal guard, were no pack of weaklings, and he shuddered inwardly as he speculated on the power she must have brought to bear to reduce them to such cowed shades.

Suddenly another noise, louder and uglier, sounded from somewhere near his feet, and from the corner of his eye he saw that the wounded sailor had sagged to his knees and was doubled over. His blood had begun to flow more copiously, and a thin scarlet stream was trickling down his chin. Pain had eclipsed his fear and he was trying to speak, pleading incoherently for help, for water, for something to staunch the bleeding. Ygorla's brilliant eyes flicked to him in a cat-swift reflex, and her lip curled.

"Ah, look! This good man is so overcome that he actually *bleeds* for me! I am touched by such a gesture, and I shall reward it. Bring him forward."

Two of the black guards stepped out of the crowd, caught the injured man by his forearms, and dragged him toward the throne, leaving a long, red smear on the hall floor. They dropped him before the dais: their mistress gazed down at him for a moment, then turned her head and made an imperious beckoning gesture. Three shadows detached themselves from the pooled darkness behind the throne. They moved so fast that at first Strann didn't realized what they were or what they were about to do; and by the time he understood, it was too late even to look away, for the sailor's pleas were already exploding into shrieks of agony as the black shadow-beasts fell on him and tore him apart.

Other screams mingled with the murdered sailor's; one woman near Strann was violently sick and another began to sob hysterically. But Strann couldn't react; all he could do was stare at the slaughter with a sense of utter unreality that shut off his emotions as though a lid had slammed down on his mind.

The sailor's shrieks had ceased after a few moments, and at last the monsters withdrew. One, as it backed away licking blood from its muzzle, seemed to smile at Strann as though sharing some private joke. Strann saw that the black beasts had left not so much as one bone from their victim's carcass, but the sight didn't affect him, it meant nothing. The woman was still sobbing; he heard Ygorla say with rancor, "Quiet her!" and the weeping cut off sharply and instantly. Beside him Fyne was breathing in huge, painful gasps, striving to maintain his self control. Ygorla's eyes glittered as she looked down at them.

"So. I am diverted, but only a little." She tilted her head almost coquettishly to one side as though considering what might most amuse her, then pointed at Fyne with a long-nailed finger. "Him," she said.

Fyne was hustled to stand before her, and she assessed him with a long, thoughtful look before addressing him. "I see you're a sea captain. Well, Captain—what entertainment do *you* mean to offer your High Margravine?"

A rattling sound came from Fyne's throat, and he jerked his head aside. *"Entertainment?"* His voice broke on the last syllable.

"Yes, entertainment. It's clear enough, Captain—you have a simple choice. You may kneel before me and swear proper allegiance, in which case you will join my court and learn to please me; or you may share your comrade's swift but painful end. Either way your carcass will be of some use."

Fyne looked up at her. Tears were streaming down his cheeks; his face was deadly white and devoid of all expression and all animation—but for his eyes. They burned with grief and they burned with rage, and above all they burned with soul-consuming loathing.

"I will not," Fyne Cais Haslo said, and his voice rang contemptuously through the hall, "make any pact with *you*. For I do not consort with demons from the Seven Hells." And he spat, with all the contempt that his fury and hatred had instilled in him, directly at her exquisite face.

Ygorla sidestepped; the spittle landed harmlessly on the dais. She gazed down at it for a moment, then shrugged, and snapped her fingers.

This time Strann couldn't look. Fyne's mad, defiant courage shook him to the core, and the fact that the sea captain made no attempt to fight the black beasts as they sprang at him somehow lent a terrible, twisted dignity to his ignominious death. But even as he shut his eyes and shrank away, one thought hammered into Strann's brain in silent, impotent but agonized protest. *He was my friend!* It didn't mean anything; it wasn't even really true . . .

but it gave him a spar to cling to in this sea of horror, for it was the first rational reaction he had been able to muster since their capture. As it sank in, piercing the miasma, he felt his innate instinct for survival creeping back into his consciousness. The numbness was fading, taking with it the sense of unreality, and a hard core of sheer common sense was forming in their place. He didn't yet know what it might lead to, but it was a shred—even if only a shred—of hope.

It was his turn now. He felt bony hands grip his arms and propel him forward, and as he was brought before the monstrous throne, he at last forced himself to look up and meet Ygorla's intense, sapphire-blue stare. She was incredibly beautiful. So beautiful, in fact, that he knew instinctively that she couldn't be fully human, for her form was too perfect. Yet neither did he believe she was a demon, for Strann knew enough about demons to be aware that, like their lower cousins the elementals, they lacked certain dimensions, certain levels of reality, which made it impossible for them to masquerade convincingly as mortals. No; this woman—this creature—was something else. But what?

Her voice broke in on his speculations, like honey and glass.

"What have we here—a rat in man's clothes, with his whiskers all a-twitch? Certainly he looks like a rat, even though he makes a good show of standing on his hind legs." She saw Strann tense involuntarily, trying to ignore the insult, and laughed; some of her court hastily followed suit. "Look at his draggled state. Look at the color of his hair, and the way it hangs about his face like rats' tails. Yes, I do believe he's not a man at all but a rodent." She leaned forward. "Are you intelligent, rat? Do you speak, or do you merely squeal?"

Strann's jaw was clenched; he forced it to relax a little and tried to keep his voice even.

"I speak, lady," he said quietly.

"Ah! So you do. Well then, rat, what fate will *you* choose? Will you nibble crumbs at my feet—or shall I spring my rat trap for you too?"

Strann hesitated. Despite his professed cowardice, every instinct he possessed was rebelling against this humiliation. He wanted to spit in her face as Fyne had tried to do, he wanted to revile her with all the vitriol his bardic skills could muster. But at the same time he knew that if he did, he'd have a mere few seconds of satisfaction before he died in the jaws of her black houndcats. Like Fyne, he had a simple choice: die with his pride and principles unsullied, or use his guile to stay alive no matter what the cost to his dignity and conscience. And he had nothing to gain from dying.

He swallowed bile, and stepped forward. "Majesty," he said in a voice that carried through the hall, "I am yours to command." Dropping to one knee, he took her outstretched hand and kissed it. As he completed the flourishing gesture and withdrew, he saw, on the periphery of his vision, the High Margravine Jianna still held rigid between her two unhuman guards. She was staring at him as though he'd risen through the floor from some sewer of the Seven Hells, and in her eyes was the loathing and misery of utter betrayal. Icy sickness washed over Strann, but there was nothing he could do to redeem himself; he couldn't take the risk of trying to indicate the truth to the Margravine, even if she would have understood or believed any sign he might make. His gaze slid away from her, breaking the link, but he could still feel the sting of her contempt like a physical wound.

Ygorla, however, was smiling. Strann's response had pleased her; she was growing irritated with the two extremes of short-lived defiance and cowering helplessness that she'd so far encountered on Summer Isle, and this nondescript little man appeared to have at least some potential to divert her.

She sat back, her posture languid but her eyes still shrewd. "So," she said. "You make a pretty flourish, rat. But what value do you think a creature like you can be to me? I want more than fealty from those who enjoy the privileges of my court, and I can easily be moved to anger by servants who fail to amuse me. My pets"—she reached out carelessly and stroked the hideous head of one of her houndcats, which made a throatily adoring sound in reply —"are always hungry."

"Majesty," Strann said obsequiously, "I make no claims to greatness, but I have a talent that I venture to think might win me the honor of entertaining you for a little while." Gods, he thought, could he truly have sunk to such depths of fawning deviousness? But if he was to survive, self-respect was a luxury he could no longer afford. He unslung the instrument case from his back—his captors had made no attempt to take it from him—and opened it, revealing the manzon inside.

"I am, Majesty, both a musician and a storyteller." He lifted the manzon and dropped to one knee again so that he could balance it, then, praying silently that the instrument wouldn't sound too sour a note, fingered a chord. The hall's natural acoustics magnified it impressively; he saw a flicker of avid interest in Ygorla's eyes and allowed himself to breathe more surely. He thought that he was beginning to get a little of this woman's measure. He didn't know the extent of her power, but he'd recognized all the signs of overweening conceit, and he was prepared to gamble that he could play outrageously to her vanity without alerting her to his true motive.

He produced another sequence of notes, rapid, complex, dazzling; and when he spoke again, he put into his voice all the richness, elegance, and persuasive ability to cajole and flatter that his Guild Academy training had instilled in him. "I will serve you as your bard, lady, if you'll only condescend to grant me that boon. I can play for you; I can sing for you. I can compose epic tales for you, tales of your own power and glory that will be whispered in awed voices throughout the world." He played new chords, stirring and with a grandiose edge, saw her involuntary responding smile, and subtly modulated his music into a shimmering cascade of sweetly plaintive notes. "Or ballads of your beauty that will drive women to suicide with envy"—*Now,* he thought, *take care; don't overdo it;* he let his head droop forward as though in embarrassment or shame and finished, in a tone of infinite reverence—"and men to distraction with desire."

Ygorla laughed delightedly. It was the reaction Strann had prayed for; he kept his head bowed and didn't move a muscle. Then the laughter subsided into a sigh and Ygorla said softly, "Do *you* desire me, little man?"

Timing, Strann thought. It was one of the earliest lessons he'd learned, and it owed more to his early fairground days than to the Guild's strictures. Very slowly, and keeping careful control, he raised his head.

"Majesty." He allowed himself to meet her gaze candidly for a calculated moment before casting his eyes down once more. "I dare not lie to you: I must tell you the truth. I would go through the tortures of fire for one instant in your arms." He looked up again. "Yet I know I can never be worthy of you. I can only pray that you will forgive my presumption."

There was a long, tense silence. Strann wondered nervously if he'd misjudged the rhetoric and given himself away, but in that at least he had overestimated Ygorla. Suddenly she laughed again, this time a peal of sheer, unfettered mirth that set the court hastening to ape her. She flung her head back, exposing her pale throat and the tantalizing swell of her breasts; her hair rippled like living jet, and as her laughter died away, she wiped her mouth with the back of one hand in a blatantly lascivious way.

"I believe I like you, rat. I believe you might have some skill to amuse me." Abruptly and imperiously her head came up and she scanned the hall, not troubling to hide her contempt for the sea of frightened faces around her. Then she rose.

"We are in need of a court jester to entertain us all, and I consider that this jongleur will be eminently suited to the role." Her eyes focused on Strann once more and he saw mockery, confidence and malevolent pleasure in their vivid gaze. "I shall add you to my menagerie and bestow on you the title of my own pet rat. As my pet, you shall sit on a velvet cushion at my feet and enjoy all the privileges of my court. But never forget that I am a demanding mistress. Please me, and you will prosper Fail"—her sweet smile changed fractionally, a hardening of her lips that left Strann in no doubt of her meaning—"and you will wish that you had never come squalling into this world."

He was given a room in one of the palace's towers, a small, circular chamber that despite the opulence of its furnishings had the atmosphere of a constricting and stifling cage. Left alone, he paced the carpeted floor, trying to forget the memories of what he'd witnessed in the hall, trying to ignore the sense of sick oppression that crowded in on him, and striving to marshal his thoughts.

He was aware that he was walking a perilously narrow bridge over a deadly and unpredictable chasm. He didn't want to speculate on what manner of snakes' nest he had fallen into. Who or what Ygorla was he didn't know and didn't want to know; he couldn't afford as yet to let his mind start down that road, for he had more immediate and more personal concerns. But certainly he had no intention of putting the power this woman seemed to wield to the test by crossing her in any way: he'd seen more than enough to know that that was the shortest and surest road to suicide. Survival. That was what mattered. Survival, whatever the cost might be. He'd negotiated the first and possibly most dangerous pitfall; now he must try to anticipate the other traps that would lie in his path and plan how best to avoid them.

Pet rat, she had called him. Disgust welled, but Strann forced it down. Pet rat. Very well, he'd play to that epithet. He'd sit up on his hind legs and wash his face with his front paws if that was what amused her, and he'd squeak when commanded while keeping prudently silent at all other times. But when his mistress's eyes were elsewhere, the pet rat's whiskers would twitch diligently for any information that might be of use to him—and he had already gleaned one important clue, for he had a strong suspicion that, however great a sorceress Ygorla might be, her intelligence didn't quite match up to her power. She'd accepted his blandishments with no more apparent discernment than a bumpkin farmgirl paid her first compliment, and that led him to believe that she was motivated by conceit above all else. Strann had his own fair share of conceit. He'd never felt particularly ashamed of it, but he also knew that such a trait, if carefully manipulated, could prove to be a weakness and therefore of potentially vital importance in his dealings with Ygorla. He wasn't prepared to gamble on his theory, but nor did he intend to overlook its potential. He'd establish himself in her favor, and—

The thought broke off as the door behind him opened. He swung around rapidly, his heart giving a painful lurch as for a split second he anticipated danger, then he relaxed a little as he saw that it was only one of the palace servants. The newcomer, a man of about his own age, was carrying a covered tray, which he set down unceremoniously on a carved table near the door.

"Your meal," he said curtly, then added with finely honed scorn, "Sir Rat."

Ah, Strann thought. Ygorla's servant in body but not in spirit. It seemed likely that most of the palace retinue who had survived Ygorla's depredations were in a similar position: privately loyal to the murdered High Margrave and the poor, widowed Jianna, but too afraid of the usurper to put up any public show of resistance. However, while they might fear their mistress, they didn't fear a fellow slave, and Strann realized suddenly that he might face other dangers than Ygorla's displeasure. His behavior in the audience hall had branded him a turncoat and a coward; he'd be a focus of hatred and therefore an obvious target for retribution, especially if it was clear that Ygorla set no especial value on his life. He couldn't fault their feelings, but neither did he relish the prospect of a strangling cord or swiftly wielded bludgeon one night as he lay among his silk sheets, and for a moment he wondered if he could take the risk of confiding in this man, telling him the truth and swearing him to secrecy.

He looked into the stony eyes and the impulse vanished. He wouldn't be believed. The charade had already gone too far; in convincing Ygorla of his willingness to serve her, he'd also convinced the survivors of the court. He was a pariah now, the lowest and most contemptible of traitors, and anything he said would be seen as an attempt either to falsely ingratiate himself or to spy on Ygorla's behalf. He could only maintain his pretense and look to Ygorla herself for protection.

He let his gaze slide away from the servant's and said quietly and distantly, "I'm obliged to you."

He could feel the sting of the man's ferocious stare. For a moment the servant stood motionless; then he lifted the domed lid of the tray and, after making sure that Strann was obliquely watching him, spat on the dish's contents. Then without a word he turned on his heel and walked out, slamming the door behind him.

Strann sighed. The man's parting gesture was no more —and in some ways a good deal less—than he'd anticipated, but it rankled nevertheless. Not the offense to his fastidious instincts; in the old fairground days he hadn't been above stealing a pig's food from its trough if he was hungry enough. But to know the depth of his peers' contempt, even if so far they showed it only by spitting in his meals, was a devastating wound to his self-esteem. And, finer feelings aside, it wouldn't stop there. Spittle one day could be poison the next. He must be very, very careful.

Slowly he crossed to the table and stared down at the

dish. It looked like an assortment of sweetmeats, rich and
dainty and not at all to his taste. But he *was* hungry. Had
his enemies put anything in this? Unlikely; they'd hardly
have had the time, and besides, if the food was poisoned,
the servant wouldn't have spat in it and risked his leaving
it uneaten. Strann picked up a two-pronged fork and
speared the delicacies on which spittle had landed, dropping them aside on the tabletop. Then he picked up the
dish and looked about him. He didn't want to sit on any of
the ornate chairs or couches; their tasseled and tinseled
vulgarity, so redolent of Ygorla's crude vanity, made him
squirm. Instead he sank down onto the floor, crossing his
legs and balancing the dish between his knees. Time for
Sir Rat to nibble the first crumbs from his mistress's table
and thereby confirm his status as her captive pet. A signifi-
cant gesture, and one that he didn't want to make. But
then he glanced around the room again and shivered. He
was a captive, whatever appearances might say to the contrary. A pet and a possession, who must now appear to
dedicate his whole existence to pleasing his patron's
whims. Ballads of her glory, paeans of praise to her beauty
. . . the prospect turned his stomach. For the time being,
though, it was a better option than death.

He selected a sweetmeat from the edge of the dish and
put it in his mouth.

The elemental writhed and a thin, pitiful sound vibrated
through the tower room. Narid-na-Gost, who was reclin-
ing in his customary place among the shadows farthest
from the window, looked around with indolent interest
and saw that Ygorla was almost done with the creature.

The task she had set it was completed and the result cooling from white- to red-hot as it hung unsupported in midair; now the elemental was pleading to be allowed to return to its natural place deep under the ground where earth and fire merged into a molten blaze. For a few moments Ygorla stared at it, considering its fate, then an unpleasant smile spread across her face and she raised both hands, forming them into the shape of a cup. The elemental's pleading turned to a shriek of terror as it realized what she meant to do; then Ygorla said a word and water fountained up from her cupped palms. The creature was engulfed; fire erupted into steam, and the hissing drowned out the elemental's screams of agony as it dissolved. Then it was gone. The water vanished and the newly made artifact, cooled now, dropped into Ygorla's hands. A sulphurous smell lingered on the air for a few seconds before fading.

Narid-na-Gost yawned. "Why do you trouble to destroy them, daughter? They're of no significance."

She looked at him over her shoulder; just for a moment a trace of resentment flickered in her blue eyes. "I find it amusing," she said.

"It achieves no purpose."

She shrugged. "My amusement is sufficient purpose for me." She tossed the artifact between her hands like a toy. "Anyway, the creature did as I bade it." She turned fully and threw the object toward him. "What do you think of it, Father?"

Her throw went wide, but the demon glanced at the object and its trajectory changed. He caught it easily and examined it. "Pretty enough. What is it—another torque to adorn your neck?"

Ygorla laughed softly. "Not quite a torque, and not for

me this time. More of a collar, I think. A collar for my new pet, to remind him of what he owes to his mistress." She crossed the room and plucked the thing from Narid-na-Gost's fingers. "Look at the workmanship, Father. Isn't it fine? See the way the gems catch the light—I chose diamonds because they're as colorless and transparent as Strann is, and rubies to ensure that he keeps in mind the color of his own blood and remembers how easily it could be shed." She laughed again, this time with an edge to the sound. "Jianna was the previous owner of these stones. They were in a necklace she used to wear; I understand that her husband gave it to her on their marriage day. I wonder if she'll recognize the gems when she sees them around my rat's throat? Wouldn't that be entertaining?"

Narid-na-Gost didn't seem particularly entertained by the thought. He said, "If you've any sense, you'll attach a chain to the collar and keep a firm hold on it." He was idly watching her body beneath the transparent silver robe that she favored for sorcerous workings. "If you trust that creature, you're a fool."

Ygorla's eyes narrowed angrily. "*Trust* him? What do you take me for? Of course I don't trust him! But I know a fawning coward when I see one. He won't cross me any more than the rest of the simpering court. He won't dare. None of them will, because they know what I can do." As she spoke, her head flicked around, and she glared at a table beneath the window. A flask of wine stood there; Ygorla made a careless gesture and the flask flew into the air, upended its contents onto the floor, and then smashed with enormous force against the wall. Ygorla watched the glass shards spinning in all directions, and when they had finally settled, she faced her father again.

"My pet will only have to displease me once and I'll do

that to him and more," she said with satisfaction. "And he knows it. They *all* know it. They watched me when my ship came sailing into Summer Isle harbor, and they learned to fear me when my crew fell on them and tore them apart. They feared me still more when my creatures killed Blis Hanmen Alacar's own army at the gates of this palace, and they fell down in fright when I held up their precious High Margrave's severed head in the audience hall and told them that a new reign had begun. And their fright became terror when I raised the seven-rayed star of Chaos above these towers to proclaim the source of my power!" She strode to the window and leaned out into the lowering, failing day. High overhead the star still pulsed; its gloomy light gave the palace grounds a brazen, nightmarish cast, and Ygorla smiled again.

"They know what I am," she continued more softly. "And they know my contempt for their human frailties."

In the dimness the demon's crimson eyes looked hot and unnatural. "You seem to have forgotten," he said quietly, "that you yourself had a human mother."

She turned to regard him, and for the first time it occurred to her that their relationship had changed in the few days since he had freed her from her long, fruitful, but intensely frustrating sojourn on the White Isle. Before that day she had held him in awe, for he was not only her father but also her mentor and teacher, and his power as a Chaos demon—even a minor one—had been far greater than her own. But since they had left the White Isle, the balance of their relationship had begun, subtly, to alter. His last remark, which she knew was a thinly disguised reprimand, would never have been delivered so mildly in the old days, and she wondered if in abandoning the Chaos realm to dwell permanently in the world of human-

kind, Narid-na-Gost felt himself to be on less certain
ground. Thinking back over the past two days, she recalled one or two other small incidents that seemed to add
weight to her suspicion, moments when they'd clashed
over minor matters and, expecting his wrath, she'd found
him more conciliatory than usual. Had his confidence
waned? Or was his power weaker in this world than in his
natural home?

She turned her head away to some degree but continued to regard him obliquely through her black lashes. "I
haven't forgotten my origins, Father," she said, choosing
her words carefully. "But that gives me all the more reason to despise those who'll never know what it is to span
both the human realm and that of Chaos. I have the best
of both worlds. Even you can't boast such a unique heritage."

Did she detect a flicker of the old anger in his eyes
then? She couldn't be sure, and when he replied, his voice
was calm and even, almost dismissive.

"Nonetheless, daughter, it's the inhabitants of this
world who should concern you above all else. You are to
reign *here*, not in Chaos."

She smiled sweetly at him. "For the time being."

He inclined his head. "As you say. But we've a long
way to go before the two worlds become one, and the
conquest of the mortal realm should be your first preoccu-
pation. Chaos,"—he returned a smile that matched sweetness with harsh confidence, and reached out to lay a hand
lightly on the casket beside him—"is for me to contend
with."

Ygorla's irritation had been growing, but the demon's
gesture distracted her. Her gaze shifted to the casket, and
she immediately forgot her annoyance as her eyes took on

a proprietorial glint. She reached out, pushing Narid-na-Gost's hand aside, and lifted the casket's lid a bare few inches. Dim and deep blue light spilled out, creating cold veins of color along the length of her fingers, and through the narrow gap she gazed at the huge sapphire that lay on a crumpled velvet cloth within. Then, gently, she lowered the lid again, and the unearthly light vanished.

"I wonder," she said thoughtfully, "if the lords of Chaos are aware of what we've done with the treasure we plucked from under their noses?"

Narid-na-Gost's eyebrows lifted faintly at her use of the word *we,* but he let it pass. "They're aware of it," he said with certainty. "They may not be able to read our minds, but you can take any wager that they know full well where the gemstone is and the nature of the trap that's been set about it. If they didn't know, they'd have tried to move against us before now and would have suffered the consequences."

"So there's nothing they can do."

"Nothing except watch every step we take, and wait." The demon grinned ferally. "Yandros must be railing furiously against the stricture, but he won't risk sacrificing his brother's soul-stone to destroy us. In that sense he's as weak as the mortals you so despise. His weakness gives us as much time as we need or desire to consolidate our place here and carry out the next stage of our plan."

Ygorla paced back toward the window. "I've been thinking about the next stage, Father. I'm becoming bored with this island—it's too small and too restricting. The people who crowd into the audience hall and grovel at my feet have accepted me as their ruler now, but that isn't enough. If I'm High Margravine not just of Summer Isle but of the entire world, then I want the entire world to know it, and to know me."

Narid-na-Gost watched her with narrowed eyes. "Don't be in too great a haste, daughter. Tread softly, and you'll spring your trap all the better."

He couldn't see her face, but he heard her sigh impatiently through clenched teeth. "You're always so cautious!" she said pettishly. "I don't *need* to tread softly! The lords of Chaos are impotent, and because of what we are, the lords of Order have no power to harm us or even impede us. We are, in effect, invincible. I have the power to take this world in my hand"—she clenched an angry fist—"and I want to *use* that power, *now!*" Abruptly she swung around to face him. "I spent seven years incarcerated on the White Isle waiting for this—I don't intend to wait any longer!"

Was he going to argue with her? She tensed, anticipating an angry storm and ready to defy him. But instead Narid-na-Gost shrugged his narrow shoulders and looked at the casket once more.

"Then if you're so set on it, Ygorla, I shan't gainsay you. As I said before, this is your domain; I have other preoccupations."

For a moment Ygorla wondered just what he meant by that careless comment. Did he have some secret, something he hadn't yet revealed to her about his own plans? Then she shook the thought off, telling herself that she was being fanciful. He was simply stating that his task was to concern himself with their eventual bid for mastery of the Chaos realm while she established their earthly dominion, and this was his way of acknowledging her supremacy in this world while trying not to let her know it. She smiled inwardly but didn't allow her outward expression to change. Narid-na-Gost had a great deal of pride, and she didn't need to wound that pride by showing that she had seen through his subterfuge. Tacitly he had given her a free hand. That was enough for now.

She returned to the window and leaned on the sill, gazing out. "I shall send a proclamation," she said, "to all the province Margraves. I shall tell them that they have a new High Margravine, and I shall demand their declarations of fealty, with a promise of retribution if they dare to defy me. For good measure I think I'll send a similar message to the Matriarch of the Sisterhood, and of course to the Star Peninsula." She paused reflectively. "I gather that the present High Initiate is quite young and inexperienced. It'll be interesting to see how he reacts to a power greater than his own."

Narid-na-Gost snorted with soft laughter. "We've nothing to fear from him. Even the highest Circle adepts are no more than conjurors, and their esteemed leader's merely another untried whelp in the litter."

"Oh, I don't doubt that. But *he* doesn't yet know it. It might be entertaining to help him learn the lesson."

The demon's laughter subsided to a thin smile. "He's a world away, Ygorla. He needn't concern us yet."

"All the same, I want him to know of me, and not just through one of the Margraves when they start to panic and turn to the Circle for help. I want our first contact to be a little more . . . personal." She straightened, tapping her fingers on the window ledge. "Birds." Then she turned, impatience radiating from her. "They use birds here, don't they, to carry messages?"

The demon shrugged lazily. "I believe so. Your tame courtiers will know the details. But you don't need such crude methods."

"I know that. However, in this case I think I'll use them. My late and unlamented great-aunt, the old Matriarch, used to tell me that wise girls shouldn't squander their energies and talents unnecessarily, and for once in her dull life I think she was right. Why show my full strength now, when I can save it for a more judicious moment?" She clasped her hands together—the many bracelets she wore jingled faintly—and stared speculatively at her fingertips. "I wonder if the Circle will capitulate without a fight? I rather hope they won't, for that would rob me of some enjoyable games. I'd like to be an angler who traps the High Initiate on her hook. It would be very pleasant to play him on my line for a while, then land him and leave him gasping out his last breath on the bank under the gaze of all those who looked upon him as their savior." Quickly her gaze flicked to the demon's face, her eyes bright and hard. "That would complete his humiliation and secure my triumph. A small but satisfying revenge."

"Revenge?" Narid-na-Gost repeated mildly. "For what?"

"For the seven years I was forced to spend in hiding, and for the fourteen years before that when I was obliged to bend the knee to authority in all its forms." Ygorla paused. "He's the last figurehead. I took my vengeance on the Sisterhood a long time ago, and the High Margravate, too, has now fallen to me. That leaves only the High Initiate of the Circle to be dealt with. The third and final member of that hateful triumvirate." A slow, cruel smile formed on her lips. "His demise will be the most satisfying victory of all. You understand that, dear Father, don't you?"

Narid-na-Gost nodded slowly, and for a moment

seemed to be looking through her and through the fabric of the physical world to another dimension, and visualizing another adversary altogether. "Oh, yes, daughter," he said emphatically. "I understand that sentiment very well."

5

The Council of Adepts was meeting that morning. As both a fifth-rank adept and the castle's senior physician, Karuth Piadar was by right a prominent council member, but after looking at the planned agenda she had decided not to attend. The meeting was simply a regular formality to discuss such matters as stores or the grading of students and Circle candidates, and as her medical supplies didn't need replenishing and she had at present no students under her tutelage, there seemed little point in creating unnecessary tensions by being present.

She was aware that not only the council but the entire Circle knew of her rift with the High Initiate, even if they didn't know the cause. She'd seen the troubled sidelong looks, sensed the awkward atmosphere whenever she and Tirand encountered each other in a public place. She didn't like the situation, for it was both discomfiting and disruptive, but at the same time she felt powerless to put matters right. The bitter acrimony of the quarrel between her and Tirand had gone too far and too deep; what had been said might be retracted but wouldn't be forgotten, and the fact that Tirand was not only the High Initiate to whom as an adept she owed fealty but also her younger brother only made matters worse. They had been so close and in such accord all their lives that to have fallen out in such a thoroughgoing way was doubly painful. Karuth would have given much to find a way of healing the wounds, yet she couldn't bring herself to make the first move without some encouraging sign from Tirand, and there had been no such sign.

The trouble was, she thought as she worked in her infirmary that morning, that both she and her brother were too proud for their own good. In truth she didn't *want* to apologize to Tirand. She might regret and be ready to rescind her cruel words on the night of their quarrel, but that didn't alter the fact that she believed she had been in the right. She wouldn't back down from that. Her conscience and her sense of justice wouldn't allow it, and doubtless Tirand was as entrenched in his point of view as she was in hers—which left them at a miserable but seemingly intractable stalemate. So the days went by without any thawing of the atmosphere, while Karuth and Tirand had nothing to say to each other beyond the barest and most fragile exchange of courtesies, and those only when circumstances made a meeting unavoidable.

Karuth finished tidying her store cupboard, then looked about her, satisfied to find that there was nothing more to be done here. She had had only one patient to attend to this morning—a freckle-faced kitchen girl, daughter of one of the castle grooms, who had slipped on a stone step and twisted her ankle—but with the cold autumn winds beginning to blow from the north she knew that it wouldn't be long before the seasonal round of agues and coughs and shivers began, and when they did, she'd have little time for anything but her medical work. In a way, that would be a blessing, for these recent days had been uncomfortably quiet, allowing her too much time to brood on her troubles. She'd be glad of the distraction, even if her patients didn't share her relief.

She took off her apron, rolled down the sleeves of her gown, and paused to tuck a few straying wisps of her long and heavy brown hair back into place. Then she left the room, not forgetting to remove the small bunch of twigs tied to the outer doorlatch—a signal that the infirmary was now unoccupied—and walked through the corridors toward the castle's main door. It was a gloomy morning, and some torches had already been lit in the main passages. Reaching the entrance hall, Karuth debated whether to fetch a shawl from her room before venturing outside, then decided against it. It would do her good to harden herself early to the colder weather and might help her to resist the winter illnesses when they came. She skimmed down the steps and began to cross the courtyard. The castle's high black walls did nothing to relieve the day's dreariness, and when she looked up beyond the towering spires to the sky, she saw tatters of thin, dark-gray cloud scudding below the grubby overcast, a sure sign that rain would set in by afternoon. She didn't linger but quickened her steps toward the stoa that led to the door of the library deep in the castle's foundations. With—barring emergencies—the rest of the day to call her own, she wanted to seek out a book on regional music and spend the afternoon in her chambers practicing some of the unusual Empty Province dance measures on her manzon. As usual she would be called upon to play a set at the castle's forthcoming Quarter-Day celebrations, and she wanted to surprise the Circle's guests, in particular a distinguished party from Empty Province who would be attending. Empty Province had contributed a generous tithe to the Circle this year, in gratitude for the adepts' help in dealing with a troublesome elemental force that had disrupted some of the deeper workings of the mineral mines, and Karuth thought that it would be a courteous and prudent gesture to show the Circle's appreciation in return.

She reached the stoa and was just about to walk under the columned canopy when something in the sky to the south caught her eye. A dark speck flying against the wind, swooping and dipping. Even with her long-focused eyesight Karuth couldn't make out any detail, but she knew what it must be and she turned from the colonnades and began to walk quickly toward the far side of the court-yard, calling for Handray the falconer. Handray emerged from the stable-block where he housed his trained birds, and Karuth pointed to the speck.

"There's a messenger coming in, Handray. Are we expecting any dispatches?"

Handray narrowed his eyes. The flier was growing closer, and now it was possible to make out the silhouettes of its wings. "Not that I know of, ma'am," he told her. "Unless it's the new-candidates list from the Lady Matriarch, though it'll be a month early if that's so." He paused. "It's a big bird, wherever it comes from. I'll fetch the lure and call it down. Should I send for you if the message is urgent?"

The council was probably still in session; these regular meetings always took an interminable time. "Yes," Karuth said. "The High Initiate is busy at the moment, so you'd best let me know if anything's amiss. I'll be in the library."

"Ma'am." Handray touched a finger to his brow and disappeared back into the stables.

Retracing her steps, Karuth heard the whining sing of the lure as Handray swung it around his head, and heard his shrill whistle calling the messenger-bird to earth. But she wasn't prepared for the sudden cawing screech that echoed from above, nor for the falconer's yell of shock and protest that followed a bare second later. She spun around and saw Handray being attacked by something the size of a mountain eagle but black, jet-black. She glimpsed tearing fangs, saw the flash of devilish scarlet eyes, and wings that weren't feathered but glistening and membranous like a bat's—

"Handray!" She ran toward him as he shouted and beat at the monster, trying to fend it off, and as she, too, flailed at it, she was suddenly assaulted by an overpowering psychic stench. This was no bird! This was something else, something from another realm—

"Handray, get back! Get away from it!" Her voice was harsh with revulsion and with fear for the falconer, who knew nothing of elementals or demons Thankfully he had the wherewithal to heed her and he dropped to a crouch, covering his head with both arms. The bird—no, the *thing* —hovered some ten feet above the ground, its wings slowly beating; and its head, which was like a travesty of a dog's head but scaled and nacreous, turned with obscene deliberation to regard her. Its expression was contemptuous; a black tongue flickered, and ropes of yellowish saliva hung from its jaws. Karuth clenched her teeth and her fists, struggling to remember the binding spell for higher elementals, which, caught unawares as she was, had fled from her mind at the moment when she needed it. But, thank Yandros, memory clicked suddenly and her voice seared out.

"Creature of unhallowed dark, spawn of the Seven Hells, in the name of Yandros and in the name of Aeoris do I charge and abjure you—"

The monstrosity laughed. The sound was so like the

giggle of a foolish girl that it threw Karuth utterly, and the power of the spell rising in her mind shattered, making her stagger back. As she tried to regather her wits, the creature laughed again—and suddenly there was the sound of booted feet scuffing on stone and an outcry of new voices from the main doors. Karuth's head whipped around and she saw her brother Tirand's broad, stocky figure, flanked by four senior adepts, emerging onto the steps.

"What in blazes is going on?" Tirand's shout rang above those of the others. "Karuth—Handray—*what in the name of Aeoris is that thing?*"

Karuth drew a gasping breath. "Help me!" she yelled back. "Bind it, *quickly*! It's demonic, it attacked us!"

Tirand swore and started down the steps, his companions on his heels. "Join!" he snapped, holding out his hands to link with the two adepts nearest to him. "Circle it, raise a power-cone!"

Someone snatched Karuth's hand and gripped it, and the six of them formed a ring beneath the hovering black creature. It didn't react, made no effort to flee or even to move, and as she felt her energies linking with her fellow adepts', Karuth had a premonition that this would prove futile. Tirand opened his mouth to pronounce the first words of the binding, as she had tried to do—and with another shriek of manic and hideously human laughter the flying thing spat a dart of venom straight at the face of the adept beside him. The man yelled with pain and shock as burning fluid grazed across his cheek; he spun around, clapping a hand to his face, and the contact was broken. The horror screeched anew; then before anyone could do anything more, it arrowed upward, spearing high above the castle wall to hover level with the spire summits, still laughing wildly. Tirand, cursing with all the savagery he possessed, stared at it while it hovered for perhaps five heartbeats—and then, so fast that it was barely more than a blur, it arrowed away into the south and was lost to sight in seconds. As it vanished, something small spun down from the spot where it had hung and thumped to the flagstones at the High Initiate's feet.

A message scroll. Karuth stared at it, mesmerized, until with a violent movement that broke the stunned hiatus Tirand bent to snatch it up.

"Tend to Ciraid!" he snapped at her. "Can't you see he's hurt?"

Karuth was furious that he should use such a tone to her, but professional instincts made her bite back a searing retort and she hastened to examine the injury. The creature's venom had raised a blister on Ciraid's cheek, and with a grimace the adept admitted that it stung painfully, but to Karuth's relief it seemed that the damage went no farther. She doubted that the venom was toxic, for she could see no telltale signs of the skin around the blister changing color, but not wanting to take chances, she said, "Best come with me to the infirmary, Ciraid, and I'll give you a salve as well as checking for any poisoning."

He took his hand gingerly from his cheek and made a negative gesture. "There's no need for you to trouble yourself, Karuth. I'll find Sanquar; I'm sure he can deal with it well enough. Stay here. You'll want to find out what's in that scroll."

Karuth didn't miss the irritable look that Tirand flashed toward Ciraid, and she knew that her brother would have preferred her to go. That decided her, and she nodded.

"All right. But I'd advise you to waste no time in seeking Sanquar out. I'll check on his ministrations later."

Ciraid hurried away. A small crowd was beginning to gather now as people, alerted by the commotion in the courtyard, came to see what was to do, and at the main door the departing adept almost collided with a tall, slim, fair-haired young man who came running from inside the castle. The young man apologized hastily, then sprang down the steps three at a time.

"Tirand! Karuth!" Calvi Alacar, brother of the High Margrave and newly qualified as a junior Master of Philosophy, slid to a halt and stared at the ring of haggard faces. "What is it? What's going on? I saw the bird from my window, and at first I thought it was a messenger, but—"

"The creature attacked Handray." Tirand and Calvi were good friends, but at this moment friendship counted for less than the need to avoid a scene, and the High Initiate's tone was brusque. "He's all right; there's no need for concern."

Baffled that such a small incident should have aroused so much curiosity, Calvi stared blankly about him. Karuth caught his eye and said quietly, "And it wasn't a bird."

Tirand glared at her. "That's enough! We'll have half the gawping servants in the castle gathered around us at any moment, so I'll thank you not to give them spice for rumor-mongering! This is a Circle matter, and not for the ears of the uninitiated."

A Circle matter . . . it was his favorite phrase these days, Karuth thought sourly, and she met his gaze with angry gray eyes. "Then I'd suggest that you allow the Circle to look to it." She nodded at the scroll. Tirand stared back at her for a few seconds, then said something under his breath and, crushing the scroll in his fist, turned back toward the doors, signaling the adepts to follow him and announcing to the growing, curious crowd that the troublesome bird had been dealt with and there was nothing more to be done. Karuth hung back as from the corner of her eye she saw Handray getting to his feet. He'd been crouching in the same protective posture throughout the skirmish, so he hadn't seen what had taken place and hadn't realized the significance of the adepts' failure to bind the creature. As well for him, she thought; and as well for Tirand's desire to keep a firm rein on any gossip.

"You're all right, Handray?" she asked.

"Thanks to you and the High Initiate, ma'am, yes." He managed a pallid smile. "The gods alone know where that bird or bat or whatever it was came from, but I hope we'll see no more of its kind around here!"

"It was probably some mountain dweller that strayed from its usual territory," she said. "There are some peculiar beasts in those crags between here and West High Land. I'll make sure that word goes out to be wary for any more sightings. Now, are you sure you're not injured?"

He assured her that he was unharmed, and she made to follow the other adepts, wanting to catch up with them before they reached Tirand's study. Even under the present circumstances Tirand wouldn't refuse her sight of the message the demonic creature had brought, and she very much wanted to know its content. As she started toward the steps, however, Calvi caught her arm.

"Karuth." His blue eyes were overbright. "You said it wasn't a bird. I know that—I saw it for myself, and I saw what you and Tirand and the others tried to do. By all the fourteen gods, what *was* it?"

She shook her head, not wanting to be curt with him

yet anxious to leave the courtyard. "In truth, Calvi, I don't know. But it left a message scroll, and I want to see what the scroll contains. Please . . ." Gently she detached his fingers from her arm.

"Do you think Tirand—?"

"No, Calvi, he wouldn't let you join us. I'm sorry; I know he wouldn't. But unless the Circle expressly forbids it, I'll tell you what's afoot as soon as I can." With that promise she left him staring after her and ran up the steps. Her heart was pounding, and it wasn't just the aftereffects of the encounter with the monstrous messenger. Something else was crawling up from the depths of her mind, something she'd tried lately to forget but that kept returning against her will to haunt her. Something that lay at the root of the quarrel with Tirand.

She caught up with her colleagues as they reached Tirand's study and, slipping in behind the others, closed the door at her back and leaned against it. Someone lit a lamp, relieving a little of the room's gloom, and Tirand sat down at his desk and spread the crumpled scroll out before him. No one had the temerity to attempt to look over his shoulder, but every gaze was fixed on his face, watching him intently as he began to read. The silence grew oppressive. Tirand didn't speak, and his face was partly in shadow, so that his expression was masked. But when at last he looked up, Karuth was appalled by what she saw. The blood had drained from his cheeks, leaving his skin a sickly gray. His eyes stared at nothing, and he looked like a man in deep shock.

"Tirand?" One of the other adepts made a tentative

move toward the High Initiate. "Tirand, what is it? What does the message say?"

Like someone dragged out of a hypnotic trance, Tirand seemed to become aware of the others' presence for the first time. Still he said nothing, but with a shaking hand he pushed the scroll toward the man who had addressed him. Then his gaze wandered to Karuth and stayed rigidly on her. She couldn't interpret his look, but she saw bitterness in his eyes. Bitterness, and fear.

The other adepts had gathered around their comrade, and someone said softly, "Sweet gods . . . this is *insane* . . ." The words brought Karuth sharply back to earth and she moved to see the scroll for herself. Her first thought was that she didn't recognize the script; whoever had written this had a bold, harsh style that seemed to spring out from the parchment and assault the eye. Then her brain began to take in the content.

"It's some warped jest!" The sharp, uneasy bark of a statement came from sixth-rank adept Sen Briaray Olvit, the eldest of the group. "Some drunken or disgruntled fool thinking they can make a mockery of the Circle! The High Margrave, *dead*? A usurper on the Summer Isle throne? Aeoris help me, if I had this evil-minded hoaxer before me in this room—"

Tirand interrupted him. "Read the rest, Sen. All of it." He was still watching Karuth, and she knew he was waiting for her to finish. What was he expecting? Why was her reaction suddenly important to him? She continued, taking in the mad words, the wild boastings, the threats, and finally the statement—the mind behind this was deluded, demented beyond belief, she thought—that the new ruler of Summer Isle now demanded the Circle's unquestioning fealty in the form of a document signed by the High Initiate's own hand and dispatched by messenger to the south without delay. Then at last she saw the flourishing signature at the foot of the scroll:

"Ordered this day in the eighty-first year of Equilibrium, by My hand, High Margravine and Regnant Supreme—Ygorla."

"Oh, gods . . ." Karuth said hollowly, and met Tirand's eyes once more.

She couldn't say it. She knew what he was thinking, what they were both thinking, but she couldn't utter it, not here and now with others to witness her words. Whatever she thought of Tirand, however much she had hated him at times during the past few days, she wouldn't humiliate him by voicing aloud what he already knew. But the shared knowledge burned in her like a cancer.

Sen spoke again, breaking the taut silence. "We must find the source of this. Find it and root it out. This is *intolerable*! High Initiate, I suggest—"

Tirand held up a hand. His composure, or at least a fair simulacrum of it, was returning. "Wait, Sen. It isn't that simple." He glanced from one to another of them, his expression tight and unhappy. "I want to reconvene the council. Now."

Sen frowned. "Surely that's not necessary, Tirand? I agree that they must be told of this, of course, but as I see it, our first priority is to set a search in train for the perpetrator of this hoax, and—"

The High Initiate interrupted him sharply. "Are you prepared to gamble that it is a hoax?"

The adept was taken aback. "You're saying that it may be *true*?"

"I'm saying that it may be very dangerous to assume it isn't."

"Aeoris"—Sen made the splay-fingered sign of the fourteen gods—"I hadn't thought—it hadn't occurred to me . . . but by all the gods, Tirand, the idea's *impossible*! We'd have had wind of it, we'd have known—" He stopped as he saw Tirand's grim expression and realized what he was driving at. Sen had been one of the senior adepts who, fifteen days ago, had helped the High Initiate to investigate Karuth's claim that something was perilously wrong in the realm of the gods. The investigation had yielded nothing; Tirand had put an interdict on the subject forbidding any further probing, and Sen suspected that this was the cause of the quarrel between him and his sister. Now, though, they had to face the thought that the Circle's conclusions might have been wrong.

He made one more attempt to argue, not wanting to let himself believe such a chilling possibility. "Tirand, there *can't* be a connection! We've had no sign, no warning, and certainly no word of trouble from the south. A usurper couldn't come from nowhere, in no time at all, and simply conquer Summer Isle!"

"And what hoaxer could summon, let alone control, a demon that laughs in the face of the Circle's most powerful binding?" Tirand countered. "Find me such a person and I might be ready to dismiss this as an evil joke. As it is, I daren't do any such thing." He stood up. "This isn't the place for further discussion. Summon the council to meet in the hall again in fifteen minutes. And emphasize the need for prudence—I don't want any whiff of this to reach outside ears for the time being."

The adepts murmured compliance and filed out of the room. Only Karuth hung back. She and Tirand hadn't addressed each other directly since leaving the courtyard, and she hoped that there might now be a chance, albeit a small one, for a step toward reconciliation between them.

Knowing that she needed an uncontentious opening gambit, she said, "Tirand—Calvi saw the demon for himself, and he saw what happened when we tried to bind it. He won't be satisfied until he knows what's afoot. And if there's any truth in this message, he . . . gods, he's not only the High Margrave's brother but also his heir. He'll have to be told."

Tirand nodded brusquely. "I know that. But I want nothing said to him yet. I won't deliver a blow like that to him unless we're certain of the facts."

"Yes." She hesitated, aware that he now seemed unwilling to look at her directly, then decided not to dissemble. Quietly she said, "Do you believe me now?"

Tirand stood very still for a few moments. Then: "No. Not without evidence."

Karuth felt something turn cold within her. "And this isn't evidence enough?" It was a futile question; she knew what he'd say and knew, too, that there would be no point in arguing with him.

"As you say, this isn't evidence enough." At last Tirand did look at her, though reluctantly, and his voice took on an angry yet at the same time almost pleading edge. "Must we go through all that again?"

Karuth shook her head. "No," she said, and turned to the door, hiding her disappointment. Hand on the latch, she paused. "I presume you don't object to my attending the council meeting?"

"Of course not." Though from his tone she knew he wished that she would stay away.

"Thank you." She smiled ironically, not letting him see her face, and went out, closing the door gently behind her. As she started toward the corridor that would lead her to the council hall, she heard someone calling her name, and she quickened her steps as she recognized the voice. Calvi. He mustn't catch up with her. She couldn't face him at this moment, because she knew that if she was forced to look into his eyes, she wouldn't be able to lie to him and tell him that nothing was wrong. For his sake as well as for her own, she must maintain a calm facade.

She heard Calvi call to her again, and a rush of emotion welled in her, catching in her throat. Putting a clenched fist to her mouth, Karuth bit down hard on the whitened knuckles as she began to run toward the council hall.

"One word." Tarod's voice was savage as he stared out of the window, and far away across the gold-and-black-checkered landscape of the Chaos realm something screamed in response to the fury that emanated from him. "Just one word, and they could *destroy* it!" He swung around to face Yandros, who stood in the center of the shifting floor. "How did it come to this, Yandros? How could we have let it happen?"

For a few moments Yandros continued to stare thoughtfully into the middle distance. Darker lights flickered in his gold hair, and his eyes changed their color through dangerous shades of the spectrum. At last he said, "The answer to your question, my brother, is painfully simple—and you know it as well as I do We were careless; we were lax; and, for what cold comfort it is to us, we have only ourselves to blame for this pass."

"We should *never* have allowed the soul-stones to be guarded so carelessly!"

"I agree. And we should have been utterly vigilant against the possibility that anyone besides ourselves might learn the one word of power that can destroy them. But done's done, Tarod." He looked up and his thin mouth curved in a faint, cynical smile. "How many times have we said all this to each other now? Thirty? Forty? More?"

Tarod's brief storm of fury subsided and he sighed. Yandros was right: There was no point in reiterating the same questions and the same answers yet again. Repetition might give him some small outlet for his rage, but it didn't change the facts.

He said, "I'm sorry. It's the inactivity that I find hard to tolerate, the knowledge that there's nothing we can do. It sticks in my throat, Yandros." He paused. "Do the Circle know yet what's afoot?"

The greatest Chaos lord frowned. "No—and even when they find out, I can't see their High Initiate willingly sanctioning an appeal to us. You know Tirand Lin's prejudices. If we're to be called on, I think we'll have to rely on that call coming from another source than the Circle."

"What of his sister? She's well disposed toward Chaos."

"True, but she's not in good odor with her brother at present." Yandros smiled cynically. "She committed the error of listening to instinct rather than logic, and that kind of unorthodoxy doesn't go down too well at the Star Peninsula these days. No, I feel there's little chance of Karuth Piadar being our instrument in this. We must look for another."

Something in his tone alerted Tarod, and his feline green eyes narrowed. "You've someone in mind?"

Yandros made an equivocal gesture. "A possibility, no more. It may come to nothing, and we can't take the risk of trying to influence any mortal's actions lest the lords of Order take that as a breach of our pledge and consider themselves free to interfere."

A heavy-bladed knife appeared in Tarod's left hand; he weighed it, bouncing it gently, in his palm. "If your assessment of Tirand Lin is right—and I don't doubt for a moment that it is—then we'll have that problem to contend with anyway, for he'll soon be yelling to Aeoris for help."

"I'm well aware of it." Yandros's expression clearly mirrored his opinion of Aeoris, who, as the highest lord of Order, was his own counterpart in that realm and also his deadliest enemy. "But I'd still prefer not to give Order any early grounds for stepping in where they're not wanted." He walked toward the window's shining arch and looked out. Fog was beginning to swirl down in thick, dark columns from the sky. Something reminiscent of a gigantic lizard with fins in place of legs hauled itself painfully, blindly over the stark checkerboard of the scenery, its toothless mouth working and drooling.

"I think," Yandros said, "that it won't be too long before the potential ally I have in mind feels a compulsion to make some move. I'm gambling on the likelihood that when that happens, Chaos will be the natural realm to turn to for aid."

"And you'll answer?"

"Oh, yes." Yandros raised one hand and touched the window lightly. The landscape outside vanished, leaving impenetrable darkness in which an eldritch chorus of voices moaned. "I'll most certainly answer."

6

Eleven messenger-falcons—every bird that Handray could muster at such short notice—left the Star Peninsula that afternoon. The operation was carried out as quickly and unobtrusively as possible, and Tirand hoped that the unwonted if brief flurry of activity wouldn't raise more than minimal curiosity in the castle.

He was relieved that the Council of Adepts had responded so positively to the news he set before them. Once they'd got over the initial confusion of being reconvened at such short notice, they had been unanimous in agreeing with the High Initiate's view that they dared not dismiss the scroll as a hoax. There were, as Tirand said, too many warning signs, not least of them the nature of the messenger itself. Word must be sent immediately to the key Margravates and Sisterhood Cots to alert them, and the fastest bird of all would fly to the Matriarch herself in Southern Chaun province to enlist her help and advice. The only point of dissent among the adepts had been over whether or not it would be wise to dispatch a message to Summer Isle. Tirand was against it; if there was any foundation to this news, he said, it would be better not to alert its perpetrator to the Circle's activities, but a strong faction, led by Sen, argued that only a letter to the High Margrave's court could confirm or deny the truth of the whole affair.

Eventually they reached a compromise: They would stay their hand for two days, but if no alarms came in from the provinces within that time, a carefully worded personal message would then be sent to Blis Hanmen Alacar without any further delay. In the meantime the more covert investigations would continue with all speed.

Tirand and Karuth didn't speak to each other after the meeting. Both told themselves that this was simply because there was no time for any discussion; the first and only priority was to see the vital letters written and dispatched. In truth, though, neither of them felt entirely able or willing to make the first breach in the barrier. In council Karuth had backed her brother emphatically and helped him to sway the doubters to his way of thinking, but although he was grateful for her support, Tirand still felt a rankling between them, a sense that she had scored a moral victory that she wouldn't allow him to forget. Karuth, for her part, resented the fact that Tirand didn't seem willing to concede open-handedly that her suspicions might after all be proved right; so, as the work of preparing the letters began, they sat at separate tables and took care not to meet each other's eyes.

With the messenger-birds launched on their way by Handray and his apprentice, there was nothing for the Circle to do but wait. Tirand had vetoed any idea of exploring the astral planes for further information, on much the same grounds as he had opposed any immediate query to Summer Isle. If there was any demonic agency at work, he said, an astral exploration would draw its attention as surely as if they shouted their intent from the tops of the spires. Two days could make no difference, other than to arm them with more desperately needed information. So they waited. But not for long.

The first falcon from the south arrived on the following evening. It carried a scrawled and barely decipherable note from the Margrave of Han Province, and as he read it, Tirand felt an ice-cold hand clutch at his gut. Theirs, it seemed, had not been the only visitation. And when at dawn the next day a second and then a third bird arrived, one from Chaun and the other from Wishet, he realized that whoever was behind this madness had done his work thoroughly and well. Then on the evening of the second day, as the communal meal was about to be served in the dining hall, a warning shout rang from the castle's barbican, and moments later came the grinding rattle of the great double gates being hauled open.

Karuth, halfway down the stairs on her way to the great hall, heard the noises from outside. She was one of the first to reach the courtyard steps and was in time to see the party of riders as they came clattering in to the shelter of the castle's black walls. White robes gleamed ghostlike in the gathering dark, and grooms ran to help four sisters and their six-strong escort down from their sweating, trembling horses. One of the sisters, a slim, middle-aged woman, saw Karuth and started forward, and Karuth hastened down the steps to meet her.

"Physician-Adept Karuth Piadar?" The woman's sharp, wind-browned face was unfamiliar, but she had seen both an adept's badge and the brooch of the Guild of Master Musicians at Karuth's shoulder and had identified her. "I am Sister-Senior Perola Beyn, deputy at the West High Land cot. Madam, we must see the High Initiate at once—it's a matter of the gravest urgency!"

An alert servant had come running to them with a lantern, and as its light spilled across them, Karuth suddenly saw that the woman was on the edge of physical collapse. Dismayed, she reached out to her. "Sister, you're utterly exhausted!"

Perola grimaced. "We've ridden all day and all through last night. We only stopped twice to change mounts and snatch a bite of food." Behind her, where the horses were milling, one of the other white-robed figures suddenly burst into tears, and Perola looked quickly over her shoulder. "Oh, gods," she said, and strain and weariness broke through her rigid self-control. "I feared this. Ette's but seventeen, one of our youngest novices; but we *had* to bring her." She would have turned and hurried back toward the weeping girl, but Karuth forestalled her as her physician's training and instinct, combined with compassion and a sudden terrible conviction that she knew what had brought these women to the castle, snapped into place and cleared all traces of confusion from her mind.

"It's all right, Sister," she said to Perola. "I'll look after her." She raised her voice, calling to the grooms. "Take these horses to the stable and give them your best attention!" Then, to the man with the lantern, "Send for the stewards: I want rooms and hot food prepared for our visitors, and servants to help them and carry their baggage. And I'll need Sanquar—tell him to come to the infirmary."

Perola tried to protest. 'Madam, we *must* see the High Initiate without any delay! I can't begin to stress how urgent—"

Karuth interrupted her kindly but firmly. "Sister, your novice is in great distress, you yourself are drained to the marrow, and I doubt if anyone else in your party fares much better. My brother will be told of your arrival straight away, but I'd be neglecting my own duty if I didn't put your immediate needs before anything else. Besides"—and suddenly her tone changed—"I think I know why you're here, Sister Perola. It's what we've all been fearing for the past two days."

———————⟩ ⟨———————

The High Initiate heard Sister Perola's story in the privacy of his study, and what she had to say was concise, calmly worded, and shattering. It seemed that the West High Land cot had also received a visit from a supernatural messenger, and immediately the cot's most skilled seers had been set to work. They had scried, Perola said, convinced that the news was a perverted joke and searching for a clue to its perpetrator's identity, and at first the information they received from the astral planes had been confusingly inconclusive. But then without warning the cot's youngest novice—who wasn't concerned with the investigation and indeed didn't even know of the message's existence—had fallen into a trance and started to babble, first about the High Margrave lying in a pool of his own blood and then about blue eyes and a woman burning. Ette, Perola told them, had been subject to uncontrolled but uncannily accurate visions since she was a small child, and the Sisterhood had great hopes of her as a seer. This fit, though, had been acute even by her standards, and as she sank deeper into the trance and her visions became more coherent, the older sisters realized that she was seeing not only the truth of the message they'd received but also glimpses of the grim events that had preceded it— including a vision of the gruesome death, seven years ago, of the old Matriarch, Ria Morys.

"There's no doubt in our minds that Ette's was a true

seeing, High Initiate," Perola said soberly when at last her story was completed. She looked up and her light blue eyes met Tirand's with painful frankness. "Then, when your own bird arrived with your letter, we felt we must come to you immediately and bring you our news."

Tirand nodded. "You've sent word of these seeings to the Matriarch?"

"Yes, sir, but even with the fastest falcons we couldn't anticipate a reply from Southern Chaun in under three days. We felt we dared not wait that long, so our party left immediately to bring Ette to the castle and ask the Circle's help."

"She'll have our help, of course," Tirand said later to Sen Briaray Olvit and a selected few of the other high-ranking adepts, "though in all honesty I doubt if any Circle rites will do much more than confirm what her seers have already discovered." Karuth had returned briefly from tending to the other sisters and their exhausted escort, but now she had left again to escort Perola to the guest wing and administer a restorative, and Tirand felt more inclined to admit the truth of his feelings than he might otherwise have done.

Sen stared out of the window at the rising first moon. "You're convinced, then, that this is no hoax?"

"I'm growing unpleasantly close to it. We've already received alarms from three Margraves and I don't doubt there'll be messages from the more distant provinces before long. With Sister-Seer Ette's visions to add to the picture, the evidence is too strong now to be ignored. We have to face the likelihood that the High Margrave has indeed been murdered and that a usurper sits on the Summer Isle throne."

There was silence for a few seconds. Then another adept spoke up, voicing what they were all thinking.

"What about Calvi Alacar, Tirand? Perhaps we should summon him now."

"No," Tirand said quietly. "I don't think we should tell him, not yet." He looked at his companions in turn, a silent appeal for support in his eyes. "I said *likelihood*. Likelihood isn't certainty, and there's still a chance that Blis Hanmen Alacar is alive and well, though the gods alone know it's a slender one. Surely it would be kinder to keep this from Calvi until we're sure?"

There were murmurs of assent, but then Sen said, "That's all well and good, Tirand, but it's also vital that we consider Calvi's own position. If Blis is dead, then as his only living brother Calvi is also his successor. If there *is* a usurper on Summer Isle, and that usurper has real power, Calvi is in great danger."

One of the younger adepts looked up sharply. "You forget, Sen, that he's also under the protection of the Circle! If we can't shield him from the ambitions of some upstart, then we've no right to call ourselves sorcerers!"

Others agreed, more readily, it seemed, than they had sided with Tirand's appeal. The High Initiate, however, made no comment, and Sen's shrewd eyes focused on him. "Tirand? You're thinking something but you seem reluctant to voice it."

Tirand stared down at his table where the scroll containing Ygorla's proclamation lay along with the province Margraves' appeals for help. "I'm recalling the nature of the messenger that brought this scroll and the contempt with which it reacted to our attempt to bind it." He looked up and met Sen's gaze. "That memory is enough to make me fear the risk of complacency."

The young adept who had spoken up shook his head emphatically. "Forgive me for being blunt, Tirand, but in my view that sounds perilously close to defeatism."

Tirand smiled, but with little humor. "I sincerely hope you're right. However, as I recall it, you weren't among the group of us who *did* try to bind that creature. As I'm sure Sen will confirm—" He stopped as someone rapped on the door. "Good grief, who's that at this hour? Come in."

The door opened, revealing one of the senior castle stewards. He touched a finger respectfully to his brow and said, "I beg your pardon, sir, but I thought I'd best alert you immediately. A second party of sisters has arrived this minute from Empty Province, and their senior is asking for an urgent interview."

Tirand's face grew very still. Sen cleared his throat and shot a meaningful glance at the dissenting adept, and the High Initiate nodded.

"I'll see her now, Kern. Perhaps you'd send word to my sister that we have new guests who may be in need of her care?"

"Yes, sir." The steward hastened away, and Tirand turned to face his fellow adepts.

"The Empty Province sisters are renowned for their scrying skills, so I imagine we can all guess what has brought them here. If any of you want to retire to your beds, please feel free to do so. I suspect there'll be little sleep tonight for anyone who chooses to stay."

Nobody moved or commented, and after a few moments Tirand acknowledged their reaction with a quick smile. "Very well—and thank you; I won't hide the fact that I appreciate your support."

But as he looked again at the parchment on the table,

he suddenly felt, despite the presence of his colleagues, more lonely than he had ever felt in his life before. Futile though it was, weak though it was, he wished that his father, Chiro, whose rank and responsibilities he had been forced so suddenly to take over two and a half years ago, were still alive to lift this burden from his unready shoulders.

As he had predicted, Tirand didn't see his bed that night. The sisters from Empty Province, headed by a young, gaunt senior with wild eyes and a disconcerting facial twitch, told much the same story as their West High Land colleagues had done. It was near dawn when the second interview finally ended and the weary sisters were shepherded to hastily prepared rooms. As soon as they had left, the argument began again over whether or not Calvi Alacar should be told the truth. Tirand, however, was still not prepared to give way, and at last even Sen was too weary to pursue his case any further, and the meeting broke up.

Tirand knew that he should have followed the others' example and tried to rest for a while before the new day began. But with the first glimmer of dawn touching the castle spires it hardly seemed worthwhile; a scant hour's sleep would probably leave him in a worse state than no sleep at all. He would, he decided, go out to the courtyard for a few minutes. The chill air would clear his head a little, and then a bath should freshen him enough to face the morning's duties with some semblance of alertness.

He turned out the lamps in his study and, not wanting to risk waking anyone by opening the main doors, which always creaked abominably, left the castle by a side exit. Emerging into the courtyard, he was surprised to see a figure standing by the central fountain. For a moment, dismayed, he thought it was Sen and was about to duck back through the door to avoid him; but then a voice hailed him, and he realized his mistake.

"Arcoro." Tirand relaxed and walked toward the fountain to join the older man. "It seems we're of the same mind."

Arcoro Raeklen Vir had been a senior member of the Council of Adepts for the past fifteen years. Chiro had considered him one of his soundest and wisest advisors, and Tirand in his turn had often found Arcoro's views to be an oasis of calm reason in the midst of dissent. Throughout tonight's upheavals Arcoro had had little to say, but as they sat down together on the parapet of the empty fountain pool—the fountain played only during the summer months—Tirand suddenly felt the need for the elder adept's opinion to bolster his own uncertain confidence.

He said, "Did I do the right thing, Arcoro?"

"In vetoing the idea of telling Calvi?" As usual Arcoro caught on to the drift of his thoughts immediately. "Yes, I think you did." One long-fingered hand tapped restlessly on the stone beside him. "I don't believe that the message from Summer Isle is false—frankly I can't believe it in the face of tonight's double dose of evidence, however much I'd like to. But I agree with you that we need to know more before we take any precipitate action." He frowned. "Any action at all, for that matter. Tirand—what are we dealing with? A lunatic, or a genuine power from outside the Circle? That's the question I keep asking myself, and I can't reach a conclusion."

"Neither can I." Tirand hesitated, wondering how frank he dared be, then decided to risk speaking his mind. "But one thing in particular troubles me, Arcoro, and though there's no logic to it, I can't shake it off."

"Ah," Arcoro said. "Her name."

Tirand looked quickly at him, taken aback. "You remember that?"

"Good gods, am I so close to my dotage that I should have forgotten? You're the one with the faulty memory, Tirand, if you don't recall that I was at the meeting your father convened after the old Matriarch's death. Or perhaps I should say, murder."

"Murder?"

Arcoro shrugged. "Just a theory, and one I've never been sufficiently sure of to pursue beyond idle speculation." He paused for a few moments, his mouth pursing, then: "Did you ever see the child during the fourteen years she was at Southern Chaun?"

"No, I didn't."

"Mm. I rather have the impression that no one from the castle ever did get to know her; certainly Ria never brought her here again, despite the fact that she was born in the shadow of these walls. Although"—he looked up shrewdly—"I gather that Ria requested that she might be initiated into the Circle?"

"That's true. My father turned the Matriarch's application down."

"On what grounds?"

"The grounds that she was too young at the time. And . . ." Tirand frowned. "My sister had a feeling that it would be unwise, and I think that, too, influenced Father's decision."

Karuth, Arcoro knew, was a sensitive topic with the

High Initiate at present, and he didn't pursue the comment.

"So," he said, "it may be that Ria Morys recognized some latent power in the girl that she hoped the Circle would take in hand and mold. Couple that with the circumstances surrounding the child's disappearance, add the results of the good sisters' scryings, and the recipe begins to look extremely murky."

Tirand thought of the suspicions that Karuth had harbored for so many years and that she had stubbornly refused to abandon despite his own and Chiro's attempts to discourage her. He thought about the bitter quarrel they'd had. He thought about omens and warnings . . .

"Of course, it may be nothing more than coincidence," Arcoro continued when it became clear that Tirand wasn't willing to share his thoughts. "Ygorla's not an uncommon name in the south, though it hasn't been particularly fashionable for a long while. To the best of our knowledge the old Matriarch's grand-niece has been dead for seven years, so we've no sound reason to think that she and this madwoman could be one and the same person. However, I'm not inclined—call it intuition or call it a helping of hardcore commonsense, I won't differentiate—I'm not inclined to rely on 'the best of our knowledge' in this instance."

Tirand nodded, staring down at the flagstones under his feet. "If they are one and the same," he said, "then it points us in one particularly ugly direction, and that is the source of this usurper's power." He hunched his shoulders against a sudden cold gust of wind that rustled the creeper on the castle walls. "As you know, my father firmly believed that what happened in Southern Chaun at that time had the whiff of Chaos about it."

Arcoro frowned, considering this, then slowly and deliberately made the splay-fingered sign of reverence to the fourteen gods.

"Tirand, I'm not qualified to comment on that. I know that Chiro felt greater fealty to Aeoris than to Yandros, and I know you feel as he did. But I don't share your bias; I'm what might best be termed a neutral bystander when it comes to a preference for either Order or Chaos." He looked up and met Tirand's gaze intently. "It's not my place to offer unsolicited advice to the High Initiate—"

"Gods, Arcoro, don't say things like that! From a man of your seniority—"

"All right, then, I'll be frank. Don't let prejudice cloud your judgment, Tirand. You may have little brief for the gods of Chaos, but bear in mind that they *are* gods all the same. Can you really believe that they'd trouble to become embroiled in anything as petty—by their standards—as this is? Can you truly see Yandros using some human megalomaniac to further his own ends?"

"No," Tirand admitted reluctantly. "You're right; it doesn't make much sense. But that demon—"

"Was nothing more than any of our higher-ranking adepts could have summoned and controlled."

"We tried to bind it, and we failed."

"Without forewarning and the chance to prepare, is that so surprising?"

"No . . . no, I suppose not. But it was proof enough that this woman, whoever she is, has power."

"Power, yes; but the blessing of Yandros? I very much doubt it."

Tirand sighed. "I hope you're right, Arcoro. In fact I pray fervently that you are, for if you're wrong, then we're faced with something far worse than a mad sorceress."

"Take my advice and don't even think about that possibility." Arcoro rose stiffly to his feet. "It's cold enough out here to make a corpse shiver. Let's go inside before we lose a few fingers."

Tirand agreed, and the two men began to walk toward the main doors. There were lights in the ground-floor windows now as the castle started to awaken to the new day. The High Initiate didn't relish the prospect of the hours that lay ahead, but he knew he must face up to them, and he was already starting to formulate the report that he would make to the full Council of Adepts, when Arcoro touched his arm.

"Tirand . . ." The older adept was frowning as he looked at something high above the southwest wall. "Your eyes are better than mine; is that a messenger-bird coming in?"

Tirand squinted into the brittle emptiness of the paling sky. "Yes," he said after a few moments. "I think it is. Gods, not more bad news!"

"I suppose it was to be expected. I'd put a wager on East Han this time, or failing that, Prospect. Shall I fetch Handray?"

"It might be as well; the bird will need food and rest. You should find him—" Tirand stopped, staring harder at the approaching speck.

"What is it?" Arcoro asked.

He couldn't be sure yet, but . . . damn it, he thought, his first instinct was right, it was far too large to be a falcon! It was—

"Arcoro, get out of the way!" the High Initiate said sharply. "Up the steps, to the shelter of the door— *quickly!*" Even as he spoke, he was starting toward the steps, pulling Arcoro with him. As they hastened under the door's arch, they heard a harsh cry echoing from be-

hind them, and Tirand swung around in time to see the
thing—for this was no bird—start its giddying dive toward the courtyard. It arrowed down with incredible
speed, so fast that it seemed it must smash onto the flagstones, but at the last instant its batlike wings fanned out,
hitting the air with a crack like a small thunderbolt, and it
was powering up again, screeching, laughing in the
nightmarishly human way that Tirand remembered so
well, hurtling skyward once more.

With a dull thump, the burden it had been carrying fell
into the dry pool of the fountain.

Arcoro swore softly and at some length under his
breath, then, taking a grip on himself, looked at Tirand.

"The same messenger?" he asked tersely.

"Or its twin." Tirand ran back down the steps and
strode toward the fountain, the older man on his heels,
and they looked into the pool.

It wasn't a message-scroll this time but something
much larger, wrapped and carefully tied to make it secure.
A folded sheet of parchment was tucked into the binding,
and Tirand jumped over the parapet to retrieve the package. It was heavier than he'd anticipated, and his cold
fingers couldn't unfasten the knots.

"Come with me to my study, Arcoro," he said as he
climbed back over the wall and the older man stepped
forward to scrutinize the offering. "I think I'd prefer to
examine this in greater privacy than here."

To his relief they encountered only servants as they
returned to Tirand's private quarters. The fire was still
burning, though sluggishly; Tirand riddled it up and put
on more fuel while Arcoro lit the lamps, then they turned
their attention to the package. As soon as he unfolded the

sheet of parchment, Tirand recognized the handwriting that sprawled across it. The message was brief and direct.

To the High Initiate Tirand Lin, greetings.

You will by now have received my first proclamation, and your lack of any fitting response to my orders greatly disappoints me. I had hoped for better from you, who are surely among the most enlightened of my subjects. I therefore send you this gift as a modest token of my sincerity, lest you might be tempted to cast doubt upon my word, and upon the fact that I am,

Your High Margravine and your indisputable Liege
Ygorla

Wordlessly Tirand passed the letter to Arcoro, then took a knife from the top drawer of his desk and slashed the package's binding with unnecessary ferocity.

"She's insane," he said savagely through clenched teeth. " 'Indisputable Liege'—by the very heart of Aeoris, she must take us for complete fools if she thinks—*ahh*!"

At the same moment as he uttered the sudden and violent cry, the stench hit both men like a wall. Stunned, Arcoro looked up—and saw, as Tirand had already seen, the nature of Ygorla's gift.

There was no blood, for the veins and arteries had been long since drained; there were only old stains now dried to brown and smearing the dead-white face and the puckered skin and flesh where the head had been severed. The ends of the fair hair were glued together into a rust-colored mat; the mouth hung open and had become grotesquely distorted; the eyes, horrible as they began to decay, and gelid like the eyes of a half-rotten fish, stared at Tirand with what seemed, hideously, like an expression of faint surprise.

Tirand shut his eyes and covered his mouth with one hand as his stomach threatened to heave up its contents. Arcoro had turned his head quickly away and was hissing prayers and oaths between tightly clamped teeth. At last, with fumbling hands, Tirand managed to cover the terrible, stinking thing from view, then stumbled to the window and flung it open. As he leaned out, sucking in great lungfuls of fresh air, images and memories rampaged uncontrollably through his mind: Summer Isle and the great wedding celebration; the music, the dancing, the laughter. The young High Margravine Jianna, holding her new husband's hand as they walked in triumphal procession through the glittering palace. Blis Hanmen Alacar himself, flushed with happiness as he received his guests' congratulations. Blis smiling. Blis laughing. Blis's severed head staring mindlessly up at him, delivered to the castle as final, shattering proof of the usurper's claim. . . .

"Tirand?" Arcoro's hand gripped the High Initiate's shoulder. "Tirand, are you all right? Are you sick, or—"

"No. No, I—I'm all right. Under control." Slowly, shakily, Tirand withdrew, carefully averting his gaze from the desk and what lay there.

"We'd better summon the council immediately," Arcoro said quietly. "Shall I . . . ?"

Tirand shook his head, holding up a hand to forestall him when for a few moments his throat wouldn't obey him and allow him to speak. "Not yet," he said at last. "There's something else we must do first, Arcoro. Not here, not in here, but . . . perhaps we could use your chambers. I think . . ." He swallowed hard. "I think it would be kinder from just two of us rather than the whole council. Send a servant to fetch Calvi. He has to be told now. And we . . . and we must pledge the Circle's fidelity to our new High Margrave."

7

A disembodied head, with the face of a deformed cat and transparent skin through which yellow veins and blue-gray muscles could be seen pulsing, skimmed along one of the sunlit corridors of the Summer Isle palace, calling out in a yowling monotone, *"Where is the rat? Where is the rat?"* A servant girl, hurrying from a side passage and almost colliding with the thing, squealed and jumped back. The monstrosity halted and snapped mindlessly at her with a thicket of teeth. *"Fetch the rat. Bring the rat."* Its order delivered, it flitted on its way, leaving her staring after it and shaking with fear.

From his room Strann heard the droning summons and knew that the palace stewards would be starting an agitated hunt for him. For a moment he was tempted to settle a few scores by not revealing his whereabouts, before reason argued that tardiness would bring Ygorla's wrath on his own head as well as on theirs. Reflexively—when he stopped to think about it, he was appalled by how quickly it had become a habitual gesture—he put a hand to his neck to ensure that the jeweled collar was still in place. As he did so, the door of his room warped suddenly and briefly, and the cat's head materialized through the solid wood, hovering some six feet above the floor.

"You are summoned," the sharp, monotonous voice

announced. *"At once. You are summoned. Bring music. Bring words. To the audience hall."*

Strann sucked air hard down into his lungs and forced himself to look at the head directly. "I understand," he said curtly, and then, when the thing made no move to depart, "I said, I *understand*! Go back to whatever pit you came from!"

It went, thankfully, and he let out his pent breath in a sigh of relief. He loathed these warped elementals that Ygorla conjured to carry her messages or simply, when the mood took her, to frighten and harass her human slaves. She seemed to favor the ugly, the malformed, the nightmarish, anything that would contrast shockingly with her own beauty. Strann knew, too, that the elementals weren't just passive messengers; he'd seen for himself what damage they were capable of inflicting on human flesh when some hapless servant failed to please his mistress.

That thought spurred him to make haste, and he crossed the room to fetch his manzon from its case. As he picked the instrument up, he paused to glance briefly at the window frame, where, half hidden by the rich brocade curtain, he'd used a spare manzon string to make a series of nicks in the soft wood, one for each day of his private hell.

Nine days now. Nine days, and still progress was frustratingly slow. He thought that Ygorla was beginning to believe his loyalty was genuine—he'd worked assiduously on that, using her one weakness, her ego, to ingratiate himself into her favor and, he hoped, her trust. But he still knew so little about her: who she truly was, where she came from, and, most importantly, the source from which she drew her awesome power.

What good his clandestine investigations could possibly do him in the long run Strann couldn't imagine, but they provided an outlet for his energies that helped to keep him sane, an antidote to his public role as Ygorla's fawning pet. In his bleaker moments he was able to console himself with the thought that at some time in the future—an unspecified time, but he preferred not to think about that—any information he could glean now might be an invaluable tool when it came to escaping from Summer Isle and finding some way of taking revenge on this monstrous woman. For revenge, pure and sweet, was the goad that drove him now. Revenge for his shame, for the lies he must tell and the pretenses he must adopt to stay alive, and most of all for the fact that Ygorla had stripped from him the one thing that he prized above all else: his self-respect. In the last few days Strann had come to loathe himself, and for that alone he yearned to exact retribution.

But retribution wasn't within his grasp yet. For now he must steel himself against sick self-disgust and a howling conscience, and continue to play the part of Strann the turncoat, Strann the traitor, Strann who had sold his loyalty to a murderess for a handful of tawdry baubles and who licked the feet of a usurper to preserve his skin in luxury. Pet rat. Very apposite, he thought bitterly as he shouldered the manzon. Rat. Nibbling rodent. Vermin.

He slammed the door savagely as he left the room and walked with a leaden heart in the direction of the audience hall.

Two shadows, man-shaped but with no visible features, intercepted Strann's path as he approached the hall's ornate double doors. Strann stood still and silent as they scrutinized him, then they moved back and the doors opened to admit him.

Ygorla was in her customary place on the raised dais,
seated on what it pleased her to call the Throne of Mortal
Dominions. In a petulant moment she had destroyed the
centuries-old ceremonial chair of the High Margrave, de-
claring it crude and unworthy of her, and had created in
its place a towering-backed sculpture of marble and precious metals and stones, upon which she reclined amid
luxurious piles of cushions. Pale bands of color moved
within the stone of the throne's shell-shaped back. They
reminded Strann uncomfortably of the colors that bled
across the sky during a Warp storm, and he'd learned
early on that they were influenced by Ygorla's moods.
Swiftly he read the shades pastel blue, silver, sea-green—
well and good; for the moment at least she was in an
amenable humor.

There were some half-dozen other people in the hall,
all gathered about their mistress's feet and deferentially
feeding her with wine, fruit, and sweetmeats. To Strann's
heartfelt relief her ghoulish houndcats were not present,
although something large and sinuous was moving sluggishly in the shadows behind the throne, and other phantasmic forms stared down at him from where they clung,
with lizardlike hands and feet, to the carvings high up on
the hall's pillars. Ghost-forms and wraiths he had learned
to cope with, but the houndcats were of another order
entirely and, goaded by awful memories of Captain Fyne's
fate, Strann went in dread of them.

At the sound of his footsteps Ygorla looked up, her
blue eyes glinting brilliantly. "Ah, my little rat! The cat
has chivvied you out of your hole and brought you patter-
ing to my side!"

"Sweet lady." Strann's trained bard's voice echoed in
the vast hall. "I come at your bidding, and with delight at

your summons." He made the flourishing bow that he'd perfected through hours of practice before his reflection in the window of his room, and saw the looks on the servants' faces as they turned to regard him. As always he felt a brief, sick sense of shame, but pushed it down as he had so many times before.

"Strann." He hated the way Ygorla enunciated his name; on her lips it sounded like an obscenity. "We are anticipating visitors, and I want to devise a small entertainment in their honor. Come here. Come and sit in your favored place."

He walked toward her, and as he approached, she snapped imperious fingers at the group around her feet. "Out," she said, and they went, scurrying like rats themselves and casting vitriolic glances at Strann as they passed. Ygorla smiled as the last of them departed through the double doors, then stretched out one graceful foot and prodded the blue velvet cushion that lay on the dais beneath her feet. Strann knew better than to wait for further prompting; he sank down cross-legged on the cushion and kissed the toe of her slipper.

Carelessly Ygorla indicated the remains of her private feast, which the slaves had left behind. "Eat, little rat. Rats are always hungry. Nibble at a sweetmeat: the head cook has quite excelled himself today."

Gods, Strann thought, but she *was* in a good mood this morning, and his alert mind immediately began to forage for a likely cause. He took one of the delicacies, looking up as he did so and venturing a smile that he hoped looked rapt. "A morsel from my lady's own table. I am the happiest of men."

Ygorla laughed; a lovely sound, but it made him squirm inwardly. "Then take another. Here, I shall feed you." She plucked a second sweetmeat from the littered tray. "Will you beg, rat?"

Thankful that—for once—there was no one else present to witness this humiliation, Strann rose to his knees, held up his hands, and twitched them in a fair imitation of a rat's paws. Ygorla's laughter increased to an uninhibited carillon, and for a moment the throne-back glowed gold.

"My predecessor was a fool not to have kept you here under lock and key for his entertainment!" She put the sweetmeat between his lips. "There. Taste."

He made a pretense of savoring the morsel, but at the same time his nostrils registered a faint and unusual scent that clung to Ygorla's fingers. Not her customary perfume, but he'd smelled it once or twice before, and something about it rang a bell deep in his psyche. Musk and hot iron, and some other, unnameable ingredient. Though he'd had little truck with occult matters, intuition told Strann that it was a whiff of the demon realms.

When and where had he caught that scent? It *was* familiar, but he couldn't pinpoint it; it wouldn't slot into place. Before he could delve into his memory, however, Ygorla's voice, nectar but with poison lurking beneath the surface, distracted him.

"Now, my favored little rodent, our visitors and their entertainment. You are composing the ballad of my triumphal arrival on Summer Isle—is it ready?"

The colors in the throne altered briefly—a momentary darkening, but it was enough to warn Strann to be cautious. He said, "It's not yet entirely as I would like it, my queen. I'm all too conscious that my efforts can never do you justice, and yet I am driven day and night by my desire to emulate your perfection." He made a self-deprecating gesture, at the same time watching her carefully from under half-lowered lashes. "I strive in my dreams and through all my waking hours, but it isn't enough."

Ygorla's smile became predatory. "I shall be the judge of that, my rat. I'll hear your ballad. Then, if it pleases me, you shall sing it to my guests when they come before me."

Strann said, "Guests, madam?"

She paused, eyeing him shrewdly. "Your whiskers are twitching. Curious, eh? Still, I'm in an indulgent mood, so I shall tell you. We have new guests in the palace. Somewhat unwilling guests, I'll grant, but I'm sure they'll soon get over their initial shyness. I mean to introduce them to my court, persuade them to spend a few days enjoying our hospitality, and then send them back to their various provinces to spread word of their experiences."

Strann began to see the picture and could imagine the circumstances under which Ygorla's "guests" had found themselves on Summer Isle. Sharp ears and a quick brain had served him well during the past few days, and he knew that Ygorla was wasting no time in spreading her net beyond Summer Isle's shores. When the first messenger-birds from the mainland provinces had arrived, each bearing a letter demanding to know the meaning of her proclamation, she had laughed, killed the birds, and retaliated with small but lethal demonstrations of her power. She had chosen her targets from the High Margrave's roll of key officials in the province Margravates, and in Shu, Southern Chaun, Prospect, and Wishet certain men and women of high standing had met untimely and gruesome deaths at the hands of demonic manifestations. Each "lesson," as Ygorla termed her depradations, had been followed by another dark messenger bearing a sardonic, salutary warning; now, though, it seemed that Ygorla had decided to change her tactics. Strann wondered how many

unfortunates had been snatched from the sanctuary of
their homes by her supernatural servants and in what state
they had arrived on Summer Isle. He also wondered—and
the thought wasn't comfortable—if there would be any
familiar faces among their number.

Abruptly Ygorla sat up, and Strann started guiltily as
he realized that he'd been in danger of letting himself become distracted, never a wise thing to do in her presence.
Luckily, however, she seemed not to have noticed his
lapse, for she had preoccupations of her own.

"We shall organize an entertainment for our guests
this evening," she said with rich satisfaction in her voice.
"Something to convince them beyond any shadow of
doubt that their masters on the mainland would be very
foolish to oppose my rule." She held out her wine-cup;
Strann hastened to refill it. "I have a number of ideas that
I think will serve to make my point very well. With those,
and your music and your bard's powers of persuasion, I
think our visitors will leave Summer Isle greatly enlightened. So, Strann: the ballad."

"Now, lady?"

"Now. I'm sure"—and suddenly there was a faintly
malevolent edge to her voice—"that it will please me. I
hope it will please me."

Strann prevaricated no further but picked up his
manzon and settled it over his knee. He had already come
to loathe his new saga of this woman's exploits. Composed
for the sole purpose of flattering her monstrous ego and
singing her praises to the heavens, it demeaned his skill
and, he felt, reduced him to something lower than the
kind of talentless huckster who would tell any number of
lies for a few coins. The fact that it was his life rather than
a few coins that Strann was trying to preserve made no

difference: he felt soiled. One day, he promised himself, he would write a parody of this obscene paean. One day . . .

He struck the opening chord, plucked an impressive and complex arpeggio, then began to play the melody that announced the ballad's first verse. It was simple—he'd discovered early on that Ygorla's appreciation of music was unsophisticated, to say the very least—but rhythmic and majestic and redolent of pomp and panoply. He saw the corners of her mouth twitch and, encouraged, he drew breath and began to sing.

Ygorla listened. Soon she began to smile.

Gods, but he would give five years of his life, Strann thought, not to have to go through that experience or anything like it again. He pressed his face against the cold, pale stone of the corridor wall, not caring whether anyone might see him but only wanting the wall's coolness to dull the pounding in his head. He wasn't drunk—or if he was, only a little. By far the worst of his sickness came not from the body but from the soul.

They were on their way to the harbor now. The ambassadors, Ygorla had dubbed them, and her mocking laughter had filled the audience hall as she bestowed the title on them. Three men and one woman, terrified almost over the brink of sanity, their eyes glazed and their brains reeling with the memory of what they had seen in their brief visit to the Summer Isle court.

Ygorla had excelled herself tonight. Excelled herself in arrogance, in spite, and in a level of childish mental cruelty that had shocked even Strann, who thought he knew her well, to the core. She had called a full assembly of her

114

court, ostensibly to welcome the distinguished visitors to Summer Isle but in truth to indulge in a veritable orgy of terror and persecution, to force home with a vengeance the lesson she wanted her guests to learn. They had learned it. And, with the shreds of their minds that were left intact, they'd remember it for the rest of their lives.

The evening's entertainment had begun harmlessly enough, at least by contrast with what was to follow. Strann, fortified with more wine that he should have allowed himself, had been led into the packed audience hall on the end of a fine gold chain attached to his jeweled collar and had prostrated himself at Ygorla's feet with the sounds of derisive laughter ringing in his ears. The visitors, to give them credit, hadn't had the wisdom to join in the hooting, sycophantic chorus from Ygorla's terrified retinue. They had merely stared, some repelled, some pitying, all baffled, as with a smiling face and a granite heart Strann acted out his part in the charade before taking his customary place on a tasseled cushion at Ygorla's feet and picking up his manzon. The ballad he had composed was received with fawning applause by his fellow slaves and in embarrassed silence by the newcomers, and when it was done, Ygorla rose to her feet and announced her intention of rewarding her pet rat by commissioning him to compose a new epic.

"The epic," she said, her blue eyes flashing as she stared at her guests with a direct and terrible challenge, "of a new reign and a new age in this world. The reign of Ygorla—Daughter of Chaos and Margravine of Mortal Dominions!"

The woman of the visiting party made a small, involuntary noise that sounded as though she were choking. Ygorla's gaze hardened and fixed on her.

"Do I hear a note of skepticism, madam? Or even of dissent?"

The woman stared up at the dais, and the words came out before she could stem them. "You are *mad* . . ."

"Mad?" Ygorla tilted her head like a bird of prey assessing a potential victim. "I think you speak from ignorance. Do you know what madness is? Have you experienced madness for yourself, in any of its grotesque forms?" The woman's lips drew back in a sharp, uncertain movement, and Ygorla smiled sweetly. "No. I see you haven't. Well, we must rectify that."

She snapped her fingers. Up near the hall's ceiling something giggled. The woman looked up, saw what was slithering down one of the marble columns and holding out its arms toward her, and screamed.

Even Strann hadn't dared to turn his head away as Ygorla's supernatural pet took its warped pleasure with the shrieking woman. No one had tried to help her, and not one of her companions had so much as raised a voice in protest. When at last it was over and the giggling, satiated thing slunk out of the hall, leaving the stink of rotting fruit in its wake, two of Ygorla's faceless sentries pulled the victim to her feet. Ygorla gazed dispassionately at the wildly distorted face staring through a matted tangle of hair, then smiled her sweet smile again.

"Was that madness, madam? Perhaps you're not yet convinced? Perhaps I can show you another of its many faces?"

Where an instant before she had been standing, a hairless dog the size of a horse, with sickly white skin and eyes of yellow flame, slavered and drooled on the dais. Its lips drew back from huge, broken teeth and it spoke in Ygorla's melodious voice.

"Enough yet, my lady? I have many more tricks if you think they'll amuse you."

The woman's eyes rolled up in their sockets and she fainted. It took three minions to revive her with aromatic phials and none too gentle slaps across the face; by the time she finally recovered her senses, Ygorla had been amused by their efforts into a more indulgent mood, and spared her further personal demonstrations of power—for a small price. The woman paid the price without an instant's hesitation, and before the entire company prostrated herself at the new High Margravine's feet and pledged her undying fealty. Her companions followed suit without demur. Strann couldn't blame them: it would, he reminded himself, have been an act of utter hypocrisy to do so, though when he watched them take turns to accept, like begging dogs, sweetmeats from Ygorla's dish as he himself had done earlier, his stomach almost rebelled.

The farce had continued from there with what Ygorla was pleased to call "a few petty conjuring tricks"; horrible, if short-lived, manifestations that left their audience reeling, terrified, and cowed. Then there had been dancing, a grim parody of Summer Isle celebrations in happier days, to the strains of unearthly music with no visible musicians to play it. The guests were partnered, willing or not, by things—Strann couldn't even dignify them with the term *creatures*—created for the occasion by Ygorla's fearsome imagination. A hunchbacked dog with eight spiderlike legs whirled the woman in a wild, contorting caper, while worm-haired, eyeless horrors cavorted with the men, alternately kissing them and biting their faces with fang-filled mouths, as around them the rest of the court made a desperate show of merriment. The mayhem continued until dawn, and then as the sun's first light crept into the hall, Ygorla gathered the shocked and bludgeoned visitors before her and delivered a speech in which she charged them to carry what they had learned of the new High Margravine back to the mainland and ensure that the word was received and understood by those who might otherwise think to defy her. The quartet had sworn to do her bidding and more, more, anything she might require of them, and at last Ygorla had let them go. Herded by Ygorla's sentries and followed by two of her black houndcats, they had shambled away to board the ship that would take them back to a saner world, and the court was dismissed.

Strann had held back, making himself as inconspicuous as possible, as the main crush of people followed Ygorla's sweeping exit through the double doors. Only when he judged that the corridor outside would be all but deserted did he unfasten the collar and chain at his throat —resisting with difficulty an urge to fling the loathesome objects down the length of the chamber—and leave in his turn. Outside the hall the torches had been extinguished and the corridor was dim with shadow. Strann stood for a minute or perhaps two until his brow cooled a little, then turned in the direction of his quarters—and stopped.

He didn't want to go back to that opulent but repellent cell. If he slept, he'd have nightmares; if he sat there wakeful, then his thoughts would crush the last remnants of his spirit out of him; and if he tried to drink himself into a stupor, he'd be ill before it ceased to matter. He wanted air. Clean, untainted air, and freedom from the palace's confining walls.

He returned to his room only to put away the manzon and throw down the jeweled collar, then made his way through the maze of passages that led to a small and little-used doorway into the palace gardens. Passing a side turning, he paused suddenly, and his nostrils flared as again he caught the frustratingly elusive smell he'd scented several times before. This side passage connected to the stairs of Ygorla's tower; Strann walked a few paces along it and the smell became distinctly stronger. Musk and iron and . . . he shook his head, his steps slowing as he realized that he was drawing perilously close to an area barred to anyone but Ygorla herself and that even now some demonic guardian might be watching him, only waiting for him to set one foot into forbidden territory. It wouldn't be wise to venture any farther, and Strann made his way back toward the outside door and let himself out into the cooler air.

The sun was beginning to climb into a clear sky, but its brilliance was dulled by another and less natural glow that distorted the colors of the morning and cast a coppery gloom over the scene. From his present vantage so close to the walls Strann couldn't see the titanic seven-rayed star that hung pulsing in the air above the palace, but he was aware of its presence, of the constant fluctuation of dark light—how light could be dark he didn't know, but this was—intensifying and fading as the star beat like a huge, slow heart.

Strann walked slowly away from the palace, under a stone arch on which a vine had flowered, faded, and was now withering with a faintly sulphurous stink, and into the first of the formal gardens. Under the star's lowering glare there was something eerie about the neat flower beds and decoratively clipped hedges: shadows seemed misshapen and in the wrong places, and it was all too easy to imagine that one of the pieces of topiary would suddenly resolve itself into some hideous living form and come scudding across the grass toward him. He tried to ignore the effect, tried to ignore the star's subliminal, insidious taint, and crossed the lawn to where a group of noble old trees would hide him from the view of anyone watching from a window. Then, careless of the ground's dampness, he sat down with his back against a tree trunk, to think.

By the time the sun set again, Ygorla's sorry little group of "ambassadors" would be back in Shu-Nhadek telling the tale of their abduction. Strann had little doubt that the rest of the world already knew of Ygorla, but the returning quartet would be the first living souls beyond Summer Isle's shores to have seen her with their own eyes and lived to carry their story back to the provinces. The Margraves' reactions, he surmised, would be mixed; some would capitulate without argument, others would flare into righteous outrage and set plans in train to invade the isle and deal summarily with the upstart pretender. The thought of what would inevitably happen to any punitive force sent against Ygorla made Strann's gut contract. The four ambassadors knew the extent of Ygorla's power. But he had an ugly intuition that some of the Margraves would refuse to take that intelligence on trust and would arm their militias and launch their fleets, and in so doing send the gods alone knew how many innocent men to their deaths while Ygorla, sprawling on her magnificent throne, laughed at their foolhardy presumption. No mortal army could hope to prevail against the powers she had at her command. And that brought Strann's reluctant mind back to the crux of his speculations.

What *was* the wellspring of Ygorla's supernatural strength? She called herself, among other grandiose titles, *Daughter of Chaos,* and the great, gloomy star pulsing above the palace like a brazen challenge implied that she did indeed pay fealty to Yandros. But Strann believed that what she might wish the world to think was not necessarily the truth. He didn't credit for one moment the idea that Ygorla felt loyalty toward anyone or anything but herself. And—though he didn't claim any expert knowledge; that was the province of the Circle and the Sisterhood—Strann doubted very much that Yandros would choose Ygorla to be his avatar in the mortal world. If the Chaos gods meant to break the pact they had established at the time of Change and take a direct hand in human affairs, what need would they have of such a creature?

So was Ygorla acting with the blessing of Chaos, or was she claiming a heritage to which she had no right? The four unwilling ambassadors would have formed their own opinions, and it didn't take a great deal of insight to guess at what those opinions would be. Before long the Margraves would surely be appealing to the Circle to call on the gods to intervene. The Circle, on the evidence given to them, would turn to Aeoris and the Lords of Order— and that, Strann was beginning to suspect, would be a fundamental mistake.

He thought again about the smell that had assailed his nostrils by the corridor to Ygorla's private quarters. The scent of demons; yet Ygorla herself, whatever else she might be, was no demon as he understood the term. What else, then, lurked in those forbidden rooms of hers? What mentor, what co-conspirator? What source of power?

He rose and began to pace across the lawn, too restless to sit still. With each minute that passed he was becoming more convinced, on an intuitive level that he couldn't logically defend, that whatever appearances suggested, whatever she might want the world to believe, Ygorla was no friend to Chaos.

In a locked room of the palace, hidden from outsiders yet kept alive by Ygorla's whim, the true High Margravine, Jianna Hanmen Alacar, grieved for her dead husband and maintained her sanity by praying for a chance to avenge him. Strann had seen her three times in recent days when she had been brought to the hall to witness some new game of Ygorla's devising, and he had seen the burning wildness in her eyes, felt the aura of fanatical resistance that radiated from her like light from the sun. Jianna would not capitulate. The flesh might be falling from her, turning her buxom prettiness to a gaunt and savage pastiche, and her mind might be on the point of breaking; but something kept her back from that final edge. She sustained herself on her hatred, feeding on it, depending on it, refusing to bow to Ygorla's will and nurturing her unshakable loathing for the usurper and all who paid her fealty. Strann had felt the scourge of her terrible stare as he performed his jester's role beside Ygorla's throne—and he had heard her whisper, over and over again as she stood rigid between her guards and tried to ignore Ygorla's humiliations, a fervent and unceasing prayer to Aeoris.

Aeoris, however, had not answered her. Jianna might spend every private moment kneeling in supplication to the great god of Order, but so far there had been no sign that her pleas had been heard, let alone that Aeoris might make any response. Though he had long forgotten most of the catechisms of his childhood, Strann knew enough about the pact between Chaos and Order to be aware that Aeoris could not take a hand in human affairs unless Yandros had first broken his side of the bargain. If Yandros's hand had guided Ygorla in any way, then surely, *surely* that would give Aeoris every justification to retaliate. Yet there had been nothing—and that, Strann felt, was further confirmation of his theory.

He was some twenty yards from the tree by now, though its trunk still concealed him from anyone in the palace. Stopping, he turned about and looked up to the treetop and the sky beyond, which was still stained with the gloomy light from the great, pulsing star.

"This isn't your doing." He spoke softly, addressing his words to a place beyond this world, beyond the reach of his imagination. He had never seen Yandros—nor, for that matter, had any living soul—but in his mind's eye he conjured an image of the great Chaos lord, as though he were speaking directly to him. "This is not your hand at work, and yet you do nothing to stop it. Why, Yandros? What holds you back?"

The sky remained impassive; the star continued to pulse. Somewhere a bird twittered, then fell silent, and Strann felt that his words had been spoken into a void. He lowered his head and stared at the grass beneath his feet for a few moments. Then, his steps slow and his shoulders a little hunched as though in defense of something he couldn't quite articulate, he began to make his reluctant way back toward the palace.

8

The punitive fleet set sail eleven days later. The Margraves of the southernmost provinces had joined forces to unite the cream of their militia; three thousand fully armed fighting men aboard a flotilla of fifteen ships crewed by the most hardened sailors that the entire southern coast could muster. They put out from Shu-Nhadek, from Port Summer in Wishet, and from the Prospect Estuary, and they joined forces in the Straits to sail on Summer Isle.

In Sisterhood Cots throughout the provinces women chanted exhortations to the gods for the fleet's success. In her own Cot in Southern Chaun the Matriarch went into retreat to pray for deliverance. And at the Star Peninsula Tirand led the higher adepts in a rite to call Aeoris's blessing on the enterprise and bring an end to Ygorla's brief but bloody reign.

At the height of the ceremony, as the Marble Hall vibrated with the power raised by the massed initiates, Karuth knew with a sure and unshakable conviction that their efforts were in vain. She couldn't put her certainty into words, nor in her present uncertain position within Tirand's estimation would she have voiced it to him even if the words had come. But her bones told her what her logical mind didn't want to acknowledge, and when the news came in five days later, she said nothing to anyone but climbed the stairs of the disused north spire and, in one of the cramped turret rooms where no one could see or hear her, wept.

The fleet hadn't reached Summer Isle. The storm, so the letter carried from Shu-Nhadek by messenger-bird said, had been the least of it. Thanks to a ragged handful of survivors who had by a miracle found their way back to the mainland in a battered dinghy, the whole ugly story was now known: Silver lightning spearing from an empty sky to strike with uncanny and devastating accuracy. Dense black clouds forming from nowhere to create a solid wall between the sea and the heavens, and within which men suffocated or died screaming as monsters materialized from the dark to rend and devour them. Elementals wreaking destruction, demonic apparitions, things that rose from the depths of the ocean to crush whole ships in their jaws. And last and most terrible of all, a dark line on the shimmering, tortured horizon that resolved into a formation of jet-black ships, towering above the remains of the fleet and bearing down on them with impossible speed. Phantom ships with sails like gigantic spiders' webs belling in a hell-born wind; ships with the phosphorescent glare of corpse-lights at their prows and ball lightning dancing atop their masts, and the bleached-bone, fleshless hands of dead men at the ropes while captains who had never been remotely human stared in deadly, smiling silence from their forecastles. The ships had plowed through the milling remnants of the mainland forces like white-hot knives through flesh. Most of those who survived the shattering onslaught were drowned as the last of the Margraves' fleet went down; an unluckier few were scooped from the sea in nets and taken, writhing and howling uselessly for help, aboard the phantom ships to meet a more gruesome fate. One small lifeboat, hurled from the deck of its sinking parent craft in a final act of desperation, was buffeted away from the scene of carnage with five men aboard and carried to shore on a strong east wind the following day. Two of the survivors died from shock by second moonset and a third was pronounced incurably mad; the remaining two were able to tell their tale with what pitiful wits were left to them. The fury of the provinces had burned out in mayhem and tragedy.

On the morning after news of the disaster reached the Star Peninsula, the High Initiate received a new missive from Summer Isle. The letter, this time, was brief and uncompromising. It said simply, *"I am your Empress."* It was signed in Ygorla's flourishing hand, and beneath her signature was the title by which she now styled herself and with which she had taunted her four captives: *Daughter of Chaos and Margravine of Mortal Dominions.*

Tirand didn't immediately show the message to any of his fellow adepts. For two hours he sat alone in his study, staring at the scrap of parchment until he felt as though the terse words had burned indelibly into his brain. *Daughter of Chaos.* He couldn't describe the emotion that that title evoked in him; it was beyond expression. *Chaos.* Lies. Deceit. Treachery. Mockery of all that he and his peers, benighted fools that they were, had believed to be sacred. It made a pitiful farce of Equilibrium; it was a filthy, depraved, and savage joke. Oh, yes, he'd heard the stories that the four unwilling ambassadors had brought back on their return. Stories of the seven-rayed star that hung over the Summer Isle palace, stories of the power that this maniacal bitch had at the tips of her fingers. Chaos power. Yandros's power. Tirand wasn't easily moved to hatred, but he felt it rising in him now, together with a sense of betrayal so great that he could barely contain it. What perverted whim had moved Yandros to this? Why had it amused him to grant such seeming omnipotence to a madwoman and set her against Margravate, Circle, and Sisterhood alike? Was this the culmination of some long-held grudge against the mortal triumvirate who ruled in the gods' names, the settling of a score against those who paid due fealty to Chaos but in their hearts still favored Order?

Tirand smacked a clenched fist down on the table as frustration momentarily overcame his self-control. He looked at Ygorla's curt message again, then carefully folded the parchment, resisting the impulse to crumple it into a ball and stamp it into the carpet. A clear head and a cool heart. That was what he needed now. He would summon the Council of Adepts—a full meeting, not just the inner coterie—in formal emergency session. The rage in him was passing now, or at least had taken second place to reason. He knew what he intended to say to the council. More crucially, he knew what he intended to do.

He clenched his hand around the folded parchment and left his study in search of the council steward.

" 'I am your Empress.' That, Adepts, is all she has to say this time." Tirand dropped Ygorla's letter on the table before him and looked steadily at the throng of grave faces in the council hall. "An arrogant and uncompromising statement that, as we now know to our bitter cost, she has the power to enforce." He picked up another handful of papers and displayed them. "For the few among you who aren't already aware of the contents of these, we have now received missives from every Margravate save for Empty Province and our own West High Land. They have all been told of the punitive fleet's fate." He sifted the letters into two piles. "The Margraves of Han, Chaun, and Southern Chaun plead for the Circle to move immediately to combat this deadly menace and are ready to put their entire resources at our disposal. The Margraves of East Han, Wishet, Shu, Prospect, and the Great Eastern Flatlands, while also begging for our help, say that unless that help can be given before Ygorla issues her next threat, they will have no choice but to capitulate for the sake of their people's safety."

Someone made a strangled sound of disbelief, and Sen Briaray Olvit looked at the High Initiate in consternation. *"Capitulate?* Tirand, they're not serious! That's craven cowardice—not to mention the fact that it's playing straight into this usurper's hands!"

Tirand had expected this from the impulsive senior adept and had an answer ready. He didn't like it any more than Sen did, but there were times when principle had to give way before necessity.

"I don't think we're in a position to accuse the Margraves of cowardice, Sen," he said. "They've already suffered one heavy blow, with the threat of worse to come if they continue to resist. And they're right; they *do* have the safety of their people to consider."

"Tirand, with all due respect, that's a fallacious argument. We in the Circle are responsible not just for one province but for the *world.*"

"Agreed. But we administer that responsibility from the safety of a virtually impenetrable stronghold, as far from Summer Isle as it's possible to be. The Margraves don't have that advantage; they are, so to speak, in the front line, and very vulnerable."

Sen frowned, still unhappy. "How can the Great Eastern Flatlands consider itself in any front line? It's one of the northernmost provinces!"

"And it has a large and unprotected coast in a direct line from Summer Isle." Tirand leaned forward over the table. "Like it or not, we have to accept that the Margraves have every justification for being frightened, and I don't think we can blame them for looking to save lives above all else." There was a murmur of agreement from the majority of the councillors at this, and, encouraged, Tirand continued, "More to the point, if the majority of provinces decide to offer fealty to this sorceress, there's nothing we can do to stop them. Our jurisdiction extends only to matters of religion; we are guardians and interpreters of the gods' laws, not those of mortals." He raised his gaze and looked to the far end of one of the long tables. "I'm sorry to have to speak of unhappy matters, but it's an inescapable fact that the provinces owe their true fealty not to the Circle but to the High Margrave."

There was a moment's awkward pause. Someone cleared his throat. Then a new voice said, "It's all right, Tirand. I'm willing to talk about it. In fact I think it's necessary."

Calvi Alacar, dressed in the purple of mourning, raised his head from where he sat beside an elderly woman councillor and gave the High Initiate a pallid smile. Though he wasn't an initiate of the Circle, let alone a council member, to exclude him from this meeting would have been unthinkable; for this slim, spare, inexperienced young man was by birthright the supreme ruler to whom the entire world was legally bound to defer.

When the news of Blis's death was broken to him, Calvi had asked to be left alone for a few hours so that he might express his grief in private before facing the official announcement of the news to the entire Circle. Worried that the strain might prove too great, Tirand had alerted Karuth to the possibility that the young man might break down, but to his surprise and relief Calvi had emerged from his room later in the day, red-eyed but with a tense and determined set to his shoulders that suggested he was aware of his new responsibilities and ready to face them.

Calvi hadn't found it easy to come to terms with the knowledge that he was now the High Margrave. He looked weary, his eyes dull, his face drawn, but despite the strain imposed on him over the past few days he was beginning to grope his way toward a degree of confidence as he realized that the Circle's attitude toward him was changing. He was no longer simply Calvi the student; he was a man whose opinion and sanction must be sought and acted upon, especially so at this time of crisis. A figurehead, yes, but a figurehead with real temporal power. He didn't want that, he would have given anything if his brother could have been restored to life to take the reins once more; but the situation had been forced upon him—upon them all—and they must make the best of it.

Tirand gestured again toward the letters before him. "The Margraves," he said, "without exception, have made two requests. They ask for the Circle's help, as I've already told you. But they also ask for the High Margrave's decree on what they should do." He looked up. "I'm sorry, Calvi. I didn't want to tax you with this, but it's a question that only you can answer."

Calvi nodded. He'd expected it, could have anticipated nothing less, and in one way at least it was reassuring, for it showed that the province Margraves had accepted him without question as Blis's successor. But he didn't know what to say. Blis, he knew, would already have formed a contingency plan; he himself had none. He felt helpless.

Gently Tirand spoke to him again. "We'll aid you in any way we can, Calvi. You know that."

Calvi did know it, just as he knew that Tirand, too, had once been in similar straits when his father's sudden death had dropped the High Initiate's mantle onto his unready shoulders. But fellow-feeling, though comforting, wasn't enough. He needed advice as never before. He wanted someone to tell him unequivocally what he should do.

Three places from him, beyond the elderly woman and a middle-aged man whose name he couldn't for the moment recall, Karuth caught his eye. She smiled reassuringly, leaned toward him with a quick apology to the others, and whispered, "Follow your instincts, Calvi. Trust them. That's the most any of us can do."

The knot of tension in Calvi's stomach eased fractionally. He couldn't find the words to thank Karuth, but he felt the paralysis of indecision loosing its hold on him, and when he looked toward the high table again, his expression was calmer.

"I can't make a decree, Tirand." He spoke clearly and without a tremor. "I may be the High Margrave, but with Summer Isle in the hands of a usurper I'm effectively in exile, even if the Margraves still look to me as their lawgiver. As you yourself said, we're safe here; we're not being asked to bear the brunt of this woman's powers. The Margraves . . ." He hesitated, then went on with greater conviction, "The Margraves must have the sanction to do as they see fit. If I had a great army at my back, if I could send them the help they need, it might be a different matter. But they have to fight this battle in their own way and with their own resources, and I don't feel that I have the right to give orders from a place of safety and expect them to be obeyed." Another pause. "I will send letters to them all, in my own hand, and tell them that, whatever they feel they must do to avoid more tragedy, they have my full blessing."

"Thank you." Tirand's eyes were warm with approval. "I think that's a very wise decision."

Calvi, however, wasn't happy. "No, Tirand, it isn't," he said. "It's cowardly." He glanced toward Sen Briaray Olvit. "Sen was right; the provinces should resist. And I should be among them, rallying—"

"No, High Margrave." Arcoro Raeklen Vir, who sat beside Tirand, spoke up. "You should not."

Calvi stared at him uncertainly. Arcoro glanced at Tirand for permission to address the gathering, received a nod.

"Under the present circumstances," he said, "the duty of the High Margrave, as I see it, is purely and simply to remain alive. To be blunt, sir, if you were to follow your heart's urgings and try to lead your subjects against this sorceress, you would die, unpleasantly and probably ignominiously, within a matter of days. With no living kin to succeed you there would then be no natural heir to the Summer Isle throne. That, I contend, would spell the complete collapse of any morale the provinces might have left."

A stirring, a murmuring in the hall. Even Sen watched Arcoro with new interest. The old adept continued.

"This raises a further issue. The world is aware that its High Margrave is here at the Star Peninsula, which means that the usurper, too, must know it—we needn't delude ourselves that any questions she might have asked won't have been truthfully answered by someone. She must also realize that Calvi Alacar's continuing existence is a potential threat to whatever grandiose plans she is hatching. The entire world might fall to its knees and give her homage, but in their hearts people will remain loyal to their rightful ruler, and her only hope of breaking the chains of that loyalty is to kill Calvi. To do that, she must first breach the defenses of this castle. So I think it reasonable to assume that before long the conquest of the Star Peninsula will become her prime goal. That, my friends, poses the question to us of how we—not the Margraves, not the militia, but the sorcerers of this Circle—are to combat her power."

Tirand expected Sen to intercede then, and he wasn't disappointed.

"You're right, Arcoro." Sen's swift, hot gaze took in the entire assembly. "Sorcery of this nature can only be met in kind. We can't expect the militia to fight this usurper, not now that we know beyond doubt what she's capable of. *Our* skills are what's needed." He looked at the High Initiate. "I don't mind admitting that I've made mistakes, Tirand. In the first place I believed that this whole affair was a hoax; now I've been proved wrong. I was also wrong just now in my initial judgment of the province Margraves. You and Calvi are right—we can't expect them to stand fast in the face of this madwoman's power. Our responsibilities are clear. We must take the battle into our own hands."

Arcoro spoke up again. "How, Sen, would you propose that we do that?"

Sen frowned sharply. "By combatting sorcery with sorcery. How else?"

"In principle I agree with you, as I'm sure we all do. But in practice it may not be so easy. Can we conjure a supernatural fleet of ships complete with demon crews? Can we spirit people away from their own hearths and transport them into our presence on a whim? Consider it. Consider what the usurper has already done and ask yourself, Are we capable of matching, let alone surpassing her?"

"We must be! The Circle is the repository of the greatest sorcerous skills known to the mortal world—and whatever else this woman may be, she *is* mortal!"

It was the opportunity for which Tirand had been waiting. Before Arcoro could answer Sen's assertion, he interjected.

"She's mortal, yes. But, my friends, there's one question we haven't yet considered. What lies behind her mortality? Whose hand has inspired her and granted her a level of power that by all reason and precedent should be beyond human reach?"

Every pair of eyes in the hall focused abruptly on him, and Tirand silently thanked both Arcoro and Sen for what they had done. This was the real issue, the heart of it. He must make the council see the truth as he saw it.

He rose to his feet. Though he wasn't consciously aware of it, this was a small strategy that his father, Chiro, had often used in debate, giving a sudden air of formality to the proceedings and thus ensuring everyone's full attention.

"Adepts, I believe that the evidence for what I am about to say is clear and unequivocal. We know from the messages we have received that the usurper pays fealty to one power and one alone." He looked up, his eyes hard and chill. "The seven-rayed star hangs above the palace on Summer Isle, like a gauntlet thrown down in our faces. The sorceress styles herself 'Daughter of Chaos' and revels in that title. And the events of the last few days, which have now been related to us in painful detail, only serve to confirm what I had already suspected. This woman may be mortal—but the power she wields has been consciously and deliberately granted to her by another agency. This is the work of Yandros!"

They had known what he would say. Tirand saw it in their faces, sensed it in the susurration of indrawn breaths that echoed his declaration, and he felt a surge of relief as he realized just how many of his fellow councillors had already, privately, reached the same conclusion. Sen was nodding vigorously; most of the other senior adepts also inclined their heads; and even Arcoro, whose loyalties were scrupulously balanced, was clearly giving the thought sober consideration.

"My friends." Tirand had their attention and, for the most part, their approval; now was the time to press his view home before any voices could dissent or dissemble. "It grieves me deeply to say this, because it goes against all the tenets that were laid down at the time of Change, the tenets that Keridil Toln himself risked his life and his soul to establish." He licked dry lips. "However, the truth can't be denied simply because it is unpalatable—and the truth is that the Chaos lords have betrayed us.

"When Equilibrium was established, the gods of both Order and Chaos pledged that they would no longer intervene in the affairs of this world. They promised us freedom to worship as we choose, they promised that they would not demand our fealty as a matter of right or coerce us into obeying their will by any means. For eighty years both sides kept faith with that promise—but now it has been broken, for Yandros has granted demonic power to a human sorceress so that she might take the place of our rightful rulers by force. Yandros's intention is clear, adepts. Ygorla is the instrument by which the lords of Chaos mean to return to the world and reign unopposed. They have cast aside their own pact, cast aside Equilibrium, and made a mockery of our faith and loyalty." He paused, then decided to dispense with rhetoric and state, bluntly, what was in his mind. "I therefore propose that the Circle should formally and ritually renounce all fealty to the gods of Chaos and call upon Aeoris of Order to aid us in bringing down the usurper before it's too late."

There was a stunned silence. Even the vociferous Sen was at a loss for words, and Tirand realized that he had made a miscalculation. The majority of the council might agree with his judgment of the situation and share his feelings of betrayal, but they hadn't anticipated such an extreme proposal. They were shocked by it, floundering, unsure of themselves. Tirand could hardly blame them; he himself had found the idea almost impossible to countenance at first, and it had taken a great deal of heart searching to bring him to his decision. But now that he *had* decided, he wouldn't turn back. His heart wouldn't allow it.

Arcoro raised a hand to his mouth and coughed. Attention focused instantly on him, and the old adept spoke.

"High Initiate." His tone was formal, the words carefully enunciated. "For the sake of clarification, so that none of us should be in any doubt . . . do we understand that you are asking the Council of Adepts to ratify that proposal?"

"Yes, Arcoro. I am."

"That we . . . revoke the principles of Equilibrium and pledge our loyalty solely to Aeoris?"

"Yes. I know it goes against all we've been taught; I know it denies everything that Keridil Toln worked for. But I believe we have no choice. Chaos has chosen to set its full might against us. Unless we stand fast, we will lose the freedom that cost our forefathers so dearly and become nothing more than the pawns of an invincible and unchallenged power." Tirand's gaze swept across the hall, and he raised his voice. "Remember the words enshrined in our records, in Keridil Toln's own hand: 'The conflict between Order and Chaos can never be resolved. The balance must be maintained, for anything that is to grow and prosper must by nature contain its intrinsic opposite.' We have lived by that tenet for nearly a century, and we've learned just how wise those words are. Now, though, that principle is threatened by the very same power that established it. I don't pretend to comprehend Yandros's motive; all I know is that our world is in danger. As High Initiate of the Circle it is my first and only duty to do battle against that danger—and I believe that our sole hope of salvation is to turn to our old gods, the gods of Order, and ask them to join with us against Chaos."

This time the adepts did react. Voices rose, a wave of murmuring that swelled rapidly toward a crescendo. Some were on their feet, signaling for Tirand's attention, wanting to speak. But it was Sen's voice that suddenly roared above the babble and carried through the hall.

"Adepts! Councillors!" His fist thumped on the table and the noise subsided a little. "Forgive me, but there are times when loudest is first, and at this moment I make no apologies for shouting anyone down! I pledge my full support for the High Initiate's proposal, for it's plain to me that even our most skilled sorcerers can't hope to prevail against Chaos itself. We must fight fire with fire! We must appeal to Aeoris! If Yandros is moving against us, then only with Aeoris's aid can we hope to stop him!" Sen drew a deep breath. "Can anyone in this hall disagree with that plain fact?"

There was a flurry of movement at one of the tables, a disturbance as someone rose to their feet, and a clear voice said, "Yes, Sen—I can, and must."

The High Initiate met his sister's gray eyes. As Karuth spoke, the hubbub died away; her rank, and her unspoken status as Tirand's blood kin, quieted the council immediately.

"Karuth." Tirand nodded courteously, but not a little reluctantly, in her direction. "What do you have to say?"

Karuth pressed her palms down on the table before her. "We run too fast and too far, Tirand. We assume that Yandros is behind Ygorla's depredations, but we have no positive proof."

"The seven-rayed star hanging above the Summer Isle palace? The usurper's self-proclaimed title? Aren't they proof enough?"

She shook her head. "I don't believe they are. Anyone can lay claim to a symbol or a title, but it doesn't necessarily follow that their claim is genuine. There's every chance that this sorceress is *not* Yandros's pawn. For all we know, she could be as much of an enemy to Chaos as she is to us."

Sen suppressed an outraged snort and Tirand shook his head. "I can't agree with that. Can you seriously imagine that Yandros would tolerate for one moment the rise to power of an enemy of Chaos who blatantly flaunts Chaos's own symbol as her banner?"

"I believe that he might," Karuth said, then added with more than a little irony, "If he is faithful to his own pact, what other choice would he have?"

"Oh, no." Tirand made a canceling gesture, aware that he was growing angry and wanting to quell the feeling before it could take root. To be drawn into a public argument with Karuth before the full council would be unseemly—and he was also anxious that the adepts shouldn't be diverted from the main debate.

"I understand your need for caution in this, Karuth," he said. "But we have enough evidence to show that you are wrong. I am certain that this usurper has Chaos's full blessing. From where else could she have gained her power? From Aeoris? I hardly think so! No; the facts are clear. Yandros won't move against Ygorla, because she is doing his will. Aeoris cannot move against her, because unlike their counterparts in Chaos the lords of Order won't break the pledge they made. Aeoris is faithful to Equilibrium—Yandros is not."

Karuth's mouth set in a tight, angry line. "Were you a lesser man, High Initiate, I might think that your viewpoint was prejudiced."

Tirand's knuckles clenched and unclenched on the table. He smiled, without a trace of humor. "I take no insult from that, Karuth. I've never pretended that I don't feel a greater loyalty to Aeoris than to Yandros, as did our father and Keridil Toln before him. The freedom to have such preferences is part of the Equilibrium that Chaos now threatens to destroy, and under the circumstances I'm confident that most of this council, whatever their particular loyalties have been until now, will feel as I do."

"I'm not so sure of that, Tirand. There are others—" she glanced pointedly at Arcoro, who was now fiddling with a quill pen and staring at his hands—"who pay at least as great a fealty to Chaos as to Order and who won't abandon their faith in Yandros so readily."

Arcoro raised his head. Though to all appearances he hadn't been watching Karuth, he hadn't missed her meaningful look and the silent appeal in it. "I'm sorry, Karuth," he said quietly, "but I'm afraid I can't stand with you. I may have an instinctive leaning toward Chaos, as you have, but in this matter I agree with Tirand. We've always known that Yandros is a mercurial god and that the moods of Chaos can't be predicted or relied on: that unpredictability is the very essence of Chaos, after all. Perhaps it was inevitable that Yandros would one day grow bored with ruling over a peaceful world—I don't know, and like Tirand I'm certainly not arrogant enough or fool enough to think that I can fathom his reasoning. But this *is* Chaos's work; I'm convinced of it. That being so, it would surely be unwise—to put it very mildly indeed—to take the risk of trying to make contact with Yandros. The chances are that that's precisely what both he and the usurper want; therefore the consequences for us could be disastrous. Our only trustworthy ally is Aeoris of Order. We *must* look to him alone."

"Thank you, Arcoro," Tirand said. "You make the point eloquently, and you're quite right." He looked at his sister again. "Aside from any other considerations, as Arcoro says we dare not risk opening ourselves to Chaos's influence. We might intend simply to test their response, but how can we predict what would result from that act alone? Under the present circumstances it's far too dangerous." He paused. "We would also be well advised to

140

consider how such a deed might affect our appeal to
Aeoris. Wouldn't it be the supreme folly to risk jeopardiz-
ing ourselves in his eyes now?"

Many other councillors, Arcoro included, murmured
agreement, but Karuth's face was a study in consternation. Even if no one else had been prepared to support her
she had expected Arcoro of all the councillors to share her
feelings, and she was adrift. Abruptly she looked away
from the old man, and Tirand spoke once more.

"I think, adepts, that there's little to be gained from
further discussion. I wish to put the proposal I've made to
the formal vote of this council."

"Is there any need, Tirand?" Sen asked. "It's obvious
that—with perhaps a very few exceptions—we're all of
one mind."

Karuth gave Sen a venomous sidelong glance, and
Tirand said, "No, Sen, I won't make that assumption."
On the table before him, untouched until now, lay an intri-
cately carved staff; he reached out, picked it up, and immediately silence fell. This was the High Initiate's staff of
office, the symbol of Tirand's indisputable and absolute
authority.

"My friends." The High Initiate's voice was solemn as
he held the staff out before him so that it was clearly
visible to the entire assembly. "The proposal I bring before
this council is that the Circle should formally renounce all
fealty to the lords of Chaos and appeal to Aeoris of Order
to send us the help and the power we need to combat the
danger that casts its shadow over our world. I ask you,
one and all, to step up now and declare for or against this
proposal."

As one, the company rose to its feet. Only Calvi remained seated, aware that he must be excluded from this

ceremony and not knowing whether he should stay in his place or leave the hall. His worried eyes met Tirand's, and the High Initiate smiled bleak acknowledgment.

"Please stay, Calvi. When the council has voted we must also seek the High Margrave's sanction. This is too serious for the Circle alone."

Calvi nodded, unable to speak. He tried to catch Karuth's eye as she moved to join the line of adepts now moving toward the high table to touch the staff and declare their votes, but she either didn't see him or didn't want to respond. As the first vote was cast, Calvi stared down at the floor and wished with all his heart that he could have turned back time and found himself safe and laughing and jesting on Summer Isle, at his brother's court.

Karuth forced herself not to run from the council hall when the meeting was formally ended. She felt desolate enough; to show her feelings before the entire gathering would have been the final humiliation. As the adepts left in twos and threes, she stood by her place at the table, avoiding all eyes and making a pretense of searching for something in the reticule at her waist. Only when someone nervously but deliberately cleared his throat behind her did she raise her head and look around.

Calvi's face was pale but for two high spots of color on his cheeks. He couldn't meet her gaze directly but said in a low, unhappy voice, "I'm sorry, Karuth. I would have supported you if I could, but . . . my conscience wouldn't allow it. Not after . . ." He swallowed. "After Blis . . ."

Slowly Karuth shook her head. "Calvi, don't apologize to me. There's no need for it. You did what your heart dictated and so did I. Just because we can't both take the same view doesn't mean that anything need change."

The young man shut his eyes momentarily. "I wanted to believe you; I really wanted to. The thought that our own gods have turned against us is almost unbearable, and I desperately don't want it to be true! But I have to think about our people. I have to do anything I can to help them, it's my duty, my responsibility . . ." He looked at her at last, miserably. "I'm not qualified for that responsibility, Karuth, but I have to take it. It would have been so easy to refuse to make a decision either way, but I couldn't have done that. It wouldn't have been right. You understand that, don't you?"

"Of course I do." She reached out and took his hand, squeezed it in an attempt at reassurance. "You did what you believe to be right. I'd be a hypocrite if I blamed you for that."

"Thank you." Calvi saw Tirand approaching and hastily squeezed Karuth's hand in return before stepping back. "I'm so relieved that you don't . . . don't feel . . ." He shook his head, released her fingers, and hurried away.

"Karuth?" Tirand stopped a pace from her. They looked at each other, then Karuth lifted her shoulders, trying to make the shrug seem careless.

"I've nothing more to say, Tirand. It was a fair vote."

"I didn't want to humiliate you. I didn't set out to do that."

"I know. You were only following the Circle's rules, as anyone would have done." She forced a smile, though it wasn't convincing. "Even me."

"All the same—"

"All the same, I didn't expect the vote to go quite so overwhelmingly against me. Just two supporters. . . . I wonder why they voted as they did? They must have had some reason for wanting to ingratiate themselves. Perhaps they're both in need of a physician."

"Don't be cynical," Tirand said gently.

"Cynical? Me?" She laughed brittlely, then looked away from him. "Please, Tirand. I don't want to talk about it, and especially not to you. I accept defeat gracefully, and I accept that you're sorry to see me defeated as well as relieved to have won the council to your point of view. Let's leave it amicably at that and say that we understand each other."

Tirand shuffled his feet. "When the ritual takes place—"

"I won't attend." She interrupted him, knowing what he wanted to ask. "I couldn't take part willingly, so I'd only be an encumbrance." Her gaze flicked to him once more. "Will you send word to the Matriarch first?"

"Yes. I must do that; we need her sanction as well as Calvi's for something so serious. In fact I'd prefer to bring her here. She'll be far safer in the castle than in Southern Chaun, if she can be persuaded to come."

"That would be wise."

Tirand paused. "She may not ratify our decision of course. If so, then—"

"No. She'll agree with you; you know she will. Don't try to be kind, Tirand." A spark of the rebellion that had led to their original quarrel showed suddenly in Karuth's eyes, though she disguised it behind another smile. "At the moment it doesn't seem to suit either of us."

Tirand watched her as with grace and dignity she left

the hall. For a moment he thought to go after her but then the impulse died. He sighed, settled the papers he carried more firmly under his arm along with his staff of office, and walked slowly toward the doors in the wake of the last stragglers.

9

Four adepts left the Star Peninsula the next morning, bound for the home of Jonakar Tan Carrik, Margrave of West High Land. They carried personal letters from the High Initiate and the High Margrave; of all the provinces West High Land had the strongest ties with the Circle, and Tirand knew that Jonakar's discretion could be trusted and his practical help relied on.

The Margrave read the messages and wasted no time. He had spent his younger days as a high-ranking officer in the militia, and West High Land's men-at-arms were among the finest. Six experienced men, Jonakar said, would accompany the adepts on to Southern Chaun, enough to provide protection if the need arose but not so many as to attract curiosity and speculation. They should travel as swiftly and inconspicuously as possible, and—it grieved him to say it, but under these unhappy circumstances he believed it was sound advice—they should ensure that no hint of their mission's nature reached the ears of his fellow Margraves to the south. It might be an unnecessary precaution, but fear was a hard master, and the southern provinces were learning fast to fear Ygorla. Beyond that he could only proffer his blessing and his earnest hope for their success.

Sobered by Jonakar's warning and armed from the

Margravate's arsenal, the adepts and their escort departed for Southern Chaun. Their journey to the Matriarch's cot was a race against time in more ways than one, for as well as the danger posed to the Matriarch by Southern Chaun's proximity to the coast and therefore to Summer Isle, there was also the weather to consider. Winter was beginning; conditions in the northern mountains would worsen rapidly now, and Sisterhood seers had predicted a hard season. If snow blocked the passes, then the returning company, with or without the Matriarch, would be cut off from the Star Peninsula perhaps for several months. The militiamen proved worthy of their reputation, guiding the party by a direct but little-known route through the forests of Chaun and avoiding the drove roads and all but the smallest villages altogether; and the travelers reached Southern Chaun without incident to find, to their intense relief, the cot as yet untouched by the troubles.

Shaill Falada listened carefully to what her unexpected visitors had to say, consulted her highest seniors, and made a painful but pragmatic decision. As Karuth's old friend Sister-Seer Fiora forcefully pointed out, a live Matriarch at the Star Peninsula was infinitely to be preferred to a dead Matriarch at Southern Chaun; and the fact that the entire Sisterhood couldn't also leave their cots for the castle was irrelevant. Besides, Fiora added darkly, if matters grew much worse, then it was quite likely that communication between the Star Peninsula and Southern Chaun would become impossible, and for one member of the ruling triumvirate to be cut off from the others was unthinkable. She and Sister Corelm Simik would cope here: Shaill must go—for all their sakes.

Eventually, though with her conscience tearing at her, Shaill capitulated. The return journey was uneventful, barring some bad weather that presaged worse to come, and at last, fifteen days after their departure, the company arrived back at the castle.

The Matriarch received an emotional welcome. The adepts had performed regular—and, it seemed, successful —rituals to safeguard the travelers, but the waiting had been hard and tension high among the castle's inhabitants, especially so as Tirand had ordered that no messenger-birds should be sent on ahead of the returning party for fear of interception. Now, though, relief at the Matriarch's safe arrival was enormous. Even Tirand, who didn't show his feelings easily, was close to tears, while Calvi cast off all pretense to his position, clinging to Shaill and weeping as though she had been his own mother.

That evening the triumvirate met for a private conference in Tirand's study. The main purpose of the meeting was to decide on a short-term strategy, and in particular on the response that should be made to Ygorla's threats and demands. Karuth, however, surmised that Tirand was also anxious to secure the Matriarch's sanction for the ceremony that would renounce the Circle's fealty to Chaos and call upon Aeoris of Order to send aid to the mortal world. Shaill's agreement was, as Karuth had already predicted, a foregone conclusion, for the Matriarch wouldn't presume to question the High Initiate's judgment on such a matter. But Tirand, being Tirand, would insist that all be done according to rule and custom; it was his way, and Karuth couldn't blame him for it.

During the afternoon it had begun to rain, and now that darkness had fallen and the temperature was dropping rapidly, the rain had turned to an icy and unpleasant sleet. Karuth had no desire to venture far from her own hearth, where a fire was burning cheerfully, but as the

evening wore on, she became increasingly restless until she
felt that she must do something more constructive than sit
in a chair and toy idly with her manzon, or she would go
quietly mad. What to do, though? The last thing she
wanted was company, and in her present mood she
doubted anyway if any of her friends would tolerate her
for long. What she *did* want—and, perhaps more to the
point, need—was a distraction from certain thoughts and
speculations that could well become dangerous unless she
quashed them.

She had already made it clear to Tirand that she would
have no part in the Circle's renunciation of Chaos. Tirand
had accepted that; each adept must be free to make his or
her own choice in such a grave matter. What Tirand
wouldn't have accepted if he'd known of it was Karuth's
embryonic but growing desire to do more than simply distance herself from the Circle's decision. Evidence or no,
she could *not* believe that Ygorla was Yandros's pawn.
Too many factors didn't fit, there were too many anoma-
lies, and she feared that by turning his back on Chaos
Tirand ran the risk not only of incurring Yandros's wrath
—which was no light matter in itself—but also of slamming the door on the one source of help that might be
vital to their cause. She couldn't explain her reasoning, it
was an instinct with no logic to back it; but she was convinced that, in the fight against the sorceress from the
south, Chaos might well prove a stronger ally than Order.
Yet if no appeal were made to Yandros—and who, after
all, would make such an appeal if the High Initiate himself
refused to do so?—how could Yandros intervene if, as she
believed, he had been true to his pact?

Karuth could see only one answer to that dilemma,
and it was an answer that she knew she must resist with

all her will. She couldn't go against Tirand's decree. It would be utterly wrong, a betrayal of the most appalling kind and one from which their relationship as adepts, let alone as brother and sister, could never recover. In recent days she'd heard enough about loyalty to be heartily sick of the subject, but there was no denying the hard fact that, whatever her affinities with Chaos, she had taken an oath years ago to be loyal above all to her High Initiate. She couldn't break that oath and still presume to call herself an adept of the Circle. It was unthinkable. She must put the idea from her, bury it, forget it.

She rose from her chair and put her manzon back in its case. Poor, neglected thing; at this rate she'd forget how to play it at all if she wasn't careful. Crossing to the window, she pulled back the curtain and looked outside. In the patches of light from the castle's many windows the falling sleet glittered with a steely look; under the sparse shelter of the stoa a hunched figure scurried, head down, toward the main doors. The icy wind crept through a gap in the window frame, nipping Karuth's fingers, and she let the curtain fall again and went to her clothes chest to pull out stout shoes and her hooded coat. A visit to the library would be the best calmative for her disquiet. She could look up those old herbalists' records she'd been meaning to read for so long. Better that task, tedious though it might be, than to let herself dwell any further on things better left untampered with.

She pulled on the shoes and coat, scrawled a hasty note that told anyone who might need her physician's skills where she might be found, and left the room.

There were four other people in the library when Karuth arrived. Three students, two boys and a girl, sat huddled together around a table, ostensibly studying for a looming examination but in reality more concerned with flirtation and gossip, and an elderly adept who was also a senior geology master had taken his chair to a dusty corner where he pored over a new treatise on mineral strata. The students rose and bowed to Karuth as she entered; the old adept looked up, blinked with myopic distraction, and returned to his reading. Karuth crossed to the medical section of the library, found the book she wanted, and carried it to a table well away from the whispering trio. She began to read but soon found she couldn't concentrate. Her eyes took in the words, but they refused to stay in her memory; she would read a paragraph, then realize moments later that she'd already forgotten its content. She persevered for some twenty minutes, then with a weary sigh she gave up as she realized that the task was beyond her in her present frame of mind. Perhaps another book, something more familiar and a little less dull. She put the herbal back in its place and was scanning the shelves when a voice behind her said quietly, "Ah. So I'm not the only one to think of looking for an answer to our dilemma down here."

Karuth turned, and saw Arcoro Raeklen Vir standing at her elbow. He'd entered the library so quietly that she hadn't been aware of his arrival, and he smiled an apology.

"I'm sorry, Karuth, I didn't mean to startle you. I must admit I didn't expect to find anyone else here on such a filthy evening. Are we, by any chance, on the same mission?"

"Mission?" She regarded him in puzzlement. "I rather doubt it, Arcoro. I came to hunt out some old records on the subject of rare medicinal herbs. I can't imagine them being of much interest to you!"

Arcoro pulled a droll face. "They sound splendidly tedious."

"They are, I assure you!" She paused. "What *does* bring you here? Did you say something about 'an answer to our dilemma?' "

"I did, though now that I've got over my initial flush of enthusiasm for the idea, it's beginning to look like a very long bowshot." He took Karuth's elbow and politely but deftly steered her a little farther away from the students' table. In a voice pitched so that only she could hear him, he added, "It concerns the Maze."

Karuth's eyes widened with interest. "The Maze? You mean—how it might be operated?"

"I mean precisely that. I was sitting in the dining hall making free with a bottle of very good Han wine when it occurred to me that, were the usurper to launch an assault on the Star Peninsula—as she might logically do in the not-too-distant future—then the Maze could prove a very effective defense against her. The snag is, of course, that no one living today has the least idea of how to manipulate it. We know what it *does*—we have plenty of documented records to tell us that. But how its powers can be called up is quite another matter." He sighed. "It's extraordinary, isn't it, how something that was commonplace less than three generations ago can have been so quickly lost and forgotten."

"Extraordinary, and foolish," Karuth agreed with some feeling.

"Well, I won't go so far as to say that. After all, we've had no need of it for the best part of a hundred years. Now, though, the situation has changed. And there must surely be some records still in existence that will return the key to the Maze to the Circle's hands."

Karuth chewed this over. Now that she considered it, it stunned her that no one had yet given the Maze a thought before this moment; and it was typical of wise old Arcoro to see the obvious where everyone else had failed. She looked speculatively around the library, asking herself where the search for such records might logically begin. Not all the Circle's books were kept here. A number of the most esoteric volumes were housed permanently in the High Initiate's private study, but she'd examined all those tomes over the years and knew that there was nothing relevant among them. The most likely source, she thought, was that small, neglected section of the library where a collection of parchments, old beyond reckoning, had lain virtually undisturbed for decades. If there was anything useful to be found, that, surely, would be its hiding place.

There was, however, one caveat that Arcoro might not have considered. She hesitated to mention it, particularly so since the students were still close enough to them that there was a risk of their overhearing. Caught in a dilemma, she was both surprised and relieved when suddenly, as though prompted by some subconscious signal, the young trio rose to their feet and gathered up their books. Arcoro caught the eye of one of the boys and smiled.

"Leaving us, Kitto?"

"Yes, sir." The student returned his smile with a shy grin. "We've an early tutorial tomorrow. Good night, sir. Good night, madam."

The scraping of chairs on flagstones as the three maneuvered from their places gave Karuth the opportunity to speak freely. Turning again to the old adept, she said, "One thing I feel I should mention, Arcoro, before your search goes any farther. You are bearing in mind the fact that if what we believe is true, the Maze was originally created by Yandros?"

Arcoro's shrewd eyes met hers. "Yes. I hadn't forgotten it."

"Then in the light of the council's vote . . ."

"It would seem like an act of sheer hypocrisy to reject Chaos on the one hand while making use of its creation with the other."

"That wasn't what I was going to say."

"Wasn't it? Don't dissemble, Karuth. Forgive me for saying this, but I'm not Tirand and you don't have to be tactful with me: I'm no threat to you."

"Tirand isn't—"

"No, no, I know that; I phrased it clumsily. What I mean is simply that you can say whatever you wish to me without risking any ramifications, because I'm not the High Initiate and I don't have the High Initiate's responsibilities toward the rest of the Circle. If you speak your mind to me, it'll go no farther."

Karuth stared at her feet. "Thank you, Arcoro. In that case I *will* be blunt." She looked directly at him, and there was a clear challenge in her eyes. "Aside from any question of hypocrisy—and I'd prefer to keep my opinions on that subject to myself—there's a factor you seem to have overlooked and that is how Chaos itself might react to any attempt to tamper with the Maze if the Circle goes ahead with Tirand's proposal. Were I—"

A small commotion by the stairs door interrupted her. Looking around, Karuth saw the students crowded in the doorway, giggling as all three tried to squeeze through the narrow gap together. Irritated by the distraction, she waited until they had finally left and their footfalls were diminishing up the spiral steps, then focused on Arcoro's face again.

"I was about to say that, were I Yandros"—she made the splay-fingered sign to show that the statement wasn't intended to be presumptuous—"I wouldn't look too kindly upon what might appear to be the application of dual standards. And if the council is right in believing that the Chaos lords have no scruples about breaking their promise not to interfere in mortal affairs, I wouldn't care to be in the shoes of whoever tries to conjure the Maze back to life."

Arcoro gazed at her for some moments, his expression unreadable. Then he uttered a short, self-deprecatory laugh.

"Karuth, you missed your true vocation," he said. "You should have become an advocate-at-law, not a physician. You've tied me in a neat parcel, and whichever way I turn, I don't believe I can extricate myself." He held up a hand. "We have two possibilities before us. One"—he told the number off on his index finger—"that the Chaos lords have broken their pledge, as all the evidence suggests; in which case Yandros will indeed be unlikely to stand by and let us meddle with his creations unimpeded. And two"—he told off a second finger—"that they have *not* broken their pledge, in which case Yandros, true to his old promise, will do nothing to punish us for our actions even if we have pronounced anathema on Chaos. So either way we're neatly trapped, aren't we? If we track down the rituals that will operate the Maze, and use them, we'll either incur retribution from the gods or realize that we've made a grievous mistake in renouncing our fealty." He pursed his lips. "That's not a happy choice."

"No," Karuth agreed somberly. "Far from happy." She paused, then her voice became more urgent. "Arcoro, you voted with Tirand in the council hall and you explained your reasons very cogently. But won't you reconsider? Don't you think the council is taking too great a risk? If Tirand's conclusions are wrong—"

"Karuth, wait." The old adept held his hands palms out as though to ward her off. "I understand your feelings, truly I do. And I *have* thought long and hard about my decision and whether I was right to vote as I did. My dear, we talk of the possible risks associated with investigating the Maze, but what of the other dangers that we haven't so much as mentioned? What, for example, if Yandros has plans to use the Maze for his own purposes, secure in the knowledge that we have forgotten how to harness its properties and will therefore be powerless to oppose him?"

Karuth frowned. "I don't see in what way he might use it."

"No, because like the rest of us you don't know for certain what its properties are. We know that in the old days it was used to move the castle's physical dimensions fractionally out of kilter with the rest of the world and therefore provide an impenetrable barrier to hostile outsiders. A potentially invaluable defense, as we both know, against the usurper if she tries to mount an assault on the Star Peninsula. But what if the dice were to fall another way? What if the sorceress were to learn—or be told of—the Maze's powers and use them against *us*, to isolate us from any hope of aid?"

"You're supposing, again, that Yandros is guiding her every move."

"I am, because I dare not suppose anything else." Arcoro took her hand, gripping her fingers hard. "Karuth, please try for a moment to look at the Circle's position without bias. If we stay our hand now and trust that Yandros has kept faith when all the evidence speaks against it, we may be playing straight into the hands of a power that means to destroy us and plunge our entire world into anarchy. Like the Margraves who feel it's better to capitulate rather than jeopardize the lives of the people for whose well-being they're responsible, we, too, must look to do what's right, not just for the Circle but for everyone. The risk of trusting Yandros is too great. We *have* to turn to Aeoris now, and Aeoris alone."

Karuth looked down at their joined hands and, very gently, pulled her fingers from his grasp. She hadn't really expected to sway Arcoro, despite the fact that she believed he still felt some qualms about the council's decision. But if he in his turn had hoped to sway her, he had failed.

They looked at each other, and both knew the truth of it. Arcoro was the first to speak again.

"I'm sorry, Karuth. Though you might find it hard to believe, I bitterly regret this necessity."

She shook her head, making a canceling gesture. "And the Maze?" she asked. "Will you still pursue that avenue?"

"Yes, I will. In fact I think it's imperative that I do so. If Chaos is now our enemy rather than our friend, then we'll be yet more vulnerable if we continue to live within the Maze's influence without knowing how that influence might manifest." Arcoro hesitated. "Despite our differences, would you be willing to help me?"

On the verge of a civil but emphatic refusal, Karuth reconsidered her view. What difference would it make?

She and Arcoro had no personal quarrel, and as he had pointed out, the Maze could be potentially invaluable to them whatever the truth of their opposing contentions. Besides, she reflected wryly, it would at least provide a surer distraction than the writings of long-dead herbalists.

She gave a nod, almost imperceptible. "I'll help you, Arcoro. I may not share your beliefs, but I can't argue with your logic."

He took her hand again, briefly this time, and patted it. The gesture reminded her of Carnon Imbro, her predecessor and mentor, and she suppressed a little shiver as she wondered what he would have had to say had he lived to witness the Circle's present straits.

Arcoro turned and surveyed the rows of shelves. "Well, we've a long task ahead of us." He nodded to the dusty corner where the elderly geology master still sat alone, his head bowed over the book on his lap. "Old Soric's fast asleep by the look of it, so we won't disturb him by rummaging in his cubbyhole. Shall we take a look at some of the old parchments?"

"It seems as good a place as any to start."

"Right. And Karuth . . ."

Already halfway to the shelves, she turned and looked back. "Yes?"

"If we find something . . . you won't consider doing anything rash, will you? Nothing that might . . ." He made a helpless gesture, either unwilling or unable to finish the sentence.

Karuth smiled with a kind of tired, defeated sympathy. "No, Arcoro," she said, and knew with an ashen feeling in her heart that she meant it. "I won't defy Tirand and the council, or do anything that might jeopardize the Circle's resolution. You have my solemn promise."

10

During the two days that they devoted to their search, Karuth and Arcoro found nothing. They had anticipated disappointment, but the failure still stung, especially so for Karuth as the day she dreaded drew ever closer.

The conclave between the three rulers on the night of the Matriarch's arrival had been, as everyone expected, a mere formality, for Shaill didn't hesitate in endorsing the council's decision. As she said privately to Calvi after the meeting, she felt that such a decision must be for the High Initiate alone. Tirand was, after all, the gods' avatar in the mortal world, and in such a matter as this the other members of the triumvirate should support him without qualm or question. Calvi, plagued by uncertainty and an unquiet conscience about Karuth, gratefully accepted her firm resolve and tried to gain strength from it. The decision was made; there was no more to be said.

The ceremony was set to take place at midnight on the fourth day after Shaill's arrival at the castle. On that night the two moons would rise in conjunction, and the Circle's astrologers had calculated that there would be no better auspice until after the winter Quarter-Day—too long, in Tirand's estimation, to wait. The adepts went quietly but efficiently about the business of preparing for what was to be the most powerful rite the castle had witnessed for the best part of a century, and tension began to build as the fateful hour drew nearer. Meanwhile, though, there were more exoteric but no less urgent plans to be made, and at a meeting in the great hall one morning Tirand set before the entire Circle the strategy that he and Calvi and Shaill had worked out at their meeting.

There would be, the High Initiate said, no overt challenge to the usurper's claims as yet. The southern Margraves had learned a bitter lesson from trying to match Ygorla's power with their own, and it was cruelly clear that no military might could prevail against the occult forces she had at her command. Messages had been sent out to all the provinces telling them that both the High Margrave and the Matriarch were safe at the Star Peninsula, but for the time being, Tirand proposed only two further moves. The first was to establish a small but vital group at each of the Margravates, consisting of one or more of the Circle's most skilled sorcerers, one or more of the Sisterhood's best seers, and a militia commander who understood the tactics of warfare and could, if the opportunity came, organize provincial manpower into a finely honed fighting force. Those Margraves who were on the brink of giving fealty to Ygorla—or who had already given it—must, Tirand said, be considered an unknown quantity; nonetheless, groups would be sent to them and must risk trusting in their true loyalties rather than those they now publicly professed. For the time being, the groups would have no work to do. They would simply establish themselves, maintain contact with the Star Peninsula via messenger-bird or whatever other means was most prudent, and wait.

The second move concerned the Circle's reaction to the missives they had received from Summer Isle. Ygorla still awaited a response to her demands for capitulation. She would not receive it, nor any other communication in the High Initiate's name no matter what threats she might make against the world. This was a harsh and possibly very dangerous decision, but the triumvirate had agreed that, whatever else might befall, the Star Peninsula must stand against any threat. To the people who now cowered before the sorceress, Tirand, Calvi, and Shaill were their one hope of salvation, and if the castle fell to Ygorla, that hope would die. She must not be provoked into striking against them now, Tirand said. They must play for time, maneuver her into staying her hand until help could be summoned from the realm of Order, and only when they had Aeoris's powers to sustain them would the Circle challenge her.

Fueled by the tension already running through the castle like taut wires, the High Initiate's announcement met with fierce approval, and Tirand found himself besieged by adepts volunteering to be a part of the groups sent to each Margravate. The parties were selected that afternoon and, to Karuth's consternation, Arcoro Raeklen Vir was among those chosen, his task to take charge of the Prospect party. Karuth greatly regretted Arcoro's departure, for he was one of the few adepts who had at least some sympathy with her views, but as one of the Circle's most talented sorcerers he was an obvious choice. Militiamen, as before, would be supplied by Jonakar Tan Carrik, and a careful selection by the Matriarch of especially gifted sister-seers included three Empty Province seniors and Sister Mysha from her own Southern Chaun cot, who would all be collected by the adepts on their way to their final destinations.

The chosen ones would leave the castle on the morning

following the great ceremony. As the last day dawned and wore through a cold, lowering morning and on into afternoon, the atmosphere within the castle's walls began to build to a suffocating pitch. There was no communal meal in the great hall that evening, nor the usual levels of talk and merriment around the vast hearth. The ancient building was uncannily, oppressively quiet.

Karuth watched the two moons rise. Silent and remote in a black sky now cleared of cloud, they lifted slowly, one after the other, above the ancient parapet, their chill light bleaching out the fainter stars. Two alien things, she thought; two observers looking down on this night's blasphemy. If she allowed her imagination just a little rein, she could see a face in the larger of the two orbs; a cruel face, an angry face, sneering at the folly that was about to be perpetrated.

Alone in her infirmary, silent now and dark but for one candle, she felt the dismal beginnings of nausea. She'd forced herself to eat a little food earlier; now she regretted it and with detached, clinical expertise she found a basin and forced herself to be sick. It eased her stomach but did nothing for her mind, and she locked the infirmary and retired to her room.

She had drunk a lot of wine by the time she heard the first sounds from outside her window. It must be nearly midnight. Karuth didn't want to look outside, but a kind of fatalism, drawing her to the inevitable, made her rise a little unsteadily from her chair near the fire and go to the window. The glass was smeared with condensation; she rubbed at it with her sleeve, but the view was still blurred, and at last she opened the casement and looked out.

She was in time to see the great doors below slowly opening. Light spilled into the deserted courtyard like a

giant, yellow-tinged sword blade, and shadows moved on
the steps. Then the procession appeared.

Tirand was at their head, and for one disconcerting
moment Karuth hardly recognized him. He hadn't worn
any of the special ceremonial robes of the High Initiate
since his inauguration—and never at all had he worn such
robes as these. There was something deeply disturbing
about the sight of her brother in the funereal purple-and-
sapphire trappings, with the massive and ancient double-
handed broadsword, the ritual weapon of a hundred
predecessors, slung at his hip. He was bareheaded, and the
moonlight glittered on a high, jeweled collar at his throat
and glowed like phosphorus in the metallic threads of the
cloak that fell from his shoulders and over his back to
sweep the frosty flagstones.

Two white-robed adepts bearing torches moved into
their positions flanking Tirand, and Karuth's breath
caught sharply in her throat as she saw the cloak more
clearly. It shone in the torchlight like burnished gold, and
she had a sudden, terrible intuition that this was not the
customary garment of High Initiates in recent years but
something far, far older. Keridil Toln had worn that cloak
when, with the then Matriarch and High Margrave whose
names were enshrined in legend, he had set foot on the
sacred rock of the White Isle to open Aeoris's casket and
call the gods of Order into the world to do battle with
Chaos. Since the time of Change, the cloak, together with
many other relics of the days when Chaos had been anathema to the Circle, had lain revered but disused in the High
Initiate's apartments, its symbolism redundant in the new
light of Equilibrium. Now, though, the circle—Karuth
couldn't laugh at the irony of her unwitting pun—had
turned again, and a new era was beginning. The purple of

death and the gold of power. Death of the Circle's old allegiance to Chaos; power that would elevate the gods of Order to the pedestal from which they had been toppled nearly a hundred years ago.

She felt bitter, impotent anger rising within her, and she wanted to fling the window wider and scream it to the figures in the courtyard below, rail at them, call them fools and blind dunderheads, spit in their faces and stamp their pomp and ceremony into the ground. Instead her body still and her face like a stone mask, she continued to watch silently as Tirand and his escort moved across the court-yard and the rest of the procession gradually came into view. Nineteen, twenty, twenty-one of the highest-ranking adepts, all clad in white, forming a double line like a tail to the comet of Tirand and his torchbearers. In their midst, looking small and a little lost among their number, were first the Matriarch, her face veiled in silver, her head bowed, and behind her Calvi, in plain, somber black that contrasted shockingly with the pale nimbus of his hair. For one bizarre second Calvi's appearance triggered old memories in Karuth's mind, and she had a momentary mental image of a portrait that hung in the great hall, of Keridil Toln as a young man. It was ridiculous; there was no physical likeness between them. It was just the shade of the hair, the set of the shoulders . . . but for that disquiet-ing instant her imagination almost fooled her into believ-ing that it was not Calvi Alacar who walked soberly in Tirand's wake, but Keridil's ghost.

The procession moved on across the courtyard, flow-ing along the stoa and toward the door that led to the library and thence the Marble Hall. For the first time in living memory, perhaps in recorded history—Karuth didn't know and doubted if anyone else did—the rule was to be broken, and other feet than those of the high-ranking adepts would tread the Marble Hall's mosaic floor tonight. What would Shaill and Ca_vi think, she wondered, when they gazed on the seven statues, and in particular on the carved face of Yandros, for the first time? What would they feel? Would they be able to meet that quirkish, darkly humorous gaze, or would they turn their own faces away in shame?

The torches, guttering, were drawing away from her now, the silent procession almost swallowed by shadow. Karuth made to move away from the window as the impulse that had made her scourge herself by watching them died away to a dull, dead feeling inside her. But before she could shut the casement, something moved among the network of guttering and buttresses outside. She paused—and saw the cat. It was sitting on an impossibly narrow ledge and had been staring alertly down into the courtyard, but as she moved, it turned its head to look at her, and the moonlight reflected in the alien orbs of its eyes. Steel-gray fur with a pattern of darker stripes showed in the gloom, and Karuth recognized the creature as one of the myriad offspring of the white cat that had, for its own inscrutable reasons, befriended her some years ago. The white cat was dead now, but this descendant, in its prime and rangily lithe and strong, seemed to have inherited some instinct from its mother that gave it an especial interest in Karuth. She had often come across it in her vicinity, in the dining hall or the courtyard or prowling a corridor; but although she'd stop to give it a kind word or to stroke its arching back, she hadn't encouraged it to become a particular friend. Now, though, something had changed. As her gaze and the cat's met, she felt the first tentative psychic probes of a clear effort to read her mind and communicate with her. Then, so unexpectedly that she jumped, the cat raised its head and uttered a long, unhappy wail.

"What is it?" Karuth's skin prickled, and she leaned dangerously out of the window, extending a hand toward the cat. It seemed it had only been waiting for a word of encouragement, for it rose to its feet and ran to her, springing lightly onto the sill and pushing its hard little head against her chin as she bent over it. Then with a chirrup it jumped down into the room, ran to the table where she kept her ritual implements, and looked back at her with an intense but unfathomable message in its green eyes.

Karuth returned its stare uncertainly. "It's no use," she said to it. "I don't understand you. I'm not a telepath, I can't communicate with your kind."

The cat opened its mouth and yowled again. It was such a dismal sound that Karuth felt the short hairs at the nape of her neck rise in response. She dropped to a crouch, holding out her hands in appeal. "Try to understand! Look into my mind; I know you can, I know what cats can do!" She tried to form a mental image of bewilderment, but she didn't have the knack of it; she felt certain her message wasn't getting through.

The cat's stare intensified and a peculiar low growl rumbled in its throat. Then, so suddenly that Karuth was caught completely unawares, a clear picture flickered through her head. She saw light dancing in a confined space, stairs winding downward, white-robed figures crowding through a narrow tunnel. . . .

"Oh, no." She scrambled to her feet, backing two rapid paces from where the cat stood motionless. "No, you can't do that!"

Another yowl, though softer, as if the animal had understood her protest but was nevertheless determined to persevere. A blurred image of Tirand moved like a ghost across Karuth's inner vision and was gone.

"Stop it! I don't want to see it!" She jerked her head aside as though by turning her back on the creature she could block the messages it was sending to her mind. Before her inner eye she saw a blaze of silver that she knew was the door to the Marble Hall. She saw it swing silently open, saw the shadows of people filing through into a shimmer of pastel mists, and the outlines of the tall, slender pillars like phantoms in the eldritch light.

"No!" Swinging around again, she confronted the cat, which stood motionless in an attitude of intense concentration before her. Its eyes locked with hers, held them, and she realized that beneath its calm demeanor lay great agitation, that it was trying to appeal to her for help.

"Help?" Karuth whispered. "How can I help? What can I do? I didn't want this! But I'm not the High Initiate, I can't rescind the order that he made! Don't show me any more—please, don't show me any more. Don't you understand, *I can't stop it!*"

The cat continued to stare at her, and for a terrible instant its green eyes took on a quality that was almost human. Karuth felt her mind lurch violently, felt that she was sliding into a vortex between worlds and that someone was waiting for her on the far side. Gripped by a fear she couldn't name, she wrenched herself back with a tremendous effort, snapping the chains of the spell that tried to pull her into another dimension, and reeled backward, losing her balance and sprawling on the floor.

As she struggled into a sitting position, her mind dazed with shock, the cat gave voice to a sad little cry. It turned and ran to the door, then stared up at the latch, clearly indicating its wish to be let out. Shakily Karuth climbed to her feet and crossed the room. Hand on the latch, she looked at the creature one last time.

"I'm sorry." Her voice was indistinct and unsteady. "I'm *sorry*."

Fool she was, talking to a cat. It didn't understand, it couldn't comprehend human speech, and she didn't have the skill to express herself in any other way. She opened the door, and it slipped out into the unlit passage, silent as a little gray ghost. Closing the door behind the flick of its tail, Karuth pressed her forehead to the cold, rough wood and bit down hard on her lower lip, only stopping short of drawing blood when the pain pulled her wits together.

She would not think about what was happening in the Marble Hall now. She would *not*. She had been shown, unwillingly, a glimpse of the events that were unfolding; that was enough. It was midnight, she was tired—wearied to the bone if truth be told. She wanted sleep. She wanted, above all, a few hours of oblivion.

On the table beside her bed stood the flagon of wine from which she'd been drinking earlier. Her stomach didn't want any more, but all the same she poured herself a fresh cup and drained it, knowing that it would help her to sleep soundly even if she suffered for it tomorrow. Then, shivering a little despite the fire's warmth, she changed into her night robe and climbed into bed, pulling the covers tightly around her. The room dimmed to firelit gloom as she snuffed out the candles, and Karuth shut her eyes.

Outside, the courtyard was empty. The two moons tracked slowly, impassively across the sky, and no sound from the Marble Hall deep under the castle's foundations

filtered up through the black flagstones. After a while—
perhaps an hour, perhaps a little less—the stillness was
broken by a shadowy form that moved among the buttresses and crenellations high up on the roof. Eyes glinted
momentarily as the moonlight caught them, and the gray
cat slipped noiselessly along the ledge to Karuth's window. It peered into the room, trying but failing to see
beyond the closed curtains; then it hooked a tentative paw
around a tiny gap in the casement and pulled gently.
Karuth hadn't fully secured the catch, and the window
swung open enough to allow the cat to slide through.
Jumping lightly to the floor, it looked back briefly into the
night, its green gaze inscrutable. Then it moved across the
room to the bed, sat down near the bedhead with its tail
curled neatly around its front paws, and stared fixedly at
the pale blur of Karuth's sleeping face on the pillow.

Karuth wasn't a natural telepath, so hers was not an
easy mind for the cat to reach. But an instinct goaded the
animal, an instinct that urged it to persevere no matter
what the obstacles. It had a message to impart that it
sensed was important to its own kind, and intuition told it
that it must impart that message to Karuth and to no
other human. Cats had always been recognized as having
an affinity with Chaos, though just how great an affinity
was something no one had yet realized. This animal,
driven by a will far beyond its own small abilities, recognized in Karuth a sympathetic spirit. It must reach her. It
must show her. It must make her understand.

Minutes passed while the cat sat motionless, staring
with intent and patient concentration. Then, in her sleep,
Karuth began to dream. It was a strange and unnatural
dream: She seemed to be floating, bodiless, just a few
inches from the ground, and she was drifting along a nar-

row passage filled with dim, gray light. Something about her surroundings was familiar, but she couldn't pinpoint it, and her vision was out of kilter, as though she were seeing the scene about her through a prism of crystal.

Abruptly the light grew in intensity, then as quickly dimmed again as though her eyes had adjusted to it with preternatural speed. A rectangular shape loomed ahead, towering above her—and she realized that she was hovering outside the silver door that led to the Marble Hall.

"No!" Karuth tried to cry out, but found she had no tongue and no lips with which to form the word. She was moving again, the door melting before and around and behind her. She felt a huge, silent vibration pulsing through her mind like the beat of a titanic heart, and she saw dim veils of color shifting and shimmering through the hues of an incredible spectrum.

"I don't want to go in! I don't want to see it!" In the bed her body twisted about, tangling in the blankets, but she didn't wake, *couldn't* wake, the dream held her fast and her cries were voiceless. "Let me go! Please, take it away, stop it!"

She drifted forward and could do nothing to halt herself. Now she could just see the seven colossal statues ahead, frightening in the pulsing fog of color. There were other shapes, too, huge to her altered perspective, moving slowly and ominously around a single dark-clad figure with a golden cloak in their midst. She knew they were chanting, but she couldn't hear the words of their ritual. The central figure held a great sword, its blade dark from disuse, before his face in a salute. The rite was nearing its climax—

Suddenly a flare of black light sent her spinning and tumbling backward like a leaf in a gale. Shocked, she saw that a dark column had erupted upward from the floor and now hung quivering in midair, turning and shuddering like a waterspout on a storm-racked sea. It emanated from the black mosaic circle in the floor that, it was believed, marked the Marble Hall's exact center. The chanting adepts seemed oblivious to it, and Karuth knew with a surging and certain instinct that this new manifestation had nothing to do with their ritual but was something else, something intended for her eyes alone.

Again she tried to cry out; again she had no voice. Her gaze was drawn to the column and she couldn't look away. The black light's shape was changing. A hand was forming, long-fingered, thin and graceful, a giant, dark, phantom hand. It curled, turning like a mirage, and it beckoned to her. Against her will, against her volition, Karuth felt herself starting to move toward it.

"Ah, NO!" From somewhere in the depths of her being came a surge of willpower. Terror fueled it, giving her new strength; her old training came back to her, and soundlessly, but with all the power she could muster, she screamed at the curling fingers as they called her inexorably toward the shimmering darkness.

"I WILL NOT BE COMMANDED! I WILL BREAK THIS SPELL! AROINT—*AROINT!*"

In the dimly lit bedroom the cat, sensing what was to come, fled to the window and was through the casement and gone in the space of a moment. Karuth hurtled out of the dream, out of sleep, and the bed coverings flew back like a heaving sea as she sat upright, her eyes snapping open.

For a few seconds she didn't know where she was. Then came recognition, and with it a rush of intense relief as she realized that she had escaped from the vision's grip.

But the relief didn't last. As shockingly as though some-one had thrust a dagger through her skull and into her brain, every detail of what she had seen in her nightmare came suddenly and violently back to her, and Karuth cov-ered her face with her hands in despair. She knew now what the cat had been trying to tell her. She understood what she had seen from that strange, changed, feline per-spective in the Marble Hall, and she understood what the creature had been urging her to do.

"I couldn't . . ." She shook her head, her unbound hair flying wildly about her shoulders. "I couldn't defy him, I *couldn't*! I took an oath—I must obey it!"

She looked up as though half expecting an answer, but the only answer she had was the sluggish hiss of an ember in the fire against the night's silence. Karuth hung her head, wanting to weep with shame and frustration and misery, but tears wouldn't come.

"Forgive me," she whispered. *"Yandros, forgive me. I can do nothing!"*

The dimensions of the hall were symmetrical to the point of perfection. Slender white columns, set at precise and aesthetically pleasing intervals, towered to a vaulted ceil-ing, and the seven high-backed chairs that were the cham-ber's only furnishing neither dominated nor were dominated by the atmosphere of airy tranquility. Pale golden light poured in through six tall windows, and at the far end of the hall a seventh and greater window, com-posed of a myriad tiny diamonds of glass, broke and scat-tered the light into a breathtaking spectral rainbow.

A breath of cool air wafting through the hall was the

only herald of the arrival of the lords of Order. The seven white-haired and white-clad figures materialized together and silently took their places in the seven chairs. Each was identical to his six brothers; only Aeoris, who ruled them all, was distinguished by a plain gold circlet around his brow.

It was rare for the lords of Order to meet together in one place; only urgent news or a momentous event called for a full gathering of the seven. Aeoris wasted no time on preamble but, as soon as the others were settled, began to speak.

"My brothers." His voice was mellifluous. "Tirand Lin has performed a high ritual in which he begs us to go to the Circle's aid in combating the sorceress who threatens the mortal world." He paused, and his pupil-less golden eyes regarded each of them in turn as though surmising their reaction to his next words. "Moreover, I have to tell you that the Circle have pronounced a formal anathema on Yandros and renounced their fealty to Chaos."

There was a ripple of astonished murmurs. Ailind, who of all of them was perhaps Aeoris's closest confidant, leaned forward in his chair. *"Renounced Chaos?"*

Aeoris smiled thinly. "Yes. I, too, was very surprised. I hadn't expected our mortal friends to act so emphatically or so soon; and this move presents us with a very interesting—not to mention curious—situation. For while this self-styled empress continues her predations under Chaos's banner, still Yandros shows no sign of making any move. This poses a question, my brothers. Have Chaos broken their part of our bargain, or have they not?"

Another of the six lords spoke up. "The Circle clearly believe that they have."

173

"The Circle are as gullible as any mortals," Aeoris reminded him. "They believe what their eyes and ears tell them; hence their appeal to us and their rejection of Chaos. I won't deny that that is greatly to our advantage, but I also ask myself: If Yandros is behind this uprising, why does he hesitate to show his power more fully? Why does he continue to use a mortal puppet to do so laboriously what he himself could achieve in moments?"

"Perhaps," Ailind suggested, "he wishes us to believe that the sorceress is not his servant, and that therefore Chaos has been true to the pact?"

Aeoris shook his head. "I don't think so. Yandros knows very well that we wouldn't be taken in by such an obvious subterfuge. No, there's another answer to this conundrum. Something is staying Yandros's hand. It's almost as if there were some stricture on him, forcing him to hold back." He rose, and paced a few steps down the length of the hall. "Consider this, my brothers. If this human sorceress is Chaos's pawn as the Circle now believe, then it seems unlikely, as I've already pointed out, that Yandros should not have taken some more direct role in the affair by now. On the other hand, if she is *not* his avatar, then it's quite out of character for Yandros to have made no move to put a stop to her activities before now."

"The pledge?" Ailind ventured.

"No." Aeoris dismissed the idea with a wave of one hand. "If she were raising Chaos's banner without Chaos's sanction, Yandros would be quite justified in putting paid to her; that would not constitute a breach of our pact, and he knows it. Unless . . ." He stalked five more paces, stopped again. "Unless it is a trap designed to lure *us* into making the first move."

174

"But surely, now that the High Initiate has called on us for aid, our intervention wouldn't be a breach of the pledge."

"True. Though Yandros may not have bargained for Tirand Lin's hasty action." Slowly, hands clasped before his face and his expression deeply thoughtful, Aeoris returned to his chair and sat down once more. "I think, brothers, that I have decided what we shall do." He looked at them each in turn. "We've known for some time that there is something untoward afoot in the realm of Chaos, and we've waited patiently for an opportunity to learn more. I believe it behoves us now to maintain that patience, at least for a while longer."

Ailind spoke again. "With all deference, brother, is it right that we should ignore the Circle's plea? They have renounced Chaos and pledged their fealty solely to us. If we fail them now——"

"We won't fail them, Ailind." There was a sharp edge to Aeoris's voice, a warning that he wasn't about to be argued with. "But we will be *prudent*. Tirand Lin will expect our response to take a ritual form." He smiled, though there was little humor in the smile. "Something similar, perhaps, to that in which we answered Keridil Toln's plea many years ago. We won't do that. Nor will our response be immediate. We have the Circle's trust; they will keep faith for a while yet before they start to doubt, and that will allow us to watch developments and temper our strategy accordingly. There's no need for haste, brothers. Yandros is both impulsive and undisciplined—let's see who grows tired of the waiting game first. If Chaos makes one move—or if the Circle show signs of losing heart and regretting their appeal to us—

175

then we will act. And when we do"—now he looked directly at Ailind—"I think that we will send them an emissary. An emissary from the very heart of our realm, to show them, and to show this upstart usurper, what the power of the gods truly means."

11

"It isn't enough!" Ygorla paced like a caged animal to the window of her high tower, turned with a furious movement, and paced back again. "It isn't *enough*! I want more, and I'm tired of waiting for it!"

Narid-na-Gost, who sat in his customary perch near the small table where the shadows were deepest, watched her agitation with calmly smoldering eyes. "Patience was never one of your virtues, daughter."

She rounded on him, her face distorted with spiteful frustration. "I spent seven interminable years being patient, waiting for the power that you promised me! Now I have that power, but what can I do with it? Use it for no better purpose than frightening fools and playing tiresome games to while away the hours!" She whirled again, strode back to the window, and glared through the glass. "I *hate* this place. It's boring and stultifying and it restricts me at every turn; I might as well be back at the Sisterhood Cot where I was incarcerated as a child!"

"There are differences," the demon said with heavy sarcasm.

"Oh, yes, there are great *differences*—but I'm still not weeping for joy at my good fortune!" Ygorla clenched her fists and thumped them down on the windowsill. "I am an empress now, but what has that brought me? Endless days of tedium incarcerated on this miserable island while I wait for the world to awaken to the truth!"

"The world is awakening. Five Margraves have already sent groveling messages of fealty."

"Damn and rot five Margraves! What are they? Nothing! I could destroy any or all of them with a word, and I would if I thought I might derive some entertainment from it. But there's no entertainment in watching the rest of the world through a crystal while I sit here in solitary splendor!" She turned once more, adopting a dramatic posture. "I want *all* my subjects to see me; *all* of them, not just the miserable handful who have been brought here! I want to ride among them in triumph and revel in their awe and their terror when they gaze into my eyes! I want to hear them crying out my name in the streets, I want to watch them falling to their knees before me like grain before the scythe! I want the cowering Margraves to kiss my feet, I want the anemic women of the Sisterhood to weep before me, I want—" Suddenly she checked herself, and spun to face the window again. "Ah, curse it, I want all that and more, *more!*"

Narid-na-Gost watched her rigid back, the quivering ripples of her black hair, but didn't speak. He knew what she had been about to say but at the last was unwilling to admit, the thing that lay at the core of her frustration. Five Margravates had already acknowledged her as their empress; the rest were sure to follow before long. With the Matriarch fled, the Sisterhood was collapsing into disarray; their authority and credibility teetered on the brink of ruin. The world lay within Ygorla's grasp—but for one small, yet utterly vital place.

At first she had anticipated with pleasure the war of wits that she planned to wage against the Star Peninsula.

The Circle promised to make far more worthy adversaries than the cowering province Margraves, and Ygorla had looked on them as a stimulating challenge. However, the novelty of that challenge had rapidly worn off when, tiring of the game, she decided to bring it to an end, only to find that Tirand Lin and the adepts under his leadership still refused to respond to her in any way at all. She had sent demands, threats, ultimatums; there had been no reply. Her demon messengers, which alone had been enough to strike terror into the provinces, had provoked not the smallest response. Whatever she did, the Circle stubbornly ignored her.

To begin with, their refusal to play by her rules irritated Ygorla. Then it angered her. Then it aroused fury. And at last came the final straw when, seething with the rage of being thwarted, she had tried to use her powers to overlook her quarry and the crystal had shown her nothing but a blank, colorless void. The castle of the Star Peninsula, and the Circle within its walls, were closed to her.

Narid-na-Gost had expected nothing less. Though their powers might be puny compared with his own or his daughter's, the adepts had enough skill to conceal from the world what they didn't wish the world to see, and the peculiar properties of the castle itself added further complexity. Ygorla, though, refused to acknowledge that any mortal bastion could stand against her, and the problem of the Star Peninsula was rapidly becoming an obsession. She had planned to confront Tirand Lin and laugh in his face as she stripped him of his strength and his standing; she wanted to usurp his place as she had usurped that of Blis Hanmen Alacar, and reduce the Circle to the role of fawning slaves. Narid-na-Gost had seen the methods she was already employing to spectacular effect in the provinces:

the fearsome supernatural strikes against anyone who even thought to defy her, the destruction by her elemental servants of crops, homes, even in one case an entire village, as punishment and a warning against further resistance. Through her crystal and through her demonic servants she watched the world like a hawk watching a desperately scuttling mouse, and as one by one the hapless Margraves capitulated, she had sent "emissaries" to take up residence in their Margravates and to enforce her will on an increasingly frightened populace. Five province capitals were now home to these shadowy, unhuman avatars, and even some Sisterhood Cots now lived under their yoke. But the Star Peninsula maintained a barrier that she couldn't breach—and now Ygorla's patience was at an end. The castle was the one prize that eluded her, so it had become the prize she craved above all others.

The demon said, quite gently, "There may be better methods of persuading the High Initiate to our way of thinking."

Ygorla's eyes blazed. "Better methods? Such as your precious caution that you never cease to lecture me about?" Breathing hard, she stared with blind fury out into the palace grounds. "What do you think I am, some milksop without the courage of my convictions? I don't fear Tirand Lin! I will *break* him—I will break his body and his mind and his soul, and he will learn the price of *daring* to resist me! Don't think, Father, don't *presume* to think for one moment that I have any intention of being *cautious*!"

Narid-na-Gost was well aware that a good measure of her anger was directed against himself, and the knowledge made him smile inwardly. His daughter was beginning to question his superiority. He had expected it and in one sense was pleased by it, for it was proof that she was, as he had long believed, ultimately willing to bow to no one, and in the long term that was precisely what he wanted. However, Ygorla still had a good deal to learn, and if her arrogance grew too great too soon, he might need to apply a measure of restraint. For now, though, he meant to tread softly, and he knew how best to placate her and turn her from one of her furious moods: a morsel from his table, fed to her as she condescendingly fed her favored slaves, to whet her appetite and give her a new diversion to ponder on and plan for.

He said, "Ygorla."

"What is it?" Her voice was still savage.

He paused just long enough to arouse a modicum of curiosity. "I counsel caution for a good reason. A reason that I haven't revealed to you before now."

He used a tone that promised intrigue and a secret to be shared, and Ygorla hesitated for a moment or two before turning slowly to face him. "What do you mean?" Beneath her irritation lay sudden cautious interest.

Amused by how easily she rose to the lure, the demon smiled conspiratorially at her. "There is something you should know, that concerns the Star Peninsula."

"What? What should I know?"

"Something about the castle itself," Narid-na-Gost told her. "I haven't spoken of it before now because it hasn't been relevant. However, in the light of the Circle's stubbornness it may now be to your advantage—to the advantage of us both—to discuss it."

Ygorla's anger fell from her as though she'd cast off a cloak, and she hastened across the room to where the demon sat. "Discuss what, Father? Is this something that might help me to break down Tirand Lin's resistance? Tell me!"

The demon changed position, hunching his misshapen body and leaning conspiratorially forward over the table. His clawed hands closed over the casket that contained the stolen soul-gem, and his eyes changed color from crimson to a hot scarlet.

"Daughter," he said huskily, "you know my ultimate ambition. I mean to rule the realm of Chaos, even as you are destined to rule the world of men. We have talked of this many times since I first revealed my plan to you before you left the White Isle. What you do *not* know, however, is that the castle of the Star Peninsula holds the key to that ambition—and not a single mortal soul is aware of that key's existence."

Ygorla's face grew avid. "What is the key?"

"It lies within the very fabric of the castle. When you were a child in Southern Chaun, you were made to learn your catechisms; you must know that the castle was built not by men but by the lords of Chaos themselves."

"So I was told. Though no one knows whether or not that's true."

"It is true. The ignorance of mortals is a marvelous thing, Ygorla, especially so when those mortals claim to be the gods' own agents in the human world yet have a barely rudimentary grasp of the powers that have been put at their disposal." He grinned ferally, and she returned the look with a vicious smile of her own.

"The Circle are fools," she said with soft venom.

"Indeed they are—and far greater fools than even you yet realize. For they have within their own walls a direct pathway that connects this world with Yandros's own realm, and they are utterly ignorant of its existence."

"A pathway?" Ygorla's eyes opened still wider.

"Yes. Used rightly, it can bridge the gulf between dimensions in the beat of a bird's wing. Now, as you know, I cannot return to Chaos as I used to, for Yandros knows of my perfidy and even with the soul-stone as hostage I dare not risk returning by the familiar way. But were we to gain control of the castle, the position would be greatly changed. Then I would have a route into his realm that Yandros would never think to suspect, for this gateway has been closed and dormant for so long that I have no doubt that the Chaos lords, like their human servants, have forgotten that it was ever created."

Ygorla didn't speak. Her eyes glittered brightly and her face was intent; she was, the demon knew, thinking deeply and rapidly.

"If we controlled the castle," she said at last, "you would know how this pathway might be found?"

"Oh, yes. I know many things that my erstwhile masters in their complacency thought beyond my humble understanding." He reached across the table and his distorted fingers took hold of her hand. "Now, daughter, I think you understand why I have always counseled caution in our dealings with the Star Peninsula. There's far more at stake than the petty affairs of Tirand Lin and his Circle of weak and foolish followers. So far you've achieved nothing by threatening the High Initiate—no, don't dare to flare at me, it's the truth, and if you're honest, you'll admit it. You've achieved *nothing*. So you must plan a new strategy."

She pulled her hand free and uttered a short, sharp laugh. "Do you think it will be as simple as that?"

Narid-na-Gost's crimson eyes grew sardonic. "Won't

183

it, to you? After all, you seem to consider yourself invincible these days."

Her mouth narrowed to a vicious line, but before she could retaliate, the demon made a sharp gesture that she knew well, and old habit silenced her.

"Words, Ygorla," Narid-na-Gost said. "That's all you've so far used in your war against Tirand Lin and his followers. Now the time has come to find a better weapon. You know the truth of that as well as I do. Think, daughter. Make full use of those powers you're so proud of and vaunt so carelessly about your court. Think, too, in the light of what I've told you, what the Circle's capitulation means for us if you succeed in breaking them." He watched her face and saw that his words had gone home. He smiled. "Whoever controls the castle also controls the Chaos Gate. And that, my child, is a prize beyond price!"

That night the Dowager High Margravine Jianna Hanmen Alacar killed herself.

By an unhappy circumstance it was Strann who found her. He hadn't wanted to obey Ygorla's sweetly phrased suggestion that he should go to her locked and guarded room and escort her to the audience hall for the empress's pleasure, but as always he knew better than to defy an order, however pleasantly veiled. Ygorla was in a particularly mischievous mood tonight; a good mood by her standards but still dangerous to anyone whom she might choose to make the butt of one of her jokes. What put into her head the idea of summoning Jianna to the court Strann didn't know; lately Ygorla had lost interest in the poor woman, and he had privately hoped that Jianna might be left to grieve in solitude. But the order was given, and Strann was charged to carry it out. Shadowed by one of the ever-present demon guards, he approached the dowager's chamber and showed Ygorla's token; the door was opened and he walked in, steeling himself to meet Jianna's eyes and feel again the silent scourge of her contempt for him.

She was hanging in front of the window, strangled by the crude but effective rope she had fashioned from torn strips of her own gown. Strann stared at her for perhaps half a minute, disbelieving, too shocked to react until the sentry, suspecting that something was amiss, moved into the room behind him. Then—he didn't remember the details later, it was as though someone else, someone with courage, someone with the spine that he had lost, had taken him over in those blind seconds—he turned screaming on the guards, flailing at them, cursing them, punching them until at last he collapsed to the floor of the corridor outside, retching into his cupped hands as the world swayed dizzily around him.

Ygorla didn't punish him for the lapse. On the contrary, when the news was carried to her in the audience hall, she merely lifted her shoulders in a shrug and announced that Strann had been quite right to castigate the guards. They had failed in their duty, which was to keep Jianna alive. She did not tolerate failure, and those responsible for the dowager's death would join her in the Seven Hells, where she hoped they would learn the folly of carelessness.

Then she looked up from her throne to where Strann stood shaking before her and said, "You'd best take yourself away, my rat. Now that Jianna is no longer with us, I suppose we must have a song to commemorate her." She smiled at him. "She might as well be more useful in death than she was in life, so I think a song advising others against copying her folly would be appropriate. Add a touch of humor: you know how greatly I enjoy an amusing ballad. You may entertain me with it tomorrow."

Strann, his vision blinded by a red film of suppressed rage, said obsequiously, "Majesty, your command does me honor as always." She dismissed him with a flick of one hand and he backed from the hall. The doors closed, and he heard her laughter.

It was the laughter, he thought later, that had provided the final catalyst. At the time he didn't stop to consider his reasoning; he wanted only to flee as far as he could from her influence and from the memory of what had happened. Instinct took him out of the side door to the palace grounds, and in the gloomy half-dark between the rising first moon and the ever-present, pulsing star of Chaos he sought sanctuary among the group of old trees in the formal garden.

The night wasn't cold—nights rarely were this far south—but Strann was shivering as though he'd suddenly found himself naked in a blizzard. It was reaction, nothing more, he told himself. It would pass in time; it always did. Don't think about it, his consciousness said, and it'll go away.

But this time he wasn't so sure that it would, and as he sat alone under the largest tree, the old, insidious impulse began to creep back into his mind. He'd thought about it before and each time dismissed it as sheer madness. Now, though, with Jianna's miserable end all too fresh in his memory, it set its claws into him and this time wouldn't let go.

How often had Jianna called on the lords of Order for

help before their silence had finally brought her to despair and suicide? Strann, and everyone else in the palace, knew how fervently and continually she had prayed to Aeoris to enter the mortal world and strike Ygorla down; and with the star of Chaos hanging over Summer Isle it was a fair bet that there must be many others across the face of the world who also begged the gods of Order to deliver them. Aeoris, however, had apparently either not heard his worshipers' pleas or had turned his back on them. So, Strann thought, if Aeoris was deaf to entreaties, what of Yandros?

No, an inner voice said, for the twentieth time. *Don't even consider it, not for a moment. It's too dangerous.*

Was it? Strann looked up through and beyond the branches above him to where the great star throbbed ominously over the palace roof. He was utterly convinced now, whatever the rest of the world might believe, that Ygorla was not Yandros's servant. He had been through the arguments time and time again, and always his conclusion was the same: Ygorla was not Chaos's friend but its enemy. Which meant—*No,* the voice said again, more emphatically. Strann ignored it—Which meant that Yandros must surely be as eager as any mortal to see her destroyed.

The whole idea was ridiculous of course. He wasn't a sorcerer; he wasn't even religious. All he had was a few old conjuring tricks left over from his early fairground days before the Guild Academy of Musicians mistakenly took him under its wing and made a bard of him. But some of those tricks were, he knew, corrupted forms of genuine occult rituals; admittedly not the high ceremonial magic practiced by the Circle, but magic nonetheless, and probably effective in their day. If he were to use one of those ancient rites, perhaps with a few subtle changes . . .

Yet again the inner voice shouted a warning in his head, but this time Strann knew it was fighting a hopeless battle. However long he might sit here arguing the logic and the sense of it, it would make no difference, for his mind —or perhaps more accurately his heart—was made up. It wasn't solely for Jianna's sake, he was honest enough to admit that. It was for what Jianna had symbolized in these last dark days: the living embodiment of the loathing and contempt that the entire, enslaved court felt for him, for the turncoat who had chosen to kneel at the usurper's feet and lick tidbits from her hand. Once, long ago it seemed now, Jianna Hanmen Alacar had loved his music and thanked him for his praises. He, in repayment, had betrayed her, and she had gone to her grave believing that his treachery was real. She'd never know the truth now, and the knowledge that her dying curse lay on his soul made Strann's heart shrivel. He had little pride in the usual sense of the word—with his background, pride was a luxury he'd rarely been able to afford. But he'd once laid claim to self-respect, and it had been precious to him. Kindly Strann, lighthearted Strann; devious and opportunistic and self-seeking perhaps, but he'd never sought to harm anyone and, until the coming of Ygorla, he believed that by and large he'd been true to that principle. Now, though, he had betrayed not only Jianna and all the others who had once liked and even admired him but also himself. And for the first time in his life Strann was bitterly, savagely, and unappeasably angry.

A light breeze stirred the leaf canopy overhead; dappled moonlight played across the grass where he sat. Suddenly he felt strangely clear-headed, as though the anger had swept the miasms of confusion from his mind and left a direct, clean shaft of light in their place. He would do it.

It might fail, it might leave him bereft and foolish, but he would do it, now, tonight. What had he to lose? For Jianna. No, he corrected, be honest: for himself; that was the truth, and there was no point in denying it. If he was ever to hold up his head again, he must at least try.

He got to his feet, brushing fragments of dry grass from his clothing and, before his nerve could fail him, started to walk rapidly across the garden, keeping the trees between himself and the palace He had long ago pinpointed an appropriate location in his mind, telling himself at the time that it was nothing more than idle speculation: a small patch of neglected woodland beyond the formal gardens, at the edge of a park that had been the High Margrave's private hunting ground. Theoretically the park was out of bounds to Ygorla's servants, but the position of relative trust that Strann had achieved allowed him a number of freedoms that were denied to others. Besides, no one dared roam the gardens at night these days for fear of meeting one of her houndcats, a fear that Strann knew to be unfounded, for the creatures seemed to dislike the outside world and only ventured beyond the palace walls when directly ordered to do so. The only real risk, in fact, was that Ygorla herself might summon him and find him gone, and even that was a predicament he could probably talk his way out of.

The second moon was rising now, adding an eldritch, pearly cast to the sky as Strann skirted the maze of clipped hedges and hurried on toward the wood, which he could see in the distance as a dark, uneven hummock against the landscape. Ground mist was forming and, emboldened by the cover it afforded him, Strann broke into a loping run. As he approached the trees, something moved ahead of him and he checked quickly, but it was only a young hind, phantasmic in the mist, leaping and darting away from his invading presence.

He was panting when he finally slowed to a halt at the edge of the wood. *Growing unfit,* he thought. *Must do something to rectify that before long.* He caught hold of a low branch, using it as a support while he got his breath back, then pushed on into the damp undergrowth. The warm, earthy smell of untrammeled greenery tingled in his nostrils and he inhaled appreciatively. Out here he could almost forget the madness of the palace and its abominable ruler. Almost—but not quite.

The belt of woodland was narrow, and within a few minutes Strann emerged on the far side. Before him the old park stretched away into dimness, mist-pale and otherworldly under the moon. A light west wind lifted his hair back from his face, and distantly he heard the churring call of a night bird. But nothing moved, nothing stirred but for the limpid rustle of leaves in the breeze. He was alone.

To his right the remains of an ancient wall—perhaps once the foundations of a lodge, though long fallen into disrepair—rose from a tangle of grass and briars. Strann moved toward it and there found what he needed: small chips of stone and flint scattered in the vegetation where the wall's cement had crumbled with age. He gathered twenty-one—seven times three—of roughly equal size, then crouched down in the lee of the wall with the fragments cupped in his hands.

Could he remember the old method? It was a little like the stone-readers' charm that had caused him such consternation once before, but stripped of the fairground chicanery with which it had become debased in recent decades. Seven stones in a pattern forming a septagon;

then three making a triangle in the center. Carefully Strann began to lay the chippings out on a relatively smooth patch of grass. The wind had dropped suddenly, and the only sound was that of his own measured but not quite steady breathing. Eleven stones left . . . seven, he knew, he must keep about his person to form the link between himself and the symbol he had described in the grass. That was the part that the hucksters had corrupted, fearing to follow the true magic too closely. Strann slipped three stones each into the pockets of his embroidered coat and palmed the seventh in his right hand, gently weighing the remaining four in his left as he searched his memory. Ah, yes—he must stand within the septagon, straddling the three central stones, and place these four in a square around his feet. His stomach felt watery as he stepped into the seven-sided figure, but he ignored the qualms and took up the proper position, bending to arrange the four stones in place. Then he clasped the one remaining chip—a piece of flint, sharp and hard and cold—between his palms and stared into the misty darkness before him.

"Yandros." His voice cracked on the second syllable; he cleared his throat, pushing down the nervous fluttering in his chest, and performed a singer's breathing exercise before trying again.

"Yandros . . ." Better; this was the voice of the bard, the musical master. Hold to that, Strann told himself. Don't let it slip. *"Yandros, Lord of Chaos, Lord of the dark hours, Master of the Seven-Rayed Star . . ."* He was sweating profusely and his eyes seemed to be losing their focus, so that the vista of the park blurred. *"Yandros, I entreat you and I call upon you, in the hours of night and in the shades of darkness, to aid this world in its time of trouble. Hear me, O highest prince of Chaos. I am no ava-*

tar and no sorcerer, but I call on you, I call on all the seven great gods of your realm, to turn to me as I have turned to you, and to help me now!"

Abruptly, unexpectedly, a surge of emotion rose from deep within Strann's psyche as the rage that he'd struggled to suppress in the palace came flooding through unchecked. He had been striving to formalize his ritual into fine words and phrases that would convey his plea in the ceremonial and orthodox ways, but suddenly his fine intentions were collapsing in the face of his feelings and he couldn't stem the tide.

"Yandros!" He turned his face up to the night sky, where the first moon now glared down from its zenith. "Don't you understand? Don't you know what this murdering whore is *doing* to us? Send Chaos, send vengeance, send thunder and lightning, and *strike her down*! She tyrannizes the world in your name, Yandros, and she's turning the world against you! Why don't you help us? *Why don't you destroy her?"*

Furious, desperate, he flung a fist up and shook it at the indifferent sky. The scrap of flint he'd been gripping fell, and the spark and sharp little sound as it struck against the triangle of stones between his feet jolted Strann back to earth.

"Oh, gods . . ." He looked down. The piece of flint had knocked the triangle out of kilter, and as he looked at it, Strann's rage, and the tide of emotion that had carried it, crumbled into self-disgust. Fool that he was, he'd lost control of himself, let his concentration be swamped by his personal feelings, and ruined the spell. There were gestures he should have made—he remembered them now, when it was too late—and the proper titles by which to address the gods, and the proper ritual words that should have closed and sealed the ceremony; but instead he had indulged in an expression of his own grief and fury and frustration, and now all that he had tried to do would be ineffective.

Or would it? Narrowing his eyes, Strann peered across the misty reaches of the park. Had he seen something moving in the distance? Hope flickered, then died as he reasoned that even if his night vision hadn't deceived him, what he had seen was nothing more than another deer, or some nocturnal predator on its solitary, silent hunt. The idea that Yandros of Chaos would even have heard, let alone reacted to, such a clumsy, haphazard, and futile attempt to call on him was utterly fatuous, and if he thought it possible, then he must have lost his wits entirely. He'd have to begin again. He had little hope of success, but he couldn't give up now. One more attempt, this time under more rigid control. Cynically he told himself that he'd at least have the cold comfort of knowing that he'd failed through incompetence rather than sheer stupidity.

He bent forward and laboriously gathered up the stones again, counting them carefully. One was missing, and after searching for it for two or three minutes without success Strann cursed roundly and turned back to the wall to find a replacement.

And froze.

A man was sitting on the wall's broken coping. He was thin, long-limbed, dressed in a dark shirt and trousers that gave him the look of a forester or gamekeeper. Strann's heart lurched horribly under his ribs as he realized that the stranger must have crept up on him, been watching him—by all that was sacred, *how much had he seen and heard?*

Then he looked at the figure's face, and his heart almost stopped altogether.

Gold hair, unnaturally, unhumanly gold, flowed in an unchecked tangle over the man's shoulders. His eyes, narrow and catlike in a sharp, aquiline, and thin-lipped face, glinted blue-violet—then changed shockingly, first to emerald green, then to the color of brass, then to a hard, glittering silver.

Strann uttered a terrible sound as his tongue seemed to swell in his mouth and threaten to choke him. "Uhhhh . . . *oh, gods* . . ."

Yandros said, "Greetings to you, Strann the Storymaker. It seems that you alone have the intelligence and resolve to tread where others have feared to venture."

12

Strann's legs gave way beneath him. He sagged to the ground, covering his face with both hands and praying that he wasn't going to lose control and pass out.

"My lord Yandros . . ." His voice was a shaking, shuddering mumble.

Yandros swung his legs over the wall's edge and sprang down to the ground. "I appear to have taken you by surprise," he said with amusement. "Do you have so little faith in your own abilities?"

"I . . . I thought I failed . . ."

"In terms of the rite you attempted, you did fail. Your performance was so farcical that under happier circumstances it would have been funny. However, I've always set greater store by men's impulses than by their ceremonies, and the speech you made was more impassioned than any tedious prescribed formality. Besides"—Strann felt air shift as the Chaos lord moved to stand over him, and he shut his eyes more tightly—"I have been waiting for one of our few remaining friends to address me directly and thereby forge the link between our worlds."

Strann didn't—couldn't—reply, and after a few moments Yandros sighed impatiently. "Strann, don't cower before me. I'm not Aeoris of Order; groveling neither interests nor impresses me. And your attitude is tiresome when we have urgent matters to discuss."

With a great effort Strann forced his eyes open and dared to part the lattice of his fingers a fraction. "Urgent . . . matters, my lord?" The idea that the supreme master of Chaos might wish to discuss anything with him was disorientating and awesome.

Yandros smiled grimly. "You may consider yourself an unlikely avatar, Strann, but remember that it was your plea that enabled me to enter this world without breaking the terms of the pact we made at the time of Change. I'm sure it will come as no surprise to you to know that no other human agency has called on Chaos; on the contrary, they seem to believe that Aeoris and his insipid brood are their only hope of salvation. So, whether you like it or whether you don't, you are for the moment the sole focus of our attention."

Strann didn't like it. For the first time he began to consider the implications of what he had done, and they terrified him.

"My lord," he began unsteadily, "I'm not fit to serve you, I'm not—"

"You have called me."

"Yes; yes—but—"

"Do you wish to rescind your words?"

"No! But—"

"Then don't be such a fool as to try my patience."

At last Strann found the courage to raise his head. Yandros was standing, arms folded, two paces away. His expression was quiet, but his eyes—emerald green again now—held a chilly light.

"My lord Yandros," Strann said, trying not to stammer, "I wouldn't be so foolish—or so audacious—as to

speak anything but the truth, particularly so since I don't
doubt that you'd see through any dissembling. But the
truth is I don't see how I can possibly be of any value to
Chaos. I'm not a sorcerer. I'm not even . . . haven't even
been . . . a man of strong religious convictions, though
I've always felt that . . . well, that . . ." Dared he say
it? He'd become used to fooling Ygorla with flattery and
obsequiousness; with Yandros that could be a lethal mistake. He swallowed. "To be honest, my lord, I've always
felt that my own interests would be served better by allegiance to Chaos than to Order."

Yandros laughed softly. On the surface it was a pleasant, musical sound; nevertheless it made Strann shiver inwardly. "I know where your interests lie, Strann, and I
assure you that I don't count it against you."

Relieved, Strann went on with a little more confidence.
"Then, my lord, you must also understand my confusion.
I believe—forgive my boldness—I believe that your wish
and mine are one and the same: to see the sorceress
Ygorla's power broken."

"More than that, Strann. *Far* more than that."

"Then surely it's a simple matter? You are Chaos.
What is she? Nothing but a usurper who claims a false
fealty to you! You could destroy her like—like . . ." He
groped for a simile.

Yandros turned to look directly at him, and for a brief
moment his eyes turned utterly black. "Like *this*?" He
snapped his fingers. Strann's world turned inside out: he
saw a black moon in a howling silver sky, felt a shrieking
vortex open beneath his feet while the entire weight of
Summer Isle seemed to hurtle down toward his unprotected head. He yelled in terror—and the world was normal again. Mist, the moon's cool light, the undisturbed

parkland. Far away, somewhere over the sea, thunder bawled dismally.

Strann sucked air into his lungs and struggled to force the contents of his stomach back to their rightful place. "Like . . . that."

Yandros turned his back and walked out from the wall's shelter to stand staring over the park. A strange, dark aura pulsed about his frame, its hues reminding Strann unpleasantly of the seven-rayed star that throbbed above the palace.

"If it were that simple," the Chaos lord said at last, "it would have been done long ago."

Strann frowned. "I don't understand."

"No, you don't. And there's a great deal more that neither you nor any other mortal understands about this miserable affair." Yandros looked back over his shoulder, considered for a few moments, then raised a thin-fingered hand and beckoned.

"Come here. Walk with me along the edge of this wood. I have something to tell you"—his eyes burned silver once more—"something that I mean to entrust to you alone among mortals. Can I be assured of your trust, Strann?"

Strann looked into his eyes and saw the price of betrayal. Pallidly he said, "I value my soul, Lord Yandros, even if these days I have little cause to value anything else."

A few seconds passed while Yandros continued to stare at him. Then the Chaos lord made a brief, careless gesture. "Very well. I see we understand each other. Come."

They began to walk along the wood's perimeter. Strann felt as though he were dreaming, caught up in a bizarre blend of nightmare, thrill, and phantasm. By all standards of reason it was impossible to believe that the tall figure at his side was no less a being than Yandros of Chaos, that a god had stepped into the mortal world and that he, one insignificant man, had been entrusted with that god's confidence. Reason, however, played no part in this. Reason had flown. Mad or not, impossible or not, this was reality.

"As you rightly surmise," Yandros said, "the sorceress Ygorla is no friend of ours. We would like nothing better than to destroy her—but as matters stand, that is impossible." He turned his head to gaze at the park, so Strann couldn't see his face. "She has in her possession a jewel that rightly belongs in our realm, and if any harm were to befall that jewel, it would spell disaster for us. It is, you see, the soul-stone of one of my brothers."

Strann hissed, a sharp shocked indrawing of breath. Yandros glanced at him. "I see you understand what that means."

Strann nodded, and swallowed. "Like all children, I learned my catechisms."

"Then I don't need to explain to you the gravity of this matter and why it is impossible for us to move against Ygorla while she holds the stone as ransom."

"Could she harm it?" Strann asked. The concept of a mortal—even a sorceress as powerful as Ygorla—being able to wreak such mayhem against the gods themselves simply didn't fit with any of his preconceptions.

"Oh, yes, she could harm it. In fact she could destroy it in less time than it takes you to draw breath. Her mentor has taught her very thoroughly."

"Her mentor?" Strann was puzzled.

"Yes. During your sojourn in the palace, has the name of Narid-na-Gost ever been spoken in your hearing?"

"No, my lord. I've not heard it before."

Yandros nodded thoughtfully. "That doesn't entirely surprise me. Such a creature doubtless prefers to stay hidden in some out-of-the-way corner where he can concoct his schemes undisturbed."

Strann suddenly remembered his own odd experiences near Ygorla's private sanctuary, and the suspicions he had harbored. "There is something . . ." he said hesitantly. "A tower, which is strictly forbidden to all palace inhabitants. Ygorla has her personal apartments there, but—" He paused again.

"But?" Yandros prompted.

Strann told him what he had sensed, the smell of musk and iron that hung about the tower and clung at times to Ygorla herself. When he finished, the Chaos lord smiled humorlessly.

" 'The scent of demons.' You phrase it aptly, Strann. So, that's where Narid-na-Gost hides, and doubtless where he and Ygorla have secreted their stolen prize."

Strann's hazel eyes narrowed and he looked hard at a tussock of rank grass, though in his mind's eye he was seeing something else entirely.

"This Narid-na-Gost—is a demon?"

Another flick of a smile from Yandros. "One of our own, though it shames me to say it now." He reached out, took hold of a twig on an overhanging branch, and turned it so that Strann saw a small insect crawling laboriously across the underside of one leaf. "We viewed Narid-na-Gost much as you view this insignificant little creature, and that was our greatest mistake." He released the twig, leaving the insect to lumber on its way. "Narid-na-Gost has ambitions far above his station. He wants power, he wants dominion; above all he bitterly envies the masters of his realm, for he believes that he is as fit to rule as we are. In reality he's fit to rule nothing; he's a twisted and corrupt little worm. But he has my brother's soul-stone, and that makes him very dangerous, for it grants him power where before he had only desire. If he should gain control of your world or ours, he would bring untold disaster on us all."

A demon in their midst, Ygorla's mentor . . . yes, Strann thought, in the light of that revelation a great number of things began to make terrible, logical sense. "He is, then, using Ygorla as a puppet to further his ambitions?"

Yandros saw where his thoughts were leading and shook his head. "Not entirely. She is much more than a mere pawn to him. You see, she is his daughter."

Strann stopped dead, and his face lost its color. *"What?"*

"You hadn't realized?" Yandros seemed grimly amused. "Surely, Strann, you didn't think she was entirely human?"

"I thought . . ." But the words died on Strann's tongue. Of course, *of course.* He'd known that no full mortal could wield such power; he simply hadn't asked himself what Ygorla's true origin might be. It fitted. It all fitted. And it terrified him.

"I think," Yandros said quietly, seeing his dismay, "that you're beginning to understand the urgency of our predicament."

"Yes . . ." Strann hunched his shoulders as though to ward off a dark shadow that he felt was closing down on him. "Yes, my lord Yandros, I believe I am." Reluctantly, unhappily, he looked up into the Chaos god's face. "But I still don't see how I can possibly help you to thwart this demon's plans."

A slow, crawling sense of dread began to take form deep down within Strann as he waited for Yandros to reply. He had a terrible premonition of what was coming, and he didn't want to be a part of it. He wasn't courageous; he wasn't a hero. He was beginning to feel as though he had dug his own grave and was about to be consigned to it.

Yandros smiled, and Strann's heart contracted.

"Ah, Strann, I know what's in your thoughts," the Chaos lord said softly. "But you must ask yourself which you fear the more: serving me, with all that that might mean, or continuing to serve the usurper. There's no third option."

The feline, unhuman eyes were glowing like banked-down furnaces, but with white-heat at their cores. Strann felt a deep, primeval shiver rack him and knew that he had no choice.

"What do you want of me, lord Yandros?"

Quiet laughter made the nearby leaves shimmer on their branches. "In truth, Storymaker, I want nothing that you are incapable of giving me. There is a way in which Ygorla and her sire might be lured to their downfall—and the means of achieving it will require your skills both as a bard and as a diplomat."

Strann looked at him in surprise. He hadn't expected this.

"The key to Narid-na-Gost's ambitions," Yandros continued, "lies not here on Summer Isle, but at the castle of the Star Peninsula. The castle is also vital to the conceit of his half-human progeny, for Tirand Lin has thus far refused to so much as acknowledge any of the messages, threats, or ultimatums she has sent to him."

Strann could well believe that of Tirand Lin. He had

met the High Initiate once and thought him stiff-necked
and arrogant, certainly not the kind of man whose pride
would allow him to make even the smallest concession to
pragmatism.

"For once Tirand's pomposity has stood him in good
stead," Yandros commented, reading Strann's thoughts
accurately. "He had two other choices: to capitulate to
Ygorla's demands or to challenge her in return, and either
path would have been suicidal. By maintaining his silence
he has bought time—and as a result Ygorla is rapidly
becoming obsessed with the desire to conquer the Star
Peninsula at any price. In matters of pride, Tirand Lin is
no match for her."

Strann couldn't suppress a smile, though it was tempered by unpleasant memories. This revelation, he
thought, went a long way toward explaining Ygorla's unpredictability in recent days, the mercurial and dangerous
shifts, from cloying sweetness to savagery and vengeful
spite, amid which her courtiers had struggled to maintain
life and sanity.

"I want Tirand Lin to break his silence," Yandros said.
"More than that, I want him to appear to capitulate to
Ygorla, to the extent of inviting her to come in triumph to
the castle."

"Gods!" Strann said, then hastily checked himself.
"Forgive me"—Yandros made an impatient gesture—"but
is that *possible*?"

"It could be," Yandros said, "if an ambassador with a
sufficiently devious mind were to act as intermediary between the two factions."

Strann's mouth was suddenly very dry. "Me . . . ?"

"Who else?" Yandros's expression grew feral. "You
alone on Summer Isle have gained a measure of the sorcer-

ess's trust—and yes, I'm well aware of how you did it;
that's yet another point in your favor."

Strann flushed, feeling the closest he dared approach
to anger in Yandros's presence. "It has cost me dearly! My
conscience—"

"Will serve you best if you continue to ignore it," Yandros interrupted acidly. "One day you may regain the
freedom to indulge in self-reproach; until and unless that
day comes, I'd strongly advise you to forget any such notions in the interests of your continuing survival. Now,
listen to what I have to say. You are in an ideal—not to
say unique—position to persuade Ygorla to send you to
the Star Peninsula as her emissary. She's not an overly
intelligent creature, despite her powers; she'll be willing
enough to believe that her bard, her pet rat"—he smiled,
not pleasantly, and Strann looked away—"can worm his
way into the Circle's stronghold and persuade the High
Initiate that he really has nothing to gain from his stubbornness. She isn't ready to challenge Tirand in person,
for she isn't entirely sure of the extent of the Circle's powers and therefore won't risk a direct confrontation. You,
however, are expendable, and if she thinks that you might
persuade the Circle to open their gates to her, she'll send
you north with her blessing. Your second task will be to
inveigle Tirand Lin into baiting the trap that will deliver
Ygorla and her sire into our hands."

Strann stared blindly at the trees. He was beginning to
feel sick. "You speak, my lord, as though that's the sim-
plest of matters."

"Oh, I'm well aware that your task won't be easy,"
Yandros said. "To begin with, you'll have Tirand's prejudices to contend with. His fundamental loyalties have always been to the lords of Order; now that he believes

Ygorla is in league with us, he has formally broken the Circle's ties with Chaos and has performed a ceremony to call on Aeoris for direct aid. If you tell him the truth, there's no guarantee that he'll be willing to listen, let alone believe you. And, of course, there's the added complication of your own position."

Strann's head came up sharply. "I don't understand."

Yandros shrugged. "You're already known in some quarters as Ygorla's pawn—enough people have seen you posturing at her feet and carried the news back to the mainland that Strann the Storymaker is a traitor. If that tale has spread to the Star Peninsula, your reception at the castle will be far from friendly. Indeed," he added carelessly, "there's a distinct possibility that you may not even reach the High Initiate with your message. But that's a risk we'll have to run."

"We?" Strann said with more than a little irony.

Yandros gave him a sharp look. "Yes, Strann, *we*. I assure you, I relish the idea of this little more than you do. Given the option, I'd take direct action to deal with Ygorla and there'd be no need for these subterfuges and the dangers they present. But the option isn't open to me —or to you. We both have to trust that you can use your particular skills to persuade Tirand Lin to listen to the truth and set the trap."

They walked on while Strann considered carefully. He felt that he had been presented with an ultimatum; but had he? To give Yandros his due, he had couched his plan in the form of a request, not a direct order. How would he react if Strann proved reluctant to cooperate?

He stopped walking and, aware that this might be a very dangerous move, said, "I could refuse."

Yandros also stopped and turned to look directly at him. "You could." His expression was inscrutable.

"If I did . . . what would you do?"

Another careless shrug of the high shoulders. "Search for another emissary with more courage than you possess."

Strann smiled wryly. "You don't insult me, Lord Yandros. I've never claimed to be anything other than a coward."

"Certainly you're honest enough about your own shortcomings," Yandros acknowledged. Then he returned the smile with such a cold, cruel curling of his lips that Strann shrank back. "Although your finer feelings will, of course, cease to have any relevance if you oblige us to look elsewhere for our allies."

Strann suddenly felt as though his mouth and throat were full of dust. He stepped back, struck his spine against the bole of a tree. Yandros watched him impassively, still smiling.

"Chaos has no interest in those who trifle with it to no purpose," he said. "You may take perverse pride in your cowardice—you've little else to be proud of these days, after all—but there's little point in invoking it now, for you've nothing to fear from us. We have far better things to do than exact petty vengeance on insignificant mortals. The facts, Strann, are simple: You called on me, and now that I am here, you may choose to help me or not, as you please. If you refuse, you can return to your precarious life as the sorceress's pet and you'll hear no more from Chaos. But I suspect that you might live—at least, until your mistress tires of you—to regret your decision."

Strann turned away, pressing his forehead against the treetrunk and whispering an oath under his breath. Yandros, doubtless quite calculatedly, had touched the one raw spot that his inner self wouldn't allow him to ignore. If the Chaos god had threatened him, coerced him, then he would have capitulated but at the same time mentally retreated into the safe shell he had built around himself, the shell that allowed him to say, *I will do this because I have no choice, because it's the only way to protect and preserve myself.* Unfortunate, helpless Strann, martyred by bad luck and blown like a leaf on the winds of fate. But instead Yandros had made him face the unpalatable reality of his own position, ripping away the comfortable, self-pitying lie that had sustained him during his sojourn on Summer Isle, and had brought him full circle, back to that same raw and emotional anger that had goaded him here in the first place. Alone in the mist, with Jianna's death still scorching his heart and his conscience—and, yes, his self-respect—the rage had taken hold of him and he had screamed it aloud in a plea to Chaos.

Self-respect. That was the nub of it. Grief for Jianna wasn't the real fulcrum, for the death, however ugly and pointless, of a virtual stranger couldn't engender such a great welter of emotion. It was what her death had meant to *him.* Loathing him, despising him, Jianna had carried her hatred of him to the grave. How many others now cursed the name of Strann the Storymaker? Strann the traitor, Strann the pariah, Strann the sniveling, groveling turncoat. Oh, he'd said the words to himself a hundred times and more, leavening the bitter hypocrisy of his existence in an orgy of self-reproach and castigation. Briefly Jianna's death had torn down the protective web that he'd woven about himself like a smug spider, but even in the few hours since her death he'd begun to rebuild it. Now Yandros had smashed it again, and this time it couldn't be repaired. For the first time Strann realized the true depth of his ravening hatred for Ygorla and what she had done to him. She had twisted him, warped him, trampled his self-esteem into the dust, and the worst of it was that he had connived with her, held up his hands in surrender and allowed her to prey on his soul for the sake of staying alive. What was it Yandros had said about the cowardice of which he made so much? *You've little else to be proud of these days, after all.* Yandros was wrong: He had *nothing* to be proud of anymore. Not one saving grace, not one mitigating argument; not even, he reminded himself, one friend in the world who might understand and excuse what he had done. It was for that reason—not any high motive, not any brave desire to be a hero or a savior, but pure, selfish fury—that he wanted to see Ygorla destroyed.

Slowly he turned around again. Yandros stood gazing out at the park, seemingly disinterested in him. The second moon was high in the sky now, while the first was sinking toward the western horizon. The mist distorted it so that it looked like a strange, misshapen phantom, hanging above the distant horizon and casting little light.

Strann said very quietly, "My lord Yandros . . ."

Yandros turned his head. "Yes, Strann the Storymaker?"

He knew. Strann could see it in his eyes, which now were the translucent fire-color of fine opals. He cast his own gaze down.

"I'll do what you ask of me."

Yandros smiled thinly. "Yes. I see that you will."

"Or at least . . ." Strann laughed, an odd, truncated sound. "I'll try." He raised his head again, daring to meet Yandros's searching gaze as for the first time since his ill-fated landing on Summer Isle a spark of his old humor came back to him. "I'll either die trying or live to write the epic that will chronicle the gods' gratitude to an insignificant minstrel."

Yandros's answering smile had a hint of mischief. "You're audacious; that's a quality Chaos appreciates." Then his expression sobered. "You will have a just reward, Strann. If, that is, you live to reap the harvest of your success; and that's something that even I can't guarantee. We'll do what we can to smooth your way, but we must take the greatest care that no scent of what's afoot should reach Ygorla's nostrils or those of her sire. If it does . . ." He shrugged, leaving Strann in no doubt of his meaning and of the consequences for himself.

Strann nodded. "I know that, Lord Yandros." He was well aware that he could anticipate little help from the Chaos realm if the plan went sour; aside from any other considerations, in the gods' eyes he was a pawn and therefore expendable. But he could accept that. In one sense it was almost refreshing, for it promised him a return to something approaching freedom, a precious commodity that he'd all but forgotten since Ygorla clamped her jeweled collar around his throat.

"Well, then." The Chaos lord regarded him with cool eyes. "I believe that you mortals traditionally clasp hands on a bargain." He extended his left hand. A little uncertainly Strann reached out and took it. He felt a sensation of intense heat followed by one of intense cold; when Yandros released his fingers, they tingled sharply.

"It is sealed," Yandros said. "There's no more to be done now—ah, but for one warning. I told you that Tirand Lin has performed a ritual to summon help from Aeoris of Order. Whether Aeoris means to answer him or not I don't know; the realm of Order is a closed book to us, as our realm is to them. But I suspect that Aeoris *will* make contact with the Circle, and that means you must take the greatest care in your dealings at the castle. The lords of Order know nothing of our predicament, and if they were to discover that Ygorla has my brother's soul-stone, they would use any means to wrest it from her before we can. That, as I'm sure you're more than intelligent enough to appreciate, would put the entire balance of Equilibrium in jeopardy."

Strann was shocked. "You mean the lords of Order would—"

"Destroy the stone? Oh, yes, and my brother with it. Aeoris hasn't forgotten his defeat, and he'll be quick to exploit any chance to tip the balance back in his own favor. He must *not* learn that we have been put at a disadvantage." Yandros paused. "Indeed, he must know nothing whatever of my involvement in this matter, at least for the time being. Which means, Strann, that whatever befalls you, there will be no further contact between us from now on. As I've already said, we'll do what we can to make your task easier, but that will be little enough. We can give you no direct help—you will, effectively, be alone."

"I understand, my lord." Strann paused. "And I thank you for being so—frank with me. I'm greatly complimented by your trust."

Yandros smiled. "It isn't a question of trust, Strann. If it were, I'd have told you nothing. It's simply that I have read your heart and know where your loyalty lies."

Strann was taken aback. He'd never thought of himself as having any particular loyalty to either Chaos or Order; he'd always been, at least consciously, too much of a pragmatist. Yandros, however, seemingly knew him better than he knew himself.

He said again, "Thank you, my lord." Then, suddenly, he frowned. Yandros saw it and looked searchingly at him.

"Something still troubles you?"

It was a small thing, Strann told himself, but . . . He looked up at Yandros again and decided to speak his mind.

"You said you believe that Aeoris will send help to the High Initiate. If that's so . . . why did he not aid Jianna?"

"The High Margravine?" A strange expression crossed the Chaos lord's face, and his eyes seemed to reflect a multitude of subdued colors.

"Yes. She . . . died today. She hanged herself."

"I know."

"Since Ygorla murdered her husband, the High Margrave, she had prayed every day to Aeoris. If he's so ready to answer the High Initiate's prayers, why didn't he answer hers?"

Yandros sighed. "I don't know. But whatever his reasons for staying silent, you can be assured that he has a motive that will serve his own interests. Perhaps he considered Jianna's plea too trivial to trouble with."

"You didn't consider my plea too trivial."

The Chaos lord shrugged. "It would seem, then, that you are a good deal more useful to us than Jianna could have been to Aeoris." Then his eyes darkened venomously. "But had she called on Chaos, we would have answered her." His gaze met Strann's candidly. "I'm sorry that she didn't. The choice, though, was hers to make."

Strann stared down at the grass under his feet. "Yes. Yes, I suppose it was."

A thin hand came to rest on his shoulder. "Don't brood about it, Strann. You can't help Jianna now, and self-pity will achieve nothing; you've indulged in it for long enough. It's time for you to go back to the palace and begin your work. Do it well—for all our sakes."

The hand lifted. Strann shut his eyes. "I'll do my best, Lord Yandros." He opened his eyes again and looked up. "But if I should—"

The words cut off. He was alone.

13

Strann didn't sleep that night. Returning to the palace, he found to his intense relief that his absence hadn't been noticed, and as he closed the door of his room behind him, he thought that he might have won a few hours' peace in which to contemplate the night's events. He was, however, too optimistic. Five minutes after his return, violet light flared under his door, the door itself turned momentarily red-hot, and an elemental that seemed to consist only of a single limb with a lipless mouth at one end materialized, hovering, in the room.

"The Empress's pet must eat. The Empress's pet must maintain his strength." The disembodied arm ended in a distorted hand, which carried a tray; the elemental drifted toward Strann and thrust the tray at his face. *"If the Empress's pet maintains his strength, the Empress will be pleased. If he does not, the Empress will be angry."*

Strann took the tray, keeping his head averted. "All right, all right, I understand! Get out of my sight, you obscenity!"

The arm floated back to the door and through it. Only when he could convince himself that it had truly gone did Strann risk looking at the room once more; then he set the tray down on the floor and slumped onto a cushion beside it.

A whole roasted bird, sweetmeats, a flask of one of the best wines in the palace's cellars. Beside the flask lay a single rosebud, once red or white or pink but now transformed by sorcery into a glowing and unrelieved black. A gift from Ygorla—and a pointed reminder of the task she had set him and that, in the light of subsequent events, he had utterly forgotten.

Strann ate the food and drank the wine; and later, when disgust at the ballad he must write melded with the delayed shock of his experiences and hit him full on, he wished to all the fourteen gods that he'd had the willpower not to touch a morsel. Stumbling back from the nearest privy with his stomach empty and twisting like a serpent inside him, he slammed his chamber door in the petty hope that it would wake anyone within earshot, sagged back onto the heap of cushions, and, with introverted eyes and coldly clinical determination, took up his manzon and concentrated on the work that must be done.

Perhaps Yandros had granted him some subtle power tonight, for the ballad came easily: a cynical and technically brilliant piece that succeeded in praising Ygorla to the four quarters of the world while at the same time mocking Jianna Hanmen Alacar's demise with a transparent pastiche of sorrow. Strann rarely wrote down his compositions, preferring to play them over and over again until they were committed to memory, but for once he made an exception. He didn't want to hear the finished piece more than once; once, in fact, would be more than enough. Ygorla would be delighted with it, he though bitterly. Tomorrow he would indeed be a favorite at her feet.

A favorite . . . . Strann stroked the manzon's strings gently, his own form of apology to the instrument for having put it to such shameful service. It gave off a discord,

which he instinctively modulated into something more
pleasing. A snatch of melody entered his head; he played
it; it seemed to lead naturally into another chord progres-
sion. . . .

A favorite. Favorites were granted favors. Yandros (he
was too tired now to feel more than a small *frisson* at the
thought that he had stood face-to-face with the greatest of
the Chaos gods a mere few hours ago) had commented on
his diplomatic skills and charged him to use them to gain
Ygorla's agreement to his plan. How better to achieve that
than by writing another new ballad—a ballad calculated
to push her monstrous ego to such heights that she'd fall
straight into the trap? Fine speeches might not be enough
to sway her; an epic song. however, was a powerful snare.

Those chords, he thought. Played slowly and with a
little more emphasis, they might form the majestic opening to a tale fit to rival the *Equilibrium* epic. Ironic to use
a composition about the Chaos gods as the basis for this,
but he suspected that Yandros would appreciate the irony.

He was beginning to feel better. Hungry again now,
but that was well and good; hunger would give his concentration an extra edge. Shifting to a more comfortable position, Strann hunched over the manzon and set to work.

He was discovered shortly before noon by a steward—
a spiteful little specimen driven by the double goad of
terror of Ygorla and envy of Strann's place as her pet—
who came at his own volition to find out why the rat
hadn't yet made his daily appearance in the court hall and
hoped to uncover some minor treachery. He found Strann
asleep and snoring gently, the neck of the manzon still
held loosely in his fingers and the manuscript of his new
ballad scattered on the floor beside him. The steward
moved carefully forward, bent down to look at the parch-

ments, then extended a cautious finger and thumb to pick up one of the pages.

The light snoring ceased. Caught stooping, the steward flushed scarlet as he saw Strann's narrow hazel eyes regarding him coldly.

Hastily he straightened, brushing at his embroidered tunic and snatching his gaze away. "Are you aware of the hour?" he demanded, his tone just a little too sharp to carry authority. "It's close on midday. Her Majesty is growing impatient."

Strann put the back of one hand to his mouth to cover a yawn. "Her Majesty may be amused to know that I've had approximately one hour's sleep," he retorted with acerbity.

The steward looked down his long nose. "If the song she ordered isn't ready—"

"Then I'll be the one to suffer for it and not you." Strann got to his feet in one economical movement, suppressing a grimace as a muscle in his back protested. "If the Empress is in the audience hall, you may tell her I'll attend on her in ten minutes. If, that is, you have the courage to address her directly."

The steward opened his mouth to make a retort, then saw Strann's eyes and thought better of it. He'd not seen such a look in the rat's gaze before. There was a new chill there, as though something else, something alien, had stepped into Strann's mind and now looked coldly out from behind the mask of his hazel irises.

He turned away. "See you waste no time," he said with asperity.

Strann watched the door shut at his back, cursing the lack of a lock or any other means to secure privacy even in his own quarters. Then he let his shoulders relax, pressed the heels of both hands against his eyes, and pushed hard in an effort to combat his weariness. He hadn't intended to fall asleep, but his body had finally rebelled against his brain and overcome him. Now he felt worse than he would have if he'd managed to stay awake, like a piece of jetsam dumped on an Eastern Flatlands beach. He must revive himself, make himself fit to appear before Ygorla, or he'd undo the potential good of his ballad even before she heard it.

A ewer and bowl stood on a small table to one side of the room, with a mirror above. The water in the ewer was yesterday's, and cold, but no matter; it would have to do. It had amused Ygorla to allow him to keep his razor—she either assumed that he wouldn't use it to slit his own wrists or anyone else's throat, or cared nothing either way —and Strann positioned himself before the mirror and began to work up a lather from the oily and overpoweringly scented soap in a small dish by the basin. Applying it to his face, he paused suddenly as, for one disconcerting moment, he seemed to be looking into the eyes of a stranger in the mirror's polished surface. Then the illusion vanished and he shook his head. Overtired. He should have let himself rest for longer. It wasn't—couldn't be— anything to do with last night. He didn't want to dwell on last night; indeed he was determined to avoid thinking about it at all for fear that if he did, he might lose his sanity altogether. Be calm, accept the necessary facts, and act according to the plan that had been laid down. That was all that mattered. The rest was best left to lie unexplored.

He looked at his reflection again and, ignoring the fact that his eyes seemed to have an unnaturally chilly cast to them, began to shave.

The colors in the great curving back of the throne behind
Ygorla's slim figure changed from russet through gold and
green to a bright and pleasant sky blue. Languidly Ygorla
stretched out one slippered foot, then reached to her
breast and unpinned a brooch that she wore on her bodice.
She smiled a shatteringly sweet smile, then tossed the
brooch to Strann, who had the presence of mind to catch
it.

"Majesty," Strann said, "you do me too much honor."

Her smile became a moue, as though she were blowing
him a kiss. "My rat, when I am pleased, I should be churl-
ish not to show it. It's simply a trifling reward for your
skills"—her eyes flicked maliciously to the small knot of
rigid-faced courtiers to one side of the throne—"and for
your loyalty. Truly I am quite touched."

Strann let out a long but silent breath of relief. He'd
walked a sword-edge during the past half hour since he'd
arrived in the hall to find the Queen—the Empress, he
corrected himself hastily and prudently—bored, impatient, and therefore only looking for the smallest opportunity to be spiteful. He'd played the undeserving penitent
under five minutes of withering sarcasm and thinly veiled
threats, managed to shift his performance into a few self-
deprecating jester's antics, which at last had elicited a
chilly though still dangerous little smile, then had finally
cajoled her into hearing the song she had ordered to mark
Jianna's passing. Now, to the disgust of his fellow slaves,
he had sung it, putting all his worth into the performance,
and Ygorla was pleased. Greatly pleased. The brooch she
had so carelessly tossed to him contained a diamond the

size of his thumbnail; with that one gem alone he could have bought Koord's tavern in Shu-Nhadek. And, far more importantly, it indicated that there might be no better time to set his plan in train.

He rose to his feet, approached the throne, and bowed low to her, having the temerity to take her fingers in his.

"Madam," he said in a voice pitched so intimately that only she could hear him, "I beg your forgiveness for my presumption, but . . . if my humble offering has pleased you, then I dare to hope that you might be still better pleased by another new ballad."

"Another?" Ygorla looked sharply at him from under her black lashes.

"Yes, Majesty. It's not yet complete, but I am bold enough to believe that it will find some small favor with you. However"—expressively his eyes indicated the others in the hall—"I wonder if, by your grace, it could be reserved for your ears alone?"

Her own eyes sparked with answering interest. "Why, rat? If it's so fine a piece, I want all my court to hear it."

Strann bowed again. "Majesty, you're too kind to me. But I . . . well, I had dearly hoped that you might do me the honor of guiding me in my work. As I said, the piece is incomplete as yet; and if I could but know how you would wish its story to be told, then it would be transformed from a creditable piece of music into a true epic."

The lure to Ygorla's ego was irresistible. She paused for a few moments, making a pretense of deigning to consider his request. Then: "Very well. I'm in a mood to be generous. You may have a few minutes of my time." She raised her head and snapped imperious fingers at the group of courtiers. "Out."

They needed no second telling. As they departed, several black shadows flowed from under Ygorla's throne, slinking out of the hall in their wake like dark water across the polished floor. The demon sentries were absent; no unhuman shapes clung and clambered among the high pillars. Ygorla sprawled back in the throne's deep seat and said, "Well?"

"Majesty." Strann lifted his manzon and took up a position on one knee at her feet. It was an awkward posture, but the effect was more important than his comfort. "I wish to tell the story of an Empress. A lady of matchless beauty and also of matchless power. A woman without peer, who has deigned to set her hand upon the world, and who makes all the world's beauty seem drab against her brilliance."

Ygorla's eyebrows lifted a fraction, but in amusement rather than irritation. "Go on."

"I wish, sweet Majesty, to write an epic for you that will rival anything composed by the greatest bards in our history. Not merely a ballad, for ballads have limitations and those limitations can only do you a gross injustice." Quietly but persuasively he began to play the opening melody he had contrived during the night. "I have it in mind to compose a symphony, a paean, a grand and magnificent hymn of praise." Time it right, he thought; change to the solemn chords . . . *now*.

Light burgeoned in Ygorla's eyes, and above the sudden power of the music Strann's voice carried richly and clearly. "But what is a hymn of praise unless it has a story to tell? A story to inspire awe, to inspire fear, to inspire reverence—the story of the Empress Ygorla's glorious and total conquest of our world."

He allowed his last words to merge into a harmonic from the manzon, and then before Ygorla could react or

even gather her thoughts, he launched into the piece he'd
composed, the opening song of his putative epic. For the
sake of expediency he'd shamelessly plagiarized elements
from the first movement of *Equilibrium*; it had saved him
a great deal of time, and he was prepared to gamble that
Ygorla, who showed no interest in artistic matters unless
they related directly to herself, wasn't familiar with the
original masterwork.

He had to admit, he thought as he played and sang,
that musically at least this was a splendid piece. The lyri-
cal content was another matter entirely, but then the
words had a quite different purpose—and it wasn't long
before they began to take effect as he'd hoped. Gradually
Ygorla's posture shifted from an affectation of aloof tolerance to the suppressed tension of genuine and eager interest. She leaned forward, feet curled under her and chin
propped on one fist, and the colors in the throne began to
agitate through a rainbow of brilliant shades as she drank
in Strann's psalm. The early verses of the song did little
more than describe her beauty, her power, her fitness to
rule as an Empress beloved and feared in equal measure
by an awed and grateful populace—hardly the most subtle
of approaches, but it had the desired effect of capturing
Ygorla's undivided attention and making her highly re-
ceptive to the suggestion that Strann had slipped into the
last verse of all, in the form of a stern warning to and
anathema against any living man who might dare to com-
mit the folly of failing to acknowledge her as their true
and unassailable queen. The verse was, effectively, a
gauntlet thrown down at the feet of any lingering doubters; and though Strann had taken care not to mention
them by name, its obvious target was the Circle, and in
particular its leader Tirand Lin.

The piece ended with a coda, which in the hands of a full complement of musicians would become a brazen fanfare. It was designed to leave its listener avid on the threshold of the next and as yet unwritten movement, ensnared by the skilfully implied promise of defeat and humiliation to her enemies —and it worked. He saw it in her expression as the last notes faded, and in the sudden violent changes of color in the throne at her back.

"Ahh . . ." The word was a soft sigh with a powerful undercurrent of venom, and Ygorla rose from her throne and slowly began to pace the dais while Strann watched her carefully from under lowered lashes. "If he but knew . . . if he but *knew* . . ."

Strann was well aware of "his" identity, and knew that he'd found the target. Yandros had been right; Tirand Lin's entrenchment was indeed beginning to obsess her, and she had snapped up his bait like a hungry pike. Suddenly she stopped and swung around to face him.

"Name your reward, my rat," she said imperiously. "Whatever you crave, it shall be yours. You have captured exactly—*exactly*—what I wanted, and more! You have told the truth!" Her eyes took on a faraway look, becoming hard and brilliant as gems. "My only regret is that the High—that those few benighted fools who still refuse to acknowledge my superiority aren't groveling before me in this hall now to hear the truth for themselves. For your words would open their eyes and *make* them see that they can't resist, whether they willed it or no." Then abruptly her gaze refocused on Strann's face. "You are a bard among bards, with a tongue of pure gold. I value gold; I prize it. So what will you have, my golden-tongued rat? What reward do you want for your service to me?"

"Madam," Strann said in a reverential voice, "your

praise is reward enough. I ask nothing more—although I share your regret that that blind and recalcitrant few of whom you spoke can't be here to witness and learn from my saga. If *that* could be achieved, my fulfillment would be complete and my work's ultimate purpose achieved."

Ygorla frowned. "So it would," she agreed, suddenly waspish, for she hadn't wanted to pursue that aspect of her personal dilemma any further. "But I think you overestimate yourself if you think for one moment that *you* could bring such a thing about."

"Of course, Majesty." Strann inclined his head in humble agreement. "But I dare to hope that I might suggest the means by which *you* might achieve it."

There was a sharp silence. Ygorla stood motionless, staring at him. Then, her tone suddenly far more menacing, she said, "Explain your meaning."

This was the moment he had hoped for, the moment to play his trump card. Very cautiously Strann said, "Madam, in the Great Eastern Flatlands the fishermen have a proverb—"

"Fishermen?" she snapped, interrupting. "What have fishermen to do with it?"

"A great deal, lady, if their maxim is applied in a new direction. They say, 'The tide will not rise for me; therefore I must rise for the tide.' "

Ygorla looked at him blankly, and the colors in the throne began to take on dangerously dark hues. "You're talking rubbish, Strann. Don't dare to trifle with me!"

Strann drew a breath. He'd feared this, feared the combination of ignorance and impatience that could so easily upset his fragile balance on this tightrope and pitch him into disaster. He *had* to win her back before her temper got the better of her curiosity.

"Majesty," he said, a pleading note in his voice now, "If you are still disposed to grant me a reward, then I beg you, let it be this: that you permit me to speak freely to you now. I may earn your contempt for my crass foolishness; I may even earn your wrath for my presumption. But I believe, fervently and deeply, that what I have to say may be of some small value to you." He raised his eyes and met her gaze candidly. "In my most cherished dreams I could want for nothing more than that."

For a few perilous moments the future of his entire plan hung in the balance. Ygorla was frowning, torn between irritation and the effect of Strann's blatant sop to her conceit. The colors of the throne were changing so fast that it was impossible to interpret them now; all Strann could do was pray silently to Yandros that he hadn't made a fatal misjudgment.

At last Ygorla's voice broke the silence. She said, "You may speak."

A shudder, tingling heat followed by violent cold, racked Strann's entire frame as relief swamped him. Quietly enough to imply submissive gratitude, he said, "My Empress, I make no claim to special knowledge, but I believe"—*careful, Strann, careful*—"that there is one man in particular whose recalcitrance shows a degree of folly unheard of in one of his calling. I refer to Tirand Lin of the Circle."

He must have injected just the right hint of contempt into his voice, for Ygorla only said, "Go on."

"The High Initiate, as he still pleases to call himself, is under the misapprehension that he has the power to deny his rightful Empress. Clearly should you choose to, you could disabuse him of this notion in less time than it takes a man to blink his eyes; but because you are merciful as

224

well as wise, you would prefer the Circle's capitulation to be . . . voluntary."

A faint smile curved the edges of Ygorla's lips. "You are astute. Continue."

So far, so good. "I, however, am not blessed with my queen's magnanimity," Strann said. "I confess it, Majesty: Tirand Lin's entrenchment *angers* me. It angers me so much that I would give a very great deal to see him laid low for the insult he has dared to pay you by his silence." He looked directly at her. "If I could help you to bring this about, then, lady, I would *gloat* at his downfall. I would *relish* it."

That surprised Ygorla. Before she could question him about his motives, though, Strann went on.

"I return now to the fishermen's proverb. The tide will not obey the command of men; therefore in order to achieve their desired ends men must adapt themselves to the ways of the tide." He smiled conspiratorially. "In other words, Majesty, if the High Initiate is reluctant to leave the Star Peninsula and come to you, then perhaps you should instead go to him and prise him out."

He knew immediately that the idea, even in such embryonic form, appealed to her. "Prise him out . . ." she said thoughtfully, and began to pace again. "Like prising a snail from its shell to expose the soft and vulnerable flesh beneath. . . . Rat, I do believe that you're an uncommonly clever rodent in more ways than one!" Then her expression changed. "But how best to do it, that's the question. It would amuse me—it would *greatly* amuse me —to make a progress to the Star Peninsula and to arrive on Tirand Lin's threshold with a fanfare of trumpets to announce my presence and my intention." Again her eyes developed a distant, avid glitter as her imagination took hold. "I would travel through the provinces and show my true power to them all. They would see *me,* not merely my servants; I would be feted, revered, adored—ah, that would be *magnificent!*" Then eagerness transmuted into a sour scowl. "But until Tirand Lin is prepared to receive me with all due honor as his Empress, I will not condescend to make any such move. *He* must give way to *me.* I have no intention of indulging his arrogance." She turned on her heel to face Strann and added challengingly, "Have you an answer to *that,* little rodent?"

Strann smiled. "Yes, Majesty, I believe I have. For while it would clearly be beneath you to make the first move, an ambassador, carefully chosen, could go before you and pave the way for your triumphal conquest. Such an ambassador might move Tirand Lin where other strategies have failed—provided, of course, that he held the right weapons at his fingertips." His left hand curled around the manzon's neck and he struck the strings gently. "Simple weapons, my Empress, but effective, for they would carry the attack from an unexpected quarter. Some well-chosen words. A story cleverly contrived and as cleverly told, to deceive the ear and dazzle the mind." A conspiratorial smile appeared on his lips. "Just a *modicum* of deviousness, Majesty. Just enough to turn the High Initiate's head and lead his unwary foot from its chosen path." And he modulated his fingers on the strings to repeat, slowly and emphatically, the opening fanfare of his epic.

Ygorla stared hard at him for an unnervingly long time. Then her eyes began to glitter, until they were as harshly bright as twin sapphire suns. "A modicum of deviousness . . ." she said thoughtfully—then her lips parted and she smiled a smile that matched Strann's own. "Oh, my rat, you are as cunning as your namesake!" Her shoulders shook; she flung her head back and uttered a savage and delighted laugh. "My ambassador, armed with a power that the Circle would never *think* to beware of—the power of a bard!" She drew a great breath, then swung about and strode back to the throne, flinging herself down among the plethora of cushions. "A bard who can concoct a tale that will bait my line and hook my elusive fish! Strann, you are the shrewdest of my servants!" She leaned forward. "Use your golden tongue to deliver Tirand Lin to me and I shall reward you with your own *weight* in gold!"

Strann bowed. "Majesty, I protest my unworthiness! If I should fail—"

"You won't fail." Ygorla gazed intently at him. "You will succeed. I want the pleasure of teaching Tirand Lin the error of his ways, and you will secure that pleasure for me. My little pet rodent will come gnawing at the castle's gates, and he will nibble at the Circle's defenses until the way is clear for his mistress to follow. That is my command to you, and I will be obeyed. You *must* succeed, my rat. Do I make my meaning clear?"

He bowed again. "Madam, you do."

"Then we understand each other well. Now"—Ygorla clasped her hands together—"to the question of how it shall be done. I see no point in wasting time, so I'll turn my mind immediately to devising my strategy. My first deed, I think, will be to dispatch a new message to the Star Peninsula." She raised one arm, snapped her fingers, and her voice rang crisply through the hall. "Servants!"

There was a dark shimmering in the air by one of the pillars, and three elementals materialized. One—the disembodied cat's head—Strann had seen before; the second was an animated green and silver flame; the third . . . he looked quickly away, feeling his stomach turn over.

Ygorla addressed the beings. "I want four scribes sent here to me at once. And tell my stewards to bring me fresh wine and more food." She eyed the silver tray beside her, then snatched it up and threw it away across the hall. "Tell them I demand something more pleasing to my palate than this tasteless ordure, or I'll have my next meal served on a cloth made from their hides!" The elementals flickered away and she turned to Strann once more. "I have no more need of you for the time being, my rat, so you may return to your quarters and continue with your compositions." She smiled. "When my plans are completed and I've decided on the day and manner of your departure, I will see you again. I assure you, you won't have very long to wait."

Strann rose to his feet. He felt queasy with a blend of emotions that didn't sit easily together, and chief among them were astonished relief that the plan—so far, at least —had gone so smoothly, and dawning dread at the thought of what now lay ahead of him. He pushed the feelings down before they could get too strong a hold and bowed again, this time a sweepingly reverential gesture of farewell.

"I shall count the moments, Majesty, until I may next have the honor of being summoned to your presence."

Even Ygorla might have been suspicious of such blatant hyperbole; but she was paying no attention. Her quicksilver mind had already moved into a new area of interest, and she merely dismissed Strann from the hall with an imperious wave of one hand. Strann left, trying to quell the uncomfortable bumping of his heart against his rib cage. In the passage outside the double doors he met the first of Ygorla's coterie of scribes hurrying toward the hall.

The scribe's steps faltered when he saw Strann. "You've just come from the Empress?" His voice was reedy with unease and his eyes searched Strann's face intently.

"Yes."

"Is she—that is—do you know what she requires?"

Strann didn't unbend. "Ask her," he said with a shrug, and walked away toward his room. He himself wanted only one thing now and was determined that nothing would keep him from it: sleep. Time to forget about Ygorla, forget about Yandros, forget about what the future might hold. Time simply to sink into blissful oblivion until the world forced its presence on him again. At this moment he didn't have the energy left to ask for anything more.

Ygorla watched her messenger rise skyward from the turret roof and wheel once over the palace as though in salute before its dark shape arrowed away into the north. When at last even her sorcerously enhanced vision could no longer detect the diminishing black silhouette of its wings, she turned from the window with a deep sigh of satisfaction.

"It's done." The sunset and the pulsing star overhead combined to cast a gory light through the glass; the light pooled around her feet like freshly spilled blood. "Tirand Lin will receive my letter by dawn, and Strann will follow it on the morning tide." She smiled, her face ghastly in the gloom. "An excellent day's work, Father, don't you agree?"

Narid-na-Gost, in his customary shadowed corner, hunched his deformed shoulders in a faintly petulant gesture. "Certainly you've acted fast enough."

"Do you blame me? Why should I waste more time than I have to?"

The demon's eyes glowed hot. "As you wish; though I still fail to see why you feel the need to be so precipitate. And as for your choice of ambassador . . ." He spat deliberately on the floor and a tongue of flame licked briefly at the edge of one of the rich rugs. "A posturing and self-seeking coward who spends his days fawning on you in the hope of reward. Do you honestly think that you can trust such a creature to carry out your orders?"

Ygorla smiled superciliously. "Ah, but you don't know Strann as I know him, Father. Fool he may be, but he has a rare and especial talent for persuasion."

"So I have observed," Narid-na-Gost interjected acidly.

She laughed. "I'm not taken in by him for one moment! But Tirand Lin will be, especially when he hears the story Strann has to tell."

She was particularly proud of that part of her strategy. It had come to her quite suddenly as she labouriously dictated the letter she intended to dispatch to the Star Peninsula, and her shrieks of delighted laughter had made the scribes cringe and brought half her court running to the audience hall to see what was to do. Snatching the scribes' pieces of parchment and tearing them to shreds, Ygorla immediately set about composing a new missal. A missal in which she hinted that her emissary, even now bound northward, came not to demand fealty but to parley with the Circle on behalf of his Empress. What was the phrase one of her terrified tame scholars had suggested? "To open negotiations toward our mutual understanding and benefit"—that was it. She had no wish to be the Circle's enemy; instead she offered the hand of friendship and cooperation, and a few well-chosen words of flattery toward Tirand Lin for good measure. This first salvo would, she was certain, ensure that the castle gates were opened to Strann, and once he was inside the Circle's stronghold, the rest of his task would be easy. The High Initiate would be curious at Ygorla's apparent change of heart; and Strann's confession—wrung from him under protest, of course, and in the greatest secrecy—that the tales of her power were exaggerated and that she would not be a match for the combined sorceries of the Circle, would provide the spark to set the fire alight. Pleading his true loyalty to the old triumvirate, Strann would persuade the High Initiate to set a trap by inviting Ygorla to come as an honored guest to the Star Peninsula—and as the castle's gates were flung wide to her, she would savor the triumph of her final conquest. Bluff and double-bluff. Yes, she thought with relish, it was all so *simple*.

The fact that Narid-na-Gost hadn't given her scheme his full blessing was an irritant, but a minor one. Lately she found herself caring less and less for his opinion, good or bad; she had enough power of her own now to have little need of him, and she suspected that he was sulking because he knew that fact as well as she did. Well and good; it would be interesting to see if he could maintain his resentment when she took control of the castle and presented him with the key to his precious Chaos Gate. That would be a very different story, and until then she was prepared to bide her time and ignore his sour moods.

For his own part, Narid-na-Gost was privately deeply amused. In truth he could find little wrong with his daughter's scheme; indeed, as she had apparently chosen to forget, he himself had counseled her in the first place to find a new tactic to overcome the Circle's resistance, and this plan had a good deal to commend it. The one flaw, though, was her choice of emissary. The demon couldn't deny Strann's talents, but those very same talents could make him an unreliable and untrustworthy servant. If he could lie convincingly to Tirand Lin, who could guarantee that he wouldn't also lie to Ygorla? And though Narid-na-Gost believed in letting his daughter learn her own hard lessons, he also had no intention of allowing anything to jeopardize his own plans for them both.

He said, his voice deliberately careless, "I don't for one moment question the jongleur's abilities, Ygorla. I merely observe that his loyalty can't be absolutely guaranteed."

She flashed him a brilliant, catlike glance. "Of course it can't. Do you think I haven't considered that and made allowance for it?"

That surprised him. Ygorla smiled.

"I have arranged a small farewell ceremony for Strann," she said. "By the time it's over and he embarks for the mainland, his loyalty to me will be assured beyond all doubt. For I will have taken something from Strann that he values above all else, and only I will have the power to restore it to him. Nothing, I promise you, will persuade him to risk forfeiting that by betraying my trust. His loyalty to me will be *absolute*."

The demon raised a querying eyebrow. "You intrigue me, daughter. What is it that your pet can possibly value so highly?"

Her smile became honey-sweet. "His music," she said.

14

"It doesn't make sense." Tirand Lin stared at the message scroll as though intense scrutiny might reveal some occluded meaning underlying the words on the parchment. Dawn was only just breaking and he hadn't had enough sleep; his mind felt fuzzy and he wasn't yet awake enough to think clearly. "This appears to be a complete contradiction of every previous letter we've received." He looked up at his two companions. "I'm honestly at a loss to know what to make of it."

The Matriarch, her chilly hands cupped around a mug of mulled ale, shook her head in sympathy, and Sen Briaray Olvit stared into the fire, which was too newly lit to be giving off any appreciable warmth.

"One thing we can be sure of," the senior adept said somberly, "and that is that there's more to it than meets the eye. A reversal like this, from implacable enmity to pledges of eternal friendship? It's like a deathbed conversion, and about as convincing!"

"I agree," the Matriarch said. "Though I must say that from what we know of the sorceress, this new ploy seems grossly out of character. I wouldn't have marked her as a woman possessed of any subtlety, not even at this childish level."

At last Tirand looked away from the parchment. "Remember, Shaill, that by now she probably has a court full of sycophants all anxious to help and advise her. Anyone intelligent enough to have preserved his or her life in the face of her depradations will also be intelligent enough to help her plan new strategies. I think we can look for other hands and other minds behind this new development." He slapped the letter with the back of his hand. "She doesn't name her ambassador. I wonder if it's anyone we know?"

"I doubt it," Sen replied. "Unless she's a complete fool, she won't have entrusted any old friend of the Circle's with a mission of this nature. No, I think it'll be a stranger who comes to our gates. Possibly even one who isn't human."

The Matriarch looked sharply at him. "You believe so?"

"I'm only saying it's possible. We don't know what manner of servants she keeps about her, or their powers. If only we did, it would be far easier to decide whether to open our gates to this envoy or slam them in his face. For my own part I'd prefer to open them," Sen added firmly. Tirand nodded; knowing Sen, he'd anticipated nothing less. There was a brief pause, then the elder adept said, "However, I wish . . ." The words trailed off, and he looked at the High Initiate warily.

"What do you wish?"

Sen sighed. "All right, I've thought it, so I suppose I'd better voice it. I wish that we'd received *some* response from the realm of Order. I was convinced—we were all convinced—that Aeoris would answer our plea, but since the ritual took place, there's been nothing, not even the smallest ripple in the ethers." He hesitated, aware of the Matriarch's steady gaze on him and of Tirand's tension, then decided that, as he'd fashioned the noose, he might as well hang himself. "Damn me for a blasphemer if you will, Tirand, but I'm beginning to wonder whether the gods are prepared to help us at all!"

Both Sen and Shaill expected an angry reaction from the High Initiate, but it didn't come. The trouble was, Tirand thought, that Sen wasn't the first senior adept to have expressed a growing doubt about the willingness of the lords of Order to come to the Circle's aid. Even he had felt the chill niggling of uncertainty in unguarded moments, though he fought hard against it, aware that he more than anyone must keep faith, and secretly terrified by the thought of what loss of that faith would imply. He had been over the arguments time and again in his mind, telling himself that Aeoris's wisdom was greater than that of any mortal and that the god would move in his own time and his own way. But always underlying his efforts to reassure himself and others was one question to which he couldn't find a rational answer. If Chaos had broken its pact—and that belief was the kingpin of the Circle's decision to sever the ties of loyalty—then the lords of Order were free to intervene when called upon. So why, *why* had they not done so?

Sen said, "I'm sorry, Tirand. I spoke out of turn."

"No, no." With an effort the High Initiate made his lips smile, though his eyes didn't reflect it. "You spoke as you feel. I, however"—he braced himself for the half-truth —"don't share your doubts. Aeoris will respond when our need is really great. I'm certain of that. Perhaps," he added, trying to interject a briskly cheerful note into his voice, "we should take comfort from his silence, for it shows that we're not yet in dire danger."

Immediately he regretted saying it, regretted making a fool of himself; for though his companions nodded and smiled agreement, he could see that they were merely humoring him. Doubt *was* setting in among the Circle, and unless it was stemmed quickly, it would soon grow out of hand. But how to stem it? That was his dilemma, and he didn't have an answer.

Turning away from Sen and Shaill so that they could no longer see his face, Tirand rolled up the message parchment and slipped it into a pouch that lay on his desk.

"For now I don't think there's any more to be done," he said in a tone that effectively cut short any thoughts of disagreement. "We'll put this letter before the Council of Adepts at our meeting this evening and discuss a proposed response. Unless he flies in on the wings of a demon, the sorceress's envoy can't hope to reach us before the new first moon, especially at this time of year; so we'll have more than enough time to deliberate over our decision." He looked up. "If there's nothing more . . . ?"

Sen left with murmured farewells; the Matriarch made to follow him, but paused at the study door. Her eyes regarded Tirand shrewdly for a few moments, then she said, "You're overworking, Tirand. I know it's unavoidable at the moment, but there are limits even to your stamina. You'll do the Circle no service if you push yourself beyond them."

Tirand stared down at his own hands. "I know, Shaill. But there just don't seem to be enough hours in the day to get everything done, especially with Arcoro and the others away." He realized that he sounded self-pitying and added, "Don't worry about me. I can cope—I think in a way I almost enjoy it."

Shaill looked skeptical. "Just as I enjoy being caught in a rainstorm without a coat? Don't be silly, Tirand. Take my advice and have a word with Karuth; I'm sure she'll be able to prescribe something that will at least allow you a decent night's sleep once in a while?"

"Maybe I will." Tirand smiled pallidly, aware—as he suspected the Matriarch was also aware—that he'd do no such thing.

"And have some breakfast," she said firmly. "I'm a great believer in breakfast. I'll see you in the dining hall."

She went out, leaving Tirand alone with his unhappy thoughts.

The symmetry and serenity of a well-tended garden were a source of great delight to Aeoris. He and Ailind walked on the perfectly smooth sward, between neat banks of flowers that no mortal gardener's wildest dreams could have encompassed, while in the air above them tiny elemental forms flitted on wings like transparent jewels.

At this moment, though, Aeoris's customary pleasure in the garden was tempered by other and more urgent considerations. He barely noticed the elementals, or the flowers, or the perfection of the lawns, or the fresh brilliance of the golden, rainbow-crossed sky that arched overhead. His gaze was fixed on the haze of the middle distance, and his mind was focused on another world.

"You said yourself," Ailind pointed out, "that doubts would begin to assail them in time."

Aeoris hunched his narrow shoulders. "Yes, I did. But it's happened sooner than I would have liked."

"Mortals are fickle at the best of times; it's one of their most irritating failings," Ailind said then added with a hint of venom, "They also have short memories. It rankles, doesn't it, to think that barely three generations ago their faith in us was absolute."

"Indeed. Still, we can do nothing to alter that—at least not for a little while yet." A faint smile played at the edges of Aeoris's mouth. "I think it's time for us to bow to circumstance, Ailind, and answer the High Initiate's plea. Especially now that Yandros seems to have stirred from his lethargy at last."

Ailind paused to gently brush one of the flitting elementals from his sleeve. "It's a pity that we weren't able to discover why he made that brief visit to the mortal world."

"Yes. I would have liked to learn more. However, it at least confirms that something's afoot in Chaos, and for the time being that's all the information we need." Aeoris stopped walking and turned to face his brother. "You're ready, I presume?"

"Oh, yes. Have you decided how it should best be done?"

"I think so. I've chosen a way that will avoid drawing more than the minimum of attention but will be unusual enough to properly impress the Circle."

Ailind made a formal bow. "Then, my brother, I am at your disposal."

"Good." Aeoris looked up at the sky, and his smile broadened. "Very good. I suggest that we begin without delay."

Strann didn't want a ceremonial farewell, but Ygorla had decreed it and there was nothing he could do. He was still recovering from the shock of her announcement that he

was to set sail this very morning, only a day after the
entire scheme had first been mooted. At first he'd found it
impossible to believe that she could have made her preparations so quickly, but when the realization really came
home to him and he learned the full details of her plans,
he began to worry in earnest.

He was, it seemed, to travel in fine style, with a fully
armed escort that would accompany him in what
amounted to a progress through the provinces. Ygorla
wanted her envoy to be seen and recognized for what he
was, and nothing but the very best, she said, would do for
him. Strann dreaded the journey, not least because it
would give him far too much time to speculate about the
reception he might receive at the castle, a reception that
would be all the worse if reports of his progress reached
the Star Peninsula before him. In other, happier days he
could have been confident that even if the High Initiate
would not welcome him under his roof—he had taken an
obvious dislike to Strann at their one brief meeting—he
could count on at least one friend among the adepts, in the
person of Tirand's sister, Karuth. Now, though, there was
little chance that even Karuth would look on him with
anything but loathing. Strann the turncoat. Strann the
traitor. She'd think it, as all the others thought it, the
moment she set eyes on his face.

He wished he'd never agreed to help Yandros. Conscience or no, surely it would have been better to stay here
on Summer Isle, well away from the rest of the world, and
continue to play the part of Ygorla's fawning pet? He
could have learned to live with himself, and at least the
abject slavery of his life would have had some compensa-
tions. It was too late now to change his mind—he would
have had Ygorla's wrath to contend with even if not Yan-

dros's, and he didn't know which prospect was worse—but Strann wished with all his heart that he could turn back time, face the Chaos god once more, and say, "I'm sorry, my lord, but no."

He was trying not to dwell on his regrets as he was admitted to the audience hall on the morning of his departure. The day was bright and fair; the tide would be turning in one hour, and Ygorla's own black ship waited for him at Summer Isle harbor with his entourage and baggage already aboard. He had one last interview to face, and then, willy-nilly, he would be on his way.

The hall doors were opened for him by the faceless shadow-sentries who stood on constant guard. Strann crossed the threshold—and stopped.

He had been led to believe that the entire court would be present for some kind of meaningless ceremony, but instead Ygorla was alone in the hall. She wasn't seated on her great throne but had stepped down from the dais and stood on the long, purple carpet that ran the length of the floor. She was watching him.

"Strann." There was something odd about her smile, something that rang an alarm bell deep in Strann's psyche. "So you're ready to embark, eh?"

Under the silk folds of his splendid clothes—ludicrous, flamboyant, and garish clothes—Strann felt sweat break out on his skin, though he didn't know why. He bowed. "I am ready, Majesty."

"Good. Then come here, my little rat, and let us say our farewells."

She extended an arm, fingers outspread, and Strann's unease suddenly flowered into terror. Something was wrong—sweet gods, he thought, had she *guessed*? Had she somehow discovered his deception? He didn't move, and Ygorla's lips pursed.

"Strann, did you hear me? Come here to me. I command it."

His legs moved of their own volition and propelled him toward her, whether through fear of disobeying or by some spell she'd cast on him he didn't know. When he stopped a single pace from her, he was trembling from head to foot.

Ygorla's eyes, blue and cold and remote as a clear winter sky, regarded him for perhaps half a minute. Then she said, "You know what you must do? You remember *everything*?"

Strann's throat was dry, and speaking was suddenly difficult. At last he managed, "Everything, Majesty."

"That's good. There is however, one last little thing that has been overlooked until now, and we must put it right before you leave. That is the question of your trustworthiness."

Strann blanched. Ygorla's smile became sweeter still.

"I trust my dear pet rat implicitly of course. I know how loyal he is; I know how dearly he loves and reveres me, and I most certainly wouldn't dream of insulting him by calling his fidelity into question in even the smallest way. But all the same, as I'm sure you appreciate, dear Strann, I can't afford to run even the *slightest* risk. So I shall extract from you a little forfeit, something for me to hold until the happy day when we meet again to enjoy my final triumph."

Strann's face was bleached of color. "Majesty, I—I don't understand . . ."

"No. But you will. Give me your hand, Strann. Let us clasp on the bargain between us."

Reflexively, before he could stop himself, Strann extended his right hand. Ygorla took it in hers—and suddenly her grip became a vise. He yelped, tried to pull away, but couldn't move; she held his wrist fast with shockingly unhuman strength, and as she began to squeeze, he felt the thin bones giving.

"Now," Ygorla said with an incredible sweetness that Strann heard through a thundering blur of pain. "My forfeit . . ."

She raised her free hand and fire sprang from her fingertips, hurling blood-red light through the hall. The light brightened as the flames grew hotter, turning through orange and yellow to a glaring white that seared Strann's watering eyes. Slowly and with terrible, deliberate relish Ygorla brought her blazing hand down to meet his, to close over it, to envelop his entire arm with a shock-wave of screaming agony as his hand caught fire and began to burn. Strann shrieked, writhing and twisting, feet slipping and scrabbling on the floor as he fought with all his strength to escape; but Ygorla held on while he screamed mad, wordless pleas and his hand blackened, charred, melted—

Suddenly the flames went out and Ygorla released him. Strann fell to the floor with a heavy impact, his senses blasted by shock and pain and his consciousness rushing down a black tunnel toward oblivion. Ygorla stared down at him; he couldn't see her, but he was aware of her presence as she stood over his twitching body and carelessly brushed a few specks of ash from her own unblemished palms. And just before he finally blacked out, he heard the last cold words she addressed to him.

"I have your music now, my dear rat, and I shall keep it as my surety. My power destroyed your hand; only my power can restore it. Remember that, little ambassador. Remember it as you go on your way, and do not *dare* to fail me!"

At their Empress's order, servants salved Strann's hand, then pulled a purple gauntlet embroidered with Ygorla's personal sigil over his ruined fingers to hide them from view. The black ship left harbor on the turning tide, and when Strann finally recovered consciousness, he found himself alone in a cabin with Summer Isle lost to view astern.

At first he thought he'd dreamed it. But when he saw the gauntlet, and pulled it off, and looked at what lay beneath, something inside him shriveled and turned as black as his hand's flesh. There was no physical pain now —Ygorla had seen to that—but no sorcery could have stemmed the mental agony he felt. For a very long time Strann sat staring at the remains of his fingers. Oh, but she had been clever. She had known unerringly the one thing that he valued above all else, even above his own life, for what use could he have from his life if he was no longer able to play his music? She had known that, and so to ensure his loyalty she had taken his music from him, and only she had the power to restore it. Yes, she had been clever. So clever.

And she had made such a grave mistake. . . .

Hatred didn't come easily to Strann. He had learned to hate Ygorla, and with good reason, but it had been a slow, simmering emotion, a desire for revenge but without direction. Now, though, he learned for the first time that hatred had another and entirely different dimension. A dimension as hard and as cold as granite, where revenge was not merely a desire but an imperative, and where nothing else—life, death, the sanctity of his soul—mattered.

At last he looked up. The cabin had one tiny window, its glass scoured by salt and almost opaque, but through it he could just make out the swell of green-gray water beating past the ship's keel. On deck the crew—and yes, he'd seen what manner of beings crewed Ygorla's fleet—would be about their silent work; doubtless in another cabin the creatures who made up his escort would be lying dormant in the uncanny way of their kind until they should be needed. Slowly, finger by finger, Strann pulled the gauntlet back over his charred and twisted hand and thought of the long journey ahead. Not with trepidation this time, but with a resolve that might under other circumstances have been almost pleasurable. He didn't regret his decision, not now. That was in the past. And that was the root of Ygorla's mistake, for she had done for him the one thing he could never have achieved for himself: She had killed his fear and replaced it with the power of hatred.

He lay back on the bunk bed, his hand placed carefully across his chest and his hazel eyes coldly expressionless, and composed himself to wait for landfall.

15

The wind's strength had been increasing since midmorning, and by the time the brief winter day began to wane, the Star Peninsula was bearing the brunt of a full-fledged northerly gale. The wind shrieked among the stones of the ancient castle and roared in every chimney on the seaward side. Fires smoked chokingly in rooms on the upper floors, driving their occupants to douse the flames in their hearths and retreat to the dining hall, where a system of cowlings protected the fire in the gigantic grate. By midafternoon rain and hail came sweeping in from the sea in driving, blinding sheets, bringing leaden and artificial twilight, and servants at last gave up any pretense of letting in daylight and hastened to draw the hall's curtains against the elements.

Calvi Alacar woke from a restless sleep to find his bedchamber filled with smoke and the fire on the verge of going out as the gale flung rain in hissing spurts down the chimney. The room was so gloomy that for a moment he thought it must be night, and he sat up with a guilty start. He'd only intended to rest for an hour or so after his midday meal, as Karuth had suggested: there was so much to do; whatever would Tirand and the Matriarch think of him? Then he saw the timepiece on the table beside his bed, and heard hailstones spattering against his window, and realized that, despite appearances, it was far earlier than he'd feared.

He swung his legs over the side of the bed and stood up. The bedchamber was as smoky as a tavern taproom at midnight; he waved ineffectually at the gray haze for a few moments, then reluctantly thumped the window open, turning his head aside as rain swirled in and the hail stung his face. Gods, what a day! He'd never grown used to the northern winters and never would; at times like this he longed for Summer Isle and the warm southern climate. . . .

The unguarded thought drove out the last remnants of drowsiness with a sharp shock as Calvi remembered that Summer Isle was no longer his home and perhaps never would be again. Shivering with more than the cold, he tried to distract himself by staring out of the window at the wild weather. Not that there was anything to see from this side of the castle but endless ocean, and that a dismal prospect now. Leaden-gray sky, leaden-gray sea, rain and wind and—

Calvi went rigid as, far in the distance—or at least so he thought, it was impossible to be sure against the blurring background of the rainstorm—a brilliant white pinpoint of light soared skyward from the sea, arced over, and winked out. Island-born as he was, Calvi knew immediately what the light must be, though it defied all reason. A distress flare—a signal from a ship in trouble.

He swung away from the window and ran to where a heavy, brass-bound chest stood against one wall. Lifting the lid, he rummaged among the collection of small personal effects inside and pulled out a polished spyglass that had been a gift from his father many years ago. Back at the window he raised the glass to his eye and trained it on the sea, but realized after a few moments that he'd been impossibly optimistic. The rain smudged everything into featureless gray; he couldn't even distinguish ocean from sky, let alone pinpoint the spot from which the flare had come, and, frustrated, he lowered the glass again and peered frantically into the storm. Was that a paler shape among the chaos of heaving waves and driving rain, the glimmer of a sail? No, he'd imagined it; no one's eyesight could be that good. . . . Then suddenly a second flare soared up into the gale, and Calvi bit hard and painfully into his lower lip in shocked excitement. It *was* a ship! North-northwest, maybe half a mile from the coast—gods, it didn't stand a chance in this; it would be swept onto the rocks—

Snatching up the spyglass again, he pelted from the room and raced along the passage toward the main staircase. As he started down the steps, jumping them three at a time, two people emerged from a side door into the hall below and he saw that, providentially, one of them was Karuth.

"Karuth!" Calvi's shout was high-pitched with excited urgency. "Karuth, there's a ship off the coast! It's in trouble!"

Karuth stopped dead. *"What?* Calvi, are you sure?"

"She's putting up distress flares; I saw them from my window."

"Yandros!" The oath was inappropriate these days, but old habits died hard. Karuth turned swiftly to the young woman with her. "Liss, find Sanquar quickly and tell him to meet me here. I'll fetch Tirand. And Calvi, you'd best alert Reyni—he's the senior steward on duty at the moment."

Thankful that he could do something more positive

than simply be the bringer of unhappy news, Calvi
sprinted away in the direction of the dining hall as Karuth
ran toward Tirand's study. Within minutes a group of
people with the High Initiate at its center had converged
by the main doors. Lookouts were dispatched to the battlements, one carrying Calvi's spyglass, and Tirand and
the steward Reyni began to issue orders for a full-scale
rescue operation.

Calvi knew that many of the adepts and servants were
trained for these rare but ever-possible emergencies; a vital
necessity, for this was a dangerous coast, and the castle
was the only human habitation between Fanaan Bay to the
west and the distant mining strongholds of Empty Province to the east. He'd never witnessed a rescue before, let
alone been directly involved in one, and he felt the peculiar sick blend of dread and excitement take hold of him as
he joined the mustering rescue party. Servants were running to place lanterns in all the castle's north-facing windows, while on the battlements others fought the elements
in an effort to fuel and light the big warning beacons that,
though unused for years, were kept in constant readiness.
Karuth had vanished but then reappeared dressed in
heavy hide trousers and a belted hide coat; more coats and
boots were brought, including Calvi's own, and as he
flailed his arms into the sleeves, Calvi listened alertly to
the rapid barrage of instructions.

"We'll go down by the stairway—it's slower, but it's
far too dangerous to rig the breech-slings down the stack
in these conditions. Ropes and other tackle are stored in
the last cellar before the stairs, but you'll need to fetch
lights from the upper storerooms. Take lanterns; not
torches, they won't stay alight for more than a moment in
the gale. Keep to your assigned teams and obey your lead-

ers implicitly and instantly. And look out for your own safety: we've enough to contend with without having to mourn over drowned heroes! Is anyone unsure of what he must do?" No voice spoke up. "Good. Then let's waste no more time!"

Tirand and half the assembly set off immediately toward the inner stairway that led down to the castle's extensive cellars, while Calvi and his companions in Reyni's party headed for the storerooms to fetch the lanterns. The next few minutes passed like a blur in Calvi's mind; with three lanterns clasped in one hand and staggering under a bulky pile of blankets—an afterthought on Reyni's part— he hastened with the others down steps and along dark, unfamiliar passages, and by the time they finally rejoined Tirand's party, he hadn't the least idea where he was. Tirand and his companions were burdened with coils of heavy rope; some carried axes, harnesses, huge iron pitons that could be driven into rock to form a stanchion for lifelines; one man gripped a crossbowlike launcher and a supply of phosphorous signal flares. Calvi glimpsed Karuth again, carrying a sledgehammer in one hand and her physician's bag in the other, and beside her was Sanquar with an armload of ropes and belaying pins. The lanterns were hastily lit, and as their illumination lifted the gloom of the cellars, the assembly moved toward a narrow door at the passage's far end. Calvi's pulse quickened as the door was opened to reveal a gaping black stairwell, but he had no time to acknowledge the sudden lurch of claustrophobic fear inside him before, borne along in the jostling, hurrying press of people, he ducked through the doorway and was on the stairs.

The flights that climbed through the castle's four spires were an intimidating enough prospect, but they were nothing compared with this. These stairs spiraled down through the stack itself, hewn an unimaginable age ago through hundreds of feet of solid rock to emerge in one of the caves on the shingle beach at the stack's base. Calvi had never dared to make the descent before. Some students and a few of the younger adepts liked to swim from the beach during the summer months, but he'd never been able to face the thought of climbing down in the knowledge that millions of tons of solid rock were poised above his head. Now that formless dread hit him with dizzying suddenness, making him lurch and almost lose his balance. A hand reached out from behind to steady him and a voice he didn't recognize said something reassuring. Calvi took a deep breath of the stale, dank air and resolutely pressed on.

The rescuers continued their hasty descent, until abruptly the atmosphere grew colder and they tasted salt and felt the first snap of the wind. Moments later the vanguard of the party reached the end of the flight, and as they stumbled out of the cave, the gale hit them in a shrieking onslaught. Leaning into it, clothes flapping madly and hair streaming as he raised an arm to protect his face from the driving hail, Tirand yelled orders in a stentorian voice as others, staggering and swaying, emerged into the mayhem. Less than twenty yards from them the sea was a churning, heaving maelstrom, mountainous waves running like wild horses, clashing in murderous crosscurrents and battering the beach with a constant, explosive booming that drowned the wind's scream. Momentarily hypnotized by the grandeur and the terror of it, Calvi stared open-mouthed at the awesome scene, thinking that surely this rescue attempt must be futile, for no ship could hope to survive this. She must have gone down, she *couldn't* still be out there—

He jumped violently and, momentarily unbalanced, was almost knocked off his feet by the gale as without warning a dazzling white light sizzled into life only feet from where he stood. Recovering his balance, he heard the thwack and clang of the flare launcher, then saw a tiny, brilliant star of burning phosphorus shoot skyward and out over the sea. The wind snatched it, flinging it off course; it winked out, and a second signal went up, while on the shingle slope, perilously close to the waves, men strained to watch for any answering flare from the stricken vessel. For a few moments there was nothing, then—

"There!" a voice bellowed, as out in the raging sea an answering star hurtled upward.

Tirand, his hair already soaked, cupped both hands to his salt-stung and streaming face and yelled back to the main party huddled in the cliff's lee, "She must be close! Spread out with those lanterns; mark the beach boundaries!"

Another bellow from the shoreline cut across him. *"There she is! There she is!"*

Looming out of the wild murk, a white sail appeared. The ship—no, not a ship Calvi realized in horror but a mere boat, barely more than a dinghy with a single, frail mast—was no more than thirty yards from shore, buffeted on the huge swell and running straight for a line of savage rocks that stretched out into the sea from the foot of the stack. For a moment she vanished as an enormous wave humped out of nowhere and hid her from view; the shoreline watchers pelted to safety as the wave crashed down where they'd been standing, and as the undertow roared back, the boat reappeared, broadside onto the rocks now and hurtling toward disaster.

"LIFELINES!" Tirand yelled with all the power his lungs could muster. "All of you, *MOVE!!"*

For one appalling moment, as the rescuers raced to obey the High Initiate, Calvi saw the outline of a man in the helplessly tossing vessel. He was fighting with the boom, struggling in one last, hopeless effort to bring the flying tatters of the sail under control, and involuntarily Calvi screamed, *"No, no! It's no use—save yourself!"* It was a futile gesture, for his cry was inaudible above the deafening sounds of the gale and the sea, and suddenly rationality came back as though one of the crashing waves had hit him full on and Calvi stumbled back up the beach to lend his strength to his frantically toiling friends. The iron stanchion was already in place and an adept with a blacksmith's build was swinging Karuth's sledgehammer, driving the metal point deep into the rock with a force that shook the ground beneath his feet. Ropes were uncoiled, made fast—then even above the storm-racket Calvi heard the terrible smashing, grinding impact as the boat struck the rocks. Though he'd known it was coming, he still cried out aloud in horror; other shouts went up from his companions, and several men surged toward the sea's edge, heedless of Reyni's bawled warning not to risk their own lives.

"Calvi!" Hands thrust a coil of rope at him, and hardly knowing what he was doing, he, too, ran down the beach, paying out the line as he went. A tall man, a servant he thought, hastened to meet him, took the end of the rope from him, and began to swing it over his head before casting it at the rocks. But the gale caught the flying rope and flung it back in their faces, and a second cast was equally useless. Calvi turned back toward the cliff and yelled desperately, *"Tirand, it's no good! The wind's too strong!"*

There was a flurry of activity by the stanchion, then a dark-haired young adept came racing toward them. Calvi had time to register the fact that he was barefoot and had exchanged his heavy coat for a harness before the young man was up with him.

"Tie this, and for Aeoris's sake make sure it's secure!" The adept's eyes were wild with a mixture of fear and determination. Fingers fumbling with cold and wet, Calvi tied the rope to the harness with a strong seaman's knot. Others had joined them, and now Tirand had Calvi's spyglass and was scanning the rocks urgently.

"I see him! This side of the reef; he's clinging on, but he can't last more than a minute!" Hands snatched up the rope, and the harnessed adept ran toward the sea, hesitated for a single moment, then launched himself into the flailing water. A wave broke over his head in a welter of spray; then he reappeared, swimming strongly toward the reef.

Tirand turned to shout instructions to those who had taken up positions on the lifeline. 'Pay the rope out slowly; not too much slack! If you see him start to drift, shout!"

Calvi stared into the hail and flying spray, tossing his head every few seconds to shake water from his hair and eyes and striving to keep the swimming man in sight through the rain's blinding veils. He couldn't see the lone sailor, but Tirand and several others could and were yelling encouragement to the adept. Then suddenly Calvi glimpsed the broken spar of the mast, with rags of white sail still clinging to it, rear up against the darker outline of the rocks, and moments later a resounding cheer vied with the sea's noise as the adept raised an arm and signaled back to the shore.

"He's got him!" Tirand's hands clenched so hard on the rope that his knuckles showed white. "Together now, *pull!"*

They dug their heels into the shingle and hauled on the lifeline. Flinging a glance over his shoulder, Calvi saw a dozen people now on the rope besides himself and Tirand, including Reyni, Karuth, Sanquar, and the powerfully built adept who'd driven home the stanchion. They were hauling against the current now and needed all their strength to overcome the sea's power; a rhythmic chant was started to keep them pulling together, and Calvi swung his body rhythmically as he threw his entire weight into the hauling. The line stung his bare hands, rubbing the skin raw as it snaked and twisted in his grip, but he barely noticed; all that mattered was to bring the adept and his burden safely to shore. He could see the swimmer's dark head now, and beside it another that looked starkly white in contrast; they drew closer, closer, then suddenly they were floundering in the shallows, and Calvi dropped the rope and ran down the beach slope, three others beside him, to pull the adept and his burden from the sea.

The adept dropped to his knees on the shingle, doubled over and coughing water. Sanquar ran to attend him, throwing a blanket over his shivering body, and Calvi and Tirand lifted the unconscious sailor and carried him up the beach as Karuth came hurrying to meet them. She directed them to the cave mouth, where they were sheltered at least from the rain if not from the wind, and they laid the man facedown with his head turned to one side.

"He's alive, but he's not breathing." Quickly Karuth

knelt over the sailor, her hands pressing down expertly on his rib cage. Seawater trickled from his mouth, and Karuth settled into the steady, concentrated movements of artificial respiration. Calvi, weary and numb now in the wake of his efforts on the lifeline, stared at the man with faintly disorientated curiosity. A stranger, white-haired yet with a paradoxically young face. He wore only a plain linen shirt and trousers; madness in such weather, Calvi thought wonderingly. Where could he have come from? And who in the name of all the gods could he possibly be?

Tirand's hand on his arm made him look up from his dazed reverie. "There's nothing we can do for him at the moment. We'll make ready for the climb back; I don't want anyone staying down here longer than necessary."

Calvi nodded wordlessly and followed him back into the teeth of the gale. The next minutes—it might have been ten or twenty, he couldn't tell—passed like a peculiarly animated but faintly unreal nightmare as the rescuers threw their waning energy into collecting their equipment and mustering for the tiring ascent back to the castle. The adept who had swum out to the reef had already gone ahead with Sanquar; shortly afterward Karuth announced that the rescued stranger was breathing again, though still unconscious, and at last, thankfully, they left the grim, gale-swept beach behind.

Back in warmth and sanctuary, the shock of the castle's quiet atmosphere after the din of the elements made the returning rescuers' ears ring. Tirand and Calvi carried the unconscious sailor to Karuth's infirmary. With the emergency over, and in the bright light of the room, Calvi had time to take in the stranger's appearance in more detail, and though he couldn't explain it even to himself, something about the man disquieted him. He was glad when Karuth summarily dismissed him and Tirand, and out in the corridor he couldn't suppress a long shiver.

Tirand, noticing, said, "Are you all right, Calvi?"

"Yes—yes, thank you. Just . . . reaction, I think." He forced a smile and hoped it was convincing. "And cold."

Tirand patted his shoulder. "We'll all be warmer for dry clothes and a seat by the fire in the main hall. Come on; we've done a good day's work."

Karuth changed her wet clothes for a loose, belted robe, toweled her hair briefly, then returned to the couch where the unknown sailor lay breathing easily now but still showing no signs of a return to consciousness. Looking at him, she wondered, first, what kind of madness could have possessed anyone to put a boat out into a northern winter gale and, second, who he could be and where he had come from. She would have taken any wager that he wasn't a West High Lander, and though pale hair was a character- istic of people from both Empty Province and the Great Eastern Flatlands, he was respectively too lightly built and too tall to be a native of either. Besides, that hair—it was truly and unmistakably *white,* despite the fact that he looked no older than she was. But for the normal pigment of his face, she thought, he could easily be taken for an albino. He was, indeed, a conundrum.

She crossed the room to her cupboard, unlocked it, and began to take out an assortment of herbs to prepare a restorative for when her patient woke. She was carefully measuring out a powdered root when something in her psyche abruptly sounded a warning. Karuth swung around—and dropped the bottle she was holding as shock took the life from her fingers.

A shimmering golden aura had sprung into being about the stranger's recumbent form. Karuth stared, her eyes wide and her mouth open. Then, quietly and calmly, like a sleeper waking from a pleasant dream, the man on the couch opened his eyes.

Karuth slapped a hand to her mouth to stop herself from crying out as two golden orbs without iris or pupil focused on the ceiling overhead. The man turned his head, and she felt a pulse of enormous power flood the room. Then the extraordinary gaze fixed on her, and the stranger sat up.

"Karuth Piadar." It was a statement, not a question; he knew her, and all her adept's training notwithstanding, Karuth felt the strength drain out of her.

"Who are you?" She hissed the words through clamped teeth. The stranger smiled an oddly remote smile and stood up, casting aside the blankets that covered him.

"Do you no longer kneel before your gods, Karuth Piadar?" he said with exquisite gentleness.

Karuth's mouth worked in a violent spasm—then suddenly she whirled, snatched at the door-latch, and flung the door open. A first-rank initiate, a boy of fifteen or so, was hurrying along the corridor toward the dining hall; she pounced on him, gripping his arm.

"Fetch the High Initiate! In the name of all the gods, *run!*"

Bewildered, but reacting instinctively to her authority, the boy pounded away. By sheer chance he met Tirand at the end of the passage, and his garbled message brought the High Initiate running. He saw Karuth on the threshold and called out, "What is it, what's happened?"

She couldn't answer him, she only gestured back into the room. Tirand pushed past her—and stopped as he saw the figure standing before the couch.

"What—?" The question died in his throat as his brain registered the aura, the eyes. The figure smiled again, a trace more warmly this time.

"High Initiate, I apologize for the unorthodox manner of my arrival here, but we felt it imperative that no untoward suspicions should be aroused. You called on us; we have answered." He extended one hand in a graceful gesture. "I am Ailind, brother to Aeoris."

Tirand began to tremble as the golden gaze held his. Then, as the truth also dawned on Karuth, he dropped to one knee and bowed his head reverently. His voice choked with shock and joy and awe together, he whispered, "My lord . . . you are a thousand times welcome!"

16

Tirand waited until a few isolated murmurings had died down and the council hall was silent. Then he rose to his feet.

"Fellow adepts and friends. You now know the full details of the usurper's newest communication, and under normal circumstances I would now ask council members to offer their proposals for the Circle's response before a final decision is made. However, present circumstances are not normal—and in addition, we are in what I think must be the unprecedented position of housing the High Margrave and the Matriarch within our walls." He gestured in turn to Calvi and Shaill, who flanked him on the dais. "We have already agreed that for the duration of this emergency the authority of the Council of Adepts will be superseded by that of the Triumvirate; but I now propose to take matters one step farther." Tirand paused. "I feel— and I'm sure you'll all agree with me—that until further notice it would be in our best interests to dispense with our tradition of debate and discussion and allow the Triumvirate's authority to become absolute, without any reference to the council."

There was silence as the assembled adepts stared at him in consternation. Only Karuth and two others cast their gazes down, their expressions immobile; to them this announcement had come as no surprise. At last a middle-aged, dark-haired councillor rose to his feet.

"Tirand . . ." The adept's expression was grave. "You've taken us somewhat unawares. I agree that these circumstances are unprecedented, but, with the greatest possible respect toward our High Margrave and Matri-arch, this suggestion is *drastic*. Do you really feel it's nec-essary to go so far?"

Tirand met his gaze steadily. "Yes. We feel it is."

Shaill and Calvi both stared down at their own hands. The adept opened his mouth to argue further, but then stopped as he saw the High Initiate's expression more clearly. Tirand's face was set in a look of resolution and determination; this was familiar enough, but there was something else, something new, an ice-cold implacability that no one had ever seen in him before.

The High Initiate watched the faltering councillor for a few moments longer, then refocused his gaze to encom-pass the entire hall. "I do realize that this decision must seem both sudden and unexpected, but I assure you that it's been taken only after a great deal of consideration and heart searching." He glanced at the dissenting adept again, and suddenly his look was icy cold. "There's noth-ing more to say. The matter has been decided, and it is, as I've already stated, for the best."

Slowly the adept sat down, and not another protesting voice was raised. Courtesy alone made argument all but impossible with Calvi and the Matriarch sitting beside Tirand, but the council's silence was more than a matter of mere protocol. Few could have reasoned it in words, even fewer could have understood it; but something in Tirand's manner had killed the possibility of any dissent.

They simply couldn't argue with him—and they didn't know why.

Tirand waited until it was patently clear to everyone that no further discussion would be forthcoming, then retook his seat behind the table. Before him was a sheet of notes; he looked briefly at what was written, then raised his head to survey the hall once more.

"Time, as I'm sure you all agree, is of the essence, so I'll come straight to the point. We have discussed the question of the usurper's latest piece of impudence and have decided on a strategy."

"The usurper's latest piece of impudence" . . . Karuth saw an older adept sitting close to her frown at the High Initiate's choice of phrasing, and guessed why. This wasn't the Tirand Lin that the council knew so well. This man, supremely confident, almost arrogant in that confidence, was a stranger, and the adept beside her wasn't the only one to have noticed and been disturbed by it. One or two speculative glances had already been directed at her, and she had little doubt that a few of her fellow initiates would lose no time in probing for any information she could give them before too long, on the assumption that she must surely know her own brother better than anyone and would have some idea as to what lay behind this sudden and startling change in him.

Karuth had more than some idea: she knew the truth as surely and as starkly as any of the small coterie who, gathered together in Tirand's study, had been sworn to secrecy earlier in the day. She hadn't wanted to take that oath, but circumstances had forced her hand. Now that she had taken it, however reluctantly, she had no choice but to obey it.

Tirand was continuing his address. "The decision of

the Triumvirate," he said, "is this. There will be no reply to the sorceress's message, but we will await—and prepare for—the arrival of her ambassador. We've received intelligence that he is now in Han Province, and allowing that the weather doesn't worsen, he should reach the Star Peninsula in another ten or twelve days. When he does, we will open our gates to him."

There was, as Karuth had anticipated, a stir at that statement. One councillor, forgetting the Matriarch's presence, swore in astonishment; another hissed under his breath, and Karuth caught the words, "This is *madness!*" She sympathized, for she knew that had they been permitted to debate the matter as normal, the council wouldn't have countenanced Tirand's plan for one moment but would have vetoed it as posing too great a risk. They didn't know the nature of the ambassador, what powers he might possess, even whether he was human at all. And they believed—how could they not, if no one had told them otherwise?—that they would have only the Circle's own sorcerous but nonetheless mortal skills with which to combat any threat the envoy might pose.

The muttering was increasing, and despite Tirand's interdict, several councillors were rising to their feet and signaling an urgent wish to speak. Karuth took the opportunity to leave her seat and, unnoticed by all but her immediate neighbors, slipped out of the hall. There seemed no point in staying only to listen to arguments whose outcome was a foregone conclusion. She knew how Tirand would counter the protests, and she knew that he would inevitably prevail. Though the vast majority didn't know it, their High Initiate's will was now reinforced by a power that the council simply couldn't argue down and overcome. It had nothing to do with the Triumvirate; that was

simply a smokescreen, a mirror to deflect attention from
the truth that had been hidden from all but a trusted,
chosen few. The reality behind this new facade took the
form of the being who had stepped so shockingly and so
unexpectedly into their midst—Ailind, lord of the realm
of Order.

She closed the door quietly behind her and turned
from the main corridor along a secondary passage that led
toward the kitchens. She didn't feel hungry but knew she
ought to eat for her health's sake, and so, not wanting to
face the risk of company in the dining hall, she resolved
to gather together a few morsels on a tray and take them
to her private quarters. Sanquar was on duty in the infirmary; she wouldn't be missed. And she certainly didn't
want to be found in any public place when the meeting
ended and the adepts emerged from the council hall with
all too many unanswered questions in the forefront of
their minds.

Ahead of her the passage crossed a broader corridor,
and as she reached the junction, Karuth's steps slowed
and faltered. To her right lay the castle's east wing and the
principal guest apartments, and it was easy to imagine
that even from this distance she could sense the new presence there, feel it like a feverish aching in her bones. It was
imagination of course; care had been taken that no psychic
undercurrent would reach beyond the wing's confines. All
the same . . .

Something moved on a level with her eyes, and Karuth
jumped back in shock. Then, in the gloom where the illumination from the wall-torches hadn't been able to reach
and banish shadow, she saw them. Four . . . no, five of
the castle's colony of cats. One—the one that had startled
her—on the embrasure of a narrow, lightless window, an-

other in a recessed alcove, three sitting or crouching on the flagstoned floor. They looked like sentries, or vigilants at a death rite. As Karuth stared at them, one turned its head to return her gaze, and she recognized the sleek little gray beast that had visited her in her room on the night that the Circle had renounced its fealty to Chaos.

The creature hissed softly. There was no aggression in the sound, rather it was a warning and an admonition to her to be as silent and stealthy as the cats themselves. Karuth dropped to a crouch and held out a hand. The cat sniffed her fingers briefly, its whiskers tickling, then looked away and resumed its watchful position.

"No," Karuth said softly. "You don't like it either, do you, little ones? And you don't like *him.*" She rose again, turned from the corridor and the silent, motionless animals, and walked on, feeling a cold sensation in the pit of her stomach. The cats, she thought, were surer judges than any human, for their peculiar and highly honed senses were tuned to psychic levels that the human mind couldn't even discern. They knew that there was a powerful new presence in the castle; they were aware of its location and well aware of its nature. With their quirkishly independent spirits and their love of the night, they had a natural affinity with Chaos, and the arrival of one of Chaos's archenemies in their midst had disturbed them greatly. Karuth had the strongest impression that the castle's entire cat colony had taken an instant and emphatic dislike to Ailind of Order. Try as she might, she couldn't help but agree with them.

She had struggled not to allow her thoughts to develop along that path, but it was impossible to ignore her own instinctive feelings. Tirand would have called it blasphemy, and doubtless he was right; yet no amount of condemnation, or simple logical argument for that matter, could change Karuth's mind. There was something about Ailind, an air of arrogant superiority bordering almost on smugness, that raised her hackles. The first words he had spoken to her—*Do you no longer kneel before your gods, Karuth Piadar?*—rankled in her memory as fiercely as dry tinder took fire. Not *I have come to your aid,* not *your prayers have been heard:* only a rebuke for her lack of reverence. The trouble was, Karuth didn't feel reverence. Perhaps she was a fool and a hypocrite; after all, wasn't it supremely arrogant of *her* to feel angered and belittled by that first, brief confrontation? Ailind was a lord of Order, brother to Aeoris himself. His statue stood with its fellows in the Marble Hall, honored and worshiped; he wasn't some elemental being but one of the fourteen gods themselves. A god, she reminded herself. A *god.*

But there was more to it than that. Her mind ranged back to the meeting that had taken place in the east wing just two hours after the sea-rescue. There had been seven people present: Ailind himself; the Triumvirate of Tirand, Calvi, and Shaill; and three senior adepts—herself, Sen Briaray Olvit, and an elderly philosopher who was one of the High Initiate's most trusted advisors. She had had the strong impression that she was allowed to participate only because circumstances had forced Ailind's hand; she had been present when he revealed his identity, so he had no choice but to include her. But beyond this small nucleus, the god had stated emphatically, no one else was to know of his presence in the mortal world. He had altered his appearance; the aura was gone, and his eyes were no longer the pupil-less golden spheres that had so shocked Karuth, but now looked as human as any mortal man's, albeit an odd shade of amber-brown and preternaturally intent. He wanted no ceremony, no panoply; he would inhabit one of the ordinary guest rooms and there would be no special provisions made for him. To all eyes and minds beyond the confines of this room he would remain simply a sailor rescued from shipwreck and enjoying the castle's hospitality until he had fully recovered from his ordeal.

Sen, in a tone of awed respect that Karuth had thought alien to his nature, had asked if they might be told the reason for the lord of Order's decision. Keeping such a secret, he pointed out, would be far from easy, and there was also the question of maintaining morale among the Circle. Surely it would be to the greater good if the other adepts knew that their prayers had been answered? Karuth remembered the exact words of Ailind's reply, and the tone in which they had been spoken, as though they were etched in her mind: "I appreciate your point, Sen, but my order will stand. The fewer who know of my presence here, the better our purpose will be served. I see no reason why your fellow adepts' morale should suffer if their faith in their gods is as genuine as they profess."

His statement had angered Karuth then, and it angered her afresh now. She understood and accepted the need to ensure that no hint of Ailind's identity should reach the ears of the usurper's envoy when he arrived, but the sting in the tail of the god's words had shocked her, for they implied that this was also a deliberate test of the Circle's fidelity. The lords of Order expected everyone in the castle, barring this small nucleus, to maintain unquestioning trust in them, yet without the comfort of knowing that their prayers had been answered. That struck Karuth as being cold, calculating, and—yes, she'd use the word again, arrogant. Did the gods really feel such contempt for their worshipers? she asked herself bitterly. Was it really more important to try the adepts' loyalty than to unite with them in defending the world against the menace that Ygorla posed to them all? Surely, she thought, *surely* Aeoris and his brothers couldn't be so petty?

She realized suddenly that she was nearing her destination and, with an effort, thrust her gloomy speculations aside for more mundane matters. Ahead of her the corridor ended in a short flight of steps; Karuth skimmed down them and entered the main kitchen. As always the great, vaulted chamber was hot, damp, hazy with steam, and bustling with activity. She sought out one of the cooks and ordered a tray to be made ready, then waited while it was prepared, trying not to catch anyone else's eye. Her manner must have indicated her mood, for to her relief no one approached her, and a few minutes later she left the kitchen with her laden, covered tray carefully balanced in both hands.

To her relief she reached her chambers without encountering any of the other adepts. She closed the door and bolted it, then set about lighting candles before crossing to the window. The gale had blown itself out earlier in the evening, taking the rain and hail with it, and the night was cold and cloudy but calm. Karuth closed the curtains, returned to where she had set down the tray, and lifted away the cloth. There was an appetizing selection of the head cook's best delicacies; desultorily, almost absently, she picked up a spiced and roasted fowl's leg, took a bite, then put it down again. She wasn't hungry, couldn't face the food, however good it might be. There was a wine flask on her bedside table; she filled a cup, drained it, filled it again, and carried it to her fireside, where she sat down in a chair and stared into the flames.

She felt, Karuth realized, desperately lonely. No, more than that; she felt *isolated,* not by her own will, but by circumstances beyond her control. In the first uneasy days after her original quarrel with Tirand, her position in the Circle had hung in the balance. Recently that balance had begun to tilt back a little in her favor as time soothed the worst of the wounds and the rift showed the first signs of healing, but in the few hours since Ailind's arrival everything had changed. Suddenly she was the maverick again, the rogue beast in the herd, the only one whose views didn't accord with those of the majority—and suddenly that mattered in a way it had never done before.

She'd already tasted the chill wine—not a very apt simile, she thought as she drank more, but it would have to do—of Ailind's contempt for her. He'd made it clear that he knew what was in her heart, just as he'd made it clear that he wouldn't tolerate any attempt on her part to step out of line. And Tirand: she had seen his feelings clearly in his eyes; doubt and disapproval mingled with fear, both for her and for himself, and underlying it a sullen kind of resentment that without the lifelong ties of blood kinship to temper it might have bordered on hatred. The others, too: at the meeting her fellow adepts hadn't addressed a single direct word to her, and several times she'd seen the Matriarch watching her obliquely, her eyes betraying shame and pity in equal measure. Even Calvi, whom she counted as one of her dearest friends, had sat studiously avoiding her gaze, his shoulders hunched guiltily as he turned his head from her.

Well, she thought, so be it. They had pledged themselves wholly to Ailind, and she could hardly blame them for that. But she wouldn't pretend, she wouldn't perjure herself to gain favor. Besides, what would be the point?

She might hide the truth from other mortals, but she couldn't hide it from a god. Provided she obeyed Ailind's dictum and bowed to his will, she'd suffer nothing worse than the sting of his contempt, and she couldn't bring herself to care about that.

She looked into her cup, saw that it was almost empty, and rose to fill it again. This time she took the flask back to her chair and set it by the fire; the wine was strong and already starting to affect her, but she was too depressed to care whether she was drunk or sober. The trouble was, she thought, the trouble was, she didn't *want* to bow to Ailind's will. Not through deluded pride but because the old doubt was still raging in her, the feeling that the Circle had made a fundamental and terrible mistake. She couldn't believe Chaos had broken its pact. She *didn't* believe it. She wanted—she drank again, draining the cup for the third time—she wanted Equilibrium, the Equilibrium of her childhood catechisms, the Equilibrium that was the fulcrum of all the Circle's power and ritual, to be restored before it was too late.

More wine splashed into the cup but her hand was unsteady now, and she spilled almost as much again onto her skirt. What would Ailind think of her now? she wondered, and wanted to laugh as she took another long swallow. Ailind and Tirand and Calvi and Shaill, and all her students, and all the lower-ranking adepts who were—or had been in the past—fool enough to look up to her. What would they think if they could see her sitting here alone, drinking her way steadily toward stupefaction? Doubtless . . . gods, her head felt as though it were filled with feathers . . . doubtless they'd tell each other sagely that this was only to be expected of one who had been hoodwinked by the machinations of Chaos. Chaos, the renegers, the betrayers, the—

"Ohhh . . ." Karuth put the near-empty cup down with a thump on the floor and stood up. The room around her looked unreal, its perspectives out of kilter, and she walked unsteadily to the window and flung it open, breathing in lungfuls of cold night air. Fool she was, *fool.* All brave words and no deeds, piss and wind, to quote a favorite vulgarity of her old teacher, Carnon Imbro. Whatever her private feelings might be, she wouldn't step out of line. She'd had that chance once and spurned it, and now it was too late. She would obey her High Initiate, obey Ailind, do all the things that were expected or demanded of her. After all, who was she to judge what was right and what was wrong? Just an ordinary adept, unimportant, expendable, and to expect anything more was to hold a dangerously deluded opinion of herself. The lords of Order had answered the Circle's plea, and one of their number was here in the castle. The help that they so desperately needed had been granted to them. Wasn't that what she, as much as any of her fellow adepts, had wanted, and shouldn't she be grateful that they now had a powerful ally in the war against Ygorla? The gods had sent one of their own to the mortal world to destroy the sorceress, and she should rejoice, not sit drunkenly sulking and carping because they were not the gods she would have chosen to call upon.

The cold air was clearing her head a little, but it was also chilling her to the marrow. She shut the window, turning back to the room and rubbing her upper arms, then picked up her cup once more and finished its contents, more as a gesture of defiance than for any other reason. But defiance of whom? Ailind? No: if that were true, then she'd leave this room now and stride to the east wing where he doubtless sat making his plans—of which he'd so far revealed so tantalizingly little—and tell him that she wouldn't dance to his tune. She wasn't about to do that, because whatever she might wish to believe to the contrary, she feared him just as much as Tirand and Calvi and Shaill did. If she was defying anyone or anything, Karuth admitted miserably, she was defying her own conscience for the sake of cowardice.

She lifted the wine flagon but found it empty. Not sure whether to be disappointed or relieved, she put both it and the drained cup with her untouched meal and draped the tray-cloth over the whole mess, hiding it from sight until a servant should clear it away in the morning. Her eyelids were heavy, and she was still viewing the room with a drunkard's distorted perspective; the only sensible thing, it seemed, was to close her mental shutters on this dreary day and hope that the morning would bring some improvement.

Too tired and dispirited to complete her customary preparations, Karuth did no more than bank down the fire before taking off her gown and climbing into bed in her smallclothes. The room swayed and heaved beyond her closed eyelids, but after a while weariness triumphed over her reeling senses and she fell asleep.

She dreamed that night that Calvi came knocking at her door, summoning her to a medical emergency. With his figure oddly wraithlike ahead of her and moving too fast for her to catch, she ran through the castle's deserted corridors to her own infirmary, where the corpse of Ygorla Morys's long-dead mother sat up from a blood-stained couch and opened her eyelids to reveal two spheres of solid, glittering brass and said, in Tirand's voice, *Do you no longer kneel before your gods, Karuth Piadar?* Beside the corpse stood Carnon Imbro, and he wagged a stern finger at her as he told her to repeat the names of the febrifuges in order of their potency or give up her life, give up her life, give up her life. Karuth fled from the infirmary and ran through more endless, unlit corridors, until far ahead down a long, sloping and ever-narrowing passage she saw the glimmer of light that told her she had almost reached the Marble Hall; and there before the silver door stood the old High Initiate from her childhood days, Keridil Toln, smiling and beckoning to her. In her mind a voice screamed, *No, it isn't Keridil, it's something else, something evil,* and she tried to stop her headlong rush, but her feet continued to move, and the finger continued to beckon, and a black, deadly shadow was emanating from Keridil's feet and stretching across the floor toward her.

And all the while, like a mad musical counterpoint, a disembodied and horribly familiar voice, yet one to which she couldn't put a name, had been laughing at her and laughing at her and *laughing* at her.

17

The first heavy snowfall of the winter started nine days later. Clouds had been massing to the north and moving slowly in from the sea, and on the afternoon of the eighth day the strong coastal winds dropped and the atmosphere became eerily still. By dusk the heavy overcast was almost colorless but for a faint pinkish-purple tinge, and shortly after midnight the slow and silent white fall began.

By morning the Star Peninsula had been transformed. Snow covered the clifftops, contrasting starkly with the black, vertical rock faces and the iron-gray sea beyond, and the West High Land mountains to the south of the castle stack were dim, white ghosts glimpsed through the snow's veils. The Matriarch, waking earlier even than the castle servants, broke the crust of ice on the washing-bowl in her bedchamber, then looked through her frost-rimmed window at the bleak, colorless dawn and smiled wryly to herself. Unless the usurper's envoy had wings, there would be no procession arriving at the castle now. Once these snows began, the mountain roads became impassable within a matter of hours, and only a madman would attempt to get through. With an innate sense of charity, even toward enemies, she hoped that the ambassador hadn't made the mistake of trying to outrun the weather only to become trapped in the passes. That wasn't a fate she would wish on anyone.

Busy with her preparations for the day, she didn't see the small disturbance in the air, the flutter of insubstantial white wings out of the mountains and across the rock bridge that separated the castle stack from the mainland. But other eyes saw, and as the air elemental skimmed over the outer wall and flickered down to the deserted court-yard, a figure emerged from the main doors and walked down the steps to meet it.

Impervious to cold, Ailind wore only a thin silk shirt and trousers, and the snow as it fell didn't touch him. He held up one arm commandingly, and the elemental flew to his hand. A sweet singing note emanated from it; Ailind nodded, said softly, "You have done well, small servant. You may go," and a rainbow of colors shimmered briefly in the air about him as the being vanished.

He turned and looked back at the castle. There was a light in the window of Tirand's study: well and good; if the High Initiate was up and about, then there would be no need to stir curiosity by sending a servant to rouse him from his bed. Ailind walked quickly back up the steps and through the main hall to Tirand's door. He didn't knock, but lifted the latch and went in, startling Tirand, who was crouched by the grate trying to coax the recalcitrant fire into life.

Tirand scrambled to his feet, recovered his composure hastily, and bowed. "Good morning, my lord." He just stopped himself from adding, "I trust you slept well"—Ailind, he knew, did not sleep.

"High Initiate." Ailind closed the door and wasted no time with preamble. "You'd best make ready your reception party. The sorceress's envoy will be at the gates within two hours."

Tirand stared at him in astonishment. *"Today?* But the snow must already have cut off the mountain passes!"

"To a human convoy, perhaps. But the elemental I set to keep watch informs me that our visitor travels by less orthodox means." The lord of Order glanced around the room. "Tell your steward to fetch the High Margrave and the Matriarch. I wish to speak to them briefly before you alert the senior adepts."

"My steward's confined to his bed with the winter rheum, my lord—that's why I'm reduced to lighting my own fire. I'll fetch Calvi and Shaill myself, if you'll do me the honor of waiting."

"Yes, yes. But we'd be well advised to waste no time."

Tirand bowed again and hurried out. As the door closed behind him, Ailind looked at the room, which showed signs of neglect, then at the hearth and the troublesome fire, which was in danger of going out altogether. His golden-brown eyes narrowed slightly, and the fuel in the grate flared suddenly into life, flames crackling and sending sparks dancing up the chimney. The god crossed the floor to Tirand's chair, fastidiously brushed a thin film of dust from it, and sat down to wait.

Strann knew that his first sight of the Star Peninsula and the Circle's stronghold should have been an awe-inspiring experience, but as he sat in his mount's saddle and stared through the swirling snowfall at the titanic vista stretching away from the mountains' feet, he felt nothing but a cold, dead aching in his soul. In the wake of all that he'd been through on his journey, not even this had the power to move him now.

The creature he was riding shifted restlessly beneath him, and he checked it with an unnecessarily vicious jerk on the reins. He'd come to loathe it, and couldn't even bear to look at it unless circumstances forced him to. He'd rather have ridden any sway-backed, broken-winded, but flesh-and-blood nag, even if it had collapsed under him in the pass and left him to die, than be shackled to this tireless monster of Ygorla's creation to which no mortal obstacles provided any bar. As for his companions . . . his mouth jerked in a mirthless spasm at the inopportune word. Demons, elementals; he didn't know what they were and he'd barely addressed a word to them, or they to him, since they had all disembarked from the black ship in Shu-Nhadek harbor under the horrified gazes of the townsfolk.

Reflexively, not thinking, he tried to clench his right hand in its purple gauntlet before he remembered that the nerves were severed and dead and could no longer control the stumps of his fingers. Memories were crowding into his mind like a pack of vicious hounds closing on their quarry, memories of things he had seen and things he had heard and things he had felt as his party progressed through the provinces on their way north. Villages where misshapen elementals patrolled the streets by day and fed on the unwary after darkness fell; towns where the militia had vanished overnight and Ygorla's unhuman servants held sway over a terrified populace; curfews, depradations, destruction, savagery . . . and he'd ridden silently through the midst of it all, his escort cleaving the way just like a harvester scythed corn. A triumphal procession of the Empress's own ambassador and his monstrous personal guard: how many hundreds, how many *thousands* of strained and stricken faces had watched Strann the Turncoat, Sir Rat, ride loftily by? And there had been nothing he could say, nothing he could do, either to help them or to exonerate himself. All he had was the burning rage within him, the rage that had no outlet but that never loosened its grip.

His companions were waiting. He could feel the heat of their stares boring into his back as his mount continued to fidget. The snow was falling heavily and steadily in the windless air, soaking his cloak and hood and making them cling clammily to his body. Ahead of him was the castle, his goal, black and forbidding and showing no signs of life but for a few thin plumes of smoke rising against the snowfall. Those great gates might never open to admit him, or if they did, he might step through them onto the point of a sword and end his life without a word spoken. But at this moment, weary and frozen and sick to the pit of his soul, Strann didn't care. Whatever fate might be in store for him on the Star Peninsula, it would at least be clean.

He flicked the reins with his unscathed left hand and felt the now-familiar fluid ripple of abnormal muscles as his mount started to move down the gentle slope. Silently his escort fell in behind him, leaving no prints in the snow in their wake. They reached the twin stone cairns that marked the way onto the rock bridge, and again they halted. Still there was no reaction from the castle—and suddenly Strann swung his feet from his stirrups and dismounted. He threw the reins aside, spoke a savage warning to his mount as it made to follow him, and walked to the cliff edge.

He could jump, fall with the snowflakes, and in a matter of seconds it would over once and for all. Yandros wouldn't pluck him out of the air before he hit the sea and the rocks far below, and then Ygorla and her legions and all the demons and gods in this realm and any other could do as they pleased and it wouldn't matter to him. But the thought was sheer bravado; Strann knew he would no more step off that dizzying edge than cut his own throat. Suicide took sterner resolve than he possessed—and besides, he hadn't yet reached the utter nadir of wanting to die.

But he *did* want to be rid of his shackles. He stepped back from the edge and turned to face his escort, narrowing his eyes against the snow that swirled into his face and forcing himself to look directly at them.

"Go back." He put all the authority he could muster into his voice, at the same gesturing southward. "Your part in this is over, and now I must go on alone. Return to your—to our Empress and report that I have reached my destination safely."

The escort leader had white, hollow eyes but no nose and no mouth; one of its fellows, lipless and toothless but able to create sounds, answered for it in a flat voice.

"We have no such order from the Empress. Without an order, we must remain."

"*I* am giving you the order!" Strann held up his ruined hand, showing Ygorla's sigil embroidered on the glove he wore. "What is this—your Empress's seal or a child's scrawl? I am her envoy, and I command you in her name. Your presence here might well jeopardize my mission, and if that should happen, then you will have the Empress's wrath to contend with. Is that what you want? No, I thought not. Go back to the White Isle!"

They hesitated, but Strann had taken their measure

well. They weren't truly intelligent but had been created only to serve, and with no clear directions from Ygorla herself—and the added threat of incurring her displeasure —they were constrained at last to obey Strann's order. He waited while, with maddening slowness, they unloaded his baggage and set it down beside him, then he harshly repeated his order and watched as they turned and went away, taking his riderless mount with him. Then, when the mountain foothills had hidden them from view, Strann turned his face once more to the castle. He ignored the bags that his guards had set so carefully by his feet. He didn't want Ygorla's silks and laces; he wanted nothing that would taint him with her influence, and would have been tempted, had the weather been kinder, to strip off even the clothes he was wearing and walk naked to the Circle's gates. The one thing he did want was not there: his manzon. She had kept that of course. Not that he had any use for it now. . . .

He hugged his cloak more tightly around him, pulled the cowl closely about his face, and stepped onto the rock bridge. It was wider than it looked, but he still took care not to glance down over the edge at the sea surging hundreds—perhaps even thousands—of feet below as he began to walk toward the stack. The castle loomed closer, its four spires dominating the sky now above the forbidding black wall. Still no movement, still no sign that his presence had been noted. Perhaps, Strann thought, the Circle didn't intend to waste time parleying and he'd be felled by a well-aimed arrow as he stepped onto the stack's sward. Or perhaps by something more emphatic: a single bolt of power to convey the clear message to Ygorla that her emissary was unwelcome. He didn't know the Circle's powers, didn't know if they were capable of such a thing, but his heart beat hard and painfully and he quickened his steps, feeling vulnerable and more than a little afraid.

No arrow came, and no power-bolt. He reached the end of the bridge, and there less than thirty yards from him were the castle's gates. Strann paused to catch his breath, but only for a moment. Paradoxical it might be, but he'd feel safer once he was under the shelter of those towering walls and therefore out of range of any archers who might be hidden on the battlements.

He approached the daunting facade—and when he was twenty paces from it, he heard the deep, rumbling grind of wood on stone and the gates began to swing open. Strann stopped, sweat breaking out on his face despite the bitter cold, as slowly a dark archway was revealed. He could see nothing in its shadows, and though a courtyard was just visible beyond the arch, the falling snow blurred any detail. *Yandros,* Strann thought desperately, *if you can hear me and if you can help me, I beg you, help me now!*

He moved forward. Ten paces, fifteen, twenty; he was walking under the arch now, and still there was no challenge, no threat, nothing. He could see the courtyard more clearly; snow-covered and with an ornately carved fountain dormant at its center, it appeared to be quite deserted. Strann slowed as he reached the arch's far mouth. He was reluctant to step out, afraid to show himself—but what had he to fear? There was no one there. Only the empty courtyard, rows of lightless windows, and beyond the silent fountain a flight of wide and shallow steps leading up to double doors, closed and, presumably, barred.

Strann hadn't expected this. He'd anticipated at best wary hostility, at worst outright aggression, but this was something for which he'd made no contingency. Someone, he thought, clenching his teeth as they threatened to start chattering in his skull, was playing with him. Very well, he'd join in the game. He'd walk past that fountain and up those steps, and he'd hammer on the barred doors and shout until they couldn't ignore him any longer.

Fired by a sudden wild rush of adrenaline that gave him reckless confidence, he strode across the courtyard, past the fountain, toward the steps. By all the Seven Hells, he hadn't made this monstrous journey only to—

The thought was cut off, and Strann jumped with shock as the double doors above him were flung open. Light flared as seven men carrying burning torches rushed from within, and behind them came some dozen more, each wearing a Circle adept's badge and each armed with a drawn sword. They spread out, forming a menacing arc at the top of the steps, with the torchbearers flanking the doorway, their brands burning with eerie steadiness despite the falling snow. Then three more figures walked out of the castle and stopped on the threshold. The torches' flickering light flung their shadows before them over the snow, and a voice that Strann recognized and that echoed between the high black walls said sternly, "Come forward, and identify yourself!"

Strann didn't move, didn't speak. He wasn't capable: all he could do was stare up, with his heart contracting to an agonizing stone in his chest, at the trio confronting him at the top of the steps.

He knew them all, and in his direst nightmares he had never imagined that he would face such an ordeal of shame as this. Shaill Falada, the Matriarch, who had once been his patroness; but in silver ceremonial garb, forbidding and stern. Calvi Alacar—oh gods, the young brother of the murdered Blis and now High Margrave in his own right, transformed from a carefree youth into an angry man with smoldering sea-chill eyes. And between them, his rank denoted only by the simple badge at his right shoulder and by the thin bronze circlet on his brow, the High Initiate, Tirand Lin. Not the wedding celebrant he'd met on Summer Isle, not even Karuth's brother radiating disapproval of an opportunistic jongleur, but stone-faced, implacable, and carrying an aura of immense and dangerous power.

Strann's bard's skills failed him, his planned speech fled from his mind. Somewhere an inner voice was shouting at him, telling him not to be a fool; this was a charade, a show put on to intimidate one whom they believed to be Ygorla's loyal servant, and all he had to do was *tell* them, explain—

"We are waiting, envoy." Tirand's voice cut through the babble in Strann's head. Clutching the cowl of his cloak, desperate that they shouldn't yet see his face, he at last gained control of his tongue.

"High Initiate . . ." He saw the Matriarch frown in surprise, and knew that she had recognized his voice even if she hadn't yet put a name to it. Gods, he couldn't couch this in fine words; there wasn't time, it couldn't work, he wasn't *capable*—

Yandros, help me, Strann thought for the second time, and flung caution to the winds. "High Initiate," he said, "I am not the usurper's puppet, whatever appearances might suggest. She sent me here to dupe you into believing that she wishes to make a pact with the Circle—but I've come instead to ask your protection, and your help in destroying her! Sir, you *must* believe me—"

The Matriarch's voice interrupted him. "Throw back your hood," she said sharply. "Let us see what manner of creature you are."

Strann hesitated for a moment, then, realizing that he could put the moment off no longer, pushed the cowl from his face. The Matriarch drew in a sharp breath, and Tirand's expression froze.

"I know you—I've seen your face somewhere before—"

Shaill caught hold of his arm. "It's Strann! Strann the Storymaker! Don't you remember, Tirand, at Blis's wedding?"

"Gods . . . you're right. It *is* him—or a clever simulacrum."

Strann's cheeks were flaming. "I'm no simulacrum, High Initiate, and no demon. I'm as human as anyone here."

Tirand's lip curled. "We'll check the truth of that for ourselves." Behind him, no more than a deeper shadow among the shadows of the interior, someone moved. Strann had a momentary glimpse of pale hair, but then he was distracted as the High Initiate pointed a finger at him and spoke five harsh syllables. A hot shock went through Strann, and he bit his tongue to stop himself from crying out. After a moment the sensation vanished, and as he stood swaying in its aftermath, Tirand nodded.

"Very well." He glanced at the armed adepts flanking the doors. "It would appear that he is human after all. Bind him and bring him inside."

Two heavyset swordsmen left the group and ran down the steps toward Strann. As they grabbed his arms and started to manhandle him toward the doors, he protested angrily. "Damn it, let go of me—I'm not about to resist you! I'm not even armed, you can see that for yourselves!"

The adepts ignored him, and as Tirand and his companions turned back inside the castle, they followed, hus-

tling Strann along between them. The great entrance hall
was unlit and gloomy, and to his chagrin Strann saw that
a great many more people were gathered there. Strangers'
faces, hard-set and hostile, watched him in silent curiosity
tinted with a good measure of contempt, and when he was
halted in the middle of the flagstoned floor, he thought
that he knew a little of how a condemned man must feel as
he was led to the public gallows or a market-square ston-
ing post.

One of his captors produced a short length of cord and
started to tie his wrists behind his back. Strann opened his
mouth to object, but thought better of it; for now passive
acquiescence was a safer option. Miserably he wondered if
Karuth Piadar was among the watching crowd, but
though he scanned the faces all around him, he saw no
sign of her and wasn't sure whether to feel dismayed or
thankful. One face, however, did catch his attention, for
reasons that he couldn't fathom: a white-haired man, with
a paradoxically young face and eyes that in the dim light
looked almost bronze. His gaze was intent, disconcertingly
steady, and with an intuitive shudder Strann looked
swiftly away.

The High Initiate turned around. He raked Strann
with a single glance that was more eloquent than any
words of condemnation and said to the two adepts, "Put
him in one of the cellars for the time being, until we've
decided what to do with him."

"No!" Strann cried out. "High Initiate, you don't understand! I have urgent news for you—"

"From your evil bitch of a mistress? Her edicts are of
no interest to us."

"Not from Ygorla! I'm trying to tell you, I'm not her

servant. I'm as much her enemy as you are, though she doesn't know it!"

"If you seriously expect us to believe that," Tirand said scornfully, "you must be as mad as she is!"

Strann gritted his teeth in an effort to keep his voice even. "I'm not mad, sir, and I am *not* the usurper's puppet." He turned in appeal to the Matriarch. "Madam, you know me well enough. Do I have it in me to be a traitor?"

Shaill stared back at him. "I don't know, Strann," she said, her tone cold and remote. "Men can be driven by all manner of motives, and you were always an opportunist."

Strann's jaw dropped, but before he could speak, Tirand intervened. "Shaill, we've nothing to gain from allowing ourselves to be drawn into an argument with scum like this. We're simply wasting time that could be put to a better use." He nodded again to Strann's captors. "Take him to the cellars, as I ordered."

Appalled both by Shaill's answer and by Tirand's blind prejudice, Strann made a last, desperate effort to get through to him. "High Initiate—please, just hear me out! Give me the chance to explain, to tell you what I have to say."

"You'll have your chance to speak at a later stage, when you're interrogated," Tirand said dismissively. "Until then, you'd be well advised to hold your tongue."

"But this can't wait!" Gods, Strann thought, would nothing sway this stiff-necked man? For all he knew, he'd be forgotten and left to rot in the castle cellars. He *must* make the High Initiate listen!

Tirand smiled at him, not pleasantly. "It will have to wait, my friend." Before Strann could say another word, he turned and walked away, with the Matriarch and High Margrave at his heels. The crowd of watchers parted for them, and they disappeared as Strann's two guards turned him around and pulled him in the opposite direction.

There was nothing Strann could do. He craned his head back as the adepts propelled him out of the hall and into a narrow passage, but Tirand was already far out of earshot, and besides, it was obvious that any further appeal would have been as useless as the first. He shut his eyes briefly, forcing down the meld of fury, frustration, and self-condemnation he felt at his own failure. There was no point in railing; that would achieve nothing. He must bide his time, wait, *think.* There had to be a way out of this predicament.

Ahead of them the passage was intersected by an arch, beyond which one of the castle's many secondary staircases spiraled to the upper floor. As they walked past the arch, footsteps clattered on the stairs and two women appeared around the last curve of the spiral. Strann, reflexively glancing in their direction, saw braided brown hair, gray eyes, a familiar face—

"Lady Karuth!"

Karuth had missed the furor of the envoy's arrival, for the pregnant wife of a third-rank adept had chosen this morning to give birth, and the labor had been difficult, necessitating her personal attention. All was now well and the mother and child comfortable, and she and the castle's senior midwife had been on their way to the dining hall for a late but well-earned breakfast. Now, surprised by the sound of a half-remembered voice so urgently calling her name, she looked up—and stopped so abruptly that the midwife only just avoided colliding with her and knocking her down the remaining steps.

"Strann?"

Strann swallowed. He was acutely, if irrelevantly,

aware of the dismal sight he must present to her, wet and
bedraggled and with his hands bound behind him like
some felonious peasant, and felt his cheeks prickle with
shame as he met her shocked stare. For a moment Karuth
was motionless, then she collected her wits and focused an
angry gaze on the two adepts.

"What in the name of all that's sacred is going on?"

The men shrank visibly at her aggressive tone. They
were both junior initiates, and Karuth's rank awed them.
One recovered sufficient confidence to make a bow and
said, "This is the usurper's emissary, madam. The High
Initiate ordered us to secure him in one of the cellars."

"He did *what*? Do you know this man's name—do you
know who he *is*?"

The adept looked nonplussed. "No, madam; only that
he's the usurper's—"

"Of course he's not the usurper's envoy!" Karuth's
voice snapped across his, cutting him off. "This is Strann
—one of our most noted bards, and a Master of my own
Musicians' Guild!"

"But, lady, he *is* the envoy," the adept persisted helplessly. "He admits it himself."

Karuth stared at Strann, suddenly confused. "Strann,
what do they mean? There must be some mistake!"

Strann took a deep breath. "There's no mistake, Lady
Karuth. The sorceress did send me here as her ambassador, but that's only the beginning of a long and unpleasant
story." He glanced sidelong at his captors. "I tried to explain to the High Initiate, but he wasn't in a mood to
listen."

Karuth's mouth pursed. "I see." Behind her the midwife was listening, agog with interest; she turned and said
pleasantly but firmly, "Go on to the dining hall without

287

me, Shuanye. I may be delayed for a while." Reluctantly the woman left them, and as she disappeared, Karuth returned her attention to the adepts. "Release him," she said.

They looked at her in consternation. "Madam, the High Initiate ordered—"

"Good gods, man, are you a complete fool? He's soaked through and shivering like a cur in a thunderstorm. Take him to the cellars in this state and he'll probably be dead by this time tomorrow! As the castle's physician I will *not* permit such barbaric disregard for his health. Cut his bonds. I'll take charge of him myself, and if the High Initiate objects, you may refer him to me!"

A little sheepishly the adepts acquiesced. Karuth stood watching sternly as they cut the cord binding Strann's wrists, then dismissed them, silencing any further protest they might have made with a dire warning look. As they hurried away, she turned at last to Strann.

"I suspect," she said with some irony, "that you have a long tale to tell. But my first priority is to find you a change of clothes and a hot, restorative drink. Come with me."

She started away along the corridor, but Strann hung back. Her tone troubled him; she seemed distant, wary, almost hostile. He hadn't expected that, and he said hesitantly, "Lady Karuth . . ."

Karuth turned around. "What is it?" Yes, he was right. She didn't trust him; he could see it reflected in her eyes, and it hurt. It *hurt.*

He said helplessly, "You don't believe that I'm a traitor? Not you. You surely can't believe that . . . ?"

She hesitated. She still hadn't entirely recovered from the shock of seeing him here in the castle and of learning the reason for his presence, and the feelings that this unexpected meeting had awaked in her were contradictory and uncertain. "I don't know, Strann," she said at last. "I hope and pray you're not, but I can't be sure." A muscle worked spasmodically in her jaw. "I ordered your release because it's my duty as a physician to protect your health, and . . . I suppose also for the sake of old times. But don't assume that I'm necessarily on your side. For all I can tell, I might be making the greatest mistake of my life."

She walked on, leaving Strann to follow her.

18

Sanquar looked up as Karuth entered the infirmary, and smiled. "Is it all over?"

"Yes, and the child safely delivered, thanks be. But I have a new patient to attend to." Karuth moved aside, allowing her assistant to see Strann standing behind her.

If Sanquar was surprised by the newcomer's disheveled appearance, he hid it well, making only a slight but formal bow in Strann's direction. Karuth crossed the room, beckoning Strann after her. "My first priority is to give him a change of clothes. You're both of a height and similarly built; could you lend him something that might suffice?"

"Of course." Sanquar looked Strann up and down again, this time with franker curiosity. "I'll go to my quarters and see what I can find."

He left the room, and Karuth went to the largest of the infirmary's store cupboards. Her back was turned to Strann, and the set of her shoulders was tense. Strann watched her uneasily. He wanted to tell his story but didn't know where to begin. Every approach he could think of seemed too glib and as likely to deepen her mistrust as to assuage it, and for once his bard's skills weren't coming to his rescue.

Karuth took an armful of towels from the cupboard, then shut the door with a bang that made Strann jump.

"Come over here and sit down," she said briskly, crossing the room to where a fire burned in the grate. "I'll set these to warm, and when Sanquar returns, you can change out of your wet clothes." Silently he did as she bade him, and she moved to a table by the window. "I'll give you a cup of wine with a restorative draft."

"Thank you." Strann's voice was dull, and he stared into the flames. He felt bereft. He'd shrunk before Tirand's contempt, shriveled under the Matriarch's hostility, but their enmity had been nothing less than he could have expected. With Karuth he'd believed it might be different, and the condemnation implicit in her voice and her manner was like an iron spike through his soul. Before anyone else he might have dissembled, put on an act to gain sympathy and trusted his powers of deception to win them over. But he couldn't attempt such a ploy with her. He had too much respect for her, and that only added to his own sense of shame.

She returned and held out a brimming cup. Unthinkingly Strann reached for it with his gloved right hand before he remembered and hastily took it with his left. "Thank you," he said again, and sipped desultorily at the drink.

Karuth stared down at him, then suddenly her own warm nature and the old memories of their previous happy encounter came to the surface, breaking through the barriers of suspicion and defensiveness.

"Oh, Strann, I can hardly believe that I'm seeing you in such a condition!" She dropped to a crouch before him and, like a mother confronted by a bedraggled and unhappy child, unfastened the clasp of his cloak and helped him to pull it off. "You're thin, you're pale, you look ill—when did you last eat?"

He shrugged awkwardly; he hadn't had much stomach for food on his journey. "I'm not sure. Yesterday morning, I think."

"Then that must be rectified."

"No." He spoke more sharply than he'd intended to, and made an apologetic gesture. "Thank you, but I'm not hungry."

Karuth's professional instincts told her that there was a good deal more to this than met the eye. "Well, we'll see about that later." She took the cloak away from him and folded it. "Take off your boots and gloves. They must be soaked through; you can at least dry your feet and hands while we wait for Sanquar."

Strann set the wine-cup down and, one-handed, pulled the boots from his feet. She gathered them up. "I'll put them to dry. And the gloves, if you'll give them to me."

"No," Strann said pallidly. "No—it's all right; I'll keep them on for the moment. My hands are still cold."

"That's hardly surprising, with those sodden gauntlets covering them!" Karuth paused as she saw his expression. "Strann? Strann, what is it, what's the matter?"

"Nothing." Chill sweat had broken out on Strann's face and torso. He didn't want her to find out the truth, didn't want her to see it with her own eyes. "I'm all right."

Suddenly Karuth reached out and gripped his left hand. He tensed violently at her touch, and her eyes narrowed. "What's wrong?" she demanded.

Strann prepared to make another denial, then realized that it would be pointless. She already suspected something; she hadn't missed his mistake with the wine-cup or the fact that he'd used only one hand to take off his boots. He'd hidden it from the world, hoping that by doing so he might also hide it from himself and not have to face or dwell on what it meant to him, but now that he was in the castle, that couldn't go on. It simply wasn't practicable.

He said quietly, "Very well." Gently freeing his hand from her grasp, he pulled the left gauntlet off with his teeth. Karuth frowned. "What's the matter with your—?"

Strann took off the right glove. There was silence. Then: *"Yandros . . ."* Karuth got to her feet and turned away, pushing a clenched fist against her mouth. Her rib cage heaved, then she swung around again.

"Who did it?" Her voice was savage.

"Ygorla." Strann picked up the cup again and drank deeply. "It's her insurance against any disloyal notions I might otherwise entertain."

"But your music—" The words caught in Karuth's throat and she couldn't finish.

"Please," he said, "don't remind me. I know."

With difficulty she recovered her composure. "How did she do it?"

"Fire," Strann told her. "Not natural fire of course. That would have been too straightforward—simple tortures don't hold much amusement for her." He turned his wrist, looking at the ugly mess with cold detachment. "I suppose I should be thankful that it's no longer painful. Not physically, anyway."

She bent swiftly toward him. "Let me examine it. It might be possible to—"

"No." He withdrew the ruined stump from her reach before she could finish. "There's no point, lady; no mortal physician could repair this damage."

"You can't be sure of that."

"Oh, but I can. She told me herself that only she has the power to reverse it, and for once I believe her." He looked up, the hand that held the wine-cup shaking slightly. "I don't think that you or the High Initiate or anyone else in the Circle has any idea of the true extent of Ygorla's power."

Karuth cast her gaze down. "We've had a small taste of it, but nothing like this." Then abruptly she focused again on his face, her eyes burning with anger. "Strann, how by all the fourteen gods did you come to such a pass? I *can't* believe you're a traitor, whatever I might have said earlier —but to be in the usurper's service, as her ambassador, after what she did to you—I don't *understand!*"

Strann sighed. Ironically the ruined hand had achieved what no words could have done. The sight of it had overcome Karuth's hostility, and now he had the all-important chance to tell his story to a sympathetic ear. There was little doubt that he could convince her of his sincerity now, he thought bitterly. Ygorla had at least done that much for him.

He said, "It's a long and tedious tale. For the moment I'll just say that I had the simple choice between dying quickly and unpleasantly or inveigling myself into her court and her favor. But I must tell you this; She's not only a threat to the mortal world but a threat to the realms of the gods as well. And especially to the realm of Chaos."

"To Chaos?" Karuth became very still. "Whatever do you mean?"

Strann drew breath. Enough time had already been wasted since his arrival here; he had to explain concisely but accurately—and she would have to make her brother listen in his turn. With intense relief he realized that the

wine he'd drunk was starting to drive out the numbness
that cold and misery had imposed on him. His head was
clearer, his mind sharper, and the urgency of the situation
was asserting itself once more.

"Karuth," he said, dropping the formal title for the
first time, "The usurper believes that I mean to use my
skills as a bard and a diplomat to persuade the Circle to
open its gates to her. But I'm not her loyal servant, nor
her slave, nor her pet rat, as it amuses her to call me. I
have a different purpose—a message to deliver" He
looked hard at her. "From Yandros."

"What?"

"I know it's hard to believe. Sometimes I can barely
credit it myself, but I swear to you on whatever sanctity's
left in this world that it's the truth. I've stood as close to
Yandros as I sit to you now, and I've spoken with him.
I'm *his* ambassador, not Ygorla's."

Karuth's hands had begun to shake. "Strann, I don't
understand this. How did Yandros make contact with
you?"

Strann grinned mirthlessly. "You'll find this even more
difficult to accept. I performed a ritual—very ineptly—to
call on him for help, and he answered."

Karuth uttered a soft oath and stood up, pacing across
the room. "He answered . . . he simply *appeared* to
you?"

"Yes."

She suppressed a peculiar sound that might have been
either a groan or a snort of bemused laughter, then suddenly sobered and turned to face him once more. "But this
sorceress is also Yandros's servant, isn't she? We've been
told that the Seven-Rayed Star hangs above the Summer

Isle palace, and we know she styles herself 'Daughter of Chaos.' "

"She's no more loyal to Yandros than I am High Initiate," Strann said with rancor. "She may have been born of Chaos, but she doesn't serve its gods."

"Born of Chaos? What do you mean?"

Strann was taken aback. "She's only half human—her father is a Chaos demon. Didn't you know?"

"No," Karuth said softly. Ailind had said nothing about that. . . . "No, we didn't know."

Strann nodded. "His name is Narid-na-Gost, so Yandros tells me. He's a minor entity, but by mortal standards he has enormous power. He fled the Chaos realm and took refuge with his daughter in our world, and it's his hand, not Yandros's, that lies behind her rise to power."

Karuth stared at him as she took this in. Of course, of *course,* it made sense . . . all the old conundrums; the mystery surrounding Ygorla's conception, her mother's untimely death and Keridil Toln's strange instinct about the child, and then the gruesome murder of her great-aunt, the old Matriarch, and Ygorla's disappearance seemingly into nowhere. The unseen hand of a demon sire. It made *sense.*

"Do you mean," she said in a tight, strained voice, "that the lords of Chaos haven't betrayed the pact they made at the time of Equilibrium?"

Strann recalled Yandros's acerbic words on the matter of the Circle's fealty, his warning that Tirand Lin believed that the Chaos lords had broken their century-old promise. Now he understood what had led the High Initiate into making such a mistake.

"Chaos hasn't betrayed us," he said. "It's they who were betrayed, by Ygorla and her sire when they snatched power in Chaos's name. Yandros wants to see them both destroyed and he wants the Circle's help to lay a trap to snare them. That's the message he charged me to carry to your brother." He leaned forward, his voice low-pitched and urgent. "But there's more, Karuth, a dangerous complication. When Narid-na-Gost—"

The door opened. Instantly Strann fell silent, and Karuth got hastily to her feet as Sanquar, carrying an armful of clothes, entered the infirmary.

"I found these," Sanquar said. "They're not among my best items, but at least they're warm." He seemed unaware of the tension in the room and turned to Strann with a courteous smile. "If there's anything more you need, please . . ." His voice tailed off, and his expression collapsed into shocked consternation as he saw Strann's hand.

Strann stared back at him. "Not pretty, is it? And, I'm sorry to say, not curable even by the castle's renowned skills."

Sanquar continued to gaze at the hand. "How did it happen?"

"Through an unpleasant combination of sorcery and vindictiveness." Strann clearly didn't feel inclined to elaborate, and Karuth touched Sanquar's arm.

"You'll learn the whole story later, Sanquar, but for now I don't think it's a subject that Strann wishes to discuss." She sounded oddly distant, not at all like her normal self, and for a moment her voice was a little unsteady before she collected herself again. "Strann will need your help to change his clothes," she went on. "I've set towels to warm. See that he's thoroughly dry before he dresses, or we'll have him down with a fever by this evening. Call me when you're finished. I'll be outside." She gave Strann an uneasy glance that Sanquar couldn't begin to interpret and left the room.

Gaining the privacy of the empty corridor, Karuth shut her eyes tightly and leaned against the wall. *"Oh, gods,"* she said, so softly that her words were barely audible even to herself, *"what have we done . . . ?"*

Her pulse was overrapid and her stomach felt queasy as her mind raced with this new revelation. If Strann was telling the truth—and if Yandros hadn't deceived him—then her own conviction that Chaos had been faithful to its pact was vindicated. The knowledge was bitter comfort now; the damage had been done and the links broken. But she couldn't stand by and do nothing, not this time.

She had to speak to Tirand. It was vital that he should be persuaded to change his mind and give Strann a hearing—and Karuth believed that only she stood a chance of persuading him. Unlike Strann, she could approach Tirand and talk to him without hindrance, and she believed—no, she corrected herself with scrupulous honesty; she *hoped*—that the old bond between them hadn't been so damaged by recent hostilities that he wouldn't listen to her. Once he did, he surely couldn't ignore the news that Strann had brought to the castle. At the very least he must hear what he had to say.

She glanced at the closed infirmary door, then at the passage. This was a gamble with dangerously high stakes, for she didn't even know if Strann's word could be believed, and though she desperately wanted to trust him, she was also wise enough to admit that her feelings were heavily colored by what she wished the truth to be. But she couldn't stop to consider that. She'd failed Yandros once; she wouldn't risk failing him again.

Quickly Karuth started to walk along the corridor.

She'd only gone a few yards when she saw the spare, gray-haired figure of Kern, the senior steward who was also Tirand's personal factotum, coming toward her.

"Kern!" She hailed him. "I'm looking for my brother. Do you know where he is?"

Kern bowed to her. "I believe he's in the dining hall, madam, or at least he was ten minutes ago."

"Thank you." Karuth hurried on to the hall. The double doors stood ajar, and muted sounds of voices and clattering plates came from inside as late breakfasters mingled with early arrivals for the lighter midday meal. Tirand was there near the fire and was fortuitously alone. Karuth hastened past the lines of tables toward him.

He rose courteously when he saw her, but his expression was wary. She didn't waste any time with preamble, but sat down uninvited and leaned toward him.

"Tirand, I must talk to you. It's urgent."

"What's wrong?" His eyes anticipated trouble; she ignored the look.

"It concerns the usurper's envoy."

"Ah." He spoke before she could get any farther. "Karuth, I don't think there's any point in what you're about to say. I'm well aware of who he is, and it doesn't make any difference. He's a traitor. He's her servant, in her pay and her confidence, and I won't make allowances for—"

"For the gods' sakes, Tirand, please listen to me and don't jump to conclusions!" she interrupted. "This has nothing to do with Strann's identity; it's *far* more important." She grasped his hands, squeezing them hard. *"Please,* just listen to what I have to tell you. Strann's in my infirmary. I intercepted his guards on their way to the cellars; and no, I'm not prepared to argue with you about that now, because as a physician it was my duty to put his well-being before any other consideration. He has a vital message for the Circle, Tirand. Not from Ygorla but from Yandros."

Tirand stared at her. "From *Yandros?*"

She nodded. "Yandros came to him—Strann called on him for help, and he answered. Tirand, he says that Ygorla is no more a friend to Chaos than she is to us. Yandros wants her destroyed, and—"

"Wait a minute." Tirand pulled his hands free and placed them palms down on the wooden arms of his chair. "He claims that Yandros has appeared to him and charged him to carry a message from Chaos to the Circle?"

"Yes."

"And you *believe* him?" His voice was incredulous.

Karuth held his gaze. "I didn't say that, Tirand. In truth I don't know, any more than you do. But what I am saying is that I think we should hear the whole of his story."

Tirand made an angrily dismissive gesture. "Hear a pack of lies trumped up by the sorceress and her fawning servants at Chaos's behest? What do you take me for?"

Biting back the retort that came to her mind, Karuth persisted with all the persuasion she could muster. "I know it sounds dubious, to say the very least; but surely we've nothing to lose simply by listening? If nothing else, it might give us some information, and that's something we're sorely lacking. I'm not asking you to trust Strann— neither of us is that gullible. I'm simply asking you to hear him out."

Tirand's eyes were narrow with suspicion. "Has he persuaded you to approach me?"

"No. He doesn't even know I'm here. I left Sanquar

helping him to change his clothes." She frowned. "He can't do it for himself. Ygorla has destroyed his right hand."

"Destroyed . . ."

"Burned it, beyond the ability of any human physician to repair." Again she met his eyes. "That's the one thing that makes me wonder if he could be telling the truth."

"I don't doubt that our friend Strann's well aware of that," Tirand pointed out acerbically.

"I know, I know. It might well be a ploy designed to gain our sympathy. But somehow I doubt it, Tirand. Strann's music is the most important thing in his life. I don't believe he'd willingly sacrifice it for any reason."

Tirand's lip curled skeptically, but he made no further comment. Aware that he was still undecided, Karuth said quietly, "Tirand, I know what you might be thinking. But I'm not trying to prove anything. I'm not trying to claim that I've been right all along and you've been wrong, nor am I trying to side with Strann against you out of some sense of pique."

He smiled, thinly and wearily. "Is your opinion of me really that low?"

Her cheeks colored. "Of course not."

"All the same, you think I'm unfairly prejudiced, don't you? Well, it's true, Karuth. I *am* prejudiced. I mistrust this envoy, I mistrust his supposed message, and above all I mistrust Chaos and anything they might have to say to him or to us. I think I have good reason for that mistrust —but at the same time my prejudices haven't blinded me to plain common sense." He rose abruptly. "He's in the infirmary?"

She, too, got to her feet, though more slowly. "You're prepared to give him a hearing?"

"Yes. As you said, I've nothing to lose by listening to what he has to tell me, whether it's true or not."

Karuth nodded. "Thank you."

Tirand smiled again. The smile wasn't warm, but she thought, though she couldn't be sure, that it at least had a touch of sour humor. "Don't waste gratitude on me. I've only two motives, and they're both selfish: prudence and sheer curiosity."

They said nothing more to each other as they left the dining hall and walked back to the infirmary. Karuth would have knocked, but Tirand simply lifted the latch and walked in. Sanquar, who was tidying one of Karuth's tables, greeted the High Initiate in some surprise, and Strann, dressed now in Sanquar's clothes, looked at Tirand with wary trepidation.

Tirand nodded brusquely to Sanquar and addressed Strann directly. "I understand you have something to tell me."

"Yes." Slowly Strann rose. As he did so, Tirand saw his right hand and flinched visibly, but made no comment. "I tried to explain on my arrival, but—"

"The little that my sister has told me changes the situation," Tirand interrupted, and gestured toward the door. "Come with me to my study, if you please."

Strann exchanged a swift look with Karuth; she nodded slightly and he shrugged. "As you wish, High Initiate."

He left the room behind Tirand. Sanquar, baffled and curious, caught Karuth's eye as she made to follow them and gave her an expressively querying look.

"I'll explain later," she told him. "If I can. . . ."

She hurried out in the two men's wake.

In his study Tirand's natural courtesy overcame dislike and suspicion, and he offered Strann a comfortable chair and a cup of wine before sitting down behind his desk.

"Well." His brown eyes met Strann's challengingly. "Karuth tells me that you claim to bring a message to the Circle from Yandros."

Strann glanced at Karuth, who had taken a seat near the window, but she gave him no help. She had, it seemed, deliberately distanced herself from the proceedings, and he focused on Tirand once more.

"That's true, High Initiate."

"I find it hard to believe."

Strann smiled faintly. "So did I at the time."

"I hardly think that this is a time for flippancy." Tirand didn't return the smile. "You'd better tell me the entire story—including how you appear to have become a trusted servant at the usurper's court."

Strann's face sobered. This, he knew, was the test, the moment for him to call upon all his bardic skills and use them to the utmost. He mustn't be intimidated, mustn't allow doubt or uncertainty to betray him. He drew breath —and as he was about to utter his first words, the study door opened.

Strann saw the surprise on Tirand's face, the consternation on Karuth's, as they both hastily rose to their feet. He looked over his shoulder, and a quick *frisson* ran through him as he recognized the white-haired man with the strange eyes whom he'd seen in the entrance hall on his arrival. The newcomer studied Strann briefly but intently, then looked at Tirand.

303

"I understand that this man has a tale to tell us," he said in a pleasant but authoritative voice. "With your permission, High Initiate, I should like to hear what he has to say."

Tirand saw the subtle gesture, hidden from Strann, that warned him not to reveal Ailind's identity. He quelled the impulse to bow and simply said, "Of course. Please, join us."

Ailind nodded coolly to Karuth and took a chair near the fire, from where he could watch Strann's face. Tirand, uncomfortable but trying his best to disguise it, sat back behind the desk again and indicated for Strann to proceed.

Strann glanced once more at the stranger with the disconcerting eyes and decided to ignore his presence. He suspected that the man was probably one of the High Initiate's confidants and that his arrival had been prearranged. So be it; he wouldn't let himself be unsettled by any such ploy.

Half closing his eyes, he began to tell his story. He told them of the *Cloudfisher*'s voyage to Summer Isle and the grisly fate of her crew and passengers; of how he had abandoned all pride and all dignity to ingratiate himself with Ygorla and become her court pet; and of the long list of outrages that had finally led him to call upon Yandros for help. He made no attempt to portray himself in a kindly light, admitting that the sole motive behind all he had done was to preserve his own life no matter what the cost. His inquisitors listened, not once interrupting, until, with a sudden catch in his voice, Strann told them of how the High Margravine, after praying ceaselessly but fruitlessly to Aeoris to intercede and help her, had committed suicide. At this Tirand's face paled.

"Jianna is *dead*?"

"You didn't know?"

"No. No, we . . . oh, gods . . ."

Strann looked away from the High Initiate's stricken face. "I'm sorry, sir. I didn't realize, or I would have tried to break the news more kindly." He grimaced. "I'm surprised that Ygorla didn't send you a triumphant message on the day that it happened."

"No," Tirand said tightly. "For once she did not.' He stared blindly down at his desk. "Could no one have done anything to save her?"

Strann was tempted to reply, "Only Aeoris," but, knowing Tirand's loyalties, held his tongue. At last Tirand looked up again.

"We will mourn Jianna in the proper way in good time," he said, his voice flat. "For now, I think you had better continue with your story." He looked at Strann. "You say it was her death that finally goaded you to call upon Chaos for aid. . . ."

Strann nodded and went on with his narrative. He was careful not to omit the smallest detail from the story of his encounter with Yandros. He related the Chaos lord's message to the Circle, and his revelations about the demonic source of Ygorla's power in the form of her sire, Narid-na-Gost. As the tale unfolded, he realized just how incomplete his own knowledge was, for Tirand began to interrupt with frequent questions, and more often than not Strann didn't have an answer to give him. At last, though, he had told them every fact he knew—save for one—and as he finished, silence fell in the room. The High Initiate was staring down at his own hands, which were clasped before him on the desktop. Karuth watched him uncertainly, and Ailind's expression was impassive. Strann waited, and at length Tirand looked up.

"You've told us quite a tale, my friend. Now I must ask myself whether a single word of it is true."

"It's true, High Initiate."

"So you say. But of course you can't prove it, can you? You may have invented the entire story, with or without the connivance of your bitch-queen of a mistress. Or, on the other hand, it may be a concoction on the part of Chaos, intended to dupe us—and possibly even you—into believing that they haven't broken the pact of Equilibrium. That makes three possibilities, and you have offered me no evidence to prove or disprove any of them."

"I can disprove the first, sir," Strann said.

"Can you?" Tirand didn't disguise his skepticism.

"I think so. At least I think I can convince you that my claim to have spoken with Yandros isn't a fiction. I believe you must already have realized that Ygorla's powers don't extend to being able to overlook this castle, so she has no knowledge of anything that takes place here. However, *I* know that at your instigation the Circle recently performed a rite that formally renounced all fealty to Chaos." He paused. "Beyond these walls only the gods themselves are aware of that."

He heard Karuth draw a sharp breath, but Tirand shook his head. "Not good enough, Strann. There are any number of ways and means by which such information might get about—including the possibility that you yourself have heard it since your arrival here."

Karuth started to protest. "Tirand, that isn't fair—" but before she could say more, Ailind spoke for the first time.

"I think, High Initiate, that perhaps we shouldn't dismiss this claim so lightly," he said. "For myself"—he exchanged a glance with Tirand that Strann noted but couldn't interpret—"I'm inclined to believe that, in this instance at least, our friend is telling the truth."

Strann was surprised to find support from such an unlikely quarter, and doubly surprised when Tirand didn't argue the point but simply made an acquiescent gesture. Ailind smiled and continued. "However, this still leaves us with the conundrum of Yandros's own motive, and that's quite another matter. We've heard nothing to persuade us beyond doubt that this usurper is not Chaos's servant; indeed all appearances suggest emphatically that she is. If Yandros wishes her dead, as he claims, then why doesn't he simply destroy her and her demon father with his own hand? Surely for him nothing could be simpler?"

Strann looked at him unhappily. He knew the answer to that question, but he also clearly remembered Yandros's warning. If the Circle were no longer loyal to Chaos, how would they react to the news that Yandros and his brothers were effectively being held to ransom by Ygorla? Dissembling, he said uncomfortably, "There is their pact to consider. . . ."

"Ah, no." Ailind smiled coldly. "I believe you must have been a poor pupil if you don't know your catechisms better than that. Order and Chaos pledged not to interfere in *human* affairs, and, in origin at least, this matter isn't the concern of mortals. If, as you claim, Narid-na-Gost is a Chaos demon and the sorceress Ygorla is his daughter, they both owe their origins to Chaos. Why, then, doesn't Chaos deal with them as it may do with any of its own kind?"

Three pairs of eyes were focused on Strann's face, and he realized that, risk or no, he must tell them the truth. He couldn't invent a plausible answer; there simply wasn't one that would convince them.

Lord Yandros, he thought, *forgive me, but I don't think there's any other way.* Aloud, he said, "Chaos can't make any move against Ygorla and her father. They dare not. You see, Narid-na-Gost has in his possession the soul-stone of one of the seven gods."

Tirand looked back at him. "He has *what*?"

"The soul-stone of—"

"Soul-stone?" Now Tirand was incredulous. "Are you trying to tell me that he simply plucked it from its rightful owner and—"

"Wait, High Initiate." Ailind raised a hand, silencing Tirand. "Let's not be too quick to doubt anything." Again they exchanged a glance; again Strann couldn't imagine what the glance might mean. Then Ailind turned to face him.

"Tell us all you know of this, Strann."

It was out now, there was nothing to be gained from evasion, so Strann told the story of Narid-na-Gost's theft of the jewel and how Chaos dared make no move against him and his daughter for fear that they would destroy the stone and its rightful owner with it. When he finished, no one said anything for some while. Then Ailind stood up.

"High Initiate—a word in private, if you please."

They moved to the far side of the room, and Ailind murmured in Tirand's ear. Strann couldn't catch what was said, nor, to judge from her expression, could Karuth, but when they were done, Tirand walked to a bell rope that hung by the fireplace and pulled it. A minute later the steward Kern answered the summons.

"Kern." Tirand indicated Strann. "Will you please conduct our guest to the upper floor and find a suitable room for him." Unseen by anyone but the steward, he made a twisting gesture with one hand that pantomimed a key turning in a lock, and Kern, understanding, nodded.

"Yes, High Initiate." He bowed slightly to Strann. "If you will come with me, sir . . . ?"

Strann hesitated, but only for a moment before logic told him that his hosts were unlikely to spring any unpleasant surprises on him now. If the High Initiate had decided that the world would be a safer place without Strann the Storymaker, he could simply order his summary execution without any need to resort to subterfuge. Reassured at least to some degree, Strann bowed to the company and followed Kern to the door. The last image he took with him from the room was that of Karuth, her head turned from him and her back rigid with tension, gazing out of the window. Then the door closed, shutting her from his sight before he could wonder why she had suddenly seemed unwilling or unable to meet his gaze.

19

For a few moments after Strann and the steward had left,
no one moved. Karuth still stared out of the window,
Tirand stood gazing down at his own feet. Only Ailind
seemed impassive as he waited for someone else to break
the silence.

At last Tirand spoke. His attitude was deferential and
his voice none too steady as he turned to Ailind and said,
"My lord, I am at a loss to know what to think."

Ailind smiled distantly. "Don't be, High Initiate. Our
jongleur friend has told nothing but the truth."

Astonished, Tirand blinked rapidly, and Ailind's smile
became a soft laugh. "My good Tirand, do you think I
couldn't see into his heart as easily as you see through
your window? He's no traitor. A coward perhaps, and a
self-seeker, but as much an enemy of the usurper as any of
your Circle adepts. Unfortunately, though, his allegiances
are not quite as favorable to our cause, for while he pays
lip service to Order, his natural loyalties are toward
Chaos."

"Which is why he called upon Yandros," Tirand said.

"Precisely." Ailind picked up one of the fire irons and
casually studied it. "That could place him at a disadvantage."

Karuth turned suddenly and unexpectedly from the

window. "A disadvantage, Lord Ailind?" she said sharply. "I don't understand. Surely Strann has as much right as any of us to give fealty to whomever he chooses?"

Tirand turned on his heel, horrified by her challenging tone and ready to rebuke her, but Ailind forestalled him.

"Certainly he has that right," he said crisply. "But the Circle has chosen a different path now, and those who are friends to Yandros are not friends to me." His voice took on an ominous note as he added, "You would do well to remember that, Adept Karuth."

For a moment Karuth stared at him, then intuition sounded a warning in her mind and she glanced quickly toward Tirand. "What do you mean to do with Strann? Where has Kern taken him?"

Her brother returned her look angrily. "You heard my order for yourself. Strann will be treated as we'd treat any guest. The only difference is that the door of his room will be locked until Lord Ailind has decided on his fate."

"His *fate*?" She was appalled. "What fate? What crime has he committed?" Suddenly furious, she rounded on Ailind, forgetting his nature and his power. "You said yourself that he's not a traitor and that everything he told us was the truth! Do you punish men for *honesty*?"

"*Karuth!*" Tirand stepped forward, grabbing her by the arm and pulling her aside. "How *dare* you speak to Lord Ailind in such a way! Apologize at once, or—"

"Or what?" She shook herself free. "What will you do, Tirand? Chastise me? Pronounce anathema on me—or ask your god to do it for you? Is that what you've come to since you abandoned the principles of Equilibrium?"

"Adept Karuth."

Ailind's voice froze them both. Very slowly Karuth turned to look at him, and as she did so, her courage abruptly collapsed. Anger had made her reckless, and in the heat of her indignation she'd forgotten that Ailind was not simply another mortal with whom she might argue as she would with any of her fellow adepts. Now, gazing at his face, she was reminded shockingly of what he was and felt a shudder of blind terror rack her as her lungs and stomach seemed to contract until she felt that a huge, invisible hand had crushed them to nothing. A cold white aura burned around the lord of Order's frame, and his eyes had lost all semblance of humanity, becoming once again two searing, golden orbs.

"Come here, Karuth," he said softly. "Come here and stand before me."

She had no choice. His power swamped her, and even without that compulsion her own newly and violently awakened fear would have forced her to obey. Shaking, she took one step toward him, another, another, and stood rigid as though trapped between ice walls while he gazed down at her. Ailind gave no sign of what he saw in her face or in her mind; he cast her fear carelessly aside, dismissed her hatred as beneath his contempt, and spoke to her in a tone that made Tirand shudder.

"You seem to have forgotten, my child, that there have been a great many changes within these walls during recent days. You may still cling to your fondness for the denizens of Chaos, but in that you are now alone among your peers. The Circle serves Order now; and while you may choose to defy your High Initiate, I warn you that you will defy *me* at your peril. Do you understand?"

Karuth's face was bloodless; her voice barely audible, she whispered, "Yes . . ."

"Then I will say what I have to say once, and I expect you to listen and take heed. From this moment onward the decisions taken by the Triumvirate under my rule will no longer be of any concern to you. You will continue your duties as a physician, but as an adept you will have no function to perform. You will take no part in the Circle's activities, and you will perform no sorcery either with others or alone. And, most importantly, you will not repeat one word of what you have heard within these walls to another living soul." He reached out, and one long finger tilted her chin up so that she was forced to look directly at him. "Don't be such a fool as to treat my warning lightly, Karuth Piadar. I know what's in your heart, but I will tolerate no disobedience. You are on sufferance—remember that, and all will be well for you; ignore it, and you'll learn that we of Order don't look kindly on those who oppose us." He released her, and abruptly his eyes returned to their human guise. "I now wish to speak to your brother, so you may leave us and go back to your work."

Shaking, her face the sickly shade of old paper, Karuth stepped back. She refused to so much as glance at Tirand but turned wordlessly and walked with what dignity she could muster toward the door. As she laid her hand on the latch, Ailind said, "I would strongly advise you to contemplate your future attitude, Karuth. In the days to come, allegiance to Chaos may not be a wise or prudent recourse for any mortal."

Karuth looked back over her shoulder, her expression a blank mask. Then she walked out of the study and slammed the door behind her.

Ailind gazed at the closed door for some moments until he knew that Karuth was no longer in the vicinity, then turned to Tirand. The High Initiate was standing by the fireplace, one arm leaning on the mantel. He seemed reluctant to look around, and when at last he did so, his face wore a mixture of fear, uncertainty, and guilt.

"Don't worry, Tirand," Ailind said, not unkindly. "You and your sister may be of the same blood, but I'm well aware that you're not of the same mind."

Tirand looked back at him unhappily. Though he was angry with Karuth for her presumption, he felt nevertheless that the lord of Order's censure had been unnecessarily hard. He wouldn't venture to say so—after all, Ailind was one of his own gods and his wisdom could not be called into question. But a reprimand, surely, would have been enough? To effectively bar Karuth from all Circle activities while at the same time forbidding her to openly worship as she chose seemed to him . . . well, not unjust, for Ailind could never be that, but . . .

"A little drastic?" Ailind's voice made him start violently, and he realized to his consternation that his thoughts had been read all too clearly. He couldn't answer, and Ailind paced slowly toward the window.

"High Initiate, your readiness to see the best in others does you credit, but it also betrays you as something less than a realist. Your sister is and will remain loyal to Chaos: she refused to abandon her loyalty when all evidence suggested that Chaos had broken its pact, and now that that evidence seems to have been disproved, she sees herself as Chaos's champion. We do not want that, Tirand. It is important—I might even say vital—to our cause that any thoughts that Karuth, or anyone else for that matter, might have of calling on Chaos for help should be crushed before they can bear fruit."

Tirand was nonplussed. "I'm sorry, my lord, but I don't understand," he said. "Surely if Chaos shares our desire to rid the world of the usurper—"

"I'm not speaking of the usurper." Ailind swung around to face him. "Her destruction will be a trivial matter. I am speaking of something else entirely." He stared hard at Tirand in a way that made the High Initiate quail. For perhaps half a minute his gaze held, then he relaxed, seemingly satisfied with what he had found.

"Yes," he said, "I see that you can be trusted, and that's as well, for we will have need of you before long. What I am about to say, High Initiate, must be repeated to no one. Not to the High Margrave, nor to the Matriarch, nor to any of your most senior adepts. Do you understand?"

Tirand was by now hopelessly out of his depth. He nodded. "I understand, my lord."

"Good. Now: although, as I have already said, Yandros's messenger told us the truth, that in itself raises the further question of whether or not Yandros's word can be relied upon. I and my brothers know our counterparts in Chaos of old; they are devious, unpredictable, and malevolent, and the tale that Yandros has fed to his servant may well be a lie with some dark, ulterior motive behind it. However, in this case I'm inclined to believe that for once our old enemy is *not* deceiving us." Glancing through the window at the courtyard, he smiled wolfishly. "In which case, Yandros will not be pleased when he discovers that his messenger has inadvertently armed us with an extremely valuable weapon."

Tirand frowned. "A weapon?"

"Indeed. We know now why the lords of Chaos have taken no action against the sorceress Ygorla and her father. They are being held to ransom."

"The soul-stone," Tirand said. "Yes . . . but *could* they destroy it, my lord? Is such a thing possible?"

"Oh, it's possible; although if Yandros and his brothers were foolish enough to use such fragile vehicles, they should have anticipated this danger and taken measures to avoid it." Ailind smiled thinly. "We of Order would never be so careless. But Chaos's loss may well become our gain if we can turn the sorceress's grandiose ambitions to our own purpose."

Tirand was horrified. "Lord Ailind, you surely don't mean to negotiate with Ygorla?"

"Negotiate with her?" Ailind raised pale eyebrows. "Indeed, High Initiate, that's exactly what I mean to do. Or rather, what I mean *you* to do." His smile, still hovering, became predatory and dangerous. "We shall, as I believe your hunters say, take two birds with one single arrow. We shall bring about the downfall of Ygorla and her demon sire and at the same time strike a blow against Chaos from which they will never recover."

He moved away from the window and walked slowly across the room. Tirand watched him. He thought he was beginning to comprehend the bones of Ailind's plan, and the realization stunned him into silence. At last Ailind stopped pacing and looked at him once more. When he spoke, his voice had lost its edge and was almost gentle.

"Tell me, Tirand, in your deepest thoughts would you not like to see the old ways restored? I believe that since you formally renounced your fealty to Chaos, you have felt as though a burden has been lifted from your shoulders, a burden that obliged you go against the urgings of your own heart and bow to the principles of Equilibrium. Isn't that so? Are you not happier, and is your soul not more at ease, now that you may openly worship Order alone?"

Tirand couldn't answer, for Ailind's words had evoked

316

the specter of a terrible mental war that had haunted his
dreams since the night of the ritual: the war between the
tearing pull of conscience and the darker yet no less powerful currents of his own desire. The catechisms he had
learned in childhood told him that Equilibrium had been
hard and bitterly won, and for eighty years that prize had
been diligently guarded, first by Keridil Toln and then by
Tirand's own father, Chiro, before he himself had inherited their noble role in his turn. He couldn't betray the
trust that they had placed upon his shoulders. And yet, he
thought . . . hadn't Keridil himself bowed to the Change
only because he had no other choice? Keridil had never
loved Chaos; he had given Yandros due reverence in his
words and in his rituals, but to the end of his long life his
soul had remained faithful to Order.

"We were the sole gods of your forefathers," Ailind
said quietly. "It takes more than a single century to wipe
out such a heritage, and more than a command from the
likes of Yandros to change men's hearts. Equilibrium is a
sham; it was never of our choosing but was imposed upon
us by Chaos's whim when they defeated us in that great
battle. We would like to see it ended, Tirand. We would
like to see the old ways restored and Chaos banished once
again to a place where it cannot threaten the peace and
harmony that this world enjoyed under the rule of Order.
And thanks to what we have learned today, we have the
means by which it might be done."

Tirand was shaking. He understood now, and he found
his voice only with the greatest of difficulty. "You mean to
destroy the Chaos lord's soul-stone. . . ."

"Yes. To destroy the stone, and its possessor with it.
To alter, beyond recall, the Equilibrium that has pre-
vented us from taking our rightful place once again as

rulers of the mortal world. We are seven; but Chaos shall be six, and their power will therefore be broken forever. Order will triumph, and the usurper, who owes her existence to Chaos, shall be our instrument."

As he spoke, Ailind had been watching Tirand carefully, but the High Initiate stood motionless, seemingly unable to respond. Suddenly Ailind reached out and laid a hand on his shoulder, noting how Tirand had to force himself not to flinch away in fear. "Don't turn your face aside, High Initiate," he said. "I know your mind better even than you know it yourself. Whatever custom may have taught you, your deeper self is aware of the truth, though until this moment you've not dared to admit it. We don't hold you to blame for that, my friend—but the time has come for honesty to take the place of self-deception. Look at me."

Tirand did. The god's eyes shone like twin stars in his skull, stars that suddenly flared into suns. Light filled the room, and for one dizzying, glorious instant the familiar walls seemed to melt away and Tirand was standing in a garden of graceful trees and perfect lawns and flowers of every color that mortal eyes could discern. Shimmering harmonies rippled from the air, rich perfumes drifted on the breeze, and beyond the garden's white, enclosing wall a colossal and breathtaking vista of tawny hills rolled away under a cloudless blue sky. Then, with a shiver, the image vanished and he was again standing before Ailind in his study in the winterbound castle, listening to the muted crackle of the fire in the grate.

Softly Ailind spoke. "Peace, Tirand Lin. That is what our realm can bring to your world. Peace and harmony, for all time, without the taint of Chaos to haunt your dreams."

Tirand's mouth worked violently, like that of a dumb man striving to speak. But there were no words he could say. This was his god, this was the being to whom his heart and soul owed allegiance. He could no longer pretend that it was otherwise.

He covered his face with both hands and dropped to one knee with his head bowed low.

"Rise, my good friend." Warmth, like the warmth of the summer sun, flooded Tirand as Ailind laid a hand lightly on the crown of his head. Slowly, uncertainly, the High Initiate got to his feet once more, and when he dared to look at the god's face, he saw that Ailind was smiling.

"We understand each other now, Tirand. You will be a faithful servant to us, I believe."

"Yes . . ." Tirand's voice quavered; with a great effort he brought it under control. "By your grace, my lord, I pray that I will."

There were five cats outside Strann's door. Karuth felt the faint touch of their telepathic probing even before she saw them, and felt, too, the eager appeal for help that they projected to her as they recognized the pattern of her mind. She turned the corner of the dimly lit passage, and her steps faltered as she saw what awaited her.

The servant who had been set to guard the door was doing his best to attract the cats to him and make much of them, but the animals would have none of it. They kept their distance, watching him with steely coldness in their eyes, tails lashing as they expressed their anger. Hearing Karuth's footsteps, the servant looked up from a futile attempt to lure one of their number to his outstretched hand, and hastily straightened.

Karuth nodded briskly by way of greeting. "Is this the room allocated to the emissary from Summer Isle?"

"Yes, madam. But—"

"Open the door, please. I have business with our guest."

The man's face colored hotly. "I'm sorry, madam, but I may not."

Karuth did her best to smile pleasantly. "I believe you know who I am. Please, open the door."

His throat worked frantically. "I'm sorry, Lady Karuth, but the High Initiate specifically ordered that no one should be admitted to this room. Not even you, madam. In fact—" He broke off hastily, and Karuth's eyes narrowed.

"In fact, *especially* not me, was that what you were about to say?"

The man didn't answer her acid question, but his deepening color was all the confirmation Karuth needed. She said nothing more but made a curt, canceling gesture, turned on her heel, and walked away. As she went, she could feel the cats' dismay; they had wanted her to make contact with Strann and she had failed them. Well, their disappointment couldn't be helped. She had set out to test Tirand's—or more accurately Ailind's—intentions, and her fears had been confirmed. Strann was a prisoner, and she was forbidden all further contact with him.

She felt the familiar tide of fury start to seethe once again within her, but this time it was directed primarily at herself. She'd been a fool to challenge Ailind, for now that he was alerted to the depth of her feelings, and therefore to her potential as a troublemaker, he would watch her as a hovering hawk might watch a rabbit and at the smallest provocation he would take retribution. Karuth couldn't pretend that she didn't fear him. His warning that he knew what was in her heart had gone home like a sword thrust; in trying to see Strann, she had taken a calculated risk of defying him, but she dared not test his tolerance any further.

Yet she must do *something*. The initial shock of Strann's revelations had been ousted from her mind by more immediate concerns, but now it was beginning to take root and its implications were horrifying. Chaos rendered powerless by the treachery of one of their own kind —it seemed impossible, beyond reason, yet Ailind himself had confirmed that Strann had spoken the truth. Karuth had seen the look in Ailind's eyes as Strann imparted the news, and she realized that it had been as much a surprise to him as to herself and Tirand. She had also seen the glint of eager delight that had followed, and though she couldn't be certain of its implications, it had chilled her to the core. Strann, in all innocence, had revealed Chaos's weakness to its deadliest and most powerful enemy, and Karuth couldn't make herself believe that Ailind, and through him Aeoris, wouldn't try to use the knowledge they had gained to their advantage and to Chaos's detriment.

The most urgent question in her mind now was whether Yandros knew of Strann's terrible and unwitting mistake. No one knew for certain how closely the gods were able to overlook the mortal world, and it was possible that even now the Chaos lords were unaware of Ailind's presence in the castle. If that was so, it was vital that they should be warned of what was afoot, and quickly. Yet how could that be achieved? Strann might still have a tenuous link with Yandros, but Strann didn't yet realize that anything was amiss—so that left only one soul in the castle with both the ability and the will to make contact with Chaos.

Sweat broke out in a cold wave over Karuth's face and body at the thought of such a responsibility resting on her shoulders, and she quickened her pace, anxious to gain the privacy of her own quarters. Reaching her door, she fumbled at the lock with unsteady hands, finally managed to turn the key, and slipped into the room beyond. The door closed with a small but emphatic sound, and she locked it once more before pacing slowly to the middle of the room, where she stood motionless, palms pressed to her cheeks and her mind racing.

Ailind had expressly forbidden her to perform any sorcerous operation. But would Ailind necessarily know if she disobeyed him? He was powerful, enormously powerful: but omnipotent? She didn't think so, for if he was, Ygorla and her demon father would by now be nothing but an ugly memory while their souls writhed and shrieked in the Seven Hells. Surely, *surely* if she did what must be done, quickly and alone, there was a chance that Ailind wouldn't realize and intervene in time to prevent her message from reaching Chaos.

Karuth knew that she would be running a dire risk, but she forced back the thought and with it her fear. She mustn't think of her own safety. Until now she'd taken the coward's option and had lived to bitterly regret it. That must change. For the sake of sanity, it must change.

She raised her head and looked around the room. The fire had gone out, and with the short day declining, the light was failing rapidly to a flat, ominous gloom. By the window, beyond which the snow was still falling, stood her work table, and on it the carved wooden box containing her personal occult tools, rarely used during the past few years. Quickly, before her nerve could fail, Karuth crossed to the table, made to brush away the film of dust and lift the box's lid—then paused. There wasn't time for the trappings of ceremony; and besides, there was a great danger that a full ritual might alert Ailind to her activities before she could hope to achieve anything. She must dispense with all formality and trust solely to her innate power.

She closed the curtains, shutting out what little light there was, and moved back to the center of the room. She took off her shoes, then on impulse also unfastened her wool gown and threw it aside, so that she was clothed only in a thin shift. Closing her eyes, she visualized a tongue of blue-green fire springing to life on the floor at her feet and surging into a snaking curve that finally formed a burning circle about her. The image was hard to hold—it had been a long time since she'd worked in this way, and the knack of it was all too easy to lose—but she concentrated with all her will, and slowly, slowly, the cold flames began to rise higher. Now she could hear, as though from a vast distance, the intermittent crackle of unchained energies, and her nostrils were filling with a sharp, clean scent, like brine and frost combined. Gooseflesh sprang up on her arms as the supernatural fire chilled her skin, and now the flames were as tall as she was, a thin, brilliant wall of translucent color flickering about her. Somewhere among the maze of sheltered crannies in the roof above her head a cat yowled a challenge to a rival, but the sound didn't so much as register in Karuth's mind. She had forged the first link with other dimensions, other worlds, and the power was coalescing within her. She was ready.

She drew breath to speak the first soft words of her call to Chaos—and with no warning, the door smashed open and a colossal blast of burning air ripped through the room. The cold fire disintegrated with a noise that shrieked up through the sonic spectrum until Karuth screamed with pain, and her consciousness was torn out of the astral world and hurled violently back to physical reality. Her feet were swept from under her by what felt like a giant hand, and she was thrown across the room to crash against her bed with stunning impact.

Dazed, sick with shock, Karuth clawed at the bed-hangings to support herself, and groggily raised her head. Her skull throbbed agonizingly where it had struck the wooden frame, her right arm was grazed and bruised if not worse, and the soles of her feet were burning. Light from the corridor spilled through the open door in a bright, hard-edged shaft, and against the light she saw a figure silhouetted. Gold burned briefly, the gold of unnatural, unhuman eyes, and Ailind's voice impinged softly through the fog that seemed to shroud her brain.

"One warning, Karuth Piadar. There won't be another."

He walked away and, without a hand to assist it, the door closed.

Karuth didn't move for a long time. One hand gripped the bed-curtain, clenching and unclenching but achieving nothing, and her face was pressed against her quilted eiderdown as though she could bury herself and hide from the world among its folds. Finally, though, she did find the strength to rise, and hauled her body onto the mattress. Another ten minutes passed before her hands stopped shaking sufficiently to allow her to sit upright and light a candle, and by its light, grimly methodical in her effort to keep all other thoughts at bay, she examined the damage she'd sustained. Her arm wasn't broken as she'd initially feared, only badly bruised. The back of her skull was painful to the touch and she'd have the grandmother of headaches to follow, but probably nothing worse. Her feet—but no, though the soles still burned as though she'd trodden on hot coals, the skin wasn't even reddened.

At last she turned over onto her back and lay staring at the canopy above her head. Her face was like stone, her eyes empty of all expression. She couldn't give vent in even the smallest way to the feelings that screamed silently inside her—the misery, the rage, the shame—and the fear that had its claws lodged so deep in her soul that she believed it might never loosen its grip. There was nothing left. Nothing.

Reaching out, Karuth snuffed out the candle and the room became dark once more. After a while she closed her eyes, and the tears dried on her cheeks as, exhausted and in desperate need of a haven in which to hide and lick her wounds, she sank into a troubled sleep.

"So our secret is out." Yandros walked slowly along an impossibly narrow ridge that overlooked a canyon where white fire flowed like a river. His eyes, at this moment a purplish black, focused on Tarod pacing a few steps behind him as he glanced back. "I should have known better than to entrust such a vital message to a mortal."

"Strann wasn't to blame," Tarod said. "He knew no better. Besides, what other choice did you have?"

Yandros sighed irritably, aware that his brother was right, but resenting the circumstances that lent weight to his argument. "I should have taken your original advice, damned the pact to the Seven Hells, and acted before Aeoris and his fellow spawn could gain the advantage. Now it's too late: Because the Circle have ritually broken their ties with us, we have no justification for intervening now as we might have had then. Order has the advantage over us, Tarod. They've been asked, with all the pomp and gravity that the Circle can muster, to take a hand in human affairs. We were not so asked. And with Ailind comfortably settled in the castle and pulling Tirand Lin's strings, there's less than a dog's chance in the Seven Hells that the call will now be made and the way opened to us."

They walked on. Far above them, hurling their shadows across the river of fire, six titanic prisms hung in the black, starless sky of Chaos, turning and pulsing with their own incandescent light. Tarod glanced speculatively up at them, then said, "There's still Karuth Piadar."

Yandros turned around. Under the ever-changing colors of the prisms' radiance his face was demonic. "Is there? She's tried once, and Ailind stepped in before she could achieve anything. If she tries again, he'll destroy her, and she knows it. She may be loyal to us, Tarod, but mortals have their limitations, and I can't seriously see her being willing to risk sacrificing her life for our cause. In truth she'd be a fool if she did."

"Unless," Tarod pointed out, "she had the protection of the Marble Hall."

Yandros stopped. His eyes turned vivid blue, then narrowed to slits as he stared at his brother. "The Marble Hall? Of course . . . our own particular creation, and a place in which the lords of Order can exert no influence. Yes, I'd overlooked the Marble Hall."

"And it has another property that might be of value to us."

"So it does, so it does." Yandros nodded, his face thoughtful. "Mind you, it wouldn't be an altogether simple matter for Karuth to gain access to the hall. Tirand Lin holds the key, and he'll hardly be willing to place it in his sister's hands under any circumstances. We'd have to make other arrangements for her. And then of course the question arises of how we might make our wishes known. Any direct move would alert Ailind to our interest, and at this stage we most certainly don't want that."

"The castle's cats?" Tarod suggested.

"I don't think so. They're faithful servants, I grant, but their ability to communicate with humans is unreliable at best. No . . . no, I have a surer notion. I think Strann himself might do us further service. We still have a link with him, albeit tenuous, and there's one sure way by which he can carry our message to Karuth without arousing suspicion from the wrong quarter." Yandros smiled. "He won't enjoy the experience, but that can't be helped. It might teach him that indiscretion brings little in the way of reward while also giving him the chance to redeem himself."

"And if your strategy is successful," Tarod said. "What will you ask of Karuth Piadar?"

His brother's smile widened until it became feral. "A very small and a very simple task. In the distant past it was a commonplace for us, but now that mortals have been given the reins of their own destiny, we must have a willing human servant to turn the key and unlock the portal." He gazed up at the sky, at the vast, slowly turning prisms pulsing like supernatural hearts of crystal far above their heads. "For the first time in many centuries, I think the time has come to reawaken the most powerful of our ancient links between this realm and the mortal world. I mean to open the Chaos Gate, Tarod. And I mean to use it."

20

Ailind lifted his gaze from the parchment laid out on the table before him and smiled at Tirand.

"Yes," he said. "It is well."

The High Initiate returned the smile pallidly. Ailind, it seemed, had either forgotten or chosen to ignore the fact that mortals needed rest in a way that gods did not, and the night's work had left Tirand wearied to the bone and light-headed from lack of sleep. Stiffly he dipped his pen into the inkwell at his side and bent to the parchment one last time. His hand shook faintly as he signed his name and title, then sealed the letter with his ring of office. He didn't need to read the message again, for he felt as though every word of it was scribed indelibly on his brain. The formal greeting with its gracious compliments, the eloquent acknowledgment of Ygorla's conciliatory message and conveyance of the Circle's willingness to reciprocate, and lastly an invitation for the Empress to visit the Star Peninsula in person, accompanied by a delicate but unmistakable hint that the Circle were nothing if not pragmatic and would favor the possibility of an alliance rather than further conflict.

He believed that Ygorla would take the bait. Strann had told him that her desire to enter the castle gates in triumph bordered on an obsession; Tirand didn't trust

Strann's word, and still less the reliability of a madwoman's whims, but Ailind had assured him that the stratagem would produce the desired result, and that was enough. It was done, they were ready, and Tirand was content.

Ailind was waiting for him. The letter was to be dispatched at first light, now less than an hour away. All that remained was to rouse Handray the falconer and instruct him to prepare his fastest bird for the journey. Tirand crossed the room to open the door, and as he did so, the candlelight reflected briefly on the gold High Initiate's badge at his right shoulder—not the badge that had been familiar to all Circle adepts for the past eighty years, but another, older brooch bearing an older emblem. It had lain untouched throughout his lifetime and his father's, but last night Ailind had granted him the sanction to wear it—the double circle bisected by a lightning flash, ancient symbol of Order's sole dominion, and the self-same badge that, long ago, had been the precious possession of Keridil Toln.

The High Initiate opened the door, bowing to usher Ailind before him, and they walked out into the dark corridor and away toward the main doors.

From an unobtrusive cranny the gray cat watched them leave. Although the lord of Order's presence had deterred it from trying to find a way into the study, it had kept vigil throughout the night, striving to glean something of what was afoot behind the door. However, the images it had picked up from Tirand's mind were vague and inconclusive, and reluctantly the cat conceded that it had learned nothing to satisfy its curiosity. Under normal circumstances it might have lost interest in the High Initiate's business and turned its attention to some more absorbing activity; but a formless imperative of which it wasn't even consciously aware still lurked deep down in its mind, and when it finally left its hiding place, it didn't simply wander away but trotted purposefully toward another part of the castle from where it could reach the outside world without waiting for dawn and the sleepy human servants who would finally unbar the doors.

The snow had stopped sometime during the night, and the cat emerged into a silent, white, and spectral courtyard. The snow shone with a faint nacre as it reflected the overcast above, and bitter cold lay like a dead weight on the world. The cat disliked snow and picked its way fastidiously by the shortest route to a windowsill and thence onto the network of ledges and gutterings that were its kind's own, undisputed kingdom. It knew instinctively where and how to find the room it was seeking, and it ran light-footedly through the maze, climbing higher until at last it reached one particular window among the many that looked out from the castle's upper floor.

The cat wasn't aware that a greater power than mere good fortune was playing its part in this mission. All it knew was that *someone* had neglected to lock the window, and as a result the casement had opened a crack, just enough for one paw to slide through and tug gently so that the window swung open. There were bars on the inside, but they presented no barrier to a small, sleek, and lithe body, and the creature squirmed through and sprang noiselessly down to the floor of the room beyond. Motionless, it waited for a few seconds until its eyes adjusted to the greater darkness, then looked for the outline of the bed and its solitary occupant. It had no need to study the sleeping man to know that he was the right one, the one it had been sent to find, and instinct told it what to do.

Strann's face was a pale oval in the darker frame of his

tangled hair. He hadn't imagined that it would be possible for him to sleep under his present unhappy circumstances, but sheer exhaustion had finally overcome all the combined burdens of fear and worry and uncertainty, and he was deeply unconscious, beyond the reach even of dreams. Only the gentle, regular hush of his breath and the slight rise and fall of the bedclothes betrayed any sign of life.

The cat sprang up onto the counterpane and stood gazing at him for a few moments. Then it padded delicately to the pillow and pushed its face toward Strann's until their noses were almost touching. Closing its eyes, it breathed steadily, one long exhalation, into Strann's nostrils. Strann murmured in his sleep, and his unmaimed hand clenched and opened under the blankets as though he were trying to grasp and hold something. Carefully lest he should wake, the cat backed away, then turned, jumped to the floor, and with no more disturbance than might have been caused by a zephyr of air, was away back through the window and out into the night.

All too many people in the castle were succumbing to the winter rheums, so when Strann's guards reported that their charge was showing the first signs of a fever, Sanquar simply added another name to his ever-growing list of the stricken to be attended to and thought no more of it.

Karuth arrived late at the infirmary, and after a sharp, swift look at her drawn face, unhealthily pale skin, and hollow eyes Sanquar said firmly that he would attend to the morning visits alone. She didn't argue, which added fuel to his suspicion that she was about to become one of the fever's next victims, and he spent the next three hours on his round, checking pulses and dispensing febrifuges and restoratives. On such a busy morning Strann was simply one sufferer among many. Sanquar confirmed that he did indeed have the early symptoms of fever, measured a herbal draft into a cup of wine, watched him drink it, and after mildly berating the guards for having left the window open in such bitter weather, departed to minister to his next patient. As the door closed behind him and the key turned in the lock, Strann sank back among his pillows, staring at the bedposts. He had a feeling that he should have known the man who had just visited him; a dim memory told him that they'd met before, but he couldn't now recall where or when or under what circumstances. He was sure one of the guards had said that the man— Yandros? No, that surely wasn't his name—was a physician. Why did he need a physician? Was there something wrong with his mind, or was it his body? He'd tried to get up a few minutes ago, but all the strength seemed to have left his limbs. Lazy fool. The day was half over, and he had so much to do. . . .

The bedposts seemed suddenly to move of their own accord, closing together and blurring, and Strann shut his eyes to escape the disorientating effect. Earlier—yes, it must have been earlier, dawn had only just broken, he remembered that—earlier he'd gone to the window and watched a falcon with a message-scroll tied to its leg leaving the courtyard. A beautiful bird, its plumage a splash of warm color among the endless monochrome that the snow had imposed on the world. He'd wondered where it was bound and whether it would reach its destination safely, and just as the thought had crossed his mind, something had happened to him, something that had brought the guards at his door hurrying in. Yes, he recalled it now: His legs had given way under him, and the guards had found him sitting in the middle of the floor shaking as though he had the ague. They thought it was the fever, but Strann knew better. Strann knew what had made him fall, what he'd seen in this very room that had so shocked him. It had been the falcon—no, *a* falcon, not the same one, for it had a gray cat's head and it was mewing loudly and urgently at him. He'd tried to tell the guards about it, but they only picked him up and carried him back to bed; then he'd fallen asleep again, and after that the physician had come.

He *wished* he knew where he'd seen the physician before. The trouble was, unless he could remember, he wouldn't know whether or not the man could be entrusted with his message, and it was vital that the message reached only the right ears. Not the High Initiate. He wouldn't listen anyway, he was too pompous and pigheaded; Strann had tried to talk to him before, but he had only turned his back and started playing that duet from the *Equilibrium* epic with his sister. His sister. What was her name? Now, he did know her well, didn't he? Very well. *Very* well. He smiled a private, lascivious smile, which abruptly faded as he recalled that the name of the High Initiate's sister was not Kiszi, and not Yya, but something else. Cyllan? *No!* Gods, no, not Cyllan! Sweat broke out on his body. Why was he frightened of that name? It was just a name, just another name for a pretty girl or a lovely woman or . . .

He felt sick. Little good that would do him; he hadn't eaten anything since . . . Han Province, was it, or Prospect? His escort kept trying to tempt him with delicacies, but he knew what they were about and he wouldn't fall for the trick. Eat his own hand? Never. *Never.* He was *proud* of his hand, for it held the secret of his music.

Suddenly at that thought he sat bolt upright. Where was his manzon? They'd taken it while he was asleep, for surely he'd left it there, at the bed-foot where he could see it when he woke. Thrusting back the bedclothes, Strann scrabbled to the end of the bed. For a moment he almost glimpsed the manzon, half-hidden under tumbled blankets, but as he reached for it, it disappeared and he sprawled facedown on the counterpane.

Behind him a voice said, "Strann."

He jerked around. There was someone lying in the bed where he himself had lain moments before. Gold hair glinted in the cold, dull daylight, and the narrow eyes in the fine-boned face changed from silver to green to amber to scarlet to black. A thin hand beckoned, and at the figure's heart light began to pulse with a slow, hypnotic rhythm. Light . . . a seven-rayed star . . . and the voice, musical and mellifluous, yet with a malevolent undertone, said, "Listen to me, Strann. Listen, and remember . . ."

Strann started to scream.

Sanquar closed the door and turned on the senior of the two guards.

"Broen, I neither know nor care about the reasons for the High Initiate's order. *I* am telling you that this is a medical emergency and that Physician-Adept Karuth's presence is necessary! The man's delirious—damn it, he's *raving.* This is no ordinary fever, it's something beyond my experience or my ability to deal with, and I *insist* on calling in my superior. For all we know, this could be the beginning of some new epidemic! Now, please, do as I ask and send for Karuth at once!"

Alarmed by such stridency from the normally self-effacing Sanquar, Broen capitulated, and Karuth was duly sent for. She arrived looking a good deal better than she had earlier in the day and, gently dismissing Sanquar's apologies for troubling her and his solicitous inquiries after her health, entered Strann's room.

"Sweet gods!" From the threshold she took one look at the white-faced figure lying in the bed and crossed the room to the bedside in three strides. Sanquar, equally horrified, followed her. "By Aeoris, Karuth, what's happened to him? He wasn't in such straits when I sent for you! Delirious and sweating as though the fever had reached crisis, but *this* . . ." He pointed to Strann's face. "Look at those blotches on his face. They weren't even *there* ten minutes ago!"

Karuth cast him an alarmed look, then snatched up Strann's limp left hand and pressed her fingers against the pulse-point at his wrist.

"There's barely a flutter. Bring the revival phial from my bag, quickly!"

Sanquar obeyed. Karuth unscrewed the phial's cap, then prised Strann's putty-colored lips apart and let three drops of liquid fall upon his tongue. Both physicians watched intently, Karuth counting the seconds under her breath. She'd reached one hundred and nine when Strann's body jerked convulsively and a gagging noise came from his throat.

Karuth hissed a sigh of relief, then nodded to Sanquar. "It's worked. Prop him upright, or he'll probably start choking on his own saliva. I'll prepare a calmative, and then we can take a closer look at him."

She was measuring an herbal tincture into a cup when Sanquar said in an odd tone of voice, "Karuth . . . those blotches. They're *fading*."

"What?" She swung around and saw the phenomenon for herself. "Good gods!"

"I've never encountered anything like it," Sanquar said as she hurried back to the bed. "Karuth, what *is* this fever?"

"I don't know, but I hope and pray that it doesn't spread." Karuth set her cup down and lifted one of Strann's eyelids. The eye beneath was bloodshot, the white almost completely crimson, but, as Sanquar said, the purplish marks on the skin of Strann's face were vanishing even as she looked at them.

Suddenly Strann's eyelids fluttered. Hastily Karuth withdrew her hand, and with an effort Strann opened his eyes unaided. He smiled foolishly at her—or at something —and said in a slurred voice, "Cat. Cat, and it had wings. I told you, but you wouldn't listen."

"Strann?" Karuth took hold of his good hand, trying by physical contact to persuade his addled wits to forge a link with reality. "Strann, it's Karuth. Karuth. Do you understand?"

"Karuth." But he was simply repeating it; it meant nothing to him.

"Strann, listen to me. You're ill with a fever, and you need—"

"Oh, no, no, no." He turned his head rapidly from side to side. "No, *I'm* not ill. It was mewing at me, you see; but at the time I didn't understand what it meant. Now I do. *Now* I do, because he told me. He was here, lying here, and he was me and I was him, just for a moment . . ." The words cut off in a high-pitched giggle. "He was me and I was him. I never thought I'd live to tell *that* tale."

Karuth sighed. He'd make no sense until the delirium passed; all she could do was finish preparing the draft and try to persuade him to swallow it. She picked up the cup once more, bent over the bed—

"Karuth."

Strann's stare had focused on her with utter intensity, and the eyes that looked out through his skull weren't human.

"Oh, gods . . ." she whispered.

Sanquar raised his head. He'd seen nothing. "What is it?"

"Karuth."

It wasn't Strann's voice. She'd never heard such a voice before, but intuition slammed up from the depths of her subconscious and told her beyond all doubt what was happening to Strann.

"Sanquar, leave the room." She snapped the words out.

"What? Karuth, are you—"

"Leave." With an effort she moderated her tone and turned to look at him. "Please don't argue with me, Sanquar, I know what I'm doing. Wait outside—and don't let anyone else enter until I give permission."

He shook his head. "Whatever you say. But if you need help—"

"I'll call for you, I promise." She watched over her shoulder until he had gone and the door closed behind him, then crouched beside the bed and renewed her grip on Strann's hand. "Strann!" she hissed urgently. "Strann, what is it that you want to tell me?"

338

Strann's eyes had closed once more and he was breathing evenly. He seemed to be asleep, and Karuth didn't know what to do. To wake him could be dangerous if her suspicion proved to be right, but at the same time she dared not linger too long or Sanquar's worry and the guards' suspicion might bring them back into the room in defiance of her order.

Suddenly Strann's fingers moved in her grasp. Startled, she glanced down at his hand, then back to his face—and saw the unhuman eyes, their color changing with every moment, gazing calmly back at her.

"My lord Yandros . . ." She could barely articulate the words; her throat had closed, and her entire body was beginning to shake.

"Hush, Karuth." The quiet voice was like molten silver, beautiful yet unnerving. "It isn't wise to speak my name aloud within these walls."

Karuth clamped her teeth hard together. "Please forgive me."

"No, no; I'm complimented by your lapse," the voice said with faint amusement. "But I will speak to you swiftly and only once, lest our mutual friend sense that all is not as he believes it should be." The eyes in Strann's face changed to silver. "It is imperative that you go to the Marble Hall. You'll have no need of the key—we shall make provision for that—but you must find the means to reach it without alerting anyone to your intention. Ailind watches, and he'll know your mind if you don't take the greatest care. However, once you do reach the hall, you'll have nothing to fear from him; in that place you'll be beyond the reach of his influence. You must perform a certain rite, a simple ceremony but one unused and forgotten for many centuries. The record of it still exists, and you will find that record among the oldest manuscripts in your library. Look for the Speaking of the Way. That will be our sanction. Do you understand me, Karuth?"

She nodded. "I . . . understand you, my lord."

"Good. Then I shall take my leave of this messenger and entrust him once again to your care." A pause, then the gentle, implacable voice added softly, "Don't fail us this time, Karuth. I rather doubt that there will be a further chance for redemption."

Something like the shadow of a vast wing passed through the room. For a second or two Karuth's vision was obscured; when her eyes cleared and, blinking, she focused on the bed once more, Strann was looking up at her. His skin was unblemished, the sweat was gone, and his hazel eyes bore a look of faint puzzlement.

"Karuth?" Even his voice was its normal light baritone, without the smallest trace of slurring. "What are you doing here? They told me I was allowed no visitors."

"Strann—" The transformation had taken place so quickly that it had left her bemused and floundering. She knew that what she had seen and heard had been no delusion, but the swift and shocking return to normality had disorientated her, and she could barely credit that it had happened at all. Then instinct took over and she put a professional hand to Strann's brow. It was cool. "But you were—"

"Asleep? I must have been. I'm sorry, that was no way to greet you." He sat up. "There's daylight outside! What's the hour?"

"Lie back!" She pushed him back against the pillows. "You've been ill!" She saw his face register incomprehension. "Don't you remember? You were delirious. Sanquar called me in because he'd never seen a fever so virulent.

And then . . ." Karuth hesitated, wondering how frank she dared be, then decided to compromise. She sat down on the bed. "Strann, listen. You spoke to me in your fever, you gave me a message. Do you remember that?"

He considered, then shook his head. "No, I can't recall any such thing. Not even a dream. . . ." Abruptly his eyes narrowed. "What did I say?"

"I can't tell you. If you don't remember, it's safer that matters stay that way for the time being."

She should have realized, should have known that Strann was no fool, for he sat up again, this time ignoring her attempt to restrain him. "Karuth, is this something to do with Yandros?"

"Shh!" Rapidly she put a finger to his lips, silencing him before he could say any more. "Don't speak his name, Strann, or you'll endanger us both!"

He caught hold of her hand, and when she tried to pull away, he wouldn't relinquish his grip. "Tell me what you mean."

She looked over her shoulder. The door was still closed; Sanquar's patience hadn't yet run out. Turning back, she made a decision. She couldn't lie to Strann. He was as involved in this as she was, however unwillingly, and she hadn't the right to pretend otherwise. For both their sakes, he had to know at least a part of the truth.

She leaned forward. "Strann, I can't explain everything, but I'll tell you as much as I can reveal without putting both our lives in jeopardy. No"—as, shocked, he made to speak—"don't interrupt me, just listen. Strann, you're a prisoner, and my situation's little better than yours. The lords of Order have sent their own emissary here, and my brother is entirely in his sway. Order knows of your message."

Strann's face lost the little color that had returned to it as realization dawned. "The adept with the white hair—"

"He's no adept."

"Oh, gods . . ." His unmaimed hand clenched into a fist. "If I'd realized, if I'd *known*—"

"I couldn't warn you at the time, and I dare not elaborate now." Again Karuth glanced nervously over her shoulder. "I don't know what Tirand and the emissary mean to do with the knowledge, and even if I did, I couldn't voice it aloud, because I'm distrusted and watched and I don't know how closely I'm being overlooked. Strann, it's *imperative* that you do what I'm going to ask of you, without questions and without argument. I can't take the risk of telling you why, but I think you're wise enough to work it out for yourself."

Strann's eyes narrowed. "This is to do with what I—or someone—said to you at the height of the fever?"

She nodded.

He hissed softly through his teeth. "I see. Well, it would seem that he's at least giving me a second chance, if nothing else. What do you want me to do?"

Karuth gave silent thanks for his quick intelligence. "Two things. Firstly, act the part of a man slowly recovering from a strange, virulent, but short-lived sickness. Your fever wasn't natural. It was visited on you as a means of bringing us into contact, but it's vital that no one else should suspect that it was anything other than a genuine illness. Secondly, keep your silence. Remember nothing, know nothing, say nothing to anyone. Just be a weary and bewildered traveler who has discharged his duty and now passively awaits whatever fate the High Initiate has decreed for him."

Strann's lip quirked. "That isn't so far from the truth."

"For the moment, yes. Within the next few days matters may change. I pray they will."

"That's your task?"

"Don't ask me, Strann."

He nodded, "Very well; I understand, and I'll do what you ask." A ghost of his old wit returned as he added, "If nothing else, it'll be good practice for me. You can rely on my discretion—and on my acting talents."

Karuth shut her eyes briefly. "Thank you."

He was still holding her hand; she started to rise, but he didn't release her. "Karuth . . ."

She looked at him. Gently but very deliberately, he raised her fingers to his lips and kissed her knuckles. "Be careful. Don't take unnecessary risks—and not just for your own sake."

She sat very still, believing she knew what he meant but not allowing herself to be entirely sure. "I won't," she said at last.

"Can I hold you to that?"

She disengaged her hand. It tingled faintly. "Yes," she told him. "You can." Then abruptly the other Karuth, the mask, the public face, reasserted itself, and she stood up. "I'm going to give you a strong sleeping draft. You'll be unconscious for some hours, and it'll make your rapid recovery more convincing. Sanquar will tend you from now on; I won't be able to come again. At least not unless . . ." She didn't finish the sentence.

Strann smiled. "You need say nothing more, Lady Karuth. I will put myself in Sanquar's hands, and I will be a model, if unusually silent, patient."

She prepared the sleeping draft and stood by as, with a grimace at the taste, Strann drank it. Then, taking the empty cup, she moved toward the door. As her hand touched the latch, Strann said, "Karuth."

"Yes?" She looked back.

"Our gods go with you."

Her smile was tentative, but warm. "With us both, Strann."

21

"I suspect," Sanquar said, "that it must have been a reaction brought on by the rigors of his journey. His body's method, if you like, of telling him that it had had quite enough."

"Yes." Karuth's voice was distracted. She was sitting at the infirmary table checking her inventory; when Sanquar glanced at her, he could only see the back of her bowed head. He tried again.

"Or possibly he contracted it on Summer Isle, and it lay dormant until exhaustion and weakness made him vulnerable. The gods alone know what manner of fevers are rife in the south, especially since the sorceress usurped the throne."

If she'd been paying more than minimal attention, Karuth might have asked him how Ygorla's depradations could have led to an increase in virulent fevers; as it was, she only said, "Possibly," and carried on with the checking of her list.

Sanquar gave up. There were a great many questions he wanted to ask her, mainly concerning the way in which she'd brought about such an extraordinarily swift remission of Strann's fever, but it seemed that they must wait. Disappointed but phlegmatic, he picked up his medical bag.

"I've a few bedridden sufferers still to see, so I'll attend to them now if you don't need me here."

This time she did at least look up, though he had the disconcerting impression that she was only half aware of his presence. "What? No, that's fine, Sanquar. A good idea." She looked away again, and with a shrug, Sanquar left.

Alone in the infirmary, Karuth tried to concentrate afresh on the inventory before her, but realized within a few minutes that the task she'd so determinedly set herself was impossible. She couldn't keep her attention on mundane matters, not with Yandros's whispered words reverberating incessantly in her mind and refusing to give her respite. "The Speaking of the Way" . . . the phrase haunted her, and for the twentieth time she felt a fear that was close to panic rise in her as she tried again, and failed again, to quash the thought of it and put it beyond reach. She *must* find a distraction. If Ailind could see into her mind with the clarity that he had implied, then it would take only a moment's carelessness at the wrong time to jeopardize everything and put herself in mortal danger into the bargain.

She looked up at the oblong of the window. Dusk was closing in, and the courtyard, still snowbound but the snow trammeled now by the crisscrossing tracks of many feet, looked dank and miserably oppressive. Karuth lit two lamps and closed the curtains, then went to the door and looked out into the corridor beyond. This passage was one of the main routes to the dining hall, and already a few adepts and students were making their way toward the hall for the evening meal. She closed the door again, thinking hard and rapidly, then made her decision. Every hour—indeed every moment—that she delayed and dissembled would increase the risk to herself and to the accomplishment of the task Yandros had set her. She couldn't hope to hide from Ailind what she knew for long, and there would be no time better suited to her mission than this evening hour, when most of her peers gathered to dine and the rest of the castle was largely deserted. She must take a tight grip on her courage and act now. Tomorrow might well be too late.

She took her shawl from behind the door and wrapped it over her head and around her shoulders. In the corridors' low light, and dressed as she was in a nondescript gray gown, anyone who saw her would be as likely as not to pass her by without a second glance, and she reached the doors to the courtyard without being hailed. The courtyard steps were slippery, and under the stoa the snow had melted then frozen again with the fall of dusk, forming a sheet of ice. Karuth slithered her way precariously to the library door, ducked under the low lintel, and started slowly down in the darkness.

As she neared the foot of the spiral, she realized to her dismay that there was not only light below but also the sound of muted voices. She'd prayed that she would find the library empty at this time of the evening, but though the gods of Chaos might be on her side, simple luck evidently was not. Karuth negotiated the last few steps, pushed the door open, and went in. There were five people in the vaulted, torchlit chamber; she knew them all, but counted none of them as especial friends, so a brief nod and smile was greeting enough. For the sake of prudence Karuth went to the shelves of medical books and took down a heavy compendium, which she tucked under her arm before moving to the cobwebbed corner where the oldest manuscripts and parchments were stored. As she looked at the dusty rows, her spirits sank. These ancient papers were uncatalogued; they had simply been stacked wherever they would fit and were in no logical sequence. It might be the work of days at the very least to find what she was searching for.

Daunted, she cast her mind back to the hours she had spent with Arcoro Raeklen Vir before he left the castle, seeking a clue to the still-unsolved secret of the Maze. She couldn't recall that search unearthing any reference to the Speaking of the Way; though of course if she'd come across the phrase she might at the time have dismissed it as irrelevant. It seemed, then, that the laborious task must begin all over again, though this time with far greater urgency.

"Researching our ancestors' methods, Karuth?"

She turned at the sound of the voice behind her and saw a fair-haired, middle-aged woman, a teaching adept by the name of Silve Rayna Cotal, watching her with quizzical interest. Karuth felt herself tense inwardly and only hoped that her outward demeanour remained calm as she replied,

"Yes. It surprises me how often the older records contain information that later scholars either dismissed or considered too trivial to include in their own works."

"Especially on the matter of rare fevers, eh?" Silve smiled. "I understand you achieved a small miracle with one of your patients today."

Some of Karuth's tension ebbed as she realized what lay behind Silve's interest. She returned the smile. "I'd hardly call it a miracle, Silve—simple luck would be closer to the truth."

"And the man's recovering?"

"Rapidly, I'm thankful to say. I don't believe the rest

of us have anything to fear; I've come to the conclusion that his was an unusual but isolated case and that the infectious stage must have passed some time before his arrival at the castle."

"Ah." Silve looked relieved. "That's good news. Well, I must be away; my stomach tells me that it's almost time for the evening meal."

Karuth smiled a farewell and turned back to the shelves as Silve headed for the door. *Calm down,* she told herself sternly, trying to quell the uncomfortable thump of her heart. *There's nothing to fear. Silve didn't suspect any duplicity, and neither will anyone else. Go on with the search, and stop believing that your secret shines about you like an aura!*

Despite her firm assurances to herself, she was nonetheless relieved when, one by one, the library's other occupants drifted away until at last she was alone. As soon as the door closed behind the last lingerer, she put aside the medical book and set about sorting through the manuscripts with urgent energy. There were so *many*. Records of births and deaths and marriages, lists of tithes brought in from the provinces, legal disputes, reports of students' progress . . . only about one document in three seemed to contain any references to Circle rites or sorcerous practices, which both surprised and worried her. Could some of the old records have been lost or even deliberately destroyed, perhaps at the time of Change? If that were so, then her quest might prove entirely futile, and what would she do then?

She was sitting at one of the long tables, poring over her third pile of musty parchments, when she heard the door creak. Hastily she opened the medical tome that still lay beside her for appearance' sake and looked up.

Calvi Alacar stood on the threshold. For a moment he gazed uncertainly at her, then ventured a hesitant smile. "Hello, Karuth. I thought everyone else was in the dining hall."

Karuth's heart thudded painfully against her ribs. Save for Ailind or Tirand, Calvi was the last person she wished to see at this moment. "I . . ." gods, her face was coloring, she could feel it. "I have some research to do." She indicated the textbook. "It's easier to concentrate without others here to distract me."

Calvi didn't take the broad hint but continued to look at her, oddly she thought—or was her nervousness driving her to imagine demons where none existed? Then he pulled out a chair on the opposite side of the table and sat down.

"I came here because I wanted to be on my own for a while too," he said. "But now, I—well, I'm glad to see you." He uttered a short, self-mocking laugh. "You're one of the few people who doesn't bow and scrape and call me High Margrave the whole time while trying to hide their conviction that I'm not fit for my office."

His gaze was roaming across the tabletop, and carefully Karuth slid the open book across the parchment before her to ensure that he couldn't read it. "Be careful, Calvi. You're beginning to sound cynical."

"Am I? I don't think I am cynical, not really. Just . . . confused." He frowned. "Very confused." A long pause, then abruptly he looked up once more, this time with painful candor. "Karuth, I *am* glad to have found you here. I've been wanting to talk to you since yesterday, but there hasn't been a chance."

Karuth's expression remained neutral. "On a medical matter?"

"No." He looked surprised and a little hurt. "No, not that at all. It's about Strann."

"Strann?" *Caution,* said an inner voice.

"Yes. I hear he's recovering from the fever, by the way. I'm glad—I liked him when we met before, at—at Blis's—" He swallowed. "And I think that's the trouble. I mean, it's so hard to stop liking someone, isn't it? Whatever they may have done, you can't simply change your entire view without at least giving them a second chance. So I have to ask, I have to know. Karuth—*is* Strann a traitor?"

Karuth sighed wearily, wondering what mischievous gremlin had made Calvi choose the worst of all possible moments to raise such a subject. She didn't want to talk about Strann. She didn't want to *think* about Strann, not here, not now. It was too dangerous.

Trying to distance herself without making the rebuff too obvious, she said, "What makes you think I can answer such a question, Calvi? I have no special knowledge, and I'm not a seeress."

"But you know Strann."

"Little better than you do. We're hardly the oldest of friends. You seem to have forgotten that I met him only once before his arrival here." Her tone was unintentionally sharp. Calvi flushed and looked away.

"I didn't mean to presume. I just thought—"

She interrupted him. "Please—this is neither the time nor the place to talk about Strann and what he might or might not be." She must shake him off, she thought. She didn't want to hurt him with a blunt rejection, but neither could she afford to worry about his finer feelings at this moment.

"Calvi, I don't wish to be unkind to you, but I have

work to do, and I need to concentrate on that and not be distracted by questions and speculations. I can't tell you anything about Strann. If you want someone to talk to, then I'll gladly spend time with you tomorrow if that's of any help. But for now, I want solitude. I'm sorry."

Calvi's chair scraped gratingly on the stone floor as he pushed it back. "No," he said in a small, distant voice, "*I'm* sorry. I didn't realize. I thought that perhaps . . . well, never mind." He rose. "Forgive me. I'll leave you in peace."

His blue eyes were watching her, and she knew that he hoped she might relent. She'd often been susceptible to his charm in the past, but this time she only said, "I'll see you tomorrow. Perhaps I'll be in a better mood then."

He inclined his head at the tacit apology and walked to the door. On the threshold he looked back.

"Is anything wrong, Karuth? Is there any way in which I might help?"

Karuth didn't unbend. "Nothing's wrong. Good night, Calvi."

He lingered as though he was about to say something more, then thought better of it. "Good night," he said dejectedly, and his footsteps faded away up the stairs.

Karuth found the parchment ten minutes later. It was among a bundle of faded and all-but-illegible manuscripts on the lowest shelf of all, and when she made out the first words, written in an elegant but archaic hand, her stomach churned with excitement.

Very cautiously, for the parchment was perilously fragile, she brushed a film of dust from the surface and bent more closely over the table. The dust made her sneeze, and as she began to read, she found that in places the script was barely decipherable, for the spelling was strange and the text contained many words and phrases that had long since fallen into disuse. This document must be centuries old; the ritual didn't follow any of the traditional forms but was completely unfamiliar in every detail, and Karuth began to realize how greatly the Circle's practices —and perhaps far more than its practices—must have changed since the day that this ancient spell had been committed to parchment.

At last she looked up. Her gaze focused on one of the torches on the far wall, but she didn't see it. The rite was so simple. It required no ceremonial cleansing, no summoning of the elemental guardians, no trance state. A novitiate child could have performed it without a second thought, and it would be completed in a matter of minutes. But as to what would result, the manuscript gave not the smallest clue. Only the name that the ancient sorcerers had given it—the Speaking of the Way—even hinted at what the spell's nature might be, and the hint meant nothing to Karuth. A mystery, an enigma. Crying in the dark.

But dared she voice that cry, knowing that it might well be answered? The Speaking of the Way would, or so she had been led to believe, at very least give the Chaos lords access to the castle—and if they entered the mortal world, they would inevitably and immediately clash head-on with Ailind of Order. What might the consequences be then? Impossible to surmise and almost as hard to imagine. For all she knew, what she was preparing to do might bring disaster on them all. Ailind must surely have his own plan for defeating the usurper; what might be the result of Chaos's sudden intervention in his scheme?

Karuth stared down at the parchment again. The truth was, she could predict nothing with any accuracy. Whatever she did, whether she performed the rite or whether she hid the scroll away again and tried to forget that she had ever seen it, she would be gambling. And whichever path she chose, the stakes were high. She thought of Yandros's eerie manifestation in Strann's bedchamber. She remembered his voice, the voice to which she felt an instinctive affinity. Then she thought of Ailind, recalling his harsh warning when she'd made her solitary, abortive attempt to call on Chaos, and her stomach contracted queasily. Whatever his plans might be, whatever the cost of her interference, she couldn't bring herself to accept that Ailind's draconian ways were right, either for the Circle in its present crisis or—more importantly—for the future. She *had* to follow her instinct, and her instinct was screaming at her to act. She must cast the die, and pray that its fall brought good and not evil.

Her legs felt as though they were made of crumbling, dessicated wood as she pushed herself up from her chair and crossed to the small door which led to the Marble Hall. The rattle of the latch sounded deafening to her ears; she closed the door carefully behind her, then swallowed saliva and started down the narrow, sloping passage. Soon the familiar dim phosphorescence began to show ahead, lighting the way and rapidly growing brighter as she progressed, until at last the corridor turned and the silver door to the hall itself lay directly ahead.

As soon as she saw it, Karuth halted in surprise. The door wasn't glowing with its usual soft, ghostly radiance; instead it seemed to be wreathed in fire—silver fire, a cold, blinding brilliance that filled the corridor. Dazzled, Karuth held a splay-fingered hand before her face to save her eyes from the worst of it. The light sparkled in the air around her and formed peculiar, coruscating patterns across her skin, and abruptly she remembered the nightmare she'd suffered in which she had stood helpless in this very spot while the old High Initiate, Keridil Toln, beckoned to her from the silver door and a long, evil shadow reached out across the floor to engulf her.

Fiercely she took a grip on her nerves, reminding herself that this was no dream and that she was in full control of her actions. Still holding a protective hand before her face, she drew breath, ignored her racing pulse, and started to move forward once more—

A terrific flash of livid whiteness blasted outward from the door, and for a split second the image of a seven-rayed star seared into Karuth's brain. Shouting with shock, she reeled back, and as she stumbled against the wall, the brilliant light vanished, leaving only a dim, grayish illumination filtering through the corridor. Gasping, Karuth pushed herself unsteadily upright, blinking as her eyes struggled to adjust to the violent change.

And the silence was broken by a faint but emphatic *click.*

She looked at the silver door and saw that it was opening, swinging back on silent hinges and revealing the Marble Hall beyond. Mist threaded with eldritch pastel colors shifted like slowly moving water, and through it the ranks of tall pillars loomed dreamlike and remote. Hardly aware of what she was doing, but driven by an unconscious blend of instinct and desire, Karuth moved slowly toward the door and hesitated on the threshold as her psychic senses took in the atmosphere. The Marble Hall was silent and serene. It felt like a place of safety, a haven where she might hide and where no power could touch her against her will. She stepped in. Her feet made a faint hushing sound as she crossed the mosaic floor, and the mist enveloped her like a strange, shimmering cloak. She passed the first rank of pillars, then the second, her gaze following the mosaic's pattern as she searched for the black circle that by repute—though no one had ever known for certain in this place of peculiar dimensions—marked the hall's exact center. There it was, a darkness like the open mouth of a deep well in the floor ahead, incongruous amid the surrounding patterns of subtle color. Swiftly Karuth moved toward it and stood at its edge, staring down. She knew that she must now steel herself to break a taboo that had existed for many generations, for the Speaking of the Way must be uttered from within that black circle, where for centuries past no adept had dared to stand. How the taboo had come into being, and why, Karuth didn't know, and she thrust all speculations about its possible origin from her mind. This was no time to procrastinate. She had memorized the ritual, she had gained the safety of the Marble Hall, and Yandros had told her that here she was beyond the influence of the lords of Order. No one could stop her now. The rite must be performed.

She began to breathe slowly and steadily in the way that she'd been taught as a novitiate, stilling her mind and allowing the muscles of her body to relax. Then as the exercise began to take effect she raised her head and looked beyond the black circle to where, vast and eerie in the mist, the seven colossi depicting the gods of Chaos and Order loomed on their pedestals. For some moments Karuth gazed at the carved figures, each standing back to back with its own counterpart from the opposing realm. Yandros and Aeoris; Aeoris stern, Yandros smiling with a hint of dark humor. And the lesser brethren, their names unknown . . . with one exception. Which, she wondered, was the figure of Ailind? Unlike the lords of Chaos, the faces of the gods of Order were all alike to the smallest detail, and any one of the six serene but unsmiling stone masks might depict the being who had come to dwell in the castle. Well, Karuth thought with the smallest of smiles, it was of no importance now. She no longer had anything to fear from Ailind or from any of his brothers.

Her mind was calm, her body pliant and at ease. Dismissing the last, lingering shreds of her old doubt and fear, she prepared to step forward into the black circle.

And from behind her a voice high-pitched with alarm cried, "Karuth! *What are you doing?*"

Karuth whirled. Coming through the agitating pastel mist toward her was Calvi.

Shock and anger made her voice savage. She caught hold of his arm as he reached her, and her nails dug viciously into his flesh. "What do you think you're about? The Marble Hall's forbidden to you without the Circle's sanction!"

Calvi shook her off with a violent movement. "And it's forbidden to you!" he countered. "I know. Tirand told me." His blue eyes were hard, and high color burned on both his cheeks. "I want to know what you're doing, Karuth. Tell me!"

"It's none of your concern," she hissed at him. "Go away, Calvi, don't try to interfere. Leave me *alone!*"

"I will not! Karuth, listen to me—I'm not trying to interfere, I'm only trying to *help* you. You're planning something, aren't you? Something that goes against Tirand's orders. You're trying to defy Lord Ailind—"

"Damn Ailind!" the contemptuous words came involuntarily, but Karuth no longer cared a whit for prudence.

"You can't say that! You *mustn't*!" Calvi grasped hold of her arms, shaking her urgently. "I beg you, Karuth, for your own sake don't be a fool! You can't disobey a god. It's wrong; it's *blasphemous*! You're putting your own life at risk!"

She stared at him, her eyes dangerous. "Let go of me, Calvi. I won't tell you twice."

He released her but didn't back off. "Come with me, Karuth," he said. "Come away from here. Whatever this is, it can't bring anything but harm to us all. That isn't what you want, is it?"

He was so naive, she thought. So well-meaning, and genuinely concerned for her. She wanted to strike him, rake her nails down his cheek and scar it, smash his blind belief in Ailind and Tirand and the Circle and all they stood for. With a great effort she choked back the desire and with it the impulse to defy reason and tell him everything and laugh in his horrified face.

"Calvi," she said, and her voice shook with the strain of keeping her temper, "why I'm here, and what I mean to do, is my business and mine alone. Not yours, not Tirand's, and most certainly not Ailind's. I will tell you once more: Go away. Don't meddle with matters that you can't even begin to comprehend."

"Oh, but I *do* comprehend. And I'm not afraid of you, Karuth. You may be a sorceress and a high-ranking adept, but you've also been my good friend for too many years for either of us to throw that away now. I ask you again: Will you leave this hall with me now and forget that this ever happened, before it's too late?"

Karuth's face was like granite, and if she'd had the

power to do it, Calvi knew, she would have blasted him where he stood. "No," she said. "I will not."

He backed away. "Then I must fetch Tirand. I'm sorry, Karuth—but you leave me no other choice." And he turned and began to run back toward the silver door.

"Calvi, no!" Karuth made a wild grab for him but missed, and she screamed his name again, starting after him. She had to stop him; if he escaped, if he sounded the alarm, everything would be in ruins!

"Calvi!" She couldn't catch him; he was too fast, too fleet—he was almost at the door and in moments he'd be through it and away. Her voice rose in near-hysterical fury. "No, Calvi, damn you, *come back!"*

Calvi raced for the door. He was five paces from it, three, one—

And with a sound like a mountain falling, the door smashed shut in his face.

"No!" He grabbed for the handle, pulling it, twisting it, thumping his fist against the door's smooth surface. "No! Open! Ailind help me, Aeoris help me, *open!"*

Ten steps behind him, Karuth stopped. She understood.

"It won't open, Calvi. There's nothing you can do."

He spun around. The color had drained from his face, and he looked sick. "You did this . . . Karuth, in the gods' names, *please*—unlock the door, let me go. Don't put us all in peril!"

She smiled at him, a strange, knowing smile. With the danger averted, her fury had fled. She was sorry that Calvi must now be an unwilling witness to what she was about to do, but there was no help for it. He'd brought it on himself.

"I didn't lock the door," she said more gently. "Something else is in control here, something far more powerful than anything that a mere Circle adept could muster. But that power knows that I daren't let you go to Tirand, and certainly not to Ailind. I'm sorry, Calvi, but you must stay here and see this through with me. Neither of us has any choice in the matter now."

Calvi stared back at her. He'd never seen Karuth like this, and he knew intuitively that there was nothing he could do either to sway her or to stop her from carrying out her intention. He might be physically stronger than she was—although that was something that had never been put to the test—but whatever possessed her now couldn't be combatted by physical means. He was trapped. He was helpless.

As Karuth turned away and began to walk with slow deliberation back toward the black mosaic, Calvi covered his face with both hands and whispered, *"Aeoris help me! Aeoris help us all!"*

22

"Hear me, O you princes. Hear me, you creators and contenders, you lords of Life and Death, you lords of Air and Earth and Fire and Water and Time and Space. I am of you and yet not of you; I am flesh and yet I am spirit; and I speak with the sanction granted to the legions who have stood before me in this place and walked before me upon this way."

The floor beneath her feet was quaking. Illusion or reality, Karuth didn't know, and she was beyond any ability to care. Around her the mists of the Marble Hall swirled like a fog rolling in from the sea, its gentle colors darkening ominously to hellish shades of purple and green and gray. Her mind was soaring; with the one faint spark that still flickered in the world of physical reality she knew that somewhere by the great statues Calvi was crouching and cowering in terror, but Calvi was nothing, he no longer mattered. The rite had taken her, and she was lost within it.

"I stand before you in this place, and I walk toward you on this way." Her voice sounded through the Marble Hall, and the mist sang back a hundred eerie echoes. "The way is long but the way is old and the way is the way of power. I am chosen and I am willing. With the feet that are my flesh I tread between dimensions, and I shall speak the way. With the hand that is my flesh I reach out across the abyss, and I shall speak the way. With the eyes that are the windows of my soul I look from world into world, and I shall speak the way."

She could feel a huge, rhythmic pulse like a titanic heart beating deep beneath the castle's foundations. Her entire body began to shudder and she shut her eyes, throwing her head back as her unbound hair fell like dark water to her waist, and her voice rang out powerfully and ecstatically.

"The locks of time are shattered and the bars of space are burned to ashes! Come, you creators—I will walk with you on the way, and I will reach to you on the way, and I will gaze upon you on the way! As it was in the days before me, it shall be again! Hear me—hear me, and let the seal be broken!" She drew a breath that hissed like a hundred serpents; then with terrible control, terrible calm, she spread her arms wide, eyes staring ahead into infinity. So softly that the words were barely audible, she uttered the final words of the rite.

"I speak the way. And the way is open."

There was a sound that went beyond sound. It rose from the depths of her soul, and it smashed up through her psyche and into her consciousness like a monstrous hammer-blow. Somewhere in another dimension Karuth screamed a scream of pain and shock and triumph together, and beneath her feet the black circle opened to a vortex of utter emptiness. A shaft of shattering black light roared through the vortex, a bolt of raw, shrieking energy that blasted into the Marble Hall as power crackled in her arteries and almost stopped her heart. She felt herself falling, pitching into a universe of lightning and spinning stars; the vortex was hurtling toward her, opening wider, wider—

Then she was standing in the center of the black circle, and around her the Marble Hall was silent and still.

Karuth blinked. It was an involuntary movement. The scene before her blanked momentarily, then returned. The pale mist, the pillars, the looming statues. Nothing had changed. All was normal.

A great shudder racked her. What had happened— what had she done? She remembered . . . but no, the recollection was gone as though a supernatural hand had brushed across her mind and erased it. Then she thought of Calvi and looked quickly toward the statues. He was there, crouching by the central pedestal with the twin figures of Yandros and Aeoris towering above his head. Their gazes locked. He looked faintly puzzled.

"Calvi . . ." Finding her voice was a strange experience; it was almost as if she'd forgotten how to speak and had to make a conscious effort to relearn. "What happened?"

The skin around Calvi's eyes tightened, and he shook his head. "Nothing happened, Karuth."

"But the ritual . . ."

"I heard the words. I watched you. But nothing happened."

She put a fist to her mouth. Surely, *surely* she hadn't made a terrible mistake? The rite had been so simple: Perhaps that was where the error lay? Perhaps she'd missed some small but vital thing—

The sound of Calvi's footsteps on the marble floor made her look up again, and she saw him walking slowly and cautiously toward her. He seemed calm, but there was a wary look in his eyes, the look of a man attempting to approach an unfamiliar, unpredictable, and possibly dangerous animal. On the edge of the circle he stopped and spoke cajolingly.

"Karuth, I think we should go. If the door will open now, I think we should leave this place." He hesitated, then reached out and touched her arm with a tentative hand. "I don't know what you were trying to do, but I think we must both agree that . . . well, that it didn't achieve what you'd hoped for. I'm sorry for you—but I'm glad too. Will you come with me now?"

Karuth stepped out of the circle. She felt light-headed, as if she'd been deprived of sleep for two days or so. She had no strength, no energy, and suddenly she acknowledged that she wanted to leave, because if she didn't, then the disappointment and despair might come welling up at any moment, and that would be more than she could bear.

"Yes," she said, in a small voice. "I'll come with you."

Calvi let out a long, gentle breath of sheer relief. "I'll say nothing," he told her. "No one need ever know, Karuth. You can trust me."

She opened her mouth to make some defeated and miserable attempt to thank him, then stopped as she saw his expression change. "Calvi? What is it, what's wrong?"

He didn't answer. His mouth was working soundlessly, and his eyes had focused behind her and were starting wildly in their sockets. Karuth turned.

Above the circle in the mosaic floor a shaft of black radiance had materialized. Glittering particles danced in it, hurtling roofward like water streaming at impossible speed, and Karuth felt an incredible force pull at her mind, compelling her toward the shaft.

"Karuth, don't!" Calvi caught hold of her as she made to follow the black light's call. She fought him, but he hung on, dragging her back, and they swayed together in silent conflict. Then suddenly Karuth put both hands to her skull and screamed. There was a noise—later Calvi couldn't describe it, save to say that it had sounded like the grinding, rumbling din of the huge chains that controlled the castle's main gates, but a thousand times more ominous—and for one moment the image of a great black door shimmered within the shaft of light. Then both it and the light vanished.

From the farthest of the statues came a sharp, echoing crack.

"Aeoris!" Calvi jumped back, loosing his hold on Karuth and instinctively making the splay-fingered sign of the gods before his own face. Karuth, though, stood utterly still. Her eyes strained through the mist, strained to see whether the forewarning that her sixth sense had given her was real or a weird and mad delusion. . . .

The mist shuddered, and darkness roiled across the statue's silhouette, obscuring it. When it cleared, someone was standing beside the pedestal. Feline eyes that glittered like emeralds regarded the two human souls who clutched each other's hands and stared back in stunned disbelief; and within a frame of wild and tangled black hair, thin lips in an aquiline face smiled. A long-fingered hand reached out with a graceful gesture, and a voice redolent with power said, "Greetings, Karuth. Chaos is in your debt."

Karuth couldn't speak. Calvi was grasping her hand so hard that her fingers were turning numb, and when she tried to free herself, his grip only tightened the more. The black-haired, black-clad figure turned his head to regard the young man, and the narrow smile flickered again.

"There's nothing to fear, High Margrave. I've no reason to wish to harm you."

Abruptly Calvi let go of Karuth's hand and backed two rapid paces. In a quavering voice he managed to ask, "Wh—who are you . . . ?"

"My name is Tarod."

Karuth's heart constricted. Calvi couldn't know it, nor for that matter could the great majority of Circle adepts, but she had heard that name before. More than twenty years ago it had been uttered by a dying man in a quiet room—and of all those who had borne witness to Keridil Toln's last words only she and Tirand now remained, and they had never spoken of what they had heard.

She found her voice at last. "Then you . . ." She swallowed. "You are the one who . . ."

Tarod's brilliant eyes focused on her face, and though she might have been deluding herself, she thought she saw a glint of faint approval in their depths. "So someone still remembers?" he said. "Yes, I am Yandros's brother, the one who took human incarnation in your world before the time of Change."

Calvi made a strangled, involuntary sound, and the color fled from his face. "Oh, no . . ." he said. "No—Karuth—Karuth, what have you done?" He turned toward her in frantic appeal. "Send him back! The links with Chaos have been broken—you can't disobey the Circle, you can't disobey Lord Ailind—"

"Ailind?" Tarod's tone changed, and the sudden malevolence in his voice cut off Calvi's words in mid-sentence. Slowly, almost carelessly, Tarod began to pace across the floor toward him. Calvi's eyes widened fearfully, and he tried to back away again, but the Chaos lord made a small gesture with one hand and the young man was held rigid, unable to move.

"High Margrave,' Tarod said, "I think there are one or two small misunderstandings that you and I should resolve before you make any more foolish statements. Ailind—or, as you please to call him, *Lord* Ailind—has no power whatever over me, and less power than he likes to believe over you. However much he might wish it otherwise, the principles of Equilibrium that we of Chaos laid down a hundred years ago can't be overthrown at the whim of one arrogant godling, or"—he glanced pointedly at Karuth—"to suit the prejudices of that godling's human followers. Inasmuch as the High Initiate chose to open the way to the Lords of Order in the Circle's time of need, so Karuth has chosen to take the opposite course and call upon Chaos."

Calvi couldn't move, but he could speak. With more courage than Karuth would have credited him, he stammered, "But she has no right—"

"On the contrary, she has every right. As a high-ranking adept of the Circle, she has the sanction of the gods."

That silenced Calvi, and from the very real terror that began to creep into his eyes Karuth knew that he was only now beginning, in the aftermath of his initial bravado, to realize just what manner of being he was dealing with.

Tarod moved to stand before the young man and looked down at him. Calvi shut his eyes.

"You're young and inexperienced, Calvi," Tarod said quite gently, "but I don't think you're a fool. Certainly not enough of a fool to think that you can wisely or safely embroil yourself in a matter that is between the Circle and its gods. Do I misjudge you?"

Calvi's jaw was quivering, but he still refused to be

367

completely cowed. Through clenched teeth he said, "I have a duty—"

"To the people of this mortal world, who look to you as their secular ruler. Not to Tirand Lin, not to the Circle, and not to the lords of Order. Now"—one hand reached out and touched Calvi's brow lightly—"leave this hall. You have no business here, and I wish to speak with Karuth alone." His green eyes narrowed as Calvi seemed about to voice another protest. "Don't try my patience, my young friend, or I may find it necessary to show you the real nature of the power you are attempting to argue with."

Again there was a slight movement of his fingers. Calvi's jaw dropped, and his face turned a ghastly shade; his eyes, bulging in their sockets, looked through Tarod's dark figure and beyond him, focusing on something invisible to Karuth.

"No . . ." His voice was shrill and incoherent, and saliva trickled from the corners of his mouth. *"No, please, not that, oh please don't—"*

Tarod blinked, and Calvi rocked on his feet as though a huge, invisible hand had slapped him hard across the face. On the far side of the hall there was a faint sound as the silver door swung open, and Tarod said softly, "Leave us."

Calvi uttered a sound like an insane sob, and fled. Watching him go, hearing the door slam shut behind him, Karuth felt a confusion of emotions. She was still angry with Calvi for trying to meddle in her affairs, however high-minded his intentions, and her anger was fueled by the chilling knowledge of how close he had come to wrecking everything she'd risked herself to achieve. But at the same time she pitied him. She didn't know and didn't want to know what manner of vision Tarod had shown him in that moment, but now, looking obliquely at the Chaos lord's impassive face as he, too, watched Calvi's departure, she experienced an ice-cold inward shudder as she realized that only his terrified capitulation had saved the young man from something far worse.

Suddenly Tarod turned his head. "Don't worry about him, Karuth. He'll suffer no lasting harm."

Her face turned white, and he laughed. "And don't fear that I'm reading every stray thought that goes through your head. Whatever Ailind might wish you to believe, we neither have nor would want such extreme insight into mortal minds. But we are as capable as any human of seeing the obvious, and your fondness for the young High Margrave is very transparent."

She continued to watch the silver door. "If he should go to my brother—"

"He won't. He'll run to the sanctuary of his own room and he'll stay there for a good while to come. He's too afraid to risk crossing me again, and too confused to know yet what he really thinks or believes. Besides, even if he were to go tattling to Tirand, it would achieve nothing, for he'd be sounding the alarm just a little too late." He smiled. "We thank you for that, Karuth. You showed great courage—and that's a quality that Chaos appreciates."

Karuth dropped her gaze at last and stared at the floor. It was hard to believe that she wasn't dreaming this, that she wouldn't wake at any moment to find herself in her own bed in the dark chill of the small hours. To converse with a god . . . but it wasn't even that, for she'd had that bitter experience before. No, it was Tarod himself who disoriented her. He was so utterly unlike Ailind of

Order. He spoke to her as though she were an equal, even a friend. And despite what he'd done to Calvi, the small demonstration of power that by all reason should have awed her, she wasn't afraid of him in the way that she was afraid of Ailind. Then she remembered what Strann had said about his own encounter with Yandros and wondered, was that the crux of it? Did the lords of Chaos, as their name implied, take a perverse delight in reversing all mortal conventions and expectations, and was this therefore nothing less than she might have anticipated?

Unable to answer the question, she said quietly, "Thank you, my lord. But if I'm to be truthful, I have to confess that I don't even know what I did."

Tarod's soft laughter stirred echoes in the mist. "No," he said, "I don't suppose you do. This castle has many properties that your adepts have either forgotten or were never aware of, and the ritual you used to open the way tonight was only one among a legion of spells that are unknown to the Circle, although they used to be a commonplace to the sorcerers of the distant past." He turned away from her and started to walk back toward the black mosaic. "I'll tell you what you did tonight, Karuth. You opened the door onto an old but disused way between your world and the realm of Chaos. It's a very ancient path; it predates anything in your history, because it was woven into these very foundations when this castle was first created thousands of years ago. The Marble Hall was built around it as a portal, and although there are many other routes by which we can travel between our world and yours, this is by far the most powerful. We call it the Chaos Gate."

"The Chaos Gate . . ." The words reverberated oddly

in the hall as Karuth thoughtfully repeated them. "I have never heard of such a thing, my lord."

"No, nor has any mortal for generations past. We used the Gate for many centuries until it was closed. How and why that came about isn't a matter that need concern you, but the way was sealed, and matters were arranged so that the seal could not be broken by us but only by our mortal servants." His lip curled faintly. "Time, however, has a habit of dimming human memory, and it wasn't long before our servants not only forgot the spell that would open the way once more, but forgot that the way even existed. Now, though, you have awakened it from its dormancy, and in doing so you have placed an old and valuable weapon in our hands." He turned on his heel to face her. "A weapon that we now urgently need to use."

"Against the usurper?"

"Yes. And not just for your sake. Also for ours."

Karuth said, "Ah—"

Tarod's face became grim. "Yes, you're aware of our predicament, aren't you? And, thanks to Strann the Storymaker, so are our enemies in the realm of Order."

Karuth nodded miserably. "But Strann wasn't to know, my lord. He was tricked, he didn't realize who Ailind was—"

He interrupted her, dismissing her plea with an impatient gesture. "Whether Strann was duped or simply careless is irrelevant. All that matters is the fact that he made a very great mistake for which we may now have to pay a terrible price."

"I don't understand."

"Don't you?" Tarod said with an edge to his voice. "Haven't you thought it out for yourself? Haven't you realized what Ailind and his scrofulous litter-mates mean to do? No, I see you haven't. You're very naive, Karuth."

Suddenly she saw it, and her face froze with shock. "Oh, but—"

"Yes?"

"The lords of Order want Ygorla to carry out her threat? They want her to destroy the stone?"

"Of course. Because if they succeed in that aim, they will destroy the balance of Equilibrium and gain the power to rule your world unchallenged."

She was aghast. "They *can't*! Surely they wouldn't want Equilibrium to be overthrown!"

He snorted derisively. "That's precisely what they want and what they've always wanted. You forget your own history, Karuth. The lords of Order didn't choose Equilibrium; we imposed it on them, and they have never, *never* submitted to it willingly!" He turned his head, staring at the statues but, Karuth suspected, not registering their presence, and a black aura flickered into life about his tall frame. "Ailind and his puppet-master, Aeoris, must be *stopped*. And they must learn their lesson over again—this time more thoroughly!"

Suddenly he looked back at her, and Karuth recoiled from the venom that burned in his eyes. In an instant all her assumptions, all her conclusions about Chaos and its overlords, fled. She'd allowed herself to look upon this being as almost human; now she knew that that had been an act of madness. Tarod might once have taken mortal incarnation in her world, but he was no more human than the elementals that haunted her most devastating nightmares, and he was a thousand times more dangerous than anything those nightmares could conjure. He had thrown off and shattered the mask, and what faced her now, with his burning emerald eyes and wild black hair and gaunt, savage face, was an incarnation of hell.

"You opened the portal to us, Karuth," Tarod said, and his voice sent a shock of terror through Karuth's bones. "You invoked the law of Equilibrium and allowed us enter your world without breaking the pact we made with your ancestors nearly a century ago. Now that I am here, I will not leave until this conflict is resolved. But what of you? Do you have the strength to see what you've begun through to its conclusion? Do you have the courage to walk with Chaos and to take its cause as your own?"

Karuth's entire body was shaking. She couldn't stop it; the spasms had hold of her and were racking her as though she were in the grip of a fever more violent than anything she'd ever known. She couldn't answer him. Words wouldn't come, and her mind was in a turmoil of terror and confusion. She couldn't face this! She was only human, she didn't have true power or true courage; she'd been a coward before, and cowardice would surely make her fail again. She couldn't live up to what he was asking of her.

An ugly, distressed sound quavered from her throat, and she covered her face with both hands. Suddenly thin fingers touched her shoulder, and she jumped as though an arrow had pierced her. Then she looked up.

Tarod was gazing down at her. The black aura and the demonic image were gone; only his green eyes still burned with an unnatural fire. "I don't demand your answer now, Karuth," he said. "We know your weaknesses, as we knew Strann's. We expect no more from any mortal than that mortal is capable of giving us."

He didn't wait for her to speak—even if she could have —but turned toward the silver door. Karuth watched him walk away, a dark wraith with the mist curling and shimmering around him, and then he was gone, and she stood alone in the Marble Hall.

Oh gods, she thought in despair, *what am I to do?* For a moment from force of habit she almost sent a silent appeal to Yandros, then laughed a wry, cracked laugh that set discordant echoes shouting between the pillars as she realized her mistake in time. As the laughter subsided, she hiccupped, wiped the back of one hand across her mouth —then stopped still as her gaze fell on the seven statues.

Chaos and Order. The mortal world's own deities, awesome in the power they wielded. She had faced a lord of Order and she had faced a lord of Chaos, and both had terrified her. Ailind, arrogant and harsh and implacable. Tarod, kinder but mercurial, and dangerous in a way that bordered on insanity. And yet . . .

She looked at Yandros's carved and smiling face. Then at Aeoris, indistinguishable from his brothers. *Do you no longer kneel to your gods, Karuth Piadar?* She bit down hard on her lower lip as Ailind's contemptuous words came back to her. *You will defy me at your peril. I will tolerate no disobedience. You are on sufferance.*

The anger surged back, the familiar, bitter and impotent anger, and its intensity astonished her. *You are on sufferance.* Sufferance to an unbending master, to one who meant to destroy Equilibrium forever and restore the rule of Order. Karuth's fury seethed to new heights, and she thought, *Better madness than that.* Better the madness she had seen in Tarod's eyes, the madness of Chaos unleashed, than to live under the stultifying yoke of Order's mistrust and hatred of all who dared oppose them. She couldn't countenance such a prospect. It was *intolerable.*

She turned her back on the statues and stared through

the mist. In her heart she knew her decision was already made and that to hesitate any longer would only delay the inevitable, and abruptly she gathered up her skirt and ran toward the silver door. It stood open. She cast one last, swift glance back at the shimmering colors behind her, then raced along the corridor to the library. The vaulted room was in darkness; carelessly, perhaps unthinkingly, Tarod had extinguished the torches with a gesture as he passed through, and Karuth groped blindly toward the door, biting back oaths of pain as she stubbed her toes and barked her shins on unseen obstacles. The door was swinging gently on its hinges and she stumbled up the spiral stairs, feeling the icy night air wash down to meet her as she neared the top. Through the outer door and into the courtyard—and she stopped in dismay. From the castle windows lights shone down on the snow, lending its graying blanket a soft golden sheen, and the lights showed her that the courtyard was empty. No new footprints led away from the door where she stood, and there was no sound but the muted growl of the sea far below the stack. Tarod had vanished.

For a few moments Karuth stood motionless, bereft. Then a shadow moved under the stoa that a moment before had been deserted.

He extended a hand as he came toward her, and she took it, though her own fingers were trembling with more than the cold. When she tried to explain, he only shook his head and smiled at her, a conspiratorial smile that almost—but not quite—made her courage desert her.

He said quietly, "Where is Ailind?"

Torches were blazing beyond the closed curtains of the dining hall, and with a small shock Karuth realized how little time must have passed since she had left the infir-

mary and ventured down to the library. Ailind would still
be in the hall, she thought, sitting with Tirand and the
other senior adepts and playing the charade of the shipwrecked mariner that he chose to maintain.

She said the words, saw Tarod nod.

"Very well. Then I think we shall pay our compliments
to our friend from the realm of Order."

He turned toward the steps that led up to the main
doors, but Karuth's voice made him halt.

"My lord Tarod . . ."

He looked back. "What is it?"

She didn't know if she dared say it, but knew she must.
She clasped her hands together, feeling sweat on her
palms. "Do you . . ." *help me,* she thought, *help me,*
". . . if Chaos is weakened by the loss it has suffered . . .
do you have the power to confront him? I'm so afraid
that . . ."

Her voice tailed off. Tarod looked thoughtfully at her
for some moments. Then he smiled again and turned his
gaze skyward. He raised his left arm, not with any drama
but in one calm movement, and beckoned.

Beyond the castle walls, beyond the stack, far, far out
to sea, a thin, eldritch wailing began to shiver through the
bitter night. On the northern edge of the world a dim
radiance shot through with dark, eerie colors began to
stain the overcast sky, and the colors coalesced into bands
that in turn formed a titanic, slowly but inexorably revolv-
ing wheel. The stones of the castle began to vibrate with
an ancient empathy, and energy crackled between two of
the towering spires, answered by a silent flash of silver
lightning far overhead. Karuth felt as though the blood
had desiccated in her veins, felt the atavistic terror bred
into her race over thousands of years, as the Warp storm,

the most ancient and most deadly herald of Chaos, gathered its power and started to move in toward the Star Peninsula. The eldritch wail was swelling now to a high, thin screaming, like the howling of damned souls, and striations of acid-green-and-blue light danced across the heavens as though the sky were a vast shell and the shell was cracking open.

Tarod caught hold of her hand, and she tore her hypnotized gaze from the monstrous phenomenon bearing down on them. A colossal crimson flash lit his face, and for one instant the mask of humanity was flung aside again and she saw the naked face of Chaos's true power.

He said, "Come, Karuth. *You* have nothing to fear tonight."

The vast, dim wheel was turning overhead, its spokes of black and green and purple and indigo rolling across the sky. Raw energy crackled once more as the spires sang their own counterpoint to the Warp's terrible song, and a network of blinding silver shattered across the firmament. Karuth's terror fell away, and in its place she felt the first stirring of a dark and thrilling excitement. She stepped toward the lord of Chaos, and the supernatural lightning flung his shadow over her as together they turned toward the steps and the castle doors beyond.

Here is a preview of

THE AVENGER
by Louise Cooper
Book 3 of *The Chaos Gate Trilogy*

Strann the Storymaker's attempt to carry Chaos's message to Tirand Lin has gone badly awry. His right hand ruined beyond repair by Ygorla's sorcery, Strann remains incarcerated at the Star Peninsula while Ailind, with the sole ear of the High Initiate, is implementing Order's plan to deal with Ygorla—and at the same time deliver a crippling blow to their old enemies in the Chaos realm.

However, through Strann Yandros has delivered a message to Karuth, who now is Chaos's only ally among the Circle adepts. With Yandros's guidance, Karuth has found and performed the ancient ritual to open the long-disused Chaos Gate, which lies at the heart of the Marble Hall. In the following scene from The Avenger, *Chaos's emissary to the mortal world makes himself known to the Circle—and to his rival from Order.*

The hour was late, but the twenty or so people still in the dining hall weren't overly anxious to leave. The fire blazing in the vast grate had been replenished yet again, the curtains were closed against the bitter winter weather, and it was more pleasant simply to sit passing the time in good company and with a few flagons of wine than to brave the castle's chilly and dimly lit corridors to retire to bed.

Most of those present were senior Circle adepts, among them the High Initiate Tirand Lin, but two non-initiates had joined the group as they gravitated to a wide semicircle of chairs around the hearth at a respectful distance from the fire's enormous heat. Shaill Falada, Matriarch of the Sisterhood, had lapsed into a comfortable semi-doze. The fire's light softened the worry-lines in her face, and her skin, its southern tan in sharp contrast to the paler complexions of the castle-dwellers, had taken on a warm, ruddy glow. Opposite the Matriarch, at the High Initiate's side, sat a tall man with a stern, serious face, considerably younger than his long white hair might imply at first glance. To all intents and purposes he was nothing more than a sailor shipwrecked on the Star Peninsula during a gale and now recuperating at the castle; only three among this company knew his true identity, and they had vowed to obey his command not to reveal the truth to their colleagues. Ailind, lord of Order and brother to Aeoris, had his own reasons for wishing to keep his presence in the mortal world a secret, and although he had cultivated the adepts' friendship he had also taken care not to exert his influence—at least, not publicly.

Servants had cleared away the remains of the evening meal, and the company's conversation had been drifting among a number of idle topics. In recent days there had been little time and less inclination for leisure, and these evening gatherings had become small and precious oases of relative peace. It wasn't that the crisis which hung over the world could be forgotten or ignored even for this short period; far from it, for there was little doubt now that Ygorla, the usurper and self-styled empress, had a hold on the land that no mortal power could break. But the castle of the Star Peninsula was the one bastion which Ygorla and her demon father couldn't breach at will. Here the Circle and those who had taken refuge with them were secure, and until now their task had been to maintain that security and keep the key players in the fight against Ygorla safe from her depredations. The enforced inactivity didn't sit well on most of the adepts' shoulders; the more hotheaded would have preferred to join battle, physical or occult, with the sorceress, while even the most prudent fretted at the fact that thus far their strategy seemed to consist of little more than an exchange of carefully worded letters between the Circle and the usurper. Only during these brief interludes, like the calm eye at the heart of a storm, did they make an effort to shake off their frustrations and their doubts and pretend for a while that life had returned to normal.

However, the hiatus couldn't last. Even at these gatherings there was always someone who, deliberately or not, introduced the sour note, the sudden reminder that cold reality was only a chance word away. This time the culprit was Sen Briaray Olvit, a senior adept with a reputation for speaking first and thinking later, and one of the only three present who was party to Ailind's secret. They'd been discussing wine, debating the relative merits of the Han and Prospect vineyards, when with a grimace Sen said, "We're assuming, of course, that the question of our preferences isn't going to become purely academic before the next harvest. By the time this business is over neither Han nor Prospect nor anywhere else may have a vineyard left for all we know."

Tirand eyed Sen sourly. He'd known that the reminder of their predicament must come but had hoped that, for tonight at least, they might have had a longer respite. He thought of trying to steer the conversation back onto a happier subject but before he could speak someone else picked up Sen's thread.

"You've a point there, Sen, and it has far greater ramifications. Wine's a luxury that we could easily survive without; but what about our more fundamental needs—the basic foodstuffs? Has anyone yet calculated how long we can continue without fresh supplies?"

Everyone looked at Tirand. The High Initiate sighed inwardly. He didn't want to turn his mind back to such unhappy matters, but duty must come first. And the question was a valid one that should have been tackled before now.

"So much depends on how long this crisis is to continue," he said. "Thankfully, all the tithe-caravans from the provinces arrived before we were effectively besieged here, so our winter stores are up to their usual level. Now, normally of course we receive fresh tithes in the spring, as soon as the weather improves enough for the mountain passes to be negotiable again. But this year . . . as you say, we can't be sure of anything. There may be no caravans: there may be no provisions for the provinces, let alone for us. You're right; it's something that we haven't previously taken into account, and it's a serious oversight."

An elderly woman spoke up. "Do you think we should ration, Tirand?"

"Until we know precisely the state of our stores I can't say for certain. But I think we'd be well advised to at least consider the possibility."

On the far side of the hearth the Matriarch set down her wine cup. "My women and I can help you there, Tirand," she said. "When I was in Wishet, years ago, we had a season of disastrous floods—you'll be too young to remember that—and there was rationing in the province for nearly half a year afterwards. What I learned then may be useful now, and it'll be some small recompense for having encumbered you with extra mouths to feed."

Tirand smiled at her. "You haven't encumbered us, Shaill, and I trust you know that as well as I do!"

"You're very chivalrous, my dear, but you won't silence my conscience, nor the nightmares I suffer about having fled here to sanctuary while Sister Fiora and the other Seniors stayed in Southern Chaun. If you'll entrust me with cataloguing the castle's supplies and drawing up a contingency, I'll feel that I'm at least contributing something practical and useful." She paused a moment, considering, then added: "I might enlist Calvi's help. It would benefit him, I think, if he had something positive to do, however mundane the task might be."

"That reminds me," Sen said, "Where is our young High Margrave tonight? I didn't see him at dinner, and it's not like him to miss a meal."

Tirand glanced around the hall. Sen was right: Calvi Alacar, brother and reluctant successor to the murdered Blis, wasn't among the gathering; in fact Tirand couldn't remember having seen him since earlier this afternoon.

"I hope he hasn't gone down with this winter rheum that's scourging the castle," the Matriarch said. "I thought he looked a little peaky this morning. I meant to mention it to Sanquar, but it—"

She stopped in mid-sentence as, so suddenly that they all started, the doors at the far end of the hall crashed open. Tirand turned in his chair, his eyes shocked and angry. "What in the name of—"

He, too, got no further as he saw the two figures who had entered the hall. One he knew all too well; his own sister, Karuth Piadar, with whom at present he was barely on speaking terms. The other . . . The High Initiate's eyes focused on the tall, black-haired man at Karuth's side, and an ice-cold shock went through him. He couldn't explain it—the man was a total stranger; he had no reason for alarm—but there was something about him, something in that cool, aquiline face, something in the intensity of the feline green eyes, that struck fear into

Tirand's heart. And Karuth: there was high color in her normally pallid cheeks; she looked defiant, almost *triumphant*. . . .

Then from behind him, Ailind of Order uttered a sharp and swiftly suppressed oath.

The black-haired man smiled. "Ah. So you recognize me, old friend, even after all these years?" He spoke quietly, but his voice carried across the hall. Then, moving with the grace of a cat, he walked toward them. Tirand saw Ailind's face flush with fury. Bewildered, he looked to the lord of Order in mute appeal but Ailind ignored him, his gaze fixed on the approaching figure. Confused and suddenly unsure of himself, Tirand rose slowly to his feet. The stranger stopped three paces from him, inclined his head and said:

"Good evening, High Initiate. My compliments to you and to the Circle." The quick green eyes focused on the Matriarch and he made a more courteous bow. "Madam."

"Sir . . ." The Matriarch's own eyes were alight with curiosity. "I'm afraid you have the advantage of me. Do I know you?"

He smiled thinly. "I believe you know *of* me, lady, though we've not met before."

If Tirand had been watching Ailind he would have seen that the god was motionless, rigid, his expression twisted and ugly. But Tirand was too caught up by the twin reactions which were rising in his own mind. He felt afraid of this stranger—and at the same time he felt that, in some subtle way, the man was mocking him.

His voice rang sharply out before Shaill could speak again. "Who are you?" His tone was aggressive. "What is your business here?"

Again that chilly smile; a smile, Tirand saw, of utter confidence. The black-haired man made a careless gesture toward Ailind.

"Ask your friend and mentor who hides behind you like a serpent behind a bush," he replied crisply. "He knows me very well."

Tirand's face purpled. *"Do you know who—"* Then, suddenly realizing what he had been about to say, he bit the furious words back. But the stranger finished the sentence for him.

"Do I know who this creature is? Yes, High Initiate, I do. Which is more than can be said for the great majority of your companions, isn't it?"

Tirand's color deepened. "Damn your insolence! Who are you to enter this hall uninvited, to—"

The stranger's eyes changed. Only Tirand saw the full impact of the change, for the green gaze was locked on his own, and it silenced him as he realized that, whatever this being might be, he was not human.

"I am Tarod," the black-haired one said softly. "Brother to Yandros of Chaos. And I do not require the invitation of one of Order's puppets to enter the hall which our own servants built an eon ago."

There was a flurry from the company: shocked exclamations, gasps, hissing intakes of breath. Sen and two others were on their feet; the Matriarch gripped the arms of her chair until her knuckles turned white. Tirand began to tremble.

"That . . ." he said in a strained voice, "is impossible. . . ."

Tarod's look grew malevolent. "Impossible, High Initiate?"

"You are . . . you're a fraud, a trickster!"

Tarod sighed. "As you wish." He snapped his fingers toward the far end of the hall, and all down its length, one by one, the torches in their wall brackets dimmed and went out. Only the firelight remained, and by its red glow Tarod scanned the half circle of stunned faces around him.

"Just a trickster's small magic, High Initiate," he said sardonically. "I assume it's nothing that a first-rank novice couldn't achieve at the blink of an eye?" Tirand didn't reply, and Tarod snapped his fingers again, this time toward the hearth. The fire went out, plunging the hall into darkness save for a thin bar of illumination shining under the doors from the passage beyond. Someone stifled a scream and there was a clatter as a chair was knocked over. Then Tarod looked up at the shadowed rafters of the great hall, and as he did so the roof seemed to melt away and the hall was open to the sky.

This time the scream was in earnest, and another voice shrieked out in terror. "Gods, no, *no!*" The Warp, which Tarod had summoned and brought sweeping down out of the north, was howling directly overhead. Shielded by the warm, bright security of the hall, by its thick walls and closed curtains, the adepts had been utterly unaware of the storm's approach, and as the sight and sound of it smashed down on them they were thrown into panic. The Warp's awesome voice, like the crying of a thousand tortured souls, beat against their senses; the high, thin hurricane-shriek that rode with and above the storm set the castle's foundations quaking in response. Crimson and emerald and silver lightning shattered across the sky, its brilliance hurling the hall and its scrambling, cowering occupants into a mayhem of savage tableaux. And over it all, far up in the tormented heavens, the great, dim bands of dark color wheeled slowly inexorably across the world.

Suddenly from somewhere near the empty fireplace a voice roared, *"Stop this!"*

Ailind was on his feet, his eyes burning gold and fired with loathing. Tarod looked back at him across a dozen huddled forms, and his own eyes narrowed. Then he glanced up—and the Warp flicked out of existence. The lightning and the dim wheel of color vanished; the howling voices shattered into nothing. Stars glared coldly down from a clear sky, and at the eastern end of the hall the faint glow of the rising first moon stained the top of the roofless wall.

Slowly, the prayers and the moaning died away as one by one the company realized that the supernatural storm had gone. The fire flared into life once more, and then the torches—and when Tirand and a few others dared to raise their heads, they saw that the hall roof was whole once more and the scene had returned to normal.

Very slowly Tirand got to his feet. He looked once at Tarod, a look of shock and fear and hatred, then turned to assist the Matriarch, whose voluminous robe was hampering her efforts to rise. The rest, too, were recovering their composure; Sen and two helpers were restoring the tipped and scattered chairs while others, finding that their legs were unwilling as yet to support them, sat shakily and mutely and tried to regain some semblance of dignity.

Behind Tarod another figure moved, and Karuth rose from where she'd been crouching, face hidden in her hands, by one of the long tables. She'd anticipated something like this, though the suddenness and violence of the Chaos lord's show of power had taken her unawares. Tarod glanced at her and smiled. She hesitated a bare moment, then returned the smile, shaking her long, dark hair back from her eyes and blinking rapidly in the renewed light. Tirand was too preoccupied to notice the look that passed between her and Tarod—but Ailind was not. Understanding dawned on the lord of Order's face and, pushing aside an adept who had inadvertantly blocked his way, he took a step towards her. *"You—"* he began. Tirand, hearing him, turned sharply; but before Ailind could say any more, Tarod stepped into his path.

"High Initiate." His eyes were as cold as the sea's depths as he turned his back on Ailind, effectively shifting the focus of attention from him to Tirand. "I trust I have proved myself to your satisfaction?"

The Matriarch, who was now reseated, made a strangled sound that might have been a sob or a near-hysterical snort of laughter. *"Proved . . ."* she said. "Gods, I— *gods!"*

Tarod looked past Tirand to where she sat and his manner changed. "Madam," he said, "I must ask your pardon for making my point so emphatically. I have no ill will towards any mortal here," he put the faintest of emphases on the word *mortal*, "but it is essential that none of you should be in any doubt of my true nature. I'm only sorry that I distressed you."

Shaill swallowed. "I—accept your apology, my lord," she replied with careful but unsteady formality. "And I trust that in return you will . . . understand why at this moment I do not rise and bow to you as protocol might otherwise dictate. . . ."

Tarod smiled. He had already taken a liking to Shaill, and admired her refusal to be intimidated. "I need no show of respect, lady. Courtesy and honesty," he flicked a pointed glance in Tirand's direction, "are quite enough." He raised his head, surveying them all. "Now that your doubts about me have been assuaged, perhaps we might turn to the matter of someone else's honesty— or lack of it." Abruptly he swung round, and as his green gaze clashed with Ailind's his voice grew venomously challenging. "It's time for your charade to stop. Either you tell our mortal friends the truth about yourself and your purpose here, or I will. The choice is entirely yours."

Ailind stared back at him. Tirand, watching them both, opened his mouth to speak then thought better of it. His face was white. Quietly, Sen Briaray Olvit moved to stand beside him and laid a hand on his shoulder, but he too said nothing.

"Well?" Tarod prompted acidly. "We are all waiting."

A shudder ran through Ailind, and those who were closest to him felt the psychic shock-wave of his fury. Though they were nonplussed by the Chaos lord's sudden and seemingly groundless challenge to the white-haired mariner, the sudden change was a warning, a first hint that Ailind might not be all he seemed, and one adept, groping at something akin to the truth, gasped, choked the sound back and gripped the arm of his nearest neighbor. Tarod and Ailind continued to face each other, and there was a sudden move backwards among the company as everyone felt the charge of raw power that was building between the two motionless figures. Suffocating, savage, lethal, that power was so alien, so unhuman that it didn't so much as acknowledge their existence. The minds of the two adversaries had shifted out of the mortal world into another, unimaginable dimension, and any mortal fool enough to get in the way would be swept aside and trampled to dust.

How long the silent challenge continued no one could later begin to calculate. To some it seemed only a matter of moments; to others it was as if a mortal lifetime had crawled by while the two adversaries stood face to face in wordless, moveless yet appalling conflict. Though the fire and the torches were undimmed, their light seemed to have no strength; vast shadows loomed through the hall, taking on shapes redolent of the most abysmal nightmares, and fevered imaginations caught the grisly echoes of unhuman laughter and monstrous whisperings. A vicious wind soughed through the hall, stirring the tangle of Tarod's black hair, the smooth shimmer of Ailind's white, chilling human flesh to the marrow before it faded into nothing. Silence gripped the hall like a steel hand. Then, so gradually that at first it seemed to the human watchers like a dream, a light began to flare into life above Tarod's heart. Cold, white, dazzling, it grew to a glare and coalesced into seven rays of blinding brilliance that began to pulse with a slow but perfect rhythm. Ailind smiled. It was the first change of expression to show on his face and it seemed to be composed of contempt and pride and resignation all at once. Then a second light began to glow above his heart. Steady and utterly symmetrical, it shone like the unbearable gold of the sun and formed the outline of a lightning flash, frozen and still and eternal—the age-old symbol of Order incarnate. Without knowing that he did so, without even knowing that his hand had moved, Tirand touched the badge at his shoulder, the ancient badge once worn by his long-dead predecessor, Keridil Toln, in the days when Order had ruled the mortal world without opposition, and his throat contracted until he could barely breathe.

Then suddenly it was over. The borderline of the moment was blurred, but in the space of three human heartbeats the psychic battle had ended and the return to normality was complete. A log shifted in the fire, crackling loudly and sending up a shimmer of bright sparks; it broke the hiatus and the watchers shook their heads like people emerging from a drugged sleep. The torches blazed along the hall's length, their brilliance restored; no monstrous shadows crawled across the walls now. And Tarod and Ailind looked for all the world like nothing more than two mortal men facing each other with the firelight dancing on their rigid figures.

Tarod was the first to breach the silence. He bowed curtly to Ailind and said, in a careless tone that didn't quite mask the underlying anger, "I salute you, cousin. It seems we are evenly matched."

Naked dislike glinted in Ailind's golden-brown eyes. "As you say, Chaos. Perhaps it's no more than either of us should have expected."

No one else dared utter a word. Tirand was breathing hard; Sen, still at his side, was whey-faced. The Matriarch's head was bowed seemingly in prayer, and, alone and away from the gathering by the fire, Karuth could only stare mutely at the scene, her face expressionless.

"So," Tarod said, "if they haven't already worked it out for themselves, as seems likely, I think it's time for one of us to tell our mortal friends a few cold facts. Will they come from your lips, or from mine?"

Ailind shrugged, affecting disinterest, and the Chaos lord looked at the strained faces of the castle dwellers. His gaze lit lastly on Tirand, and held there.

"Or maybe the High Initiate would prefer to tell the tale in his own words?" he said softly. "You understand my meaning, don't you, Tirand? You and two others present in this hall know what manner of being you harbor within your walls. Not some poor shipwrecked mariner rescued from a winter storm, but a lord of Order, a brother to Aeoris, who swore you to secrecy on pain of his displeasure and seduced you with his promises of a return to the old ways for which your heart privately hankers. Isn't that so?"

Tirand colored hotly. "You twist the truth—"

"No, I *tell* the truth. It's an unpleasant habit but one

which we of Chaos often choose to indulge against all mortal expectations. That's our nature, High Initiate, as you would know if you'd learned your catechisms a little less onesidedly. Now I ask you again, as I also ask the lady Matriarch and the adept who stands at your side and lends you his moral support: do you acknowledge that I'm right in what I say?"

The eyes of the entire company were on Tirand, and he felt suddenly like a young student brought before his teaching master to answer for some shameful deed. Then hard on the heels of that feeling came anger—righteous anger, not only on his own behalf but on that of the whole Circle. He was the High Initiate! He had renounced any loyalty he might once have professed to Chaos, and in that renunciation he had been supported by the Council of Adepts and by the other two members of the ruling triumvirate. Now a lord of Chaos stood before him and accused him of deceiving his fellow adepts—but by what right? He'd done his duty to the Circle and to his own conscience. His fealty was to Ailind and the lords of Order. *They* were his gods, his only gods.

Ailind spoke, quietly but with emphasis. "You've nothing to fear from Chaos, Tirand. Whatever Tarod might wish you to believe, he has no power over you. You are under *my* protection." He gestured carelessly, almost contemptuously towards the watching adepts. "Answer his question. It's of no moment to me."

The lord of Order was smiling, and Tirand met Tarod's chilly gaze with a sudden surge of confidence that wasn't entirely of his own creation.

"Yes," he said clearly. "It's the truth. And it changes nothing."

There was a harsh susurration as his listeners heard him. Then an elderly woman adept rose abruptly from her chair. Her face was ashen.

"Tirand—are you telling us that . . . that all this time, a lord of Order has been in our midst, and yet you kept his presence a *secret?*"

Tarod glanced at her. "That is precisely what the

High Initiate is telling you, madam. On the order of this being in whom the Circle has been foolish enough to put its trust, he—and a few others—have deceived you."

A heavyset, dark-haired man spoke up. He looked from the High Initiate to Tarod and finally to Ailind and, with an effort, addressed the lord of Order directly. "Is it true, sir? Are you . . ." He swallowed. "Are you one of our seven gods?"

Ailind's expression was unreadable as he inclined his head. "I am."

"Gods!" Then, realizing what he'd said, the adept's face colored. "Forgive me, I meant no disrespect, I didn't—"

Tarod interrupted his flustering with a wry smile. "Save your embarrassment, adept. Your oath is a compliment."

The man collected himself and nodded. Then, his composure still uncertain, he turned back to the High Initiate. "Why did you keep this a secret, Tirand? Why didn't you *tell* us? All this time, unknowing—"

From a short way off a new voice said, "He had no choice. None of us did."

They'd forgotten Karuth. She came forward into the firelight, and Tirand abruptly stiffened as he saw the steely glint in her eyes. Karuth ignored him and looked directly at the disconcerted adept. "I can't deny my own involvement," she said. "I, too, kept the secret." She flicked a glance in Ailind's direction which might have contained a measure of contempt, though the unsteady light made it impossible to be certain. "My brother is no more to blame than any of us. As I said, we had no choice in the matter."

The elderly woman spoke again. "How many others were there, Karuth? Who else knows?"

Karuth hesitated, and Tarod spoke for her. "There are four others, madam. The Matriarch, though I regret to say it. Your High Margrave. This good adept here," he indicated Sen, who couldn't meet his gaze, "and one other senior member of your council who isn't present at this gathering. For reasons best known to himself your god chose to withhold the knowledge of his presence here from the rest of his worshippers." His feline eyes narrowed abruptly. "You must thank physician-adept Karuth Piadar for the fact that he has been unmasked. She alone had the courage to defy the strictures that were laid upon you all, and call on Chaos to . . . shall we say, redress the balance."

Tirand's jaw clenched and he stared at Tarod. For a moment his eyes were blank as though with shock. Then, as though neither the Chaos lord nor Ailind nor any of the watching adepts existed, he turned slowly to face his sister. His voice shook with fury and he said: "From this moment you are no longer an adept! I pronounce anathema on you. I cast you from the Circle—and I only wish that present circumstances didn't prevent me from banishing you from this castle to rot in obscurity!"

Karuth's cheeks flamed as Tirand's words brought all the grudges, the resentments and the bitterness of the old quarrel between them flaring back to the surface. She couldn't control her tongue and she didn't even try, but retaliated with a venom that matched his. "You may be Ailind's puppet, but Ailind no longer has a free hand here!" she retorted savagely. "And I'd remind you that the Circle doesn't consist only of its High Initiate. Your word is not immutable law, brother, and your anathema doesn't impress me!"

"Don't *dare* to call me brother!" Tirand exploded. "I have no sister! Do you understand me? The lying whore who stands before me now is no kin of mine!"

There was an ugly silence. Like two warring cats Tirand and Karuth faced one another, oblivious to their shocked audience. No one else spoke, no one made the smallest attempt to intervene. This had suddenly focused into a vicious personal quarrel, and though the entire Circle might be well aware of the rift between the High Initiate and his sister, to see it revealed before them in such an embarrassing public display was quite another matter. Then with a violent gesture Karuth put one hand to her own shoulder. There was the sound of fabric ripping as she tore the gold adept's badge from her dress. She clenched it in one fist, and her voice cut through the tense atmosphere like vitriol.

"We understand each other, Tirand Lin. I spit on the Circle—and I spit on the fawning coward who calls himself its leader!"

She hurled the badge at Tirand. It struck him above the right eye; Tirand clapped a hand to his face with a shout of outrage, and at the same moment Tarod and Ailind both started forward—

"*Karuth! Tirand!*" The Matriarch's chair scraped back and Shaill was on her feet. She strode forward, ignoring the two lords, and interposed herself between brother and sister.

"This is *disgraceful!*" Shaill so rarely showed real anger that her fury now was all the more startling, and it stopped them all in their tracks. The Matriarch treated Karuth and Tirand to a searing look. "I'd expect more civilized behavior from two mewling infants! It's not to be tolerated!"

There was a long pause. At last Tirand looked away, and muttered something that might have been an apology. Karuth tried to hold Shaill's gaze but failed, and stared down at her own feet. Shaill continued to watch them intently until she was satisfied that neither was about to launch into a fresh assault, then allowed her rigid posture to relax a fraction.

"I think we have all had quite enough to contend with for one night." Her voice wasn't entirely steady but her stare was still sharp as she scanned the gathering, challenging her colleagues to disagree. No one did. "I *strongly* suggest—with respect to you both, my lords," she bowed stiffly first to Ailind, then to Tarod, "that our most prudent course would be to withdraw with what little grace is still left to us, before matters become completely out of hand." She sucked in breath between clenched teeth. "We will say nothing more about this unfortunate display but will excuse both physician-adept

Karuth and the High Initiate, and trust that a sound night's sleep will give them both cause to feel rightly ashamed." Another pause, then: "Indeed, we would *all* benefit from a sound night's sleep. Very grave matters have come to light this evening. We will be better equipped to face them, as regrettably it seems we must, with clear and cool heads."

She gave them all one last look, flinching only a little as she met the gazes of Tarod and Ailind, then turned and, with great dignity, began to walk toward the doors. Halfway, she stopped and looked back.

"If in the midst of this deadly crisis we can do no more than sink to the level of squabblings and tantrums," she said, "then whatever our loyalties, I fear there's little hope for any of us."

* * *

In *The Avenger*, the gripping finale to *The Chaos Gate Trilogy*, men and gods together must join forces against the twisted power of Ygorla and her demonic father. The battle will be long and deadly. But there is no alternative to war—for the only other choice is submission to Ygorla and her monstrous plans for total control.

All too soon she will arrive on the Star Peninsula—but the Circle is only now learning about the gods' predicament. Both sides are at stalemate. Ailind can do nothing to interfere with Ygorla and Narid-na-Gost, for they are of Chaos and therefore beyond the reach of Order's powers. Chaos, in its turn, is helpless because the soul-stone of one of its lords is in Ygorla's possession; if she destroys it, the lord will die. Neither side as yet has a strategy to defeat the usurper; but at the same time they flatly refuse to cooperate. Caught in the middle, the humans face Ygorla's demonic wrath with no help in view. . . .

Watch for *The Avenger*, on sale from Bantam Books in October 1991.

Other Vista SF titles include

Robot Dreams Isaac Asimov 0 575 60180 9
Robot Visions Isaac Asimov 0 575 60152 3
Tangents Greg Bear 0 575 60159 0
Blood Music Greg Bear 0 575 60280 5
Eon Greg Bear 0 575 60266 X
The Forge of God Greg Bear 0 575 60265 1
In the Ocean of Night Gregory Benford 0 575 60035 7
Sailing Bright Eternity Gregory Benford 0 575 60047 0
Imperial Earth Arthur C. Clarke 0 575 60158 2
The Deep Range Arthur C. Clarke 0 575 60291 0
Reach for Tomorrow Arthur C. Clarke 0 575 60046 2
The Wind from the Sun Arthur C. Clarke 0 575 60052 7
The Fountains of Paradise Arthur C. Clarke 0 575 60153 1
Richter 10 Arthur C. Clarke & Mike McQuay 0 575 60110 8
Golden Witchbreed Mary Gentle 0 575 60033 0
Ancient Light Mary Gentle 0 575 60112 4
City of Illusions Ursula K. Le Guin 0 575 60128 0
Four Ways to Forgiveness Ursula K. Le Guin 0 575 60175 2
Red Dust Paul J. McAuley 0 575 60213 9
Secret Harmonies Paul J. McAuley 0 575 60372 0
More Than Human Theodore Sturgeon 0 575 60207 4
Hard Questions Ian Watson 0 575 60067 5
Oracle Ian Watson 0 575 60226 0
The Knights of the Black Earth Margaret Weis &
Don Perrin 0 575 60037 3
Robot Blues Margaret Weis & Don Perrin 0 575 60068 3
Faraday's Orphans N. Lee Wood 0 575 60130 2

VISTA books are available from all good bookshops or from:
Cassell C.S.
Book Service By Post
PO Box 29, Douglas I-O-M
IM99 1BQ
telephone: 01624 675137, fax: 01624 670923

VISTA